ANGER!

Its underbelly was heaving, turning purple. Then its wings fanned the air, backwards. It drifted off the ledge, hovering. The long neck snaked around, and two nearsighted eyes sought mine. The nose expanded, catching my scent. The Dragon hissed triumphantly.

A dozen delicious tales about the most frightening, and the most lovable, monsters ever imagined by man.

Fawcett Crest Books
Edited by Isaac Asimov, Charles G. Waugh,
and Martin Harry Greenberg:

DRAGON TALES
FLYING SAUCERS
THE LAST MAN ON EARTH
THE SEVEN DEADLY SINS OF SCIENCE FICTION
SPACE MAIL II
STARSHIPS
TV: 2000

DRAGON TALES

edited by
Isaac Asimov,
Charles G. Waugh, and
Martin Harry Greenberg

Introduction by Isaac Asimov

FAWCETT CREST • NEW YORK

A Fawcett Crest Book
Published by Ballantine Books
Copyright © 1982 by Isaac Asimov, Martin Harry Green-
berg and Charles G. Waugh

ISBN 0-449-21306-4

Printed in Canada

First Ballantine Books Edition: July 1982
Fourth Printing: July 1986

CONTENTS

CONTENTS

DRAGON TALES

INTRODUCTION

by Isaac Asimov

HUMAN BEINGS have invented many an imaginary monster, but of them all the most fearsome and impressive is the dragon.

In our western tradition, the dragon is a long, large, scaly monster, with wings and fiery breath, malignant in nature, and deadly in deed. It is the supreme act of a hero (whether divine, semidivine, or human) that he slay a dragon. The Greek god Apollo slew one in establishing his temple at Delphi. The Teutonic hero Siegfried slew one, and so did the Christian hero St. George.

Dragons were worth slaying for several reasons. For one thing, they tended to guard precious hoards. In the Greek myths, a dragon guarded the Golden Fleece and had to be killed by Jason, while another dragon guarded the golden apples of the Hesperides and had to be killed by Heracles. Fafnir, the dragon Siegfried slew, also guarded a fortune in gold.

Other dragons had to be killed because they had an unpleasant habit of dining on virgins (who were highly valued, then as now, for their scarcity, and who were thoroughly wasted when merely an item on a menu). Or they could be the embodiment of evil, for in the Bible, the dragon is mentioned two or three times as a primal enemy of God.

Dragons, in a broad sense, could be any large and fearsome monster; one, for instance, inhabiting the sea rather than the air. The sea monster that threatened the beautiful Andromeda and was slain by Perseus in the Greek myths is sometimes spoken of as a dragon. So is Leviathan, the great sea monster mentioned in the Bible.

Some dragons were abnormally monstrous, such as the

many-headed Hydra, slain by Heracles, or the six-headed Scylla, whose gauntlet Odysseus had to run.

On the other hand, the Chinese had dragons that superficially resembled the flying dragons of the western tradition. Chinese dragons, however, tended to be beneficent spirits.

Where did all these dragons come from? How did they arise in the human imagination?

One possibility we can dismiss at once. They were not versions of the dinosaurs. The most fearsome land animals of all time were the huge reptiles of the Mesozoic. Knights who routinely faced and destroyed dragons in the medieval romances might well have quailed if they had had to face an angry tyrannosaur. There were even flying reptiles, the pterosaurs, the largest flyers that ever lived.

However, all these monster lizards died out 65,000,000 years ago and human beings had absolutely no knowledge of them until the nineteenth century.

Can we be sure? Isn't it possible that some survived into early human times and formed the basis of the legend?

No. The chances of survival are so small that we might as well utterly ignore the possibility.

What, then, was the birth of the dragon?

Undoubtedly, it started as an actually existing animal and was improved upon. For one thing, there is the snake. "Dragon" is from the Greek word *drakon,* which originally referred to a sharp-eyed earth spirit of some sort and was later applied to snakes.

Snakes have unwinking eyes, and that gives them the impression of being able to see much, of being sharp-eyed. They slither noiselessly underfoot and, if poisonous, are apt to strike without warning when frightened. This makes them seem evil and malevolent. Furthermore, if a poisonous snake strikes, the bite, if not fatal, will inflame and pain badly, and it is not far from that to the notion of a fiery breath.

And snakes can be improved on. Exaggerate the poisonous nature and you get the cockatrice or basilisk that kills not only by means of poisoned fangs, but by poisoned breath, or even a poisoned look. An easier exaggeration is to make the snake monstrous in size (and some snakes are indeed ten meters long). It is difficult to imagine monster snakes slithering along the ground, but they can easily be made even more dangerous if allowed to slither through the air on wings.

(The wings are often pictured as bat wings, since bats—

those creatures of the night—are also viewed as ill-omened creatures. It is perhaps the bat origin that makes dragon wings so oddly small in most illustrations, but then what do the myth-makers know of aerodynamics?)

And the sea dragons—what of them? The real animal that serves as the model there is surely the crocodile, the deadly monster of the Nile. The description of Leviathan in the Book of Job is almost surely inspired by the crocodile.

The crocodile, like the snake, is a reptile, and both contribute to the scaly hide of the dragon. If the breath of the airborne dragon is pure snake, the short legs it is often pictured as having are pure crocodile. (And contributing to the many-headed sea monsters such as Hydra and Scylla is, undoubtedly, the many-tentacled octopus.)

In ancient and medieval times, it was thought that dragons (as well as other fanciful creatures) really existed, and it wasn't totally irrational to think so, since so much of the world was undiscovered. Who knew what could exist in the strange, misty lands beyond the horizon?

In modern times, however, we know well that dragons don't exist and never existed (unless you want to count the pterosaurs).

Nevertheless, they are still to be found in the imagination, and the dread dragon Smaug in Tolkien's *The Hobbit* is no less fearsome for being imaginary.

On the other hand, the gift of nonexistence is this: We can, if we wish, make our dragons bumbling, well-meaning creatures, or even entirely kindly. There is Walt Disney's *Pete's Dragon*, in which the dragon is rather an overgrown puppydog; and *The Reluctant Dragon*, which only wants to be left in peace; and the altogether kindly and ill-used *Puff, the Magic Dragon* of the affecting ballad.

In the end, then, dragons have become the most lovable as well as the most frightening monsters of all, and those of us who write science fiction and fantasy have the broadest possible range of plots—and dragons—to deal with. The stories here included will amply demonstrate the point.

EVELYN E. SMITH

Evelyn E. Smith is the author of two science-fiction novels and approximately fifty shorter works of science fiction and fantasy. Once employed as a science-fiction crossword puzzle compiler, she specializes in work of broad social satire, skewering such targets as society ("Tea Tray in the Sky"), hippies ("Calliope and Gerkin and the Yankee Doodle Thing"), horseracing ("Nightmare on the Nose"), and colleges. Indeed, the following enchanting story might even have been called "A Taste of Academia."

GERDA

by Evelyn E. Smith

SHE WAS beautiful: she had golden hair and blue eyes like a fairy-tale princess's. In fact, she might even have been a real princess, for she came of a noble Middle European family so highly placed that there not impossibly was a thread of royal purple mingling with the azure in their veins. But she never spoke of it. When she spoke, it was always about her work.

Currently she was a Biology Major. Her interest in Biology seemed to be quite objective, for, although virtually every male heart at the University—from ancient Professor down to fuzz-faced Freshman—beat as one for her, she spurned their attentions to devote herself to her science.

Not least among her admirers was Peter Loomis, a Junior and a Psychology Major, with a B-minus average. The reason that he did not have an A-plus average, even though he was brilliant at Psychology, was that he kept flunking Mathematics and Physical Training term after term. These subjects were required of all students by the University officials, who operated on the theory that happiness was not good for the young.

But, as far as Peter was concerned, the miseries of Gym and Calculus, although great, were as nothing compared to the pangs of unrequited love. For, in view of the fact that Gerda had already refused to attend the Senior Prom with the Captain of the Football Team, take in a nightclub with the handsomest of the Dramatics teachers, or visit whatever era she chose with the Head of the Physics Department in his Time Machine, it should have seemed presumptuous to him to dare to ask her to go to the Student Union with him for a chocolate malted. But ask her he did.

True worth did not win out over crass comeliness or intellectual attainment. It seldom does in real life. "No, thank you," she said politely, as she had said to the Football Captain, the Dramatics teacher, and the Physicist. "I am too busy with my Biological experiments, which are of a momentous and world-shaking nature."

This unnatural speech should have warned Peter, but the poor fool was blinded by his mad infatuation. All he knew was that her accent was fascinating. She was fascinating. Why couldn't she see the rare qualities in him that he himself was able so easily to discern? How could such a lovely creature be as imperceptive as the Math and Gym teachers, who were, of course, quite unlovely, but who also exerted a powerful influence on his life?

But it was of Gerda he mostly thought—not of them. Obviously there was something wrong with her, he was forced to admit to himself; otherwise she could not have failed to succumb to the battery of male charm—not only his, he conceded modestly—with which she had been bombarded. But using Psychological wiles on her would be useless, for she had also, with equal tact, spurned the whole Psychology Department. Something stronger was needed.

Peter betook himself to the Department of Necromancy, to which he had the entrée since every Psychology Major was required to Minor in that subject. There he found the Head of the Department muttering to himself in Latin as he stirred the contents of a crucible.

"Professor Tenebroso—" Peter began.

"Oh, drat!" the Professor said petulantly. "You've spoiled my incantation. Now I'll have to start all over again. Go away, won't you?"

"I wanted to ask you a question, sir. I need help."

"In my day," the old man snarled, "we worked out our own problems or we were turned into field mice. Well, what do you want?"

Peter told his story. Professor Tenebroso actually appeared to be paying a limited amount of attention, which was the most anyone could expect from him. He interrupted the youth before he had finished. "Obviously she's under a spell!" he snapped, waving his rod petulantly. "Any fool could see that."

"Of course, of course, sir," Peter replied eagerly. "An enchanted princess," he said to himself. "Now, how could I have missed that? . . . But how can I break the spell, sir?" he asked aloud.

Professor Tenebroso was agitating the contents of his crucible again. "Oh, it's one of those elementary things," he said vaguely. "I should think just a kiss would do it."

Peter bounded off, without stopping to thank the Professor or to point out to him that the end of his beard had crept into the crucible. A kiss! What a simple, traditional, and altogether satisfactory way of breaking a spell!

He sped light-footed to the Science Building. There, by good luck, he found Gerda alone in one of the Biology Laboratories meticulously vivisecting a frog.

"Gerda!" he announced dramatically, "I have come to break the spell that binds you!"

The princess drew back, her eyes indigo with alarm. "No, no! I beg of you, Peter," she protested, trying to fend him off with a pair of forceps. "You do not know what you are planning to do!"

"I am going to take you in my arms, little one," Peter breathed, tenderly wrenching the forceps out of her delicate hand."

"No, Peter," she protested, struggling. "I implore you. . . . I warn you. . . . You will be sorry, I tell you, mad, impetuous youth!"

But she was no match for his superior strength. That term of compulsory Physical Education which he was now repeating for the fifth time had done its work well, in spite of the teacher's opinion.

"Ha, ha!" Peter laughed contemptuously, as he folded her in his arms and pressed his lips against hers.

There was a flash of lightning, a clap of thunder. The earth trembled. So did Peter, although he had not been entirely unprepared for some such manifestation.

And then Gerda was released from her enchantment.

Even if Peter had not recoiled in horror, he would have found it difficult to continue to clasp her in his arms, for she was now at least twenty times as big as he, and finding the Biology Lab rather a tight fit.

"Sorry, Peter," Gerda apologized, choking slightly on a mouthful of smoke and flame. "I was under a spell all right, and a kiss was needed to release me. However, I wasn't an enchanted princess at all, but an enchanted dragon."

Peter backed away.

"Ah, fickleness, your name is man!" the dragon said. "Just the other day you were pledging me eternal faith. And now, when I really need you, you recoil from me!" She sighed, and the room swirled with clouds of smoke. "I fear it was for my beauty of person you loved me, Peter, and not for my beauty of soul."

On a dragon, the Middle European accent wasn't nearly as charming.

"I'm awfully sorry," Peter explained, trying to retreat imperceptibly, "but I thought you were going to eat me."

She coughed, and gouts of fire flew all over the room. "I am."

"Listen to me for a moment, will you!" Peter shrieked, dodging around a table. "Just a minute, for old times' sake! Remember, we were in Modern European History together!"

"Very well," she conceded. "You have touched the core of sentimentality that lies deep within the heart of every dragon. Because we were classmates, I will listen. But hurry up; I'm hungry!"

Peter took a deep breath. "Actually I want to ask you a question: why do you have to eat *me?* You aren't bound to eat the person who breaks the spell are you?"

"It's not in the rules, if that's what you mean. But there's no law against it either."

"But you could eat lots of other people instead. There's Professor Quaternion, for instance. . . ."

"Why should . . . ? Hmmmm," she mused. "He gave me a D in Trig and spoiled my chances of making Phi Beta."

"This University has, as you know, a very large Mathematics Department," he tempted her, "full of stout and juicy instructors. And then there's the Physical Ed Department!"

The dragon licked her lips again. "That Miss Teres," she said. "Making *me* do a double forward somersault!"

"I will hold them in conversation while you snake up on them from behind!" Peter promised enthusiastically. "It will spare you from having to expend any undue effort. Besides, most people, unaware of the golden heart that beats beneath your saurian exterior, would tend to flee as soon as they caught sight of you."

"*You* don't have to worry, Peter," the dragon said tenderly. "You have convinced me. Why, with a whole University full of overfed pedagogues and succulent, toothsome adolescents, need I devour my only friend? Come, let us away before I forget myself!"

"I think Mathematics first," Peter decided, "as the Gym teachers are apt to be somewhat stringy as a result of excessive exercise."

"I shall do my Master's Thesis," he said happily to himself, "on the Psychology of Dragons. It will be a milestone in the History of Learning."

And hand in hand, they wandered off into the sunset.

DAVID DRAKE

An inveterate lover of Roman history, handsome David Drake is a Vietnam veteran who is pursuing a full-time writing career after having recently resigned his job as assistant town attorney for Chapel Hill, North Carolina. Much of his work consists of war and adventure stories set in the future, such as *Hammer's Slammers,* or the distant past, such as the following condensed version of a tale originally published in *Midnight Sun.*

DRAGONS' TEETH

by David Drake

THE SOUND of squealing axles drifted closer on the freezing wind. The watching Roman raised his eyes an inch above the rim of his brush-screened trench. A dozen Sarmatian wagons were hulking toward him into the twilight. Their wheels of uncured oak, gapped and irregular at the fellies, rumbled complainingly as they smashed stiff grass and bushes into the unyielding soil.

A smile of grim satisfaction brushed Vettius's lips as the Sarmatians approached. He did not touch the bow that lay beside him; it was still too soon.

The enormous weight of the wagons turned every finger's breadth of rise into a steep escarpment up which the oxen had to plod. They grunted out great plumes of breath as they threw their weight into the traces. Sexless, almost lifeless in their poses of stolid acceptance, the drivers hunched on the high wagon seats. Like the oxen, they had been at their killing work since dawn. The wind slashed and eddied about the canopies of aurochs hide that covered the boxes. Tendrils of smoke from heating fires within squirmed through the peaks. They hung for a moment in the sunset before scudding off into invisibility.

The last of the wagons was almost within the defile, Vettius noted. It would be very soon now.

Among the Sarmatians the whole family traveled together, even to war. The children and nursing mothers huddled inside the wagons. So did the warriors; their work, like that of the horses tethered behind each wain, was yet to come. Soon the wagons would halt and laager up in the darkness. Using night as a shroud, the reivers would mount and thunder across the frozen Danube. Laughingly they would return before dawn with booty and fresh Roman ears.

The only picket Vettius could see from where he lay was a single rider slightly ahead and to the left of the wagons. Earlier in the day he might have been guide or outrider. Hours had passed. Wagons had bunched or straggled according to the strength of their teams and the temper of their drivers. Now, while the sun bled like an open wound in the western sky, the rider was almost a part of the jumbled line and no protection for it. Vettius smiled again, and his hand was on the bow.

The wind that moaned around the wagons scuffed up crystals from the snow crusts lying in undulant rills among the brush. The shaggy pony's rump and belly sparkled. The beast's torso, like its rider's, was hidden under armor of broad horn scales, each one painstakingly sewn onto a leather backing by the women of the family. Across his pommel rested a slender lance more than eighteen feet long. The Sarmatian fondled its grip as he nodded over his mount's neck, neglecting to watch the bushes that clawed spike shadows from the sun.

A sound that trickled through the wind made him straighten; unexpected movement caught his eye. Then the Roman archer rose up from behind a bush far too small to conceal a man the way it had. The Sarmatian, spurring his horse in incredulous panic, heard the slap of the bowstring, heard the loud pop as one scale of his cuirass shattered. After the bodkin-pointed arrow ripped through his chest he heard nothing at all.

"Let's get 'em!" Vettius shouted, nocking another arrow as his first target pitched out of the saddle. The trumpeter crouching behind him set the silver-mounted warhorn to his lips and blasted out the attack. Already the shallow hillsides were spilling soldiers down on the unprepared Sarmatians.

The driver of the lead wagon stood up, screaming a warning. The nearest Roman thrust her through the body with his spear. With two slashes of his shortsword, the legionary cut open the canopy behind her and plunged inside with a howl of triumph.

Sarmatians leaped out the back of the second wagon, trying to reach their horses. Three legionaries met them instead. Vettius had set fifty men in ambush, all picked veterans in full armor. None of the others had bows—the legate had feared a crossfire in the dusk—but sword and spear did the butcher's work on the startled nomads. The

Sarmatians were dressed for war in armor of boiled leather or aurochs horn, but they had no shields and their light swords were no match for the heavy Roman cut-and-thrust blades. One at a time the nomads jumped down to be stretched on the ground by a stab, a quick chop, or even the heavy smash of a shield rim. Death trebled, the legionaries stood waiting for each victim. The fading sunlight gleamed from their polished helmets and greaves and touched with fire the wheels of bronze and vermilioned leather that marked their shields.

The legate's practiced eye scanned the fighting. The wrack showed the Sarmatians had battled with futile desperation. A baby lay beside the fourth wagon. Its skull had been dashed in on the wagon box but its nails were stained with Roman blood. The oxen bellowed, hamstrung in the yoke. One was spurting black jets through a heart-deep channel. This day was Rome's vengeance; retribution for a thousand sudden raids, a thousand comrades crumpled from a chance arrow or a dagger thrust in the night.

Only toward the rear where three wagons had bunched together was there real fighting. Vettius ran down the line of wagons though his quiver was almost emptied when he saw one of his men hurtle through the air in a lifeless somersault. The legionary crashed to the ground like a load of scrap metal. His whole chest and body armor had been caved in by an enormous blow. Measurably later the man's sword completed its own parabola and clanked thirty feet away.

"Get back!" Vettius shouted when he saw the windrow of ruined bodies strewn in front of him. "Stand clear!" Before he could say more, the killer was lumbering toward him around the back of the wagon.

The horsehair crest wobbling in the waning sunlight increased the figure's titanic height, but even bareheaded the giant would have been half again as tall as the six-foot soldier. Worse, he was much heavier-built than a man, a squat dwarf taller than the wagon. Though he carried no shield, his whole body shone with a covering of smooth bronze plates. Both gauntleted hands gripped the haft of an iron-headed mace. The six-foot helve was as thick as a man's calf and the head could have served as an anvil.

The giant strode toward Vettius with terrifying agility.

Vettius arced his bow. The shaft of his arrow splintered on the monster's breastplate. It left only a bright scar on the metal. Vettius stepped back, nocking another missile and

shifting his aim to the oddly sloped helmet. The face was
completely covered except for a T-shaped slot over the eyes
and nose. The light was very dim but the narrow gap stood
out dead black against the helmet's luster. As the giant
started to swing his mace parallel to the ground, Vettius shot
again.

The arrow glanced off the bronze and howled away into the
darkness.

Vettius leaped upward and fell across the wagon seat as
the giant's mace hurtled toward him. The spiked head smashed
into a wheel with awesome force, scattering fragments of
wood and making the whole wagon shudder. As it rocked, the
driver's hacked corpse tumbled to the ground, leaving the
Roman alone on the seat as he sighted along his last arrow.
He released it.

The giant had reversed his grip on the mace. Now he
swung his weapon upward with no more effort than a man
with a flywhisk. As the head came level with the giant's hips,
the mace slipped from his fingers to fly forward and burst
through the side of the wagon. The titan reeled backwards. A
small tuft of feathers was barely visible where the helmet
slot crossed the bridge of his nose.

The earth trembled when he fell.

Shaking with reaction himself, Vettius dropped his now-
useless bow and craned his neck to peer over the wagon's
canopy at the remaining fighting. Some of the wains were
already burning. Confusion or the victors had spilled the
heating fires from their earthenware pots and scattered coals
in the cloth and straw of the bedding.

"Save me a prisoner!" Vettius bellowed against the wind.
"For Mithra's sake, save me a prisoner!"

He jumped to the ground and cautiously approached the
fallen giant. The helmet came off easily when he grasped it
by the crest and yanked. Beneath the bronze the face was
almost human. The jaw was square and massive; death's
rictus had drawn thin lips back from leonine tushes, yellowed
and stark. The nose squatted centrally like a smashed toad,
and from it the face rose past high flat eyesockets to enormous ridges of bone. There was virtually no forehead, so that
the brows sloped shallowly to a point on the back of the skull.
Only their short tight coils distinguished the eyebrows from
the black strands that covered the rest of the head.

No wonder the helmet looked odd, Vettius thought bleakly.

He would believe in the face, in a man so large, because they were there for him to touch; but he would have called another man a liar for claiming the existence of something so impossible. Perhaps believing in the impossible was the secret of the success of the Christians whose god, dead three hundred years, was now beginning to rule the Empire.

The trumpeter approached from behind with his horn slung and a bloody sword in his right hand. The torque he now wore was of gold so pure and soft that he had spread it by hand to get it off a dead nomad and rebent it around his own neck.

"Sir!" he called, "are you all right?"

"Give me a hand here," Vettius grunted unresponsively as he tugged at the mace. Together the men pulled the weapon from the fabric of the wagon. Vettius gave a curt order and hefted it alone as his subordinate stepped back. "Ha!" he snorted in disbelief. The mace weighed at least two talents, the weight of a small man or a fair-sized woman.

He let it thud to the ground and walked away from it. "May the Bull bugger me if I don't learn more about this," he swore.

The doorkeeper had difficulty slamming the door against the gust of wind that followed Vettius into the anteroom. Moist air from the baths within condensed to bead the decorated tiles and rime the soldier's cape of black bearskin. He wore the bear's head as a cowl. The beast's glass eyes usually glared out above Vettius's own; now they too were frosted and the doorkeeper, turning, shuddered at the look of blank agony they gave him.

Vettius shrugged off the cape and stamped his muddy boots on the floor. The doorkeeper sighed inwardly and picked up his twig broom. The damned man had been stomping through the muck like a common soldier instead of riding decently in a litter as befit his rank. The slave said nothing aloud as he swept, though; the legate had a reputation for violence and he already wore a dark glower this afternoon.

Walking through the door of the changing room, Vettius tossed his cape to one of the obsequious attendants and began to unlace his boots. While he sat on a bench and stripped off his thick woolen leggings, the other attendant looked delicately at the miry leather and asked with faint disdain, "Will you have these cleaned while you bathe, sir?"

"Dis, why should I?" the soldier snarled. "I've got to wear them out of here, don't I?"

The attendant started at his tone. Vettius chuckled at the man's fear and threw the filthy leggings in his face. Laying both his tunics on the bench, he surveyed the now apprehensive slaves and asked, "Either of you know where Dama is?"

"The Legate Vettius?" called a voice from the inner hallway. A third attendant poked his head into the changing room. "Sir? If you will follow me . . ."

The attendant's sandals slapped nervously down the hallway past steam rooms on the right and the wall of the great pool on the left. Tiles of glaucous gray covered the floors and most of the walls, set off by horizontal bands of mosaic. A craftsman of Naisso who had never been to the coast had inset octopi and dolphins cavorting on a bright green sea. The civilization I protect, Vettius thought disgustedly. The reason I bow to fat fools.

At the corner of the hall the attendant stopped and opened one of the right-hand doors. Steam puffed out. Vettius peered in with his hand on the jamb to keep from slipping on the slick tile. Through the hot fog he could make out the figure of the small man who lay on one of the benches.

"Dama?" the soldier called uncertainly.

"Come on in, Lucius," invited the other. He rose to his elbow and the light on his head of tight blond curls identified him. "How did it go?"

"The interrogation was fine," Vettius answered; but his tone was savage, that of a man used to taking out his frustrations in slaughter and very close to the point of doing so again. "We didn't need much persuasion to get the prisoner to tell us everything he knew about the giant. It came from a tent village called Torgu, and he says the shaman running the place has ten more just like it."

"If one, why not eleven?" Dama mused. "But I didn't think the Sarmatians ever made a shaman chief."

"I didn't either," Vettius agreed darkly, "and that wasn't the last strange thing he told us about this wizard, this Hydaspes. He was at Torgu when the family we ambushed got there late in the fall, nervous as the Emperor's taster and fussing around the village to look over each new arrival. He wasn't claiming much authority, either. Then about two months ago a horseman rode in from the east. Our prisoner didn't talk with the fellow but he saw him give a package the

size of his fist to Hydaspes. That was what the wizard had
been waiting for. He laughed and capered all the way to his
tent and didn't come out again for a week. When he did, he
started giving orders like a king. Since now he had a nine-
foot giant behind him, everyone obeyed. In back of Hydaspes's
tent there was a long trench in the frozen ground and a lot of
dirt was missing. Nobody the prisoner knew hung about
behind there to see if the wizard really was digging up giants
there night after night—they were all scared to death by
then."

"So a one-time hedge wizard gets a giant bodyguard," the
merchant said softly, "and he unites a tribe under him. If he
can do that, he may just as easily become king of the whole
nation. What would happen, Lucius, if the Sarmatians got a
real king, a real leader who stopped their squabbling and
sent them across the Danube together?"

The white fear that had been shimmering around the edges
of Vettius's mind broke through again and tensed all his
muscles. "A century ago the Persians unified Mesopotamia
against us," he said. "Constant fighting. Some victories, more
losses. But we could accept that on one frontier—it's a big
empire. On two at the same time . . . I can't say what would
happen."

"We'd better deal with Hydaspes soon," Dama summarized
flatly, "or Hydaspes will deal with us. Have you told Celsus?"

"Oh, I told the Count," Vettius snapped, "but he didn't
believe me—and besides, he was too busy reaming me out for
leading the ambush myself. It was *undignified* for a legate,
he said."

Dama crowed, trying to imagine Vettius too dignified for a
fight.

"That's the sort he is," the soldier agreed with a rueful
smile. "He expects me to keep my cutthroats in line without
dirtying my boots. A popular attitude this side of the river, it
seems."

Knuckles slammed on the steam-room door. Both men
looked up sharply.

"Sirs, quickly!" the attendant hissed from outside.

Dama threw the door open, his face blank.

"Sirs," the frightened slave explained, "the Count has come
for the legate Vettius. I misdirected him, thinking you might
want to prepare, but he'll be here any moment."

"I'll put on a tunic and meet him in the changing room,"

the soldier decided. "I've no desire to be arrested in the nude."

The frightened changing room attendants had disappeared into the far reaches of the building, leaving the friends to pull on their linen tunics undisturbed. Celsus burst in on them without ceremony, followed by two of his runners. *He's not here to charge me after all,* Vettius thought, not without at least a squad of troops. Though Mithra knew, his wishes would have supported a treason indictment.

"Where have you been?" the official stormed. His round face was almost the color of his toga's broad maroon hem.

"Right here in the bath, your excellency," Vettius replied without difference.

"Word just came by heliograph," the Count sputtered. "There were ten attacks last night, *ten!* Impregnable monsters leading them—Punicum, Novae, Frasuli, Anarti—posts wiped out!"

"I told you there were other attacks planned," the soldier replied calmly. "None of them was in my sector. I told you the why of that, too."

"But you lied when you said you killed a monster, didn't you?" accused Celsus, stamping his foot. "At Novae they hit one with a catapult and the bolt only bounced off!"

"Then they didn't hit him squarely," Vettius retorted. "The armor isn't that heavy. And I told you, I shot mine through the viewslit in his helmet."

The Count motioned his runners away. Noticing Dama for the first time he screamed, "Get out! Get out!"

The merchant bowed and exited behind the runners. He stood near the door.

"Listen," Celsus whispered, plucking at the soldier's sleeve to bring his ear lower, "you've got to do something about the giants. It'll look bad if these raids continue."

"Fine," Vettius said in surprise. "Give me my regiment and the Fifth Macedonian, and some cavalry—say the Old Germans. I'll level Torgu and everyone in it."

"Oh no," his pudgy superior gasped, "not so much! The Emperor will hear about it and the gods know what he'll think. Oh, no—fifty men, that was enough before."

"Are you—" Vettius began, then rephrased his thought. "This isn't an ambush for one family, your excellency. This is disposing of a powerful chief and maybe a thousand of his followers, a hundred miles into Sarmatia. I might as well go alone as with fifty men."

"Fifty men," Celsus repeated. Then, beaming as if he were making a promise, he added, "You'll manage, I'm sure."

The two riders were within a few miles of Torgu before they were noticed.

"I shouldn't have let you come," Vettius grumbled to his companion. "Either I should have gone myself or else marched my regiment in and told Celsus to bugger himself."

Dama smiled. "You don't have any curiosity, Lucius. You only see the job to be done. Myself, I want to know where a nine-foot giant comes from."

They eyed the sprawling herd of black cattle finding some unimaginable pasturage beneath the snow crust. Perhaps they were stripping bark from the brush that scarred the landscape with its black rigidity. A cow scented the unfamiliar horses approaching it. The animal blatted and scrambled to its feet, splashing dung behind it. When it had bustled twenty feet away, the cow regained enough composure to turn and stare at the riders, focusing the ripple of disturbance that moved sluggishly through other bovine minds. Face after drooling, vacant face rotated toward them; after long moments, even the distant herdsman looked up from where he huddled over his fire in the lee of a hill.

Dama's chest grew tight. There was still another moment's silence while the Sarmatian made up his mind that there really were Romans riding through his herd toward Torgu. When at last he grasped that fact, he leaped to his feet yipping his amazement. For an instant he crouched bowlegged, waiting for a hostile move. When the intruders ignored him, the Sarmatian scampered to his horse and lashed it into a startled gallop for home.

The merchant chewed at his cheeks, trying to work saliva into a mouth that had gone dry when he realized they would be noticed. He'd known they were going to meet Sarmatians: that was their whole purpose. But now it was too late to back out. "About time we got an escort," he said with false bravado. "I'm surprised the Sarmatians don't patrol more carefully."

"Why should they?" Vettius snorted. "They know they're safe over here so long as a brainless scut like Celsus is in charge of the border."

They jogged beyond the last of the cattle. Without the Sarmatian's presence the beasts were slowly drifting away from the trampled area where they had been herded. If they wandered far they would be loose at night when the wolves hunted.

"Cows," Vettius muttered. "It's getting hard to find men, my friend."

Half a mile away on the top of the next rolling hill an armored horseman reined up in a spatter of snow. He turned his head and gave a series of short yelps that carried over the plain like bugle calls. Moments later a full score of lancers topped the brow of the hill and pounded down toward the interlopers.

"I think we'll wait here," the soldier said.

"Sure, give them a sitting target," Dama agreed with a tense smile.

Seconds short of slaughter, the leading Sarmatian raised his lance. The rest of the troop followed his signal. The whole group swept around Vettius and Dama to halt in neighing, skidding chaos. One horse lost its footing and spilled its rider on the snow with a clatter of weapons. Cursing, the disgruntled Sarmatian lurched toward the Romans with his short, crooked sword out. From behind Dama, the leader barked a denial and laid his lance in front of the man. The merchant breathed deeply but did not relax his grip on the queerly shaped crossbow resting on his saddle until the glowering Sarmatian had remounted.

The leader rode alongside Vettius and looked up at the soldier on his taller horse. "You come with us to Torgu," he ordered in passable Greek.

"That's right," Vettius agreed in Sarmatian. "We're going to Torgu to see Hydaspes."

There was a murmur from the Sarmatians. One of them leaned forward to shake an amulet bag in the soldier's face, gabbling something too swiftly to be understood.

The leader had frowned when Vettius spoke. He snapped another order and kicked his horse forward. Romans and Sarmatians together jogged up the hill, toward the offal and frozen muck of Torgu.

On the back of a nameless, icebound stream stood the village's central hall and only real building. Dama glanced at it as they rode past. Its roughly squared logs were gray and streaked with odd splits along the twisted grain. Any caulking there might have been in the seams had fallen out over the years. The sides rose to a flaring roof of scummed thatch, open under the eaves to emit smoke and the stink of packed bodies. The hall would have seemed crude in the most stagnant backwaters of the Empire; the merchant could scarcely believe there could be a threat from a people to whom it was the height of civilization.

Around the timber structure sprawled the nomad wagons in filthy confusion. Their sloping canopies were shingled with cow droppings set out to dry in the wan sunlight before being burned for fuel. The light soot that had settled out of thousands of cooking fires permeated the camp with an unclean, sweetish odor. Nothing in the village but the untethered horses watching the patrol looked cared for.

Long lances had been butted into the ground beside each wagon. As he stared back at the flat gazes directed at him by idle Sarmatians, Dama realized what was wrong with the scene. Normally, only a handful of each family group would have been armored lancers. The rest would be horse archers, able to afford only a bow and padded linen protection. Most of their escort hung cased bows from their saddles, but all bore the lance and most wore scale mail.

"Lucius," the merchant whispered in Latin, "are all of these nobles?"

"You noticed that," Vettius replied approvingly. "No, you can see from their looks that almost all of them were merely herdsmen recently. Somebody made them his retainers, paid for their equipment and their keep."

"Hydaspes?" the merchant queried.

"I guess. He must have more personal retainers than the king, then."

"You will be silent!" ordered the Sarmatian leader.

They had ridden almost completely through the camp and were approaching a tent of gaily pennoned furs on the edge of the plains. At each corner squatted an octagonal stump of basalt a few feet high. The stones were unmarked and of uncertain significance, altars or boundary markers or both. No wains had been parked within fifty paces of the tent. A pair of guards stood before its entrance. Dama glanced at the streamers and said, "You know, there really is a market for silk in this forsaken country. A shame that—"

"Silence!" the Sarmatian repeated as he drew up in front of the tent. He threw a rapid greeting to the guards, one of whom bowed and ducked inside. He returned quickly, followed by a tall man in a robe of fine black Spanish wool. The

newcomer's face was thin for a Sarmatian and bore a smile
that mixed triumph—and something else. On his shoulder,
covered by the dark hood, clung a tiny monkey with great
brown eyes. From time to time it put its mouth to its master's
ear and murmured secretly.

"Hydaspes," Vettius whispered. "He always wears black."

"Have they been disarmed?" the wizard questioned. The
escort's leader flushed in embarrassment at his oversight and
angrily demanded the Romans' weapons. Vettius said nothing as he handed over his bow and the long cavalry sword he
carried even now that he commanded an infantry unit. The
merchant added his crossbow and a handful of bolts to the
collection.

"What is that?" Hydaspes asked, motioning his man to
hand him the crossbow.

"It comes from the east where I get my silk," Dama
explained, speaking directly to the wizard. "You just drop a
bolt into the tall slot on top. That holds it while you pull back
on the handle, cocking and firing it all in one motion."

"From the east? I get weapons from the east," the Sarmatian
said with a nasty quirk of his lip. "But this, this is only a toy,
surely? The arrow is so light and scarcely a handspan long.
What could a man do with such a thing?"

Dama shrugged. "I'm not a warrior. For my own part, I
wouldn't care to be shot with this or anything else."

The wizard gestured an end to the conversation, setting the
weapon inside his tent for later perusal. "Dismount, gentlemen, dismount," he continued in excellent Greek. "Perhaps
you have heard of me?"

"Hydaspes the wizard. Yes," Vettius lied, "even within the
Empire we think of you when we think of a powerful sorcerer.
That's why we've come for help."

"In whose name?" the Sarmatian demanded. "Constantius
the emperor?"

"Celsus, Count of Dacia," Vettius snapped back. "The Empire
has suffered the bloody absurdities of Constantius and his
brothers long enough. Eunuchs run the army, priests rule the
state, and the people pray to the tax gatherers. We'll have
support when we get started, but first we need some standard
to rally to, something to convince everyone that we have
more than mere hopes behind us. We want your giants, and
we'll pay you a part of the Empire to get them."

"And you, little man?" Hydaspes asked the merchant unexpectedly.

Dama had been imagining the Count's face if he learned his name was being linked with raw treason, but he recovered swiftly and fumbled at his sash while replying, "We merchants have little cause to love Constantius. The roads are ruinous, the coinage base, and the rapacity of local officials leaves little profit for even the most daring adventure."

"So you came to add your promise of future gain?"

"Future? Who knows the future?" Dama grunted. Gold gleamed in his hand. A shower of coins arced unerringly from his right palm to his left and back again. "If you can supply what we need, you'll not lament your present payment."

"Ho! Such confidence," the wizard said, laughing cheerfully. The monkey chittered, stroking its master's hair with bulbous fingertips. "You really believe that I can raise giants from the past?

I can!"

Hydaspes's face became a mask of unreason. Dama shifted nervously from one foot to the other, realizing that the wizard was far from the clever illusionist they had assumed back at Naisso he must be. This man wasn't sane enough to impose successfully on so many people, even ignorant barbarians. Or was the madness a recent thing?

"Subradas, gather the village behind my tent," Hydaspes ordered abruptly, "but leave space in the middle as wide and long as the tent itself."

The leader of the escort dipped his lance in acknowledgment. "The women, Lord?"

"All—women, slaves, everyone. I'm going to show you how I raise the giants."

"Ho!" gasped the listening Sarmatians. The leader saluted again and rode off shouting. Hydaspes turned to re-enter his tent, then paused. "Take the Romans, too," he directed the guards. "Put them by the flap and watch them well.

"Yes," he continued, glancing back at Vettius, "it is a very easy thing to raise giants, if you have the equipment and the knowledge. Like drawing a bow for a man like you."

The Hell-lit afterimage of the wizard's eyes continued to blaze in the soldier's mind when the furs had closed behind the black figure.

As the rest of the Sarmatians dismounted and began to jostle them around the long tent, Dama whispered, "This isn't working. If it gets too tight, break for the tent. You know about my bow?"

Vettius nodded, but his mind was chilled by a foretaste of death.

As the prisoner had said, eleven long trenches bristled outward from the wall of Hydaspes's tent. Each was shallow but too extensive for the wizard to have dug it in the frozen ground in one night. Dama disliked the way the surface slumped over the ditches, as if enormous corpses had clawed their way out of their graves . . .

Which was what the wizard seemed to claim had happened.

The guards positioned the two Romans at the center of the back wall of the tent where laces indicated another entrance. Later comers crowded about anxiously, held back in a rough circle by officers with drawn swords. Twenty feet to either side of the Romans stretched the straight walls of the tent paralleled by a single row of warriors. From the basalt posts at either corner curved the rest of the tribe in milling excitement, warriors in front and women and children squirming as close as they could get before being elbowed back.

The Sarmatians were still pushing for position when Hydaspes entered the cleared space, grinning ironically at Vettius and Dama as he stepped between them. A guard laced the tent back up. In the wizard's left hand was a stoppered copper flask; his right gripped a small packet of supple cowhide.

"The life!" Hydaspes shouted to the goggle-eyed throng, waving the flask above his head from the center of the circle. He set the vessel down on the dirt and carefully unrolled the leather wrappings from the other objects.

"And the seed!" the wizard cried at last. In his palm lay a pair of teeth. They were a dull, stony gray without any of the sheen of ivory. One was a molar, human but inhumanly large. The other tooth, even less credible, seemed to be a canine fully four inches long. With one tooth in either hand, Hydaspes goat-footed about the flask in an impromptu dance of triumph.

His monkey rider clacked its teeth in glee.

The wizard stopped abruptly and faced the Romans. "Oh, yes. The seed. I got them, all thirteen teeth, from the Chinese— the people who sell you your silk, merchant. Dragons' teeth they call them—hee hee! And I plant them just like Cadmus did when he built Thebes. But I'm the greater prince, oh yes, for I'll build an *empire* where he built a city."

Dama licked his lips. "We'll help you build your empire," he began, but the wizard ignored him and spoke only to Vettius.

"You want my giants, Roman, my darlings? Watch!"

Hydaspes plucked a small dagger from his sash and poked a hole in the ground. Like a farmer planting a nut, the wizard popped the molar into the hole and patted the earth back down. When he straightened he shouted a few words at the sky. The villagers gasped, but Dama doubted whether they understood any more of the invocation than he did. Perhaps less—the merchant thought he recognized the language, at least, one he had heard chanted on the shores of the Persian Gulf on a dead, starless night. He shuddered.

Now the wizard was unstoppering his flask and crooning under his breath. His cowl had fallen back to display the monkey clinging fiercely to his long oily hair. When the wizard turned, Dama could see the beast's lips miming its master obscenely.

Droplets spattered from the flask, bloody red and glowing. The merchant guessed wine or blood, changed his mind when the fluid popped and sizzled on the ground. The frozen dirt trembled like a stricken gong.

The monkey leaped from Hydaspes's shoulder, strangely unaffected by the cold. It faced the wizard across the patch of fluid-scarred ground. It was chanting terrible squeaky words that thundered back from Hydaspes.

The ground split.

The monkey collapsed. Hydaspes leaped over the earth's sudden gape and scooped up the little creature, wrapping it in his cloak.

Through the crack in the soil thrust an enormous hand. Earth heaved upward again. The giant's whole torso appeared, dribbling dirt back into the trench. Vettius recognized the same thrusting jaw, the same high flat eyesockets, as those of the giant he had killed.

The eyes were Hydaspes's own.

"Oh yes, Roman," the wizard cackled. "The life and the seed—and the mind too, hey? There must be the mind."

The giant rose carefully in a cascade of earth. Even standing in the trench left by his body, he raised his pointed skull eight feet into the air.

"My mind!" Hydaspes shrieked, oblivious to everyone but
the soldier. "Part of me in each of my darlings, you see?
Flowing from me through my pet here to them."

One of the wizard's hands caressed the monkey until it
murmured lasciviously. The beast's huge eyes were seas of
steaming brown mud, barely flecked by pinpoint pupils.

"You said you knew me," continued the wizard. "Well, I
know you too, Lucius Vettius. I saw you bend your bow, I saw
you kill my darling—

"I saw you kill me, Roman!"

Vettius unclasped his cape, let it slip to the ground. Hydaspes
wiped a streak of spittle from his lips and stepped back to lay
a hand on the giant's forearm. "Kill me again, Roman," the
wizard said softly. "Go ahead; no one will interfere. But this
time you don't have a bow. Watch the little one!" he snapped
to the guard on Dama's right.

The Sarmatian gripped the merchant's shoulder.

Then the giant charged.

Vettius dived forward at an angle, rolling beyond the
torn-up section of the clearing. The giant spun, stumbling in
a ditch that had cradled one of his brothers. The soldier had
gained the room he wanted in the center of the open space
and waited in a loosearmed crouch. The giant sidled toward
him splay-footed.

"Hey!" the Roman shouted and lunged for his opponent's
dangling genitalia. The giant struck with shocking speed,
swatting Vettius in midair like a man playing handball.
Before the Roman's thrusting fingers could make contact, the
giant's open-handed blow had crashed into his ribs and
hurled him a dozen feet away. Only the giant's clumsy rush
saved Vettius from being pulped before he could jump to his
feet again. The soldier was panting heavily but his eyes were
fixed on the giant's. A thread of blood dribbled off the point of
his jaw. Only a lip split on the hard ground—thus far.

The giant charged.

Two faces in the crowd were not fixed on the one-sided
battle. Dama fingered the hem of his cloak unobtrusively,
following the fight only from the corners of his eyes. It would
be pointless to watch his friend die. Instead the merchant
eyed Hydaspes, who had dug another hole across the clearing
and inserted the last and largest tooth into it. The wizard
seemed to ignore the fighting. If he watched at all, it was
through the giant's eyes as he claimed; surely, mad as he

was Hydaspes would not otherwise have turned his back on
his revenge. For the first time Dama thought he recognized
an unease about the monkey that rode again on the wizard's
shoulder. It might only have been fatigue. Certainly Hydaspes
seemed to notice nothing unusual as he tamped down the soil
and began his thirteenth invocation.

Dama's guard was wholly caught up in the fight. He began
to pound the merchant on the back in excitement, yelling
bloodthirsty curses at Vettius. Dama freed the slender sti-
letto from his cloak and palmed it. He did not turn his head
lest the movement catch the guard's attention. Instead he
raised his hand to the Sarmatian's neck, delicately fingered
his spine. Before the moth-light touch could register on the
enthusiastic Sarmatian, Dama slammed the thin blade into
the base of his brain and gave it a twist. The guard died
instantly. The merchant supported the slumping body, guid-
ing it back against the tent. Hydaspes continued chanting a
litany with the monkey, though the noise of the crowd
drowned out his words. The wizard formed the inaudible
syllables without noticing either Dama or the stumbling way
his beast answered him. There was a look of puzzlement,
almost fear, in the monkey's eyes. The crowd continued to
cheer as the merchant opened the flap with a quick slash and
backed inside Hydaspes's tent.

Inside a pair of chalcedony oil lamps burned with tawny
light. The floor was covered with lush furs, some of which
draped wooden benches. On a table at one end rested a pair of
human skulls, unusually small but adult in proportions.
More surprising were the cedar book chests holding parch-
ments and papyri and even the strange pleated leaf-books of
India. Dama's crossbow stood beside the front entrance. He
ran to it and loosed the bundle of stubby, unfletched darts
beside it. From his wallet came a vial of pungent tarry
matter into which he jabbed the head of each dart. The
uncovered portions of the bronze points began to turn green.
Careful not to touch the smears of venom, the merchant
slipped all ten missiles into the crossbow's awkward vertical
magazine.

Only then did he peer through the tent flap.

Vettius leaped sideways, kicking at the giant's knee. The
ragged hobnails scored his opponent's calf, but the giant's
deceptively swift hand closed on the Roman's outer tunic. For
a heartsick instant the heavy fabric held; then it ripped and

Vettius tumbled free. The giant lunged after him. Vettius backpedaled and, as his enemy straightened, launched himself across the intervening space. The heel of his outstretched boot slammed into the pit of the giant's stomach. Again the iron nails made a bloody ruin of the skin. The titan's breath whooshed out, but its half-ton bulk did not falter at the blow. Vettius, thrown back by the futile impact, twisted away from the giant's unchecked rush. The creature's heels grazed past, thudded with mastodonic force. The soldier took a shuddering breath and lurched to his feet. A long arm clawed for his face. The Roman staggered back, barely clear of the spadelike talons. The monster pressed after him relentlessly, and Vettius was forced at last to recognize what should have been hopelessly obvious from the first: he could not possibly kill the giant with his bare hands.

A final strategem took shape. With desperate purpose Vettius began to circle and retreat before his adversary. He should have planned it, measured it, but now he could only trust to luck and the giant's incredible weight. Backed almost against a corner post, he crouched and waited. Arms wide, the giant hesitated—then rushed in for the kill. Vettius met him low, diving straight at his opponent instead of making a vain effort to get clear again. The Roman's arms locked about the great ankles and the giant wavered, then began to topple forward. As he fell his taloned fingers clamped crushingly on Vettius's ribs.

The unyielding basalt altar met the giant's skull with shattering force. Bone slammed dense rock with the sound of a maul on a wedge. Warm fluids spattered the snow while the Sarmatians moaned in disbelief. Hydaspes knelt screaming on the ground, his fists pummeling terror from a mind that had forgotten even the invocation it had just completed. The earth began pitching like an unmastered horse. It split in front of the wizard where the tooth had been planted. The crack raced jaggedly through the crowd and beyond.

"Lucius!" Dama cried, lifting the corner of the tent.

The soldier pulled his leg free from the giant's pinioning body and rolled toward the voice, spilling endwise the only Sarmatian alert enough to try to stop him. Dama dropped the tent wall and nodded toward the front, his hands full of crossbow.

"There're horses waiting out there. I'll slow them up."

Vettius stamped on a hand that thrust into the tent.

"Get out, damn you!" the merchant screamed. "There aren't any more weapons in here."

A Sarmatian rolled under the furs with a feral grimace and a dagger in his hand. The soldier hefted a full case of books and hurled it at his chest. Wood and bone splintered loudly. Vettius turned and ran toward the horses.

The back flap ripped apart in the haste of the Sarmatians who had remembered its existence. The first died with a dart through his eye as Dama jerked the cocking handle of his weapon. The next missile fell into position. The merchant levered back the bow again. At full cock the sear released, snapped the dart out into the throat of the next man. The Sarmatian's life dissolved in a rush of red flame as the bolt pricked his carotid to speed its load of poison to the brain. The third man stumbled over his body, screamed. Two darts pinged off his mail before one caught the armpit he bared when he threw his hands over his face.

Relentless as a falling obelisk, Dama stroked out the full magazine of lethal missiles, shredding six screaming victims in the space of a short breath. The entrance was plugged by a clot of men dying in puling agony. Tossing his empty bow at the writhing chaos behind him, Dama ran through the front flap and vaulted onto his horse.

"We'll never get clear!" Vettius shouted as he whipped his mount. "They'll run us down in relays before we reach the Danube."

Wailing Sarmatians boiled around both ends of the tent, shedding helmets, weapons—any encumbrance. Their voices honed a narrow blade of terror.

"The control," Dama shouted back as the pair dodged among the crazy pattern of wagon tongues. "He used his own mind and a monkey's to control something not quite a man."

"So what?"

"That last tooth didn't come from a man. It didn't come from anything like a man."

Something scaly, savage and huge towered over the wreckage of the tent. It cocked its head to glare at the disappearing riders while scrabbling with one stubby foreleg to stuff a black-robed figure farther into its maw. Vettius twisted in his saddle to stare in amazement at the coffin-long jaws gaping twenty feet in the air and the spined backfin like that of no reptile of the past seventy million years.

The dragon hissed, leaving a scarlet mist of blood to hang in the air as it ducked its head for another victim.

L. SPRAGUE DE CAMP

One of the most erudite men in science fiction and fantasy, L. Sprague de Camp is the author of such noted works as *Lest Darkness Fall*, *The Incomplete Enchanter* (along with Fletcher Pratt), and *The Tritonian Ring*. However, he has also written popular historical fiction and nonfiction such as *The Dragon of Ishtar Gates* and *Lost Continents*.

The following story is a good example of his ability to combine humor and intelligence with sword and sorcery and is the first of a series set in an alternate medieval world.

TWO YARDS OF DRAGON

by L. Sprague de Camp

EUDORIC DAMBERTON, Esquire, rode home from his courting of Lusina, daughter of the enchanter Baldonius, with a
face as long as an olifant's nose. Eudoric's sire, Sir Dambert,
said:

"Well, how fared thy suit, boy? Ill, eh?"

"I—" began Eudoric.

"I told you 'twas an asinine notion, eh? Was I not right?
When Baron Emmerhard has more daughters than he can
count, any one of which would fetch a pretty parcel of land
with her, eh? Well, why answerest not?"

"I—" said Eudoric.

"Come on, lad, speak up!"

"How can he, when ye talk all the time?" said Eudoric's
mother, the Lady Aniset.

"Oh," said Sir Dambert. "Your pardon, son. Moreover and
furthermore, as I've told you, an ye were Emmerhard's son-
in-law, he'd use his influence to get you your spurs. Here ye
be, a strapping youth of three-and-twenty, not yet knighted.
'Tis a disgarce to our lineage."

"There are no wars toward, to afford opportunity for deeds
of knightly dought," said Eudoric.

"Aye, 'tis true. Certes, we all hail the blessings of peace,
which the wise governance of our sovran emperor hath given
us for lo these thirteen years. Howsomever, to perform a
knightly deed, our young men must needs waylay banditti,
disperse rioters, and do suchlike fribbling feats."

As Sir Dambert paused, Eudoric interjected, "Sir, that
problem now seems on its way to solution."

"How meanest thou?"

"If you'll but hear me, Father! Doctor Baldonius has set me

47

a task, ere he'll bestow Lusina on me, which should fit me for
knighthood in any jurisdiction."

"And that is?"

"He's fain to have two square yards of dragon hide. Says he
needs 'em for his magical mummeries."

"But there have been no dragons in these parts for a
century or more!"

"True; but, quoth Baldonius, the monstrous reptiles still
abound far to eastward, in the lands of Pathenia and
Pantorozia. Forsooth, he's given me a letter of introduction to
his colleague, Doctor Raspiudus, in Pathenia."

"What?" cried the Lady Aniset. "Thou, to set forth on
some year-long journey to parts unknown, where, 'tis said,
men hop on a single leg or have faces in their bellies? I'll not
have it! Besides, Baldonius may be privy wizard to Baron
Emmerhard, but 'tis not to be denied that he is of no gentle
blood."

"Well," said Eudoric, "so who was gentle when the Divine
Pair created the world?"

"Our forebears were, I'm sure, whate'er were the case with
those of the learned Doctor Baldonius. You young people are
always full of idealistic notions. Belike thou'lt fall into heretical delusions, for I hear that the Easterlings have not the
true religion. They falsely believe that God is one, instead of
two as we truly understand."

"Let's not wander into the mazes of theology," said Sir
Dambert, his chin in his fist. "To be sure, the paynim Southrons
believe that God is three, an even more pernicious notion
than that of the Easterlings."

"An I meet God in my travels, I'll ask him the truth o't,"
said Eudoric.

"Be not sacrilegious, thou impertinent whelp! Still and all
and notwithstanding, Doctor Baldonius were a man of influence to have in the family, be his origin never so humble.
Methinks I could prevail upon him to utter spells to cause my
crops, my neat, and my villeins to thrive, whilst casting
poxes and murrains on my enemies. Like that caitiff Rainmar,
eh? What of the bad seasons we've had? The God and Goddess
know we need all the supernatural help we can get to keep us
from penury. Else we may some fine day awaken to find that
we've lost the holding to some greasy tradesman with a
purchased title, with pen for lance and tally sheet for shield."

"Then I have your leave, sire?" cried Eudoric, a broad grin splitting his square, bronzed young face.

The Lady Aniset still objected, and the argument raged for another hour. Eudoric pointed out that it was not as if he were an only child, having two younger brothers and a sister. In the end, Sir Dambert and his lady agreed to Eudoric's quest, provided he return in time to help with the harvest, and take a manservant of their choice.

"Whom have you in mind?" asked Eurodic.

"I fancy Jillo the trainer," said Sir Dambert.

Eudoric groaned. "That old mossback, ever canting and haranguing me on the duties and dignities of my station?"

"He's but a decade older than ye," said Sir Dambert. "Moreover and furthermore, ye'll need an older man, with a sense of order and propriety, to keep you on the path of a gentleman. Class loyalty above all, my boy! Young men are wont to swallow every new idea that flits past, like a frog snapping at flies. Betimes they find they've engulfed a wasp, to their scathe and dolor."

"He's an awkward wight, Father, and not overbrained."

"Aye, but he's honest and true, no small virtues in our degenerate days. In my sire's time there was none of this newfangled saying the courteous 'ye' and 'you' even to mere churls and scullions. 'Twas always 'thou' and 'thee.' "

"How you do go on, Dambert dear," said the Lady Aniset.

"Aye, I ramble. 'Tis the penalty of age. At least, Eudoric, the faithful Jillo knows horses and will keep your beasts in prime fettle." Sir Dambert smiled. "Moreover and furthermore, if I know Jillo Godmarson, he'll be glad to get away from his nagging wife for a spell."

So Eudoric and Jillo set forth to eastward, from the knight's holding of Arduen, in the barony of Zurgau, in the county of Treveria, in the kingdom of Locania, in the New Napolitanian Empire. Eudoric—of medium height, powerful build, dark, with square-jawed but otherwise undistinguished features—rode his palfrey and led his mighty destrier Morgrim. The lank, lean Jillo bestrode another palfrey and led a sumpter mule. Morgrim was piled with Eudoric's panoply of plate, carefully nested into a compact bundle and lashed down under a canvas cover. The mule bore the rest of their supplies.

For a fortnight they wended uneventfully through the duchies and counties of the Empire. When they reached lands where they could no longer understand the local dia-

lects, they made shift with Helladic; the tongue of the Old
Napolitanian Empire, which lettered men spoke everywhere.

They stopped at inns where inns were to be had. For the
first fortnight, Eudoric was too preoccupied with dreams of
his beloved Lusina to notice the tavern wenches. After that,
his urges began to fever him, and he bedded one in Zerbstat,
to their mutual satisfaction. Thereafter, however, he forebore,
not as a matter of sexual morals but as a matter of thrift.

When benighted on the road, they slept under the stars—
or, as befell them on the marches of Avaria, under a rain-
dripping canopy of clouds. As they bedded down in the wet,
Eudoric asked his companion:

"Jillo, why did you not remind me to bring a tent?"

Jillo sneezed. "Why, sir, come rain, come snow, I never
thought that so sturdy a springald as ye be would ever need
one. The heroes in the romances never travel with tents."

"To the nethermost hell with heroes of the romances! They
go clattering around on their destriers for a thousand cantos.
Weather is ever fine. Food, shelter, and a change of clothing
appear, as by magic, whenever desired. Their armor never
rusts. They suffer no tisics and fluxes. They pick up no fleas
or lice at the inns. They're never swindled by merchants, for
none does aught so vulgar as buying and selling."

"If ye'll pardon me, sir," said Jillo, "that were no knightly
way to speak. It becomes not your station."

"Well, to the nethermost hells with my station, too! Wherever these paladins go, they find damsels in distress to
rescue, or have other agreeable, thrilling and sanitary adventures. What adventures have we had? The time we fled from
robbers in the Turonian Forest. The time I fished you out of
the Albis half drowned. The time we ran out of food in the
Asciburgi Mountains and had to plod fodderless over those
hair-raising peaks for three days on empty stomachs."

"The Divine Pair do but seek to try the mettle of a valorous
aspirant knight, sir. Ye should welcome these petty adversi-
ties as a chance to prove your manhood."

Eudoric made a rude noise with his mouth. "That for my
manhood! Right now, I'd fainer have a stout roof overhead, a
warm fire before me, and a hot repast in my belly. An ever I
go on such a silly jaunt again, I'll find one of those
versemongers—like that troubadour, Landwin of Kromnitch,
that visited us yesteryear—and drag him along, to show him
how little real adventures are like those of the romances.

And if he fall into the Albis, he may drown, for all of me. Were it not for my darling Lusina—"

Eudoric lapsed into gloomy silence, punctuated by sneezes.

They plodded on until they came to the village of Liptai, on the border of Pathenia. After the border guards had questioned and passed them, they walked their animals down the deep mud of the main street. Most of the slatternly houses were of logs or of crudely hewn planks, innocent of paint.

"Heaven above!" said Jillo. "Look at that, sir!"

"That" was a gigantic snail shell, converted into a small house.

"Knew you not of the giant snails of Pathenia?" asked Eudoric. "I've read of them in Doctor Boldonius' encyclopedia. When full grown, they—or rather their shells—are ofttimes used for dwellings in this land."

Jillo shook his head. " 'Twere better had ye spent more of your time on your knightly exercises and less on reading. Your sire hath never learnt his letters, yet he doth his duties well enow."

"Times change, Jillo. I may not clang rhymes so featly as Doctor Baldonius, or that ass Landwin of Kromnitch; but in these days a stroke of the pen were oft more fell than the slash of a sword. Here's a hostelry that looks not too slummocky. Do you dismount and inquire within as to their tallage."

"Why, sir?"

"Because I am fain to know, ere we put our necks in the noose! Go ahead. An I go in, they'll double the scot at sight of me."

When Jillo came out and quote prices, Eudoric said, "Too dear. We'll try the other."

"But, Master! Mean ye to put us in some flea-bitten hovel, like that which we suffered in Bitava?"

"Aye. Didst not prate to me on the virtues of petty adversity in strengthening one's knightly mettle?"

" 'Tis not that, sir."

"What, then?"

"Why, when better quarters are to be had, to make do with the worse were an insult to your rank and station. No gentleman—"

"Ah, here we are!" said Eudoric. "Suitably squalid, too! You see, good Jillo, I did but yester'en count our money, and lo! more than half is gone, and our journey not yet half completed."

"But, noble Master, no man of knightly mettle would so debase himself as to tally his silver, like some base-born commercial—"

"Then I must needs lack true knightly mettle. Here we be!"

For a dozen leagues beyond Liptai rose the great, dense Motolian Forest. Beyond the forest lay the provincial capital of Velitchovo. Beyond Velitchovo, the forest thinned out *gradatim* to the great grassy plains of Pathenia. Beyond Pathenia, Eudoric had been told, stretched the boundless deserts of Pantorozia, over which a man might ride for months without seeing a city.

Yes, the innkeeper told him, there were plenty of dragons in the Motolian Forest. "But fear them not," said Kasmar in broken Helladic. "From being hunted, they have become wary and even timid. An ye stick to the road and move yarely, they'll pester you not unless ye surprise or corner one."

"Have any dragons been devouring maidens fair lately?" asked Eudoric.

Kasmar laughed. "Nay, good Master. What were maidens fair doing, traipsing round the woods to stir up the beasties? Leave them be, I say, and they'll do the same by you."

A cautious instinct warned Eudoric not to speak of his quest. After he and Jillo had rested and had renewed their equipment, they set out, two days later, into the Motolian Forest. They rode for a league along the Velitchovo road. Then Eudoric, accoutered in full plate and riding Morgrim, led his companion off the road into the woods to southward. They threaded their way among the trees, ducking branches, in a wide sweep around. Steering by the sun, Eudoric brought them back to the road near Liptai.

The next day they did the same, except that their circuit was to the north of the highway.

After three more days of this exploration, Jillo became restless. "Good Master, what do we, circling round and about so bootlessly? The dragons dwell farther east, away from the haunts of men, they say."

"Having once been lost in the woods," said Eudoric, "I would not repeat the experience. Therefore do we scout our field of action, like a general scouting a future battlefield."

" 'Tis an arid business," said Jillo with a shrug. "But then, ye were always one to see further into a millstone than most."

At last, having thoroughly committed the byways of the nearer forest to memory. Eudoric led Jillo farther east. After casting about, they came at last upon the unmistakable tracks of a dragon. The animal had beaten a path through the brush, along which they could ride almost as well as on the road. When they had followed this track for above an hour, Eudoric became aware of a strong, musky stench.

"My lance, Jillo!" said Eudoric, trying to keep his voice from rising with nervousness.

The next bend in the path brought them into full view of the dragon, a thirty-footer facing them on the trail.

"Ha!" said Eudoric. "Meseems 'tis a mere cockadrill, albeit longer of neck and of limb than those that dwell in the rivers of Agisymba—if the pictures in Doctor Baldonius' books lie not. Have at thee, vile worm!"

Eudoric couched his lance and put spurs to Morgrim. The destrier bounded forward.

The dragon raised its head and peered this way and that, as if it could not see well. As the hoofbeats drew nearer, the dragon opened its jaws and uttered a loud, hoarse, groaning bellow.

At that, Morgrim checked his rush with stiffened forelegs, spun ponderously on his haunches, and veered off the trail into the woods. Jillo's palfrey bolted likewise, but in another direction. The dragon set out after Eudoric at a shambling trot.

Eudoric had not gone fifty yards when Morgrim passed close aboard a massive old oak, a thick limb of which jutted into their path. The horse ducked beneath the bough. The branch caught Eudoric across the breastplate, flipped him backwards over the high cantle of his saddle, and swept him to earth with a great clatter.

Half stunned, he saw the dragon trot closer and closer— and then lumber past him, almost within arm's length, and disappear on the trail of the fleeing horse. The next that Eudoric knew, Jillo was bending over him, crying:

"Alas, my poor heroic Master! Be any bones broke, sir?"

"All of them, methinks," groaned Eudoric. "What's befallen Morgrim?"

"That I know not. And look at this dreadful dent in your beauteous cuirass!"

"Help me out of the thing. The dent pokes most sorely into my ribs. The misadventures I suffer for my dear Lusina!"

"We must get your breatsplate to a smith to have it hammered out and filed smooth again."

"Fiends take the smiths! They'd charge half the cost of a new one. I'll fix it myself, if I can find a flat rock to set it on and a big stone wherewith to pound it."

"Well, sir," said Jillo, "ye were always a good man of your hands. But the mar will show, and that were not suitable for one of your quality."

"Thou mayst take my quality and stuff it!" cried Eudoric. "Canst speak of nought else? Help me up, pray." He got slowly to his feet, wincing, and limped a few steps.

"At least," he said, "nought seems fractured. But I misdoubt I can walk back to Liptai."

"Oh, sir, that were not to be thought of! Me allow you to wend afoot whilst I ride? Fiends take the thought!" Jillo unhitched the palfrey from the tree to which he had tethered it and led it to Eudoric.

"I accept your courtesy, good Jillo, only because I must. To plod the distance afoot were but a condign punishment for so bungling my charge. Give me a boost, will you?" Eudoric grunted as Jillo helped him into the saddle.

"Tell me, sir," said Jillo, "why did the beast ramp on past you without stopping to devour you as ye lay helpless? Was't that Morgrim promised a more bounteous repast? Or that the monster feared that your plate would give him a disorder of the bowels?"

"Meseems 'twas neither. Marked you how gray and milky appeared its eyes? According to Doctor Baldonius' book, dragons shed their skins from time to time, like serpents. This one neared the time of its skin change, wherefore the skin over its eyeballs had become thickened and opaque, like glass of poor quality. Therefore it could not plainly discern objects lying still, and pursued only those that moved."

They got back to Liptai after dark. Both were barely able to stagger, Eudoric from his sprains and bruises and Jillo footsore from the unaccustomed three-league hike.

Two days later, when they had recovered, they set out on the two palfreys to hunt for Morgrim. "For," Eudoric said, "that nag is worth more in solid money than all the rest of my possessions together."

Eudoric rode unarmored save for a shirt of light mesh mail, since the palfrey could not carry the extra weight of the plate all day at a brisk pace. He bore his lance and sword, however, in case they should again encounter a dragon.

They found the site of the previous encounter, but no sign either of the dragon or of the destrier. Eudoric and Jillo tracked the horse by its prints in the soft mold for a few bowshots, but then the slot faded out on harder ground.

"Still, I misdoubt Morgrim fell victim to the beast," said Eudoric. "He could show clean heels to many a steed of lighter build, and from its looks the dragon was no courser."

After hours of fruitless searching, whistling, and calling, they returned to Liptai. For a small free, Eudoric was allowed to post a notice in Helladic on the town notice board, offering a reward for the return of his horse.

No word, however, came of the sighting of Morgrim. For all that Eudoric could tell, the destrier might have run clear to Velitchovo.

"You are free with advice, good Jillo," said Eudoric. "Well, rede me this riddle. We've established that our steeds will bolt from the sight and smell of dragon, for which I blame them little. Had we all the time in the world, we could doubtless train them to face the monsters, beginning with a stuffed dragon, and then, perchance, one in a cage in some monarch's menagerie. But our lucre dwindles like the snow in spring. What's to do?"

"Well, if the nags won't stand, needs we must face the worms on foot," said Jillo.

"That seems to me to throw away our lives to no good purpose, for these vasty lizards can outrun and outturn us and are well harnessed to boot. Barring the luckiest of lucky thrusts with the spear—as, say, into the eye or down the gullet—that fellow we erst encountered could make one mouthful of my lance and another of me."

Your knightly courage were sufficient defense, sir. The Divine Pair would surely grant victory to the right."

"From all I've read of battles and feuds," said Eudoric, "methinks the Holy Couple's attention oft strays elsewhither when they should be deciding the outcome of some mundane fray."

"That is the trouble with reading; it undermines one's faith in the True Religion. But ye could be at least as well armored as the dragon, in your panoply of plate."

"Aye, but then poor Daisy could not bear so much weight to the site—or, at least, bear it thither and have breath left for a charge. We must be as chary of our beasts' welfare as of our own, for without them 'tis a long walk back to Treveria. Nor do I deem that we should like to pass our lives in Liptai."

"Then, sir, we could pack the armor on the mule, for you to do on in dragon country."

"I like it not," said Eudoric. "Afoot, weighted down by that lobster's habit, I could move no more spryly than a tortoise. 'Twere small comfort to know that if the dragon ate me, he'd suffer indigestion afterward."

Jillo sighed. "Not the knightly attitude, sir, if ye'll pardon my saying so."

"Say what you please, but I'll follow the course of what meseems were common sense. What we need is a brace of those heavy steel crossbows for sieges. At close range, they'll punch a hole in a breastplate as 'twere a sheet of papyrus."

"They take too long to crank up," said Jillo. "By the time ye've readied your second shot, the battle's over."

"Oh, it would behoove us to shoot straight the first time; but better one shot that pierces the monster's scales than a score that bounce off. Howsomever, we have these fell little hand catapults not, and they don't make them in this barbarous land."

A few days later, while Eudoric still fretted over the lack of means to his goal, he heard a sudden sound like a single thunderclap from close at hand. Hastening out from Kasmar's Inn, Eudoric and Jillo found a crowd of Pathenians around the border guard's barracks.

In the drill yard, the guard was drawn up to watch a man demonstrate a weapon. Eudoric, whose few words of Pathenian were not up to conversation, asked among the crowd for somebody who could speak Helladic. When he found one, he learned that the demonstrator was a Pantorozian. The man was a stocky, snub-nosed fellow in a bulbous fur hat, a jacket of coarse undyed wool, and baggy trousers tucked into soft boots.

"He says the device was invented by the Sericans," said the villager. "They live half a world away, across the Pantorozian deserts. He puts some powder into that thing, touches a flame to it, and *boom!* it spits a leaden ball through the target as neatly as you please."

The Pantorozian demonstrated again, pouring black powder from the small end of a horn down his brass barrel. He placed a wad of rag over the mouth of the tube, then a leaden ball, and pushed both ball and wad down the tube with a rod. He poured a pinch of powder into a hole on the upper side of the tube near its rear, closed end.

Then he set a forked rest in the ground before him, rested the barrel in the fork, and took a small torch that a guardsman handed him. He pressed the wooden stock of the device against his shoulder, sighted along the tube, and with his free hand touched the torch to the touchhole. Ffft, *bang!* A cloud of smoke, and another hole appeared in the target.

The Pantorozian spoke with the captain of the guard, but they were too far for Eudoric to hear, even if he could have understood their Pathenian. After a while, the Pantorozian picked up his tube and rest, slung his bag of powder over his shoulder, and walked with downcast air to a cart hitched to a shade tree.

Eudoric approached the man, who was climbing into his cart. "God den, fair sir!" began Eudoric, but the Pantorozian spread his hands with a smile of incomprehension.

"Kasmar!" cried Eudoric, sighting the innkeeper in the crowd. "Will you have the goodness to interpret for me and this fellow?"

"He says," said Kasmar, "that he started out with a wainload of these devices and has sold all but one. He hoped to dispose of his last one in Liptai, but our gallant Captain Boriswaf will have nought to do with it."

"Why?" asked Eudoric. "Meseems 'twere a fell weapon in practiced hands."

"That is the trouble, quoth Master Vlek. Boriswaf says that should so fiendish a weapon come into use, 'twill utterly extinguish the noble art of war, for all men will down weapons and refuse to fight rather than face so devilish a device. Then what should he, a lifelong soldier, do for his bread? Beg?"

"Ask Master Vlek where he thinks to pass the night."

"I have already persuaded him to lodge with us, Master Eudoric."

"Good, for I would fain have further converse with him."

Over dinner, Eudoric sounded out the Pantorozian on the

price he asked for his device. Acting as translator, Kasmar said, "If ye strike a bargain on this, I should get ten per centum as a broker's commission, for ye were helpless without me."

Eudoric got the gun, with thirty pounds of powder and a bag of leaden balls and wadding, for less than half of what Vlek had asked of Captain Boriswaf. As Vlek explained, he had not done badly on this peddling trip and was eager to get home to his wives and children.

"Only remember," he said through Kasmar, "overcharge it not, lest it blow apart and take your head off. Press the stock firmly against your shoulder, lest it knock you on your arse like a mule's kick. And keep fire away from the spare powder, lest it explode all at once and blast you to gobbets."

Later, Eudoric told Jillo, "That deal all but wiped out our funds."

"After the tradesmanlike way ye chaffered that barbarian down?"

"Aye. The scheme had better work, or we shall find ourselves choosing betwixt starving and seeking employment as collectors of offal or diggers of ditches. Assuming, that is, that in this reeky place they even bother to collect offal."

"Master Eudoric!" said Jillo. "Ye would not really lower yourself to accept menial wage labor?"

"Sooner than starve, aye. As Helvolius the philosopher said, no rider wears sharper spurs than Necessity."

"But if 'twere known at home, they'd hack off your gilded spurs, break your sword over your head, and degrade you to base varlet!"

"Well, till now I've had no knightly spurs to hack off, but only the plain silvered ones of an esquire. For the rest, I count on you to see that they don't find out. Now go to sleep and cease your grumbling."

The next day found Eudoric and Jillo deep into the Motolian Forest. At the noonday halt, Jillo kindled a fire. Eudoric made a small torch of a stick whose end was wound with a rag soaked in bacon fat. Then he loaded the device as he had been shown how to do and fired three balls at a mark on a tree. The third time, he hit the mark squarely, although the noise caused the palfreys frantically to tug and rear.

They remounted and went on to where they had met the dragon. Jillo rekindled the torch, and they cast up and down the beast's trail. For two hours they saw no wildlife save a fleeing sow with a farrow of piglets and several huge snails with boulder-sized shells.

Then the horses became unruly. "Methinks they scent our quarry," said Eudoric.

When the riders themselves could detect the odor and the horses became almost unmanageable, Eudoric and Jillo dismounted.

"Tie the nags securely," said Eudoric. " 'Twould never do to slay our beast and then find that our horses had fled, leaving us to drag this land cockadrill home afoot."

As if in answer, a deep grunt came from ahead. While Jillo secured the horses. Eudoric laid out his new equipment and methodically loaded his piece.

"Here it comes," said Eudoric. "Stand by with that torch. Apply it not ere I give the word!"

The dragon came in sight, plodding along the trail and swinging its head from side to side. Having just shed its skin, the dragon gleamed in a reticular pattern of green and black, as if it had been freshly painted. Its great, golden, slit-pupiled eyes were now keen.

The horses screamed, causing the dragon to look up and speed its approach.

"Ready?" said Eudoric, setting the device in its rest.

"Aye, sir. Here goeth!" Without awaiting further command, Jillo applied the torch to the touchhole.

With a great boom and a cloud of smoke, the device discharged, rocking Eudoric back a pace. When the smoke cleared, the dragon was still rushing upon them, unharmed.

"Thou idiot!" screamed Eudoric. "I told thee not to give fire until I commanded! Thou hast made me miss it clean!"

"I'm s-sorry, sir. I was palsied with fear. What shall we do now?"

"Run, fool!" Dropping the device, Eudoric turned and fled. Jillo also ran. Eudoric tripped over a root and fell sprawling. Jillo stopped to guard his fallen master and turned to face the dragon. As Eudoric scrambled up, Jillo hurled the torch at the dragon's open maw.

The throw fell just short of its target. It happened, however, that the dragon was just passing over the bag of black powder in its charge. The whirling torch, descending in its flight beneath the monster's head, struck this sack.

BOOM!

When the dragon hunters returned, they found the dragon

writhing in its death throes. Its whole underside had been blown open, and blood and guts spilled out.

"Well!" said Eudoric, drawing a long breath. "That is enough knightly adventure to last me for many a year. Fall to; we must flay the creature. Belike we can sell that part of the hide that we take not home ourselves."

"How do ye propose to get it back to Liptai? Its hide alone must weigh in the hundreds."

"We shall hitch the dragon's tail to our two nags and lead them, dragging it behind. 'Twill be a weary swink, but we must needs recover as much as we can to recoup our losses."

An hour later, blood-spattered from head to foot, they were still struggling with the vast hide. Then, a man in forester's garb, with a large gilt medallion on his breast, rode up and dismounted. He was a big, rugged-looking man with a rat-trap mouth.

"Who slew this beast, good my sirs?" he inquired.

Jillo spoke: "My noble master, the squire Eudoric Dambertson here. He is the hero who hath brought this accursed beast to book."

"Be that sooth?" said the man to Eudoric.

"Well, ah," said Eudoric, "I must not claim much credit for the deed."

"But ye were the slayer, yea? Then, sir, ye are under arrest."

"What? But wherefore?"

"Ye shall see." From his garments, the stranger produced a length of cord with knots at intervals. With this he measured the dragon from nose to tail. Then the man stood up again.

"To answer your question, on three grounds: *imprimis,* for slaying a dragon out of lawful season; *secundus,* for slaying a dragon below the minimum size permitted; and *tertius,* for slaying a female dragon, which is protected the year round."

"You say this is a female?"

"Aye, 'tis as plain as the nose on your face."

"How does one tell with dragons?"

"Know, knave, that the male hath small horns behind the eyes, the which this specimen patently lacks."

"Who are you anyway?" demanded Eudoric.

"Senior game warden Voytsik of Prath, at your service. My credentials." The man fingered his medallion. "Now, show me your licenses, pray!"

"Licenses?" said Eudoric blankly.

"Hunting licenses, oaf!"

"None told us that such were required, sir," said Jillo.

"Ignorance of the law is no pretext; ye should have asked. That makes four counts of illegality."

Eudoric said, "But why—why in the name of the God and Goddess—"

"Pray, swear not by your false, heretical deities."

"Well, why should you Pathenians wish to preserve these monstrous reptiles."

"*Imprimis,* because their hides and other parts have commercial value, which would perish were the whole race extirpated. *Secundus,* because they help to maintain the balance of nature by devouring the giant snails, which otherwise would issue forth nightly from the forest in such numbers as to strip bare our crops, orchards, and gardens and reduce our folk to hunger. And *tertius,* because they add a picturesque element to the landscape, thus luring foreigners to visit our land and spend their gold therein. Doth that explanation satisfy you?"

Eudoric had a fleeting thought of assaulting the stranger and either killing him or rendering him helpless while Eudoric and Jillo salvaged their prize. Even as he thought, three more tough-looking fellows, clad like Voytsik and armed with crossbows, rode out of the trees and formed up behind their leader.

"Now come along, ye two," said Voytsik.

"Whither?" asked Eudoric.

"Back to Liptai. On the morrow, we take the stage to Velitchovo, where your case will be tried."

"Your pardon, sir; we take the what?"

"The stagecoach."

"What's that, good my sir?"

"By the only God, ye must come from a barbarous land indeed! Ye shall see. Now come along, lest we be benighted in the woods."

The stagecoach made a regular round trip between Liptai and Velitchovo thrice a sennight. Jillo made the journey sunk in gloom, Eudoric kept busy viewing the passing countryside and, when opportunity offered, asking the driver about his occupation: pay, hours, fares, the cost of the vehicle, and so forth. By the time the prisoners reached their destination, both stank mightily because they had had no chance to wash the dragon's blood from their blood-soaked garments.

As they neared the capital, the driver whipped up his team to a gallop. They rattled along the road beside the muddy river Pshora until the river made a bend. Then they thundered across the planks of a bridge.

Velitchovo was a real city, with a roughly paved main street and an onion-domed, brightly colored cathedral of the One God. In a massively timbered municipal palace, a bewhiskered magistrate asked, "Which of you two aliens truly slew the beast?"

"The younger, hight Eudoric," said Voytsik.

"Nay, Your Honor, 'twas I!" said Jillo.

"That is not what he said when we came upon them red-handed from their crime," said Voytsik. "This lean fellow plainly averred that his companion had done the deed, and the other denied it not."

"I can explain that," said Jillo. "I am the servant of the most worshipful squire Eudoric Dambertson of Arduen. We set forth to slay the creature, thinking this a noble and heroic deed that should redound to our glory on earth and our credit in Heaven. Whereas we both had a part in the act, the fatal stroke was delivered by your humble servant here. Howsomever, wishing like a good servant for all the glory to go to my master. I gave him the full credit, not knowing that this credit should be counted as blame."

"What say ye to that, Master Eudoric?" asked the judge.

"Jillo's account is essentially true," said Eudoric. "I must, however, confess that my failure to slay the beast was due to mischance and not want of intent."

"Methinks they utter a pack of lies to confuse the court," said Voytsik. "I have told Your Honor of the circumstance of their arrest, whence ye may judge how matters stand."

The judge put his fingertips together. "Master Eudoric," he said, "ye may plead innocent, or as incurring sole guilt, or as guilty in company with your servant. I do not think that you can escape some guilt, since Master Jillo, being your servant, acted under your orders. Ye be therefore responsible for his acts and at the very least a fautor of dragocide."

"What happens if I plead innocent?" said Eudoric.

"Why, in that case, an ye can find an attorney, ye shall be tried in due course. Bail can plainly not be allowed to foreign travelers, who can so easily slip through the law's fingers."

"In other words, I needs must stay in jail until my case comes up. How long will that take?"

"Since our calendar be crowded, 'twill be at least a year and a half. Whereas, an ye plead guilty, all is settled in a trice."

"Then I plead sole guilt," said Eudoric.

"But, dear Master—" wailed Jillo.

"Hold thy tongue, Jillo. I know what I do."

The judge chuckled. "An old head on young shoulders, I perceive. Well, Master Eudoric. I find you guilty on all four counts and amerce you the wonted fine, which is one hundred marks on each count."

"Four hundred marks!" exclaimed Eudoric. "Our total combined wealth at this moment amounts to fourteen marks and thirty-seven pence, plus some items of property left with Master Kasmar in Liptai."

"So, ye'll have to serve out the corresponding prison term, which comes to one mark a day—unless ye can find someone to pay the balance of the fine for you. Taken him away, jailer."

"But, Your Honor!" cried Jillo, "what shall I do without my noble master? When shall I see him again?"

"Ye may visit him any day during the regular visiting hours. It were well if ye brought him somewhat to eat, for our prison fare is not of the daintiest."

At the first visiting hour, when Jillo pleaded to be allowed to share Eudoric's sentence, Eudoric said, "Be not a bigger fool than thou canst help! I took sole blame so that ye should be free to run mine errands; whereas had I shared my guilt with you, we had both been mewed up here. Here, take this letter to Doctor Raspiudus; seek him out and acquaint him with our plight. If he be in sooth a true friend of our own Doctor Baldonius, belike he'll come to our rescue."

Doctor Raspiudus was short and fat, with a bushy white beard to his waist. "Ah, dear old Baldonius!" he cried in good Helladic. "I mind me of when we were lads together at the Arcane College of Saalingen University! Doth he still string verses together?"

"Aye, that he does," said Eudoric.

"Now, young man, I daresay that your chiefest desire is to get out of this foul hole, is't not?"

"That, *and* to recover our three remaining animals and other possessions left behind in Liptai, *and* to depart with the two square yards of dragon hide that I've promised to Doctor Baldonius, with enough money to see us home."

"Methinks all these matters were easily arranged, young sir. I need only your power of attorney to enable me to go to Liptai, recover the objects in question, and return hither to pay your fine and release you. Your firearm is, I fear, lost to you, having been confiscated by the law."

"'Twere of little use without a new supply of the magical powder," said Eudoric. "Your plan sounds splendid. But, sir, what do you get out of this?"

The enchanter rubbed his hands together. "Why, the pleasure of favoring an old friend—and also the chance to acquire a complete dragon hide for my own purposes. I know somewhat of Baldonius' experiments. As he can do thus and so with two yards of dragon, I can surely do more with a score."

"How will you obtain this dragon hide?"

"By now the foresters will have skinned the beast and salvaged the other parts of monetary worth, all of which will be put up at auction for the benefit of the kingdom. And I shall bid them in." Raspiudus chuckled. "When the other bidders know against whom they bid, I think not that they'll force the price up very far."

"Why can't you get me out of here now and then go to Liptai?"

Another chuckle. "My dear boy, first I must see that all is as ye say in Liptai. After all, I have only your word that ye be in sooth the Eudoric Dambertson of whom Baldonius writes. So bide ye in patience a few days more. I'll see that ye be sent better aliment than the slop they serve here. And now, pray, your authorization. Here are pen and ink."

To keep from starvation, Jillo got a job as a paver's helper and worked in hasty visits to the jail during his lunch hour. When a fortnight had passed without word from Doctor Raspiudus, Eudoric told Jillo to go to the wizard's home for an explanation.

"They turned me away at the door," reported Jillo. "They told me that the learned doctor had never heard of us."

As the import of this news sank in, Eudoric cursed and beat the wall in his rage. "That filthy, treacherous he-witch! He gets me to sign that power of attorney; then, when he has my property in his grubby paws, he conveniently forgets about us! By the God and Goddess, if ever I catch him—"

"Here, here, what's all this noise?" said the jailer. "Ye disturb the other prisoners."

When Jillo explained the cause of his master's outrage, the jailer laughed. "Why, everyone knows that Raspiudus is the worst skinflint and treacher in Velitchovo! Had ye asked me, I'd have warned you."

"Why has none of his victims slain him?" asked Eudoric.

"We are a law-abiding folk, sir. We do not permit private persons to indulge their feuds on their own, and we have some *most* ingenious penalties for homicide."

"Mean ye," said Jillo, "that amongst you Pathenians a gentleman may not avenge an insult by the gage of battle?"

"Of course not! We are not bloodthirsty barbarians."

"Ye mean there are no true gentlemen amongst you," sniffed Jillo.

"Then, Master Tiolkhof," said Eudoric, calming himself by force of will, "am I stuck here for a year and more?"

"Aye, but ye may get time off for good behavior at the end—three or four days, belike."

When the jailer had gone, Jillo said, "When ye get out, Master, ye must needs uphold your honor by challenging this runagate to the trial of battle, to the death."

Eudoric shook his head. "Heard you not what Tiolkhof said? They deem dueling barbarous and boil the duelists in oil, or something equally entertaining. Anyway, Raspiudus could beg off on grounds of age. We must, instead, use what wits the Holy Couple gave us. I wish now that I'd sent you back to Liptai to fetch our belongings and never meddled with his rolypoly sorcerer."

"True, but how could ye know, dear Master? I should probably have bungled the task in any case, what with my ignorance of the tongue and all."

After another fortnight, King Vladmor of Pathenia died. When his son Yogor ascended the throne, he declared a general amnesty for all crimes less than murder. Thus Eudoric found himself out in the street again, but without horse, armor, weapons, or money beyond a few marks.

"Jillo," he said that night in their mean little cubicle, "we must needs get into Raspiudus' house somehow. As we saw this afternoon, 'tis a big place with a stout, high wall around it."

"An ye could get a supply of that black powder, we could blast a breach in the wall."

"But we have no such stuff, nor means of getting it, unless we raid the royal armory, which I do not think we can do."

"Then how about climbing a tree near the wall and letting ourselves down by ropes inside the wall from a convenient branch?"

"A promising plan, *if* there were such an overhanging tree. But there isn't, as you saw as well as I when we scouted the place. Let me think. Raspiudus must have supplies borne into his stronghold from time to time. I misdoubt his wizardry is potent enough to conjure foodstuffs out of air."

"Mean ye that we should gain entrance as, say, a brace of chicken farmers with eggs to sell?"

"Just so. But nay, that won't do. Raspiudus is no fool. Knowing of this amnesty that enlarged me, he'll be on the watch for such a trick. At least, so should I be, in his room, and I credit him with no less wit than mine own. . . . I have it! What visitor would logically be likely to call upon him now, whom he will not have seen for many a year and whom he would hasten to welcome?"

"That I know not, sir."

"Who would wonder what had become of us and, detecting our troubles in his magical scryglass, would follow upon our track by uncanny means?"

"Oh, ye mean Doctor Baldonius!"

"Aye. My whiskers have grown nigh as long as his since last I shaved. And we're much of a size."

"But I never heard that your old tutor could fly about on an enchanted broomstick, as some of the mightiest magicians are said to do."

"Belike he can't, but Doctor Raspiudus wouldn't know that."

"Mean ye," said Jillo, "that ye've a mind to play Doctor Baldonius? Or to have me play him? The latter would never do."

"I know it wouldn't, good my Jillo. You know not the learned patter proper to wizards and other philosophers."

"Won't Raspiudus know you, sir? As ye say he's a shrewd old villain."

"He's seen me but once, in that dark, dank cell, and that for a mere quarter hour. You he's never seen at all. Methinks I can disguise myself well enough to befool him—unless you have a better notion."

"Alack, I have none! Then what part shall I play?"

"I had thought of going in alone."

"Nay, sir, dismiss the thought! Me let my master risk his mortal body and immortal soul in a witch's lair without my being there to help him!"

"If you help me the way you did by touching off that firearm whilst our dragon was out of range—"

"Ah, but who threw the torch and saved us in the end? What disguise shall I wear?"

"Since Raspiudus knows you not, there's no need for any. You shall be Baldonius' servant, as you are mine."

"Ye forget, sir, that if Raspiudus knows me not, his gate-keepers might. Forsooth, they're likely to recall me because of the noisy protests I made when they barred me out."

"Hm. Well, you're too old for a page, too lank for a body-guard, and too unlearned for a wizard's assistant. I have it! You shall go as my concubine!"

"Oh, Heaven above, sir, not that! I am a normal man! I should never live it down!"

To the massive gate before Raspiudus' house came Eudoric, with a patch over one eye, and his beard, uncut for a month, dyed white. A white wig cascaded down from under his hat. He presented a note, in a plausible imitation of Baldonius' hand, to the gatekeeper:

Doctor Baldonius of Treveria presents his compliments to his old friend and colleague Doctor Raspiudus of Velitchovo, and begs the favor of an audience to discuss the apparent disappearance of two young protégés of his.

A pace behind, stooping to disguise his stature, slouched a rouged and powdered Jillo in woman's dress. If Jillo was a homely man, he made a hideous woman, least as far as his face could be seen under the headcloth. Nor was his beauty enhanced by the dress, which Eudoric had stitched together out of cheap cloth. The garment looked like what it was: the work of a rank amateur at dressmaking.

"My master begs you to enter," said the gatekeeper.

"Why, dear old Baldonius!" cried Raspiudus, rubbing his hands together. "Ye've not changed a mite since those glad, mad days at Saalingen! Do ye still string verses?"

"Ye've withstood the ravages of time well yourself, Raspiudus," said Eudoric, in an imitation of Baldonius' voice.

"'As fly the years, the geese fly north in spring; Ah, would the years, like geese, return awing!'"

Raspiudus roared with laughter, patting his paunch. "The same old Baldonius! Made ye that one up?"

Eudoric made a deprecatory motion. "I am a mere poetaster; but had not the higher wisdom claimed my allegiance, I might have made my mark in poesy."

"What befell your poor eye?"

"My own carelessness in leaving a corner of a pentacle open. The demon got in a swipe of his claws ere I could banish him. But now, good Raspiudus, I have a matter to discuss whereof I told you in my note."

"Yea, yea, time enow for that. Be ye weary from the road? Need ye baths? Aliment? Drink?"

"Not yet, old friend. We have but now come from Velitchovo's best hostelry."

"Then let me show you my house and grounds. Your lady . . . ?"

"She'll stay with me. She speaks nought but Treverian and fears being separated from me among strangers. A mere swineherd's chick, but a faithful creature. At my age, that is of more moment than a pretty face."

Presently, Eudoric was looking at his and Jillo's palfreys and their sumpter mule in Raspiudus' stables. Eudoric made a few hesitant efforts, as if he were Baldonius seeking his young friends, to inquire after their disappearance. Each time Raspiudus smoothly turned the question aside, promising enlightenment later.

An hour later, Raspiudus was showing off his magical sanctum. With obvious interest, Eudoric examined a number of squares of dragon hide spread out on a workbench. He asked:

"Be this the integument of one of those Pathenian dragons, whereof I have heard?"

"Certes, good Baldonius. Are they extinct in your part of the world?"

"Aye. 'Twas for that reason that I sent my young friend and former pupil, of whom I'm waiting to tell you, eastward to fetch me some of this hide for use in my work. How does one cure this hide?"

"With salt, and —*unh!*"

Raspiudus collapsed, Eudoric having just struck him on

the head with a short bludgeon that he whisked out of his voluminous sleeves.

"Bind and gag him and roll him behind the bench!" said Eudoric.

"Were it not better to cut his throat, sir?" said Jillo.

"Nay. The jailer told us that they have ingenious ways of punishing homicide, and I have no wish to prove them by experiment."

While Jillo bound the unconscious Raspiudus, Eudoric chose two pieces of dragon hide, each about a yard square. He rolled them together into a bundle and lashed them with a length of rope from inside his robe. As an afterthought, he helped himself to the contents of Raspiudus' purse. Then he hoisted the roll of hide to his shoulder and issued from the laboratory. He called to the nearest stableboy.

"Doctor Raspiudus," he said, "asks that ye saddle up those two nags." He pointed. "Good saddles, mind you! Are the animals well shod?"

"Hasten, sir," muttered Jillo. "Every instant we hang about here—"

"Hold thy peace! The appearance of haste were the surest way to arouse suspicion." Eudoric raised his voice. "Another heave on that girth, fellow! I am not minded to have my aged bones shattered by a tumble into the roadway."

Jillo whispered, "Can't we recover the mule and your armor, to boot?"

Eudoric shook his head. "Too risky," he murmured. "Be glad if we get away with whole skins."

When the horses had been saddled to his satisfaction, he said, "Lend me some of your strength in mounting, youngster." He groaned as he swung awkwardly into the saddle. "A murrain on thy master, to send us off on this footling errand— me that hasn't sat a horse in years! Now hand me that accursed roll of hide. I thank thee, youth; here's a little for thy trouble. Run ahead and tell the gatekeeper to have his portal well opened. I fear that if this beast pulls up of a sudden, I shall go flying over its head!"

A few minutes later, when they had turned a corner and were out of sight of Raspiudus' house, Eudoric said, "Now trot!"

"If I could but get out of this damned gown," muttered Jillo. "I can't ride decently in it."

"Wait till we're out of the city gate."

When Jillo had shed the offending garment, Eudoric said, "Now ride, man, as never before in your life!"

They pounded off on the Liptai road. Looking back, Jillo gave a screech. "There's a thing flying after us! It looks like a giant bat!"

"One of Raspiudus' sendings," said Eudoric. "I knew he'd get loose. Use your spurs! Can we but gain the bridge . . ."

They fled at a mad gallop. The sending came closer and closer, until Eudoric thought he could feel the wind of its wings.

Then their hooves thundered across the bridge over the Pshora.

"Those things will not cross running water," said Eudoric, looking back. "Slow down, Jillo. These nags must bear us many leagues, and we must not founder them at the start."

". . . so here we are," Eudoric told Doctor Baldonius.

"Ye've seen your family, lad?"

"Certes. They thrive, praise to the Divine Pair. Where's Lusina?"

"Well—ah—ahem—the fact is, she is not here."

"Oh? Then where?"

"Ye put me to shame, Eudoric. I promised you her hand in return for the two yards of dragon hide. Well, ye've fetched me the hide, at no small effort and risk, but I cannot fulfill my side of the bargain."

"Wherefore?"

"Alas! My undutiful daughter ran off with a strolling player last summer, whilst ye were chasing dragons—or perchance 'twas the other way round. I'm right truly sorry. . . ."

Eudoric frowned silently for an instant, then said, "Fret not, esteemed Doctor. I shall recover from the wound—provided, that is, that you salve it by making up my losses in more materialistic fashion."

Baldonius raised bushy gray brows. "So? Ye seem not so grief-stricken as I should have expected, to judge from the lover's sighs and tears wherewith ye parted from the jade last spring. Now ye'll accept money instead?"

"Aye, sir. I admit that my passion had somewhat cooled during our long separation. Was it likewise with her? What said she of me?"

"Aye, her sentiments did indeed change. She said you were

too much an opportunist altogether to please her. I would not wound your feelings. . . ."

Eudoric waved a deprecatory hand. "Continue, pray. I have been somewhat toughened by my months in the rude, rough world, and I am interested."

"Well, I told her she was being foolish; that ye were a shrewd lad who, an ye survived the dragon hunt, would go far. But her words were: 'That is just the trouble, Father. He is too shrewd to be very lovable.'"

"Hmph," grunted Eudoric. "As one might say: I am a man of enterprise, thou art an opportunist, he is a conniving scoundrel. 'Tis all in the point of view. Well, if she prefers the fools of this world, I wish her joy of them. As a man of honor, I would have wedded Lusina had she wished. As things stand, trouble is saved all around."

"To you, belike, though I misdoubt my headstrong lass'll find the life of an actor's wife a bed of violets:

'Who'd wed on a whim is soon filled to the brim
Of worry and doubt, till he longs for an out.
So if ye would wive, beware of the gyve
Of an ill-chosen mate; 'tis a harrowing fate.'

But enough of that. What sum had ye in mind?"

"Enough to cover the cost of my good destrier Morgrim and my panoply of plate, together with lance and sword, plus a few other chattels and incidental expenses of travel. Fifteen hundred marks should cover the lot."

"Fif-teen *hundred!* Whew! I could ne'er afford—nor are these moldy patches of dragon hide worth a fraction of the sum."

Eudoric sighed and rose. "You know what you can afford, good my sage." He picked up the roll of dragon hide. "Your colleague Doctor Calporio, wizard to the Count of Treveria, expressed a keen interest in this material. In fact, he offered me more than I have asked of you, but I thought it only honorable to give you the first chance."

"What!" cried Baldonius. "That mountebank, charlatan, that faker? Misusing the hide and not deriving a tenth of the magical benefits from it that I should? Sit down, Eudoric; we will discuss these things."

An hour's haggling got Eudoric his fifteen hundred marks.

Baldonius said, "Well, praise the Divine Couple that's over.
And now, beloved pupil, what are your plans?"

"Would ye believe it, Doctor Baldonius," said Jillo, "that
my poor, deluded master is about to disgrace his lineage and
betray his class by a base commercial enterprise?"

"Forsooth, Jillo? What's this?"

"He means my proposed coach line," said Eudoric.

"Good Heaven, what's that?"

"My plan to run a carriage on a weekly schedule from
Zurgau to Kromnitch, taking all who can pay the fare, as
they do in Pathenia. We can't let the heathen Easterlings get
ahead of us."

"What an extraordinary idea! Need ye a partner?"

"Thanks, but nay. Baron Emmerhard has already thrown
in with me. He's promised me my knighthood in exchange for
the partnership."

"There is no nobility anymore," said Jillo.

Eudoric grinned. "Emmerhard said much the same sort of
thing, but I convinced him that anything to do with horses is
a proper pursuit for a gentleman. Jillo, you can spell me at
driving the coach, which will make you a gentleman, too!"

Jillo sighed. "Alas! The true spirit of knighthood is dying
in this degenerate age. Woe is me that I should live to see the
end of chivalry! How much did ye think of paying me, sir?"

GREGORY BENFORD & MARC LAIDLAW

A physicist at the University of California at Irvine, Gregory Benford has won two Nebula Awards for his stylishly written hard science fiction. Most interested in the theme of alien contact, he often introduces philosophic issues into his stories. He has collaborated with others such as his twin brother James, Gordon Eklund, William Rotsler, and Marc Laidlaw.

A HISS OF DRAGON

by Gregory Benford & Marc Laidlaw

"INCOMING DRAGON!" Leopold yelled, and ducked to the left. I went right.

Dragons come in slow and easy. A blimp with wings, this one settled down like a wrinkled brown sky falling. I scrambled over boulders, trying to be inconspicuous and fast at the same time. It didn't seem like a promising beginning for a new job.

Leopold and I had been working on the ledge in front of the Dragon's Lair, stacking berry pods. This Dragon must have flown toward its Lair from the other side of the mountain spire, so our radio tag on him didn't transmit through all the rock. Usually they're not so direct. Most Dragons circle their Lairs a few times, checking for scavengers and egg stealers. If they don't circle, they're usually too tired. And when they're tired, they're irritable. Something told me I didn't want to be within reach of this one's throat flame.

I dropped my berrybag rig and went down the rocks feet first. The boulders were slippery with green moss for about 20 meters below the ledge, so I slid down on them. I tried to keep the falls to under four meters and banged my butt when I missed. I could hear Leopold knocking loose rocks on the other side, moving down toward where our skimmer was parked.

A shadow fell over me, blotting out Beta's big yellow disk. The brown bag above thrashed its wings and gave a trumpeting shriek. It had caught sight of the berry bags and knew something was up. Most likely, with its weak eyes, the Dragon thought the bags were eggers—off season, but what do Dragons know about seasons?—and would attack them. That was the optimistic theory. The pessimistic one was that the Dragon had seen one of us. I smacked painfully into a

75

splintered boulder and glanced up. Its underbelly was heaving, turning purple: anger. Not a reassuring sign. Eggers don't bother Dragons that much.

Then its wings fanned the air, backwards. It drifted off the ledge, hovering. The long neck snaked around, and two nearsighted eyes sought mine. The nose expanded, catching my scent. The Dragon hissed triumphantly.

Our skimmer was set for a fast takeoff. But it was 200 meters down, on the only wide spot we could find. I made a megaphone of my hands and shouted into the thin mountain mist, "Leopold! Grab air!"

I jumped down to a long boulder that jutted into space. Below and a little to the left I could make out the skimmer's shiny wings through the shifting green fog. I sucked in a breath and ran off the end of the boulder.

Dragons are clumsy at level flight, but they can drop like a brick. The only way to beat this one down to the skimmer was by falling most of the way.

I banked down, arms out. Our gravity is only a third of Earth normal. Even when falling, you have time to think things over. I can do the calculations fast enough—it came out to nine seconds—but getting the count right with a Dragon on your tail is another matter. I ticked the seconds off and then popped the chute. It fanned and filled. The skimmer came rushing up, wind whipped my face. Then my harness jerked me to a halt. I drifted down. I thumped the release and fell free. Above me, a trumpeting bellow. Something was coming in at four o'clock and I turned, snatching for my blaser. Could it be that fast? But it was Leopold, on chute. I sprinted for the skimmer. It was pointed along the best outbound wind, flaps already down, a standard precaution. I belted in, sliding my feet into the pedals. I caught a dank, foul reek of Dragon. More high shrieking, closer. Leopold came running up, panting. He wriggled into the rear seat. A thumping of wings. A ceiling of wrinkled leather. Something hissing overhead.

Dragons don't fly, they float. They have a big green hydrogen-filled dome on their backs to give them lift. They make the hydrogen in their stomachs and can dive quickly by venting it out the ass. This one was farting and falling as we zoomed away. I banked, turned to get a look at the huffing brown mountain hooting its anger at us, and grinned.

"I take back what I said this morning," Leopold gasped.

"You'll draw full wages *and* commissions, from the start."

I didn't say anything. I'd just noticed that somewhere back there I had pissed my boots full.

I covered it pretty well back at the strip. I twisted out of the skimmer and slipped into the maintenance bay. I had extra clothes in my bag, so I slipped on some fresh socks and thongs.

When I was sure I smelled approximately human, I tromped back out to Leopold. I was damned if I would let my morning's success be blotted out by an embarrassing accident. It was a hirer's market these days. My training at crop dusting out in the flat farmlands had given me an edge over the other guys who had applied. I was determined to hang on to this job.

Leopold was the guy who "invented" the Dragons, five years ago. He took a life form native to Lex, the bloats, and tinkered with their DNA. Bloats are balloonlike and nasty. Leopold made them bigger, tougher, and spliced in a lust for thistleberries that makes Dragons hoard them compulsively. It had been a brilliant job of bioengineering. The Dragons gathered thistleberries, and Leopold stole them from the Lairs.

Thistleberries are a luxury good, high in protein, and delicious. The market for them might collapse if Lex's economy got worse—the copper seams over in Bahinin had run out last month. This was nearly the only good flying job left. More than anything else, I wanted to keep flying. And *not* as a crop duster. Clod-grubber work is a pain.

Leopold was leaning against his skimmer, a little pale, watching his men husk thistleberries. His thigh muscles were still thick; he was clearly an airman by ancestry, but he looked tired.

"Goddamn," he said. "I can't figure it out, kid. The Dragons are hauling in more berries than normal. We can't get into the Lairs, though. You'd think it was mating season around here, the way they're attacking my men."

"Mating season? When's that?"

"Oh, in about another six months, when the puffbushes bloom in the treetops. The pollen sets off the mating urges in Dragons—steps up their harvest, but it also makes 'em meaner."

"Great," I said. "I'm allergic to puffbush pollen. I'll have to fight off Dragons with running eyes and a stuffy nose."

Leopold shook his head absently; he hadn't heard me. "I can't understand it—there's nothing wrong with my Dragon designs."

"Seems to me you could have toned down the behavior plexes," I said. "Calm them down a bit—I mean, they've outgrown their competition to the point that they don't even *need* to be mean anymore. They don't browse much as it is . . . nobody's going to bother them."

"No way—there's just not the money for it, Drake. Look, I'm operating on the margin here. My five-year rights to the genetic patents just ran out, and now I'm in competition with Kwalan Rhiang, who owns the other half of the forest. Besides, you think gene splicing is easy?"

"Still, if they can bioengineer *humans* . . . I mean, we were beefed up for strength and oxy burning nearly a thousand years ago."

"But we weren't blown up to five times the size of our progenitors, Drake. I made those Dragons out of mean sons of bitches—blimps with teeth is what they were. It gets tricky when you mess with the life cycles of something that's already that unstable. You just don't understand what's involved here."

I nodded. "I'm no bioengineer—granted."

He looked at me and grinned, a spreading warm grin on his deeply lined face. "Yeah, Drake, but you're good at what you do—really good. What happened today, well, I'm getting too old for that sort of thing, and it's happening more and more often. If you hadn't been there I'd probably be stewing in that Dragon's stomach right now—skimmer and all."

I shrugged. That gave me a chance to roll the slabs of muscle in my shoulders, neck, and pectorals—a subtle advertisement that I had enough to keep a skimmer aloft for hours.

"So," he continued, "I'm giving you full pilot rank. The skimmer's yours. You can fly it home tonight, on the condition that you meet me at the Angis Tavern for a drink later on. And bring your girl Evelaine, too, if you want."

"It's a deal, Leopold. See you there."

I whistled like a dungwarbler all the way home, pedaling my new skimmer over the treetops toward the city. I nearly wrapped myself in a floating thicket of windbrambles, but not even this could destroy my good mood.

I didn't notice any Dragons roaming around, though I saw that the treetops had been plucked of their berries and then scorched. Leopold had at least had the foresight, when he was gene tinkering, to provide for the thistleberries' constant replenishment. He gave the Dragons a throat flame to singe the treetops with, which makes the berries regrow quickly. A nice touch.

It would have been simpler, of course, to have men harvest the thistleberries themselves, but that never worked out, economically. Thistleberries grow on top of virtually un-climbable thorntrees, where you can't even maneuver a skim-mer without great difficulty. And if a man fell to the ground . . . well, if it's on the ground, it has spines, that's the rule on Lex. There's nothing soft to fall on down there. Sky life is more complex than ground life. You can actually do some-thing useful with sky life—namely, bioengineering. Lex may be a low-metal world—which means low-technology—but our bioengineers are the best.

A clapping sound, to the left. I stopped whistling. Down through the greenish haze I could see a dark form coming in over the treetops, its wide rubbery wings slapping together at the top of each stroke. A smackwing. Good meat, spicy and moist. But hard to catch. Evelaine and I had good news to celebrate tonight; I decided to bring her home smackwing for dinner. I took the skimmer down in the path of the smackwing, meanwhile slipping my blaser from its holster.

The trick to hunting in the air is to get beneath your prey so that you can grab it while it falls, but this smackwing was flying too low. I headed in fast, hoping to frighten it into rising above me, but it was no use. The smackwing saw me, red eyes rolling. It missed a beat in its flapping and dived toward the treetops. At that instant a snagger shot into view from the topmost branches, rising with a low farting sound. The smackwing spotted this blimplike thing that had leaped into its path but apparently didn't think it too threatening. It swerved about a meter under the bobbing creature—

And stopped flat, in midair.

I laughed aloud, sheathing my blaser. The snagger had won his meal like a real hunter.

Beneath the snagger's wide blimplike body was a dangling sheet of transparent sticky material. The smackwing struggled in the moist folds as the snagger drew the sheet upward. To the unwary smackwing that clear sheet must have been invisible until the instant he flew into it.

Within another minute, as I pedaled past the spot, the snagger had entirely engulfed the smackwing, and was unrolling its sticky sheet as it drifted back into the treetops. Pale yellow eyes considered me and rejected the notion of me as food. A ponderous predator, wise with years.

I flew into the spired city: Kalatin.

I parked on the deck of our apartment building, high above the jumbled wooden buildings of the city. Now that my interview had been successful, we'd be able to stay in Kalatin, though I hoped we could find a better apartment. This one was as old as the city—which in turn had been around for a great deal of the 1,200 years humans had been on Lex. As the wood of the lower stories rotted, and as the building crumbled away, new quarters were just built on top of it and settled into place. Someday this city would be an archaeologist's dream. In the meantime, it was an inhabitant's nightmare.

Five minutes later, having negotiated several treacherous ladders and a splintering shinny pole into the depths of the old building, I crept quietly to the wooden door of my apartment and let myself in, clutching the mudskater steaks that I'd picked up on the way home. It was dark and cramped inside, the smell of rubbed wood strong. I could hear Evelaine moving around in the kitchen, so I sneaked to the doorway and looked in. She was turned away, chopping thistleberries with a thorn-knife.

I grabbed her, throwing the steaks into the kitchen, and kissed her.

"Got the job, Evey!" I said. "Leopold took me out himself and I ended up saving his—"

"It *is* you!" She covered her nose, squirming away from me. "What is that smell, Drake?"

"Smell?"

"Like something died. It's all over you."

I remembered the afternoon's events. It was either the smell of Dragon, which I'd got from scrambling around in a Lair, or that of urine. I played it safe and said, "I think it's Dragon."

"Well take it somewhere else. I'm cooking dinner."

"I'll hop in the cycler. You can cook up the steaks I brought, then we're going out to celebrate."

* * *

The Angis Tavern is no skiff joint, good for a stale senso on the way home from work. It's the best. The Angis is a vast old place, perched on a pyramid of rock. Orange fog nestles at the base, a misty collar separating it from the jumble of the city below.

Evelaine pedaled the skimmer with me, having trouble in her gown. We made a wobbly landing on the rickety side deck. It would've been easier to coast down to the city, where there was more room for a glide approach, but that's pointless. There are thick cactus and thornbushes around the Angis base, hard to negotiate at night. In the old days it kept away predators; now it keeps away the riffraff.

But not completely: two beggars accosted us as we dismounted, offering to shine up the skimmer's aluminum skin. I growled convincingly at them, and they skittered away. The Angis is so big, so full of crannies to hide out in, they can't keep it clear of beggars, I guess.

We went in a balcony entrance. Fat balloons nudged against the ceiling, ten meters overhead, dangling their cords. I snagged one and stepped off into space. Evelaine hooked it as I fell. We rode it down, past alcoves set in the rock walls. Well-dressed patrons nodded as we eased down, the balloon following. The Angis is a spire, broadening gradually as we descended. Phosphors cast creamy glows on the tables set into the walls. I spotted Leopold sprawled in a webbing, two empty tankards lying discarded underneath.

"You're late," he called. We stepped off onto his ledge. Our balloons, released, shot back to the roof.

"You didn't set a time. Evelaine, Leopold." Nods, introductory phrases.

"It seems quite crowded here tonight," Evelaine murmured. A plausible social remark, except she'd never been to an inn of this class before.

Leopold shrugged. "Hard times mean full taverns. Booze or sensos or tinglers—pick your poison."

Evelaine has the directness of a country girl and knows her own limitations; she stuck to a mild tingler. Service was running slow, so I went to log our orders. I slid down a shinny pole to the first bar level. Mice zipped by me, eating up tablescraps left by the patrons; it saves on labor. Amid the jam and babble I placed our order with a steward and turned to go back.

"You looking for work?" a thick voice said.

I glanced at its owner. "No." The man was big, swarthy, and sure of himself.

"Thought you wanted Dragon work." His eyes had a look of distant amusement.

"How'd you know that?" I wasn't known in the city.

"Friends told me."

"Leopold hired me today."

"So I hear. I'll top whatever he's paying."

"I didn't think business was that good."

"It's going to get better. Much better, once Leopold's out of the action. A monopoly can always sell goods at a higher price. You can start tomorrow."

So this was Kwalan Rhiang. "No thanks. I'm signed up." Actually, I hadn't signed anything, but there was something about this man I didn't like. Maybe the way he was so sure I'd work for him.

"Flying for Leopold is dangerous. He doesn't know what he's doing."

"See you around," I said. A senso was starting in a nearby booth. I took advantage of it to step into the expanding blue cloud, so Rhiang couldn't follow and see where we were sitting. I got a lifting, bright sensation of pleasure, and then I was out of the misty confusion, moving away among the packed crowd.

I saw them on the stairway. They were picking their way down it delicately. I thought they were deformed, but the funny tight clothes gave them away. Offworlders, here for the flying. That was the only reason anybody came to Lex. We're still the only place men can seriously fly longer than a few minutes. Even so, our lack of machines keeps most offworlders away; they like it easy, everything done for them. I watched them pick their way down the stairs, thinking that if the depression got worse, offworlders would be able to hire servants here, even though it was illegal. It could come to that.

They were short as children but heavyset, with narrow chests and skinny limbs. Spindly people, unaugmented for Lex oxy levels. But men like that had colonized here long ago, paying for it in reduced lifetimes. I felt as though I was watching my own ancestors.

Lex shouldn't have any oxy at all, by the usual rules of planetary evolution. It's a small planet, 0.21 Earth masses, a third gee of gravity. Rules of thumb say we shouldn't have any atmosphere to speak of. But our sun, Beta, is a K-type star, redder than Sol. Beta doesn't heat our upper atmosphere very much with ultraviolet, so we retain gases. Even then, Lex would be airless except for accidents of birth. It started out with a dense cloak of gas, just as Earth did. But dim old Beta didn't blow the atmosphere away, and there wasn't enough compressional heating by Lex itself to boil away the gases. So they stuck around, shrouding the planet, causing faster erosion than on Earth. The winds moved dust horizontally, exposing crustal rock. That upset the isostatic balance in the surface, and split open faults. Volcanoes poked up. They belched water and gas onto the surface, keeping the atmosphere dense. So Lex ended up with low gravity and a thick atmosphere. Fine, except that Beta's wan light also never pushed many heavy elements out this far, so Lex is metal-poor. Without iron and the rest you can't build machines, and without technology you're a backwater. You sell your tourist attraction—flying—and hope for the best.

One of the offworlders came up to me and said, "You got any sparkers in this place?"

I shook my head. Maybe he didn't know that getting a sendup by tying your frontal lobes into an animal's is illegal here. Maybe he didn't care. Ancestor or not, he just looked like a misshapen dwarf to me, and I walked away.

Evelaine was describing life in the flatlands when I got back. Leopold was rapt, the worry lines in his face nearly gone. Evelaine does that to people. She's natural and straightforward, so she was telling him right out that she wasn't much impressed with city life. "Farmlands are quiet and restful. Everybody has a job," she murmured. "You're right that getting around is harder—but we can glide in the updrafts, in summer. It's heaven."

"Speaking of the farmlands," I said, "an old friend of mine came out here five years ago. He wanted in on your operations."

"I was hiring like crazy five years ago. What was his name?"

"Lorn Kramer. Great pilot."

Leopold shook his head. "Can't remember. He's not with me now, anyway. Maybe Rhiang got him."

Our drinks arrived. The steward was bribable, though—Rhiang was right behind him.

"You haven't answered my 'gram," Rhiang said directly to

Leopold, ignoring us. I guess he didn't figure I was worth any more time.

"Didn't need to," Leopold said tersely.

"Sell out. I'll give you a good price." Rhiang casually sank his massive flank on our table edge. "You're getting too old."

Something flickered in Leopold's eyes; he said nothing.

"Talk is," Rhiang went on mildly, "market's falling."

"Maybe," Leopold said. "What you been getting for a kilo?"

"Not saying."

"Tight lips and narrow minds go together."

Rhiang stood, his barrel chest bulging. "You could use a little instruction in politeness."

"From you?" Leopold chuckled. "You paid off that patent clerk to release my gene configs early. Was that polite?"

Rhiang shrugged. "That's the past. The present reality is that there may be an oversupply of thistleberries. Market isn't big enough for two big operations like ours. There's too much—"

"Too much of you, that's my problem. Lift off, Rhiang."

To my surprise, he did. He nodded to me, ignored Evelaine, and gave Leopold a look of contempt. Then he was gone.

I heard them first. We were taking one of the outside walks that corkscrew around the Angis spire, gawking at the phosphored streets below. A stone slide clattered behind us. I saw two men duck behind a jutting ledge. One of them had something in his hand that glittered.

"You're jumpy, Drake," Evelaine said.

"Maybe." It occurred to me that if we went over the edge of this spire, hundreds of meters into the thorn scrabble below, it would be very convenient for Rhiang. "Let's move on."

Leopold glanced at me, then back at the inky shadows. We strolled along the trail of volcanic rock, part of the natural formation that made the spire. Rough black pebbles slipped underfoot. In the distant star-flecked night, skylight called and boomed.

We passed under a phosphor. At the next turn Leopold looked back and said, "I saw one of them. Rhiang's right-hand man."

We hurried away. I wished for a pair of wings to get us off this place. Evelaine understood instantly that this was serious. "There's a split in the trail ahead," Leopold said. "If they follow, we'll know . . ." He didn't finish.

We turned. They followed. "I think I know a way to slow

them down," I said. Leopold looked at me. We were trying to avoid slipping in the darkness and yet make good time. "Collect some of these obsidian frags," I said.

We got a bundle of them together. "Go on up ahead," I said. We were on a narrow ledge. I sank back into the shadows and waited. The two men appeared. Before they noticed me I threw the obsidian high into the air. In low gravity it takes a long time for them to come back down. In the darkness the two men couldn't see them coming.

I stepped out into the wan light. "Hey!" I yelled to them. They stopped, precisely where I thought they would. "What's going on?" I said, to stall.

The biggest one produced a knife. "This."

The first rock hit, coming down from over a hundred meters above. It slammed into the boulder next to him. Then three more crashed down, striking the big one in the shoulder, braining the second. They both crumpled.

I turned and hurried along the path. If they'd seen me throw they'd have had time to dodge. It was an old schoolboy trick, but it worked.

The implications, though, were sobering. If Rhiang felt this way, my new job might not last long.

I was bagging berries in the cavernous Paramount Lair when the warning buzzer in my pocket went off. A Dragon was coming in. I still had time, but not much. I decided to finish this particular bag rather than abandon the bagging-pistol. The last bit of fluid sprayed over the heap of berries and began to congeal instantly, its tremendously high surface tension drawing it around the irregular pile and sealing perfectly. I holstered the gun, leaving the bag for later. I turned—

A slow flapping boom. Outside, a wrinkled brown wall.

Well, I'd fooled around long enough—now I dived for safety. The Dragon's Lair was carpeted with a thick collection of nesting materials. None were very pleasant to burrow through, but I didn't have any choice. Behind me I could hear the Dragon moving around; if I didn't move out of his way in a hurry I might get stepped on. The emergency chute on my back tangled in a branch, just as the stench in the Lair intensified. I hurried out of it and went on. I'd just have to be sure not to fall from any great heights. I didn't worry about it, because my skimmer was parked on the ledge just outside the Lair.

I stuck my head up through the nest to judge my position. The bulk of the Dragon was silhouetted against the glare of the sky, which was clear of fog today. The beast seemed to be preening itself. That was something I never thought they did outside of the mating season—which was six months away.

I scrambled backward into the nest. The buzzer in my pocket went off again, though it was supposed to signal just once, for ten seconds. I figured the thing must have broken. It quieted and I moved on, thinking. For one thing, the Dragon that occupied this Lair was supposed to have been far from home right now—which meant that my guest didn't really belong here. Dragons never used the wrong Lair unless it was the mating season.

I frowned. Why did that keep coming up?

Suddenly there was a rush of wind and a low, thrumming sound. The light from outside was cut off. I poked my head into the open.

Another Dragon was lumbering into the Lair. *This* was really impossible. Two Dragons sharing a Lair—and the wrong one at that! Whatever their reasons for being here, I was sure they were going to start fighting pretty soon, so I burrowed deeper, moving toward the nearest wall.

My elbow caught on something. Cloth. I brushed it away, then looked again. A Dragonrobber uniform like my own. It was directly beneath me, half-buried in the nesting material. I caught my breath, then poked at the uniform. Something glittered near one empty sleeve: an identification bracelet. I picked it up, shifted it in the light, and read the name on it: *Lorn Kramer.*

Lorn Kramer! So he had been in Leopold's group after all. But that still didn't explain why he'd left his clothes here.

I tugged at the uniform, dragging it toward me. It was limp, but tangled in the nest. I jerked harder and some long, pale things rattled out of the sleeve.

Bones.

I winced. I was suddenly aware that my present situation must be somewhat like the one that had brought him here.

I looked into the Lair again. One of the Dragons was prodding its snout at the other, making low, whuffling sounds. It didn't look like a hostile gesture to me. In fact, it looked like they were playing. The other Dragon wheeled about and headed for the entrance. The first one followed, and in a minute both of them had left the Lair again—as abruptly and inexplicably as they had entered it.

I saw my chance. I ran across the Lair, grabbed my skimmer, and took off. I moved out, pedaling furiously away from the Dragons, and glanced down.

For a minute I thought I was seeing things. The landscape below me was blurred, though the day had been clear and crisp when I'd flown into the Lair. I blinked. It didn't go away, but got clearer. There was a cloud of yellowish dust spreading high above the forest, billowing up and around the Lairs I could see. Where had it come from?

I sneezed, passing through a high plume of the dust. Then my eyes began to sting and I sneezed again. I brought the skimmer out of the cloud, but by this time my vision was distorted with tears. I began to cough and choke all at once, until the skimmer faltered as I fought to stay in control, my eyes streaming.

I knew what that dust was.

Nothing affected me as fiercely as puffbush pollen: it was the only thing I was really allergic to.

I stopped pedaling.

It affected Dragons, too. It set off their mating urges.

But where was the damned stuff coming from? It was six months out of season. I started pedaling again, legs straining. I turned to get a better view.

A flash of light needled past my head, and I knew. Three skimmers shot into view from around the spire of Paramount Lair. The tip of one of my wings was seared away by a blaser. My skimmer lurched wildly, but I held on and brought it up just as the fist skimmer came toward me. Its pilot was wearing a filtermask. Attached to the skimmer were some empty bags that must have held the puffbush pollen. But what I was looking at was the guy's blaser. It was aimed at me.

I reeled into an updraft, pulling over my attacker, grabbing for my own blaser. The skimmer soared beneath me, then careened into a sharp turn. It was too sharp. The guy turned straight into the path of his companion. The two skimmers crashed together with a satisfying sound, then the scattered parts and pilots fell slowly toward the treetops. Seconds later, the forest swallowed them up.

I looked for the third man, just as he came up beside me. The bastard was grinning, and I recognized that grin. It was Kwalan Rhiang's.

He nodded once, affably, and before I could remember to use my blaser, Rhiang took a single, precise shot at the chainguard of my skimmer. The pedals rolled uselessly. I was out of control. Rhiang lifted away and cruised out of sight, leaving me flailing at the air in a ruined skimmer.

I had exactly one chance, and this was to get back to the Lair I'd just abandoned. I was slightly higher than the opening, so I glided in, backpedaled for the drop—and crashed straight into the wall, thanks to my ruined pedals. But I made it in alive, still able to stand up and brush the dirt from my uniform. I stood at the mouth of the Lair, staring out over the forest, considering the long climb that lay below me.

And just then the Dragons returned.

Not one, this time—not even two. *Five* shadows wheeled overhead; five huge beasts headed toward the Lair where I was standing. And finally, five Dragons dropped right on top of me.

I leaped back just in time, scrambling into the blue shadows as the first Dragon thumped to the ledge. It waddled inside, reeking. I moved back farther. Its four friends were right behind. I kept moving back.

Well, at least now I knew *why* they were doing this. Kwalan Rhiang had been setting off their mating urges by dusting the Dragons with puffbush-pollen, messing up their whole life cycle, fooling with their already nasty tempers. It made sense. Anything less subtle might have gotten Rhiang into a lot of trouble. As it was, he'd doubtless fly safely home, waiting for Leopold's Dragons to kill off Leopold's men.

Out in the cavernous Lair, the Dragons began to move around, prodding at each other like scramblemice, hooting their airy courting sounds. The ground shook with their movement. Two seemed to be females, which suggested that I might look forward to some fighting between the other three. Great.

I fumbled at my pockets for something that might be of help. My warning buzzer had shattered in my rough landing; I threw it away. I still had my bagging-gun, but it wouldn't do me a lot of good. My blaser seemed okay. I unholstered it and began to move along the wall. If I went carefully, I might be able to get onto the outer ledge.

Two of the males were fighting now, lunging, the sounds of their efforts thundering around me. I made a short run and gained a bit of ground. One of the Dragons retreated from the battle—apparently the loser. I groaned. He had moved directly into my path.

A huge tail pounded at the ground near me and a female started backing my way, not looking at me. There was no place to go. And I was getting tired of this. I decided to warn her off. I made a quick shot at her back, nipping her in the hydrogen dome. She squawked and shuffled away, confused. I went on.

I stopped. There was a hissing sound behind me. Turning, I could see nothing but the Dragon I'd just shot. She didn't appear to be making the sound, but it was coming from her direction. I peered closer, through the blue gloom, and then saw where the noise was coming from.

Her hydrogen dome was deflating.

I nearly laughed aloud. Here was the answer to my problem. I could deflate the Dragons, leaving them stranded, unable to fly, while I climbed down this spire without fear of pursuit. I lifted my blaser and aimed at the male nearest the rear of the Lair. A near miss, then a hit. Hydrogen hissed out of his dome as well. Then I got the second female, and another male who was directly across from me.

One Dragon to go. The others were roaring and waddling. The Lair was full of the hissing sound.

I turned to my last opponent. He wasn't looking my way, but he was blocking my exit. I moved in closer and lifted my blaser.

Then he saw me.

I flung myself aside just as he bellowed and pounded forward, filling the entrance to the Lair, blocking out the sunlight. I rolled into the thorny nest. I fired once, hitting him in the snout. He swung his head toward me, pushing me around toward the outer ledge, bellowing. I fired again, and once more missed his hydrogen dome. I made a dash around his rump just as he spun my way, tail lashing against me. His dark little eyes narrowed as he sighted me, and his throat began to ripple.

My time was up. He was about to blast me with his throat flame.

The Dragon opened his mouth, belched hydrogen, and ignited it by striking a spark from his molars—

That was the wrong thing to do.

I saw it coming and ducked.

The cavern shuddered and blew up. The orange explosion rumbled out, catching the Dragons in a huge rolling flame. I buried myself in the nesting strands and grabbed onto the lashing tail of my attacker. Terrified by the blast, he took off. My eyebrows were singed, my wrists burned.

The world spun beneath me. A tendril of smoke drifted into view just below, mingled with flaming bits of nesting material and the leathery hide of Dragons. Then my view spun again and I was looking at the sky. It gradually dawned on me that I was clinging to a Dragon's tail.

It occurred to the Dragon at the same time. I saw his head swing toward me, snapping angrily. His belly was flashing purple. Every now and then he let out a tongue of flame, but he couldn't quite get at me. Meanwhile, I held on for my life.

The Dragon flew on, but my weight seemed to be too much for it. We were dropping slowly toward the trees, as easily as if I'd punctured his bony dome with my blaser. But it would be a rough landing. And I'd have to deal with the Dragon afterward.

I spied something rising from the trees below us. It shot swiftly into the air after a high-flying bulletbird, its transparent sheet rippling beneath its blimplike body. It was a huge snagger—as big as my own skimmer. I kicked on the Dragon's tail, dragging it sideways. The Dragon lurched and spun and then we were directly over the snagger.

I let go of the tail and dropped, my eyes closed.

In a second, something soft rumpled beneath me. I had landed safely atop the snagger. I opened my eyes as the Dragon—having lost my weight—shot suddenly upward. I watched it glide away, then looked down at the snagger, my savior. I patted its wide, rubbery body. My weight was pushing it slowly down, as if I were riding the balloons in the Angis Tavern. I looked forward to a comfortable trip to the ground.

"I like your style, kid."

I jumped, nearly losing my place on the snagger. The voice had come out of midair. Literally.

"You," I said. No more was necessary. He was banking around behind me.

Kwalan Rhiang had returned in his skimmer. He circled easily about me as I fell toward the treetops. He came in close, smiling, his huge legs pedaling him on a gentle course. I had to turn my head to keep an eye on him.

"I said before I'd top what Leopold was paying you," he shouted, his thick voice cutting the high air. "After today, I think I'd pay *double*. I could use someone like you."

I felt my face harden. "You bastard. You're responsible for what just happened. Why would I work for someone who's tried to kill me?"

He shrugged. "Gave you a chance to prove yourself. Come on, you're wasting your time with Leopold."

"And you're wasting your time with me."

He shrugged again, utterly sure of himself. "As you wish. I gave you a chance."

I nodded. "Now just go away."

"And leave you to tell Leopold about all this? You don't think I'm going to let you back alive, do you?"

I froze. Rhiang slid a blaser from its holster at his waist and aimed it at my head. His grin widened. The muzzle dropped a fraction, and I breathed a little easier.

"No," he said distantly, "why kill you straight off? Slow deaths are more interesting, I think. And harder to trace."

He aimed at the snagger. If he punctured it I'd drop into the trees. It was a long fall. I wouldn't make it.

I growled and grabbed for the gun at my waist, bringing it up before Rhiang could move. He stared at me for a moment, then started laughing. I looked at what I was holding.

"What're you going to do with that?" he said. "Bag me?"

It was my bagging-pistol, all right. I'd dropped the blaser back in the Lair. But it would still serve a purpose.

"Exactly," I said, and fired.

The gray fluid squirted across the narrow gap between us, sealing instantly over Rhiang's hands. He fired the blaser but succeeded only in melting the bag enough to let the weapon break away. It fell out of sight.

His eyes were wide. He was considering death by suffocation.

"No," he choked.

But I didn't fire at his head. I put the next bag right over his feet, sealing the pedal mechanism tight. His legs jerked convulsively. They slowed. Rhiang began to whimper, and then he was out of control. His skimmer turned and glided away as he hurried to catch any updraft he could. He vanished behind Paramount Lair, and was gone.

I turned back to observe the treetops. Rhiang might be back, but I doubted it. First he'd have a long walk ahead of him, over unpleasant terrain, back to his base . . . *if* he could maneuver his skimmer well enough to land in the treetops, and make the long, painful climb down.

But I didn't worry about it. I watched the thorntrees rise about me, and presently the snagger brought me gently to the ground. I dismounted, leaving the snagger to bob back into the air, and began to walk gingerly across the inhospitable ground, avoiding the spines. A daggerbush snapped at me. I danced away. It was going to be a rough walk out. Somewhere behind me, Rhiang might be facing the same problem. And he wanted me dead.

But I didn't have as far to go.

FITZ-JAMES O'BRIEN

A very popular nineteenth-century fantasist, Fitz-James O'Brien grew up in Ireland, but fled to the United States in 1852 to escape the ire of an angry husband. During the next nine years he produced a number of surprisingly modern classics such as "The Diamond Lens," "The Lost Room," and "The Wondersmith." In 1861, however, his career ended when the Civil War broke out. He volunteered for a commission in the Union Army, foolhardily led a charge against superior odds, and died of lockjaw from his wounds.

THE DRAGON FANG POSSESSED BY THE CONJURER PIOU-LU

by Fitz-James O'Brien

Chapter of the Miraculous Dragon Fang

"COME MEN and women, and little people of Tching-tou, come and listen. The small and ignoble person who annoys you by his presence is the miserable conjurer known as Piou-Lu. Everything that can possibly be desired he can give you;—charms to heal dissensions in your noble and illustrious families;—spells by which beautiful little people without style may become learned Bachelors, and reign high in the palaces of literary composition;—Supernatural red pills, with which you can cure your elegant and renowned diseases;—wonderful incantations, by which the assassins of any members of your shining and virtuous families can be discovered and made to yield compensation, or be brought under the just eye of the Brother of the Sun. What is it that you want? This mean little conjurer, who now addresses you, can supply all your charming and refreshing desires; for he is known everywhere as Piou-Lu, the possessor of the ever-renowned and miraculous Dragon Fang!"

There was a little, dry laugh, and a murmur among the crowd of idlers that surrounded the stage erected by Piou-Lu in front of the Hotel of the Thirty-two Virtues. Fifth-class Mandarins looked at fourth-class Mandarins and smiled, as much as to say, "We who are educated men know what to think of this fellow." But the fourth-class Mandarins looked haughtily at the fifth-class, as if they had no business to smile at their superiors. The crowd, however, composed as it was principally of small traders, barbers, porcelain-tinkers, and country people, gazed with open mouths upon the conjurer, who, clad in a radiant garment of many colors, strutted proudly up and down upon his temporary stage.

"What is a Dragon Fang, ingenious and well-educated conjurer?" at last inquired Wei-chang-tze, a solemn-looking Mandarin of the third class, who was adorned with a sapphire button, and a one-eyed peacock's feather. "What is a Dragon Fang?"

"Is it possible," asked Piou-Lu, "that the wise and illustrious son of virtue, the Mandarin Wei-chang-tze, does not know what a Dragon Fang is?" and the conjurer pricked up his ears at the Mandarin, as a hare at a barking dog.

"Of course, of course," said the Mandarin Wei-chang-tze, looking rather ashamed of his having betrayed such ignorance, "one does not pass his examinations for nothing. I merely wished that you should explain to those ignorant people here what a Dragon Fang is; that was why I asked."

"I thought that the Soul of Wisdom must have known," said Piou-Lu, triumphantly, looking as if he believed firmly in the knowledge of Wei-chang-tze. "The noble commands of Wei-chang-tze shall be obeyed. You all know," said he, looking round upon the people, "that there are three great and powerful Dragons inhabiting the universe. Lung, or the Dragon of the Sky; Li, or the Dragon of the Sea; and Kiau, or the Dragon of the Marshes. All these Dragons are wise, strong, and terrible. They are wondrously formed, and can take any shape that pleases them. Well, good people, a great many moons ago, in the season of spiked grain, I was following the profession of a barber in the mean and unmentionable town of Siho, when one morning, as I was sitting in my shop waiting for customers, I heard a great noise of tamtams, and a princely palanquin stopped before my door. I hastened, of course, to observe the honorable Rites toward this new-comer, but before I could reach the street a Mandarin, splendidly attired, descended from the palanquin. The ball on his cap was of a stone and color that I had never seen before, and three feathers of some unknown bird hung down behind his head-dress. He held his hand to his jaw, and walked into my house with a lordly step. I was greatly confused, for I knew not what rank he was of, and felt puzzled how to address him. He put an end to my embarrassment.

"'I am in the house of Piou-Lu, the barber,' he said, in a haughty voice that sounded like the roll of a copper drum amidst the hills.

"'That disgraceful and ill-conditioned person stands before you,' I replied, bowing as low as I could.

"'It is well,' said he, seating himself in my operating-chair, while two of his attendants fanned him. 'Piou-Lu, I have the toothache!'

"'Does your lordship,' said I, 'wish that I should remove your noble and illustrious pain?'

"'You must draw my tooth,' said he. 'Woe to you if you draw the wrong one!'

"'It is too much honor,' I replied; 'but I will make my abominable and ill-conducted instruments entice your lordship's beautiful tooth out of your high-born jaw with much rapidity.'

"So I got my big pincers, and my opium-bottle, and opened the strange Mandarin's mouth. Ah! it was then that my low-born and despicable heart descended into my bowels. I should have dropped my pincers from sheer fright if they had not caught by their hooked ends in my wide sleeve. The Mandarin's mouth was all on fire inside. As he breathed, the flames rolled up and down his throat, like the flames that gather on the Yellow Grass Plains in the season of Much Heat. His palate glowed like red-hot copper, and his tongue was like a brass stewpan that had been on the salt-fire for thirty days. But it was his teeth that affrighted me most. They were a serpent's teeth. They were long, and curved inward, and seemed to be made of transparent crystal, in the centre of which small tongues of orange-colored fire leaped up and down out of some cavity in the gums.

"'Well, dilatory barber,' said the Mandarin, in a horrible tone, while I stood pale and trembling before him, 'why don't you draw my tooth? Hasten, or I will have you sliced lengthwise and fried in the sun.'

"'O, my lord!' said I, terrified at this threat, 'I fear that my vicious and unendurable pincers are not sufficiently strong.'

"'Slave!' answered he in a voice of thunder, 'if you do not fulfil my desires, you will not see another moon rise.'

"I saw that I should be killed any way, so I might as well make the attempt. I made a dart with my pincers at the first tooth that came, closed them firmly on the crystal fang, and began to pull with all my strength. The Mandarin bellowed like an ox of Thibet. The flames rolled from his throat in such volumes that I thought they would singe my eyebrows. His two attendants and his four palanquin-bearers put their arms round my waist to help me to pull, and there we tugged for three or four minutes, until at last I heard a report as loud as nine thousand nine hundred and ninety-nine fire-crackers. The attendants, the palanquin-bearers, and myself all fell flat on the floor, and the crystal fang glittered between the jaws of the pincers.

"The Mandarin was smiling pleasantly as I got up from the floor. 'Piou-Lu,' said he, 'you had a narrow escape. You have removed my toothache, but had you failed, you would have perished miserably; for I am the Dragon Lung, who rules the sky and the heavenly bodies, and I am as powerful as I am wise. Take as a reward the Dragon Fang which you drew from my jaw. You will find it a magical charm with which you can work miracles. Honor your parents, observe the Rites, and live in peace.'

"So saying, he breathed a whole cloud of fire and smoke from his throat, that filled my poor and despicable mansion. The light dazzled and the smoke suffocated me, and when I recovered my sight and breath the Dragon Lung, the attendants, the palanquin, and the four bearers had all departed, how and whither I knew not. Thus was it, elegant and refined people of Tching-tou, that this small and evil-minded person who stands before you became possessed of the wonderful Dragon Fang, with which he can work miracles."

This story, delivered as it was with much graceful and dramatic gesticulation, and a volubility that seemed almost supernatural, had its effect upon the crowd, and a poor little tailor, named Hang-pou, who was known to be always in debt, was heard to say that he wished he had the Dragon Fang, wherewith to work miracles with his creditors. But the Mandarins, blue, crystal, and gilt, smiled contemptuously, and said to themselves, "We who are learned men know how to esteem these things."

The Mandarin Wei-chang-tze, however, seemed to be of an inquiring disposition, and evinced a desire to continue his investigations.

"Supremely visited conjurer," said he to Piou-Lu, "your story is indeed wonderful. To have been visited by the Dragon Lung must have been truly refreshing and enchanting. Though not in the least doubting your marvelous relation, I am sure this virtuous assemblage would like to see some proof of the miraculous power of your Dragon Fang."

The crowd gave an immediate assent to this sentiment by pressing closer to the platform on which Piou-Lu strutted, and exclaiming with one voice, "The lofty Mandarin says wisely. We would like to behold."

Piou-Lu did not seem in the slightest degree disconcerted. His narrow black eyes glistened like the dark edges of the seeds of the water-melon, and he looked haughtily around him.

"Is there any one of you who would like to have a miracle performed, and of what nature?" he asked, with a triumphant wave of his arms.

"I would like to see my debts paid," murmured the little tailor, Hang-pou.

"O Hang-pou," replied the conjurer, "this unworthy personage is not going to pay your debts. Go home and sit in your shop, and drink no more rice-wine, and your debts will be paid; for labor is the Dragon Fang that works miracles for idle tailors!"

There was a laugh through the crowd at this sally, because Hang-pou was well known to be fond of intoxicating drinks, and spent more of his time in the street than on his shopboard.

"Would either of you like to be changed into a camel?" continued Piou-Lu. "Say the word, and there shall not be a finer beast in all Thibet!"

No one, however, seemed to be particularly anxious to experience this transformation. Perhaps it was because it was warm weather, and camels bear heavy burdens.

"I will change the whole honorable assemblage into turkey-buzzards, if it only agrees," continued the conjurer; "or I will make the Lake Tung come up into the town in the shape of a water-melon, and then burst and overflow everything."

"But we should all be drowned!" exclaimed Hang-pou, who was cowardly as well as intemperate.

"That's true," said Piou-Lu, "but then you need not fear your creditors,"—and he gave such a dart of his long arm at the poor little tailor, that the wretched man thought he was going to claw him up and change him into some frightful animal.

"Well, since this illustrious assembly will not have turkey-buzzards or camels, this weak-minded, ill-shapen personage must work a miracle on himself," said Piou-Lu, descending from his platform into the street, and bringing with him a little three-legged stool made of bamboo rods.

The crowd retreated as he approached, and even the solemn Wei-chang-tze seemed rather afraid of this miraculous conjurer. Piou-Lu placed the bamboo stool firmly on the ground, and then mounted upon it.

"Elegant and symmetrical bamboo stool," he said, lifting his arms, and exhibiting something in his hand that seemed like a piece of polished jade-stone,—"elegant and symmetrical bamboo stool, the justly despised conjurer, named Piou-Lu, entreats that you will immediately grow tall, in the name of the Dragon Lung!"

Truly the stool began to grow, in the presence of the astonished crowd. The three legs of bamboo lengthened and lengthened with great rapidity, bearing Piou-Lu high up into the air. As he ascended he bowed gracefully to the open-mouthed assembly.

"It is delightful!" he cried; "the air up here is so fresh! I smell the tea-winds from Fuh-kien. I can see the spot where the heavens and the earth cease to run parallel. I hear the gongs of Pekin, and listen to the lowing of the herds in Thibet. Who would not have an elegant bamboo stool that knew how to grow?"

By this time Piou-Lu had risen to an enormous height. The legs of the slender tripod on which he was mounted seemed like silkworm's threads, so thin were they compared with their length. The crowd began to tremble for Piou-Lu.

"Will he never stop?" said a Mandarin with a gilt ball, named Lin.

"O, yes!" shouted Piou-Lu from the dizzy height of his bamboo stool. "O, yes! this ugly little person will immediately stop. Elegant stool, the poor conjurer entreats you to stop growing; but he also begs that you will afford some satisfaction to this beautifying assemblage down below, who have honored you with their inspection."

The bamboo stool, with the utmost complaisance, ceased to lengthen out its attenuated limbs, but on the moment experienced another change as terrifying to the crowd. The three legs began to approach each other rapidly, and before the eye could very well follow their motions had blended mysteriously and inexplicably into one, the stool still retaining a miraculous equilibrium. Immediately this single stem began to thicken most marvellously, and instead of the dark shining skin of a bamboo stick, it seemed gradually to be incased in overlapping rings of a rough bark. Meanwhile a faint rustling noise continued overhead, and when the crowd, attracted by the sound, looked up, instead of the flat disk of cane-work on which Piou-Lu had so wondrously ascended, they beheld a cabbage-shaped mass of green, which shot forth every moment long, pointed satiny leaves of the tenderest green, and the most graceful shape imaginable. But where was Piou-Lu? Some fancied that in the yellow crown that topped the cabbage-shaped bud of this strange tree they could see the tip of his cap, and distinguish his black, roguish eyes, but that may have been all fancy; and they were quickly diverted from their search for the conjurer by a shower of red, pulpy fruits, that began to fall with great rapidity from the miraculous tree. Of course there was a scramble, in which the Mandarins themselves did not disdain to join; and the crimson fruits—the like of which no one in Tching-tou had ever seen before—proved delightfully sweet and palatable to the taste.

"That's right! that's right! perfectly bred and very polite people," cried a shrill voice while they were all scrambling for the crimson fruits; "pick fruit while it is fresh, and tea while it is tender. For the sun wilts, and the chills toughen, and the bluest plum blooms only for a day."

Everybody looked up, and lo! there was Piou-Lu, as large as life, strutting upon the stage, waving a large green fan in his hand. While the crowd was yet considering this wonderful reappearance of the conjurer, there was heard a very great outcry at the end of the street, and a tall thin man in a coarse blue gown came running up at full speed.

"Where are my plums, sons of thieves?" he cried, almost breathless with haste. "Alas! alas! I am completely ruined. My wife will perish miserably for want of food, and my sons will inherit nothing but empty baskets at my death! Where are my plums?"

"Who is it that dares to address the virtuous and well-disposed people of Tching-tou after this fashion?" demanded the Mandarin Lin, in a haughty voice, as he confronted the new-comer.

The poor man, seeing the gilt ball, became immediately very humble, and bowed several times to the Mandarin.

"O, my lord!" said he, "I am an incapable and undeserving plum-seller, named Liho. I was just now sitting at my stall in a neighboring street selling five cash worth of plums to a customer, when suddenly all the plums rose out of my baskets as if they had the wings of hawks, and flew through the air over the tops of the houses in this direction. Thinking myself the sport of demons, I ran after them, hoping to catch them, and— Ah! there are my plums," he cried, suddenly interrupting himself, and making a dart at some of the

crimson fruits that the tailor Hang held in his hand, intend-
ing to carry them home to his wife.

"These your plums!" screamed Hang, defending his treasure
vigorously. "Mole that you are, did you ever see scarlet plums?"

"This man is stricken by Heaven," said Piou-Lu, gravely.
"He is a fool who hides his plums and then thinks that they
fly away. Let some one shake his gown."

A porcelain-cobbler who stood near the fruiterer immediately seized the long blue robe and gave it a lusty pull, when,
to the wonder of everybody, thousands of the most beautiful
plums fell out, as from a tree shaken by the winds of autumn.
At this moment a great gust of wind arose in the street, and a
pillar of dust mounted up to the very top of the strange tree,
that still stood waving its long satiny leaves languidly above
the house-tops. For an instant every one was blinded, and
when the dust had subsided so as to permit the people to use
their eyes again the wonderful tree had completely vanished,
and all that could be seen was a little bamboo stool flying
along the road, where it was blown by the storm. The poor
fruiterer, Liho, stood aghast, looking at the plums, in which
he stood knee-deep.

The Mandarin, addressing him, said sternly, "Let us hear
no more such folly from Liho, otherwise he will get twenty
strokes of the stick."

"Gather your plums, Liho," said Piou-Lu kindly, "and
think this one of your fortunate days; for he who runs after
his losses with open mouth does not always overtake them."

And as the conjurer descended from his platform it did not
escape the sharp eyes of the little tailor Hang that Piou-Lu ex-
changed a mysterious signal with the Mandarin Wei-chang-tze.

The Chapter of the Shadow of the Duck

IT was close on nightfall when Piou-Lu stopped before
Wei-chang-tze's house. The lanterns were already lit, and the
porter dozed in a bamboo chair so soundly, that Piou-Lu
entered the porch and passed the screen without awaking
him. The inner room was dimly lighted by some horn lanterns elegantly painted with hunting scenes; but despite the
obscurity the conjurer could discover Wei-chang-tze seated at
the farther end of the apartment on an inclined couch covered
with blue and yellow satin. Along the corridor that led to the

women's apartments the shadows lay thick; but Piou-Lu fancied he could hear the pattering of little feet upon the matted floor, and see the twinkle of curious eyes illuminating the solemn darkness. Yet, after all, he may have been mistaken, for the corridor opened on a garden wealthy in the rarest flowers, and he may have conceived the silver dripping of the fountain to be the pattering of dainty feet, and have mistaken the moonlight shining on the moist leaves of the lotus for the sparkle of women's eyes.

"Has Piou-Lu arrived in my dwelling?" asked Wei-chang-tze from the dim corner in which he lay.

"That ignoble and wrath-deserving personage bows his head before you," answered Piou-Lu, advancing and saluting the Mandarin in accordance with the laws of the Book of Rites.

"I hope that you performed your journey hither in great safety and peace of mind," said Wei-chang-tze, gracefully motioning to the conjurer to seat himself on a small blue sofa that stood at a little distance.

"When so mean an individual as Piou-Lu is honored by the request of the noble Wei-chang-tze, good fortune must attend him. How could it be otherwise?" replied Piou-Lu, seating himself not on the small blue sofa, but on the satin one which was partly occupied by the Mandarin himself.

"Piou-Lu did not send in his name, as the Rites direct," said Wei-chang-tze, looking rather disgusted by this impertinent freedom on the part of the conjurer.

"The elegant porter that adorns the noble porch of Wei-chang-tze was fast asleep," answered Piou-Lu, "and Piou-Lu knew that the great Mandarin expected him with impatience."

"Yes," said Wei-chang-tze; "I am oppressed by a thousand demons; devils sleep in my hair, and my ears are overflowing with evil spirit; I cannot rest at night, and feel no pleasure in the day. Therefore was it that I wished to see you, in hopes that you would, by amusing the demon that inhabits my stomach, induce him to depart."

"I will endeavor to delight the respectable demon who lodges in your stomach with my unworthy conjurations," replied Piou-Lu. "But first I must go into the garden to gather flowers."

"Go," said Wei-chang-tze. "The moon shines, and you will see there very many rare and beautiful plants that are beloved by my daughter Wu."

"The moonlight itself cannot shine brighter on the lilies than the glances of your lordship's daughter," said the conjurer, bowing and proceeding to the garden.

Ah! what a garden it was that Piou-Lu now entered! The walls that surrounded it were lofty, and built of a rosy stone brought from the mountains of Mantchouria. This wall, on whose inner face flowery designs and triumphal processions were sculptured at regular intervals, sustained the long and richly laden shoots of the white magnolia, which spread its large snowy chalices in myriads over the surface. Tamarisks and palms sprang up in various parts of the grounds, like dark columns supporting the silvery sky; while the tender and mournful willow drooped its delicate limbs over numberless fish-ponds, whose waters seemed to repose peacefully in the bosom of the emerald turf. The air was distracted with innumerable perfumes, each more fragrant than the other. The blue convolvulus, the crimson ipomea, the prodigal azaleas, the spotted tiger-lilies, the timid and half-hidden jasmine, all poured forth, during the day and night, streams of perfume from the inexhaustible fountains of their chalices. The heavy odors of the tube-rose floated languidly through the leaves, as a richly-plumaged bird would float through summer air, borne down by his own splendor. The blue lotus slept on the smooth waves of the fish-ponds in sublime repose. There seemed an odor of enchantment over the entire place. The flowers whispered their secrets in the perfumed silence; the inmost heart of every blossom was unclosed at that mystic hour; all the magic and mystery of plants floated abroad, and the garden seemed filled with the breath of a thousand spells. But amidst the lilies and lotuses, amidst the scented roses and the drooping convolvuli, there moved a flower fairer than all.

"I am here," whispered a low voice, and a dusky figure came gliding toward Piou-Lu, as he stood by the fountain.

"Ah!" said the conjurer, in a tender tone, far different from the shrill one in which he addressed the crowd opposite the Hotel of the Thirty-two Virtues. "The garden is now complete. Wu, the Rose of Completed Beauty, has blossomed on the night."

"Let Piou-Lu shelter her under his mantle from the cold winds of evening, and bear her company for a little while, for she has grown up under a lonely wall," said Wu, laying her little hand gently on the conjurer's arm, and nestling up to his side as a bird nestles into the fallen leaves warmed by the sun.

"She can lie there but a little while," answered Piou-Lu, folding the Mandarin's daughter in a passionate embrace, "for Wei-chang-tze awaits the coming of Piou-Lu impatiently, in order to have a conjuration with a devil that inhabits his stomach."

"Alas!" said Wu, sadly, "why do you not seek some other and more distinguished employment than that of a conjurer? Why do you not seek distinction in the Palace of Literary Composition, and obtain a style? Then we need not meet in secret, and you might without fear demand my hand from my father."

Piou-Lu smiled, almost scornfully. He seemed to gain an inch in stature, and looked around him with an air of command.

"The marble from which the statue is to be carved must lie in the quarry until the workman finds it," he answered, "and the hour of my destiny has not yet arrived."

"Well, we must wait, I suppose," said Wu, with a sigh. "Meantime, Piou-Lu, I love you."

"The hour will come sooner than you think," said Piou-Lu, returning her caress; "and now go, for the Mandarin waits."

Wu glided away through the gloom to her own apartment, while the conjurer passed rapidly through the garden and gathered the blossoms of certain flowers as he went. He seemed to linger with a strange delight over the buds bathed in the moonlight and the dew; their perfume ascended into his nostrils like incense, and he breathed it with a voluptuous pleasure.

"Now let the demon tremble in the noble stomach of Wei-chang-tze," said Piou-Lu, as he re-entered the hall of reception laden with flowers. "This ill-favored personage will make such conjurations as shall delight the soul of the elegant and well-born Mandarin, and cause his illustrious persecutor to fly terrified."

Piou-Lu then stripped off the petals from many of the flowers, and gathered them in a heap on the floor. The mass of leaves was indeed variegated. The red of the quamoclit, the blue of the convolvulus, the tender pink of the camellia, the waxen white of the magnolia, were all mingled together like the thousand hues in the Scarfs of Felicity. Having built this confused mass of petals in the shape of a pyramid, Piou-Lu unwound a scarf from his waist and flung it over the heap. He then drew the piece of jade-stone from his pocket, and said,—

"This personage of outrageous presence desires that what will be may be shown to the lofty Mandarin, Wei-chang-tze."

As he pronounced these words, he twitched the scarf away with a rapid jerk, and lo! the flower-leaves were gone, and in their place stood a beautiful mandarin duck, in whose gorgeous plumage one might trace the brilliant hues of the flowers. Piou-Lu now approached the duck, caught it up with one hand, while with the other he drew a sharp knife from his girdle and severed the bird's head from its body at a single stroke. To the great astonishment of Wei-chang-tze, the body and dismembered head of the bird vanished the moment the knife had passed through the neck; but at the same instant a duck, resembling it in every respect, escaped from the conjurer's hands and flew across the room. When I say that this duck resembled the other in every respect, I mean only in shape, size, and colors. For the rest, it was no bodily duck. It was impalpable and transparent, and even when it flew it made no noise with its wings.

"This is indeed wonderful!" said Wei-chang-tze. "Let the marvellous conjurer explain."

"The duck formed out of flowers was a duck pure in body and in spirit, most lofty Mandarin," said Piou-Lu, "and when it died under the knife, I ordered its soul to pass into its shadow, which can never be killed. Hence the shadow of the duck has all the colors as well as the intelligence of the real duck that gave it birth."

"And to what end has the very wise Piou-Lu created this beautiful duck-shadow?" asked the Mandarin.

"The cultivated Wei-chang-tze shall immediately behold," answered the conjurer, drawing from his wide sleeve a piece of rock-salt and flinging it to the farther end of the room. He had hardly done this when a terrific sound, between a bark and a howl, issued from the dim corner into which he had cast the rock-salt, and immediately a large gray wolf issued wonderfully from out of the twilight, and rushed with savage fangs upon the shadow of the beautiful duck.

"Why, it is a wolf from the forests of Mantchouria!" exclaimed Wei-chang-tze, rather alarmed at this frightful apparition. "This is no shadow, but a living and bloodthirsty beast."

"Let my lord observe and have no fear," said Piou-Lu, tranquilly.

The wolf seemed rather confounded when, on making a snap at the beautiful duck, his sharp fangs met no resistance, while the bird flew with wonderful venom straight at his fiery eyes. He growled, and snapped, and tore with his claws at the agile shadow that fluttered around and over him, but all to no purpose. As well might the hound leap at the reflection of the deer in the pool where he drinks. The shadow of the beautiful duck seemed all the while to possess some strange, deadly influence over the savage wolf. His growls grew fainter and fainter, and his red and flaming eyes seemed to drop blood. His limbs quivered all over, and the rough hairs of his coat stood on end with terror and pain, —the shadow of the beautiful duck never ceasing all the time to fly straight at his eyes.

"The wolf is dying!" exclaimed Wei-chang-tze.

"He will die,—die like a dog," said Piou-Lu, in a tone of savage triumph.

And presently, as he predicted, the wolf gave two or three faint howls, turned himself round in a circle as if making a bed to sleep on, and then laid down and died. The shadow of the beautiful duck seemed now to be radiant with glory. It shook its bright wings, that were lovely and transparent as a rainbow, and, mounting on the dead body of the wolf, sat in majesty upon his grim and shaggy throne.

"And what means this strange exhibition, learned and wise conjurer?" asked Wei-chang-tze, with a sorely troubled air.

"I will tell you," said Piou-Lu, suddenly dropping his respectful and ceremonious language, and lifting his hand with an air of supreme power. "The mandarin duck, elegant, faithful, and courageous, is an emblem of the dynasty of Ming, that true Chinese race that ruled so splendidly in this land before the invaders usurped the throne. The cowardly and savage wolf is a symbol of the Mantchou Tartar robbers who slew our liberties, shaved our heads, and enchained our people. The time has now arrived when the duck has recovered its splendor and its courage, and is going to kill the wolf; for the wolf cannot bite it, as it works like a shadow in the twilight and mystery of secret association. This you know, Wei-chang-tze, as well as I."

"I have indeed heard of a rebel Chinese named Tién-té, who has raised a flame in our peaceful land, and who, proclaiming himself a lineal descendant of the dynasty of Ming, seeks to dethrone our wise and heavenly sovereign, Hién-foung."

"Lie not to me, Wei-chang-tze, for I know your inmost

thoughts. Chinese as you are, I know that you hate the Tartar in your heart, but you are afraid to say so for fear of losing your head."

The Mandarin was so stupefied at this audacious address that he could not reply, while the conjurer continued: "I come to make you an offer. Join the forces of the heaven-descended Emperor Tién-té. Join with him in expelling this tyrannical Tartar race from the Central Kingdom, and driving them back again to their cold hills and barren deserts. Fly with me to the Imperial camp, and bring with you your daughter Wu, the Golden Heart of the Lily, and I promise you the command of one third of the Imperial forces, and the Presidency of the College of Ceremonies."

"And who are you, who dare to ask of Wei-chang-tze to bestow on you his nobly-born daughter?" said Wei-chang-tze, starting in a rage from his couch.

"I!" replied Piou-Lu, shaking his conjurer's gown from his shoulders and displaying a splendid garment of yellow satin, on the breast of which was emblazoned the Imperial Dragon, —"I am your Emperor, Tién-té!"

"Ha!" screamed a shrill voice behind him at this moment, "here he is. The elegant and noble rebel for whose head our worthy Emperor has offered a reward of ten thousand silver tales. Here he is. Catch! beautiful and noble Mandarins, catch him! and I will pay my creditors with the head-money."

Piou-Lu turned, and beheld the little tailor Hang-pou, at whose back were a whole file of soldiers and a number of Mandarins. Wei-chang-tze shuddered, for in this compromise of his character he knew that his death was written if he fell into the Imperial hands.

The Chapter of "All Is Over"

"STATELY and temperate tailor," said Piou-Lu, calmly, "why do you wish to arrest me?"

"Ho! because I will get a reward, and I want to pay my debts," said Hang-pou, grinning spitefully.

"A reward for me, the miserable and marrowless conjurer, Piou-Lu! O, elegant cutter of summer gowns, your well-educated brains are not at home!"

"O, we know you well enough, mighty conjurer. You are none other than the contumacious rebel, Tién-té, who dares to claim the throne held by the wise and merciful Hién-foung; and we will bear you to the court of Pekin in chains, so that you may wither in the light of his terrible eyes."

"You think you will get a reward of ten thousand silver tales for my head?" said Piou-Lu.

"Certainly," replied the little tailor, rubbing his hands with glee,—"certainly. His Unmatched and Isolated Majesty has promised it, and the Brother of the Sun never lies."

"Listen, inventive closer of symmetrical seams! Listen, and I will tell you what will become of your ten thousand silver tales. There is a long avenue leading to the Imperial treasury, and at every second step is an open hand. When the ten thousand tales are poured out, the first hand grasps a half, the second hand an eighth of the remaining half, the third hand grasps a fourth of the rest, and when the money-bags get down a little lower, all the hands grasp together; so that when the bags reach the little tailor Hang-pou, who stands stamping his feet very far down indeed, they are entirely empty; for Tartar robbers surround the throne, and a Tartar usurper sits upon it, and the great Chinese nation toils in its rice-fields to gild their palaces, and fill their seraglios, and for all they give get neither justice nor mercy. But I, Tién-té, the Heavenly Emperor of this Central Land, will ordain it otherwise, and hurl the false Dragon from his throne; for it is written in the Book of Prognostics, a copy of which was brought to me on the wings of a yellow serpent, that the dynasty of Han shall rule once more, and the Tartar wolves perish miserably out of the Land of Flowers."

"This is treason against the Light of the Universe, our most gracious Emperor," said the Mandarin Lin. "You shall have seventy times seven pounds of cold iron put upon your neck for these blasphemies, and I will promise you that many bamboo splinters shall be driven up under your rebellious nails."

"Let our ears be no longer filled with these atrocious utterances!" cried Hang-pou. "O brave and splendid Mandarins, order your terrifying tigers to arrest this depraved rebel, in order that we may hasten with him to Pekin."

"Before you throw the chains of sorrow around my neck, O tailor of celestial inspirations," said Piou-Lu, with calm mockery,—"before the terrible weight of your just hand falls upon me, I pray you, if you would oblige me, to look at that duck." So saying, Piou-Lu pointed to where the shadow of the duck was sitting on the body of the wolf.

"O, what a beautiful duck!" cried Hang-pou, with glistening eyes, and clapping his hands. "Let us try and catch him!"

"It is indeed a majestic duck," said Mandarin Lin, gravely stroking his mustache. "I am favorable to his capture."

"You will wait until we catch the duck, illustrious rebel!" said Hang-pou to Piou-Lu, very innocently, never turning his eyes from the duck, to which they seemed to be glued by some singular spell of attraction.

"I will talk with the Mandarin Wei-chang-tze while you put your noble manœuvres into motion," answered Piou-Lu.

"Now let us steal upon the duck," said Hang-pou. "Handsomely-formed duck, we entreat of you to remain as quiet as possible, in order that we may grasp you in our hands."

Then, as if actuated by a single impulse, the entire crowd, with the exception of Wei-chang-tze and Piou-Lu, moved toward the duck. The Mandarins stepped on tiptoe, with bent bodies, and little black eyes glistening with eagerness; Hang-pou crawled on his belly like a serpent; and the soldiers, casting aside their bows and shields, crept, with their hands upon their sides, toward the beautiful bird. The duck remained perfectly quiet, its variegated wings shining like painted tale, and its neck lustrous as the court robe of a first-class Mandarin. The crowd scarcely breathed, so intense was their eagerness to capture the duck; and they moved slowly forward, gradually surrounding it.

Hang-pou was the first to make a clutch at the bird, but he was very much astonished to find his hand closing on empty air, while the duck remained seated on the wolf, as still as a picture.

"Miserable tailor!" cried Mandarin Lin, "your hand is a sieve, with meshes wide enough to strain elephants. How can you catch the beautiful duck? Behold me!" and Mandarin Lin made a rapid and well-calculated dive at the duck. To the wonderment of every one except Piou-Lu and Wei-chang-tze, the duck seemed to ooze through his fingers, and, escaping, flew away to the other end of the room.

"If my hand is a sieve," said Hang-pou, "it is evident that the noble Mandarin's hand is not a wall of beaten copper, for it lets ducks fly through with wonderful ease."

"It is a depraved and abominable duck, of criminal parentage," said Mandarin Lin, in a terrible rage; "and I vow, by the whiskers of the Dragon, that I will catch it and burn it on a spit."

"O, yes!" cried the entire crowd,—Mandarins, soldiers, and the little tailor,—all now attracted to the chase of the duck by a power that they could no longer resist. "O, yes! we will most assuredly capture this little duck, and, depriving him of his feathers, punish him on a spit that is exceedingly hot."

So the chase commenced. Here and there, from one corner to the other, up the walls, on the altar of the household gods,—in short, in every possible portion of the large room, did the Mandarins, the little tailor, and the soldiers pursue the shadow of the beautiful duck. Never was seen such a duck. It seemed to be in twenty places at a time. One moment Mandarin Lin would throw himself bodily on the bird, in hopes of crushing it, and would call out triumphantly that now indeed he had the duck; but the words would be hardly out of his mouth when a loud shout from the rest of the party would disabuse his mind, and, turning, he would behold the duck marching proudly down the centre of the floor. Another time a soldier would declare that he had the duck in his breeches pocket; but while his neighbors were carefully probing that recess the duck would be seen calmly emerging from his right-hand sleeve. One time Hang-pou sat down suddenly on the mouth of a large china jar, and resolutely refused to stir, declaring that he had seen the duck enter the jar, and that he was determined to sit upon the mouth until the demon of a duck was starved to death. But even while uttering his heroic determination, his mouth was seen to open very wide, and, to the astonishment of all, the duck flew out. In an instant the whole crowd was after him again; Mandarin Hy-le tumbled over Mandarin Ching-tze, and Mandarin Lin nearly drove his head through Hang-pou's stomach. The unhappy wretches began now to perspire and grow faint with fatigue, but the longer the chase went on the hotter it grew. There was no rest for any of them. From corner to corner, from side to side,—now in one direction, now in another,—no matter whither the duck flew, they were compelled to follow. Their faces streamed, and their legs seemed ready to sink under them. Their eyeballs were ready to start out of their heads, and they had the air of government couriers who had travelled five hundred *li* in eleven days. They were nearly dead.

"Those men will surely perish, illustrious claimant of the

throne," said Wei-chang-tze, gazing with astonishment at this mad chase.

"Let them perish!" said the conjurer; "so will perish all the enemies of the Celestial sovereign, Tién-té. Wei-chang-tze, once more, do you accept my offer? If you remain here, you will be sent to Pekin in chains; if you come with me, I will gird your waist with the scarf of Perpetual Delight. We want wise men like you to guide our armies, and—"

"And the illustrious Tién-té loves the Mandarin's daughter," said Wei-chang-tze, roguishly finishing the sentence. "Light of the Universe and Son of Heaven, Wei-chang-tze is your slave!"

Piou-Lu—for I still call him by his conjurer's name—gave a low whistle, and, obedient to the summons, Wu's delicate shape came gliding from the corridor toward her lover, with the dainty step of a young fawn going to the fountain.

"Wu," said Piou-Lu, "the marble is carved, and the hour is come."

"My father, then, has consented?" said Wu, looking timidly at her father.

"When the Emperor of the Central Land condescends to woo, what father dare refuse?" said Wei-chang-tze.

"Emperor!" said Wu, opening her black eyes with wonder. "My Piou-Lu an Emperor!"

"I am indeed the son of the Dragon," said Piou-Lu, folding her to his breast, "and you shall sit upon a throne of ivory and gold."

"And I thought you were only a conjurer!" murmured Wu, hiding her head in his yellow gown.

"But how are we to leave this place?" asked Wei-chang-tze, looking alarmed. "The guard will seize us if they get knowledge of your presence."

"We shall be at my castle in the mountains of Tse-Hing, near the Kouéï-Lin, in less than a minute," answered Piou-Lu; "for to the possessor of the Dragon Fang all things are possible."

Even as he spoke the ground began to slide from under their feet with wonderful rapidity, leaving them motionless and upright. Houses, walls, gardens, fields, all passed by them with the swiftness of a dream, until, in a few seconds, they found themselves in the mountain castle of Tién-té, where they were welcomed with a splendid hospitality. Wu became the favorite wife of the adventurous Emperor, and Wei-chang-tze one of his most famous generals.

The day after these events some Tartar soldiers entered Wei-chang-tze's house to search for the Mandarin, when, in the reception-hall, they were confounded at finding a number of men lying dead upon the floor, while in the midst sat a beautiful duck, that immediately on their entrance flew out through a window, and was seen no more. The dead men were soon recgonized, and it was the opinion of the people of Tching-tou that Wei-chang-tze had poisoned all the soldiers and Mandarins, and then fled. The tailor, Hang-pou, being among the corpses, was found to have given his creditors the slip forever.

Victory still sits on the banner of Tién-té, and he will, without doubt, by the time that the tea is again fit to gather, sit upon the ancient throne of his ancestors.

Everything is now gracefully concluded.

ORSON SCOTT CARD

Winner of the 1978 John W. Campbell, Jr., Award for best
new science fiction writer, Orson Scott Card has published
several novels and many short stories since then. Fantasy
lovers will undoubtably recognize him as the editor of *Dragons of Light* and *Dragons of Darkness*—two fine, original
anthologies. However, he is also capable of creating his own
poignant visions of dragons, heroism, and common sense, as
the following novella illustrates.

THE BULLY AND THE BEAST

by Orson Scott Card

THE PAGE entered the Count's chamber at a dead run. He had long ago given up sauntering—when the Count called, he expected a page to appear immediately, and any delay at all made the Count irritable and likely to assign a page to stable duty.

"My lord," said the page.

"My lord indeed," said the Count. "What kept you?" The Count stood at the window, his back to the boy. In his arms he held a velvet gown, incredibly embroidered with gold and silver thread. "I think I need to call a council," said the Count. "On the other hand, I haven't the slightest desire to submit myself to a gaggle of jabbering knights. They'll be quite angry. What do you think?"

No one had ever asked the page for advice before, and he wasn't quite sure what was expected of him. "Why should they be angry, my lord?"

"Do you see this gown?" the Count asked, turning around and holding it up.

"Yes, my lord."

"What do you think of it?"

"Depends, doesn't it, my lord, on who wears it."

"It cost eleven pounds of silver."

The page smiled sickly. Eleven pounds of silver would keep the average knight in arms, food, women, clothing, and shelter for a year with six pounds left over for spending money.

"There are more," said the Count. "Many more."

"But who are they for? Are you going to marry?"

"None of your business!" roared the Count. "If there's anything I hate, it's a meddler!" The Count turned again to the window and looked out. He was shaded by a huge oak tree

117

that grew forty feet from the castle walls. "What's today?" asked the Count.

"Thursday, my lord."

"The day, the day!"

"Eleventh past Easter Feast."

"The tribute's due today," said the Count. "Due on Easter, in fact, but today the Duke will be certain I'm not paying."

"Not paying the tribute, my lord?"

"How? Turn me upside down and shake me, but I haven't a farthing. The tribute money's gone. The money for new arms is gone. The travel money is gone. The money for new horses is gone. Haven't got any money at all. But gad, boy, what a wardrobe." The Count sat on the sill of the window. "The Duke will be here very quickly, I'm afraid. And he has the latest in debt collection equipment."

"What's that?"

"An army." The Count sighed. "Call a council, boy. My knights may jabber and scream, but they'll fight. I know they will."

The page wasn't sure. "They'll be very angry, my lord. Are you sure they'll fight?"

"Oh, yes," said the Count. "If they don't, the Duke will kill them."

"Why?"

"For not honoring their oath to me. Do go now, boy, and call a council."

The page nodded. Kind of felt sorry for the old boy. Not much of a Count, as things went, but he could have been worse, and it was pretty plain the castle would be sacked and the Count imprisoned and the women raped and the page sent off home to his parents. "A council!" he cried as he left the Count's chamber. "A council!"

In the cold cavern of the pantry under the kitchen, Bork pulled a huge keg of ale from its resting place and lifted it, not easily, but without much strain, and rested it on his shoulders. Head bowed, he walked slowly up the stairs. Before Bork worked in the kitchen, it used to take two men most of an afternoon to move the huge kegs. But Bork was a giant, or what passed for a giant in those days. The Count himself was of average height, barely past five feet. Bork was nearly seven feet tall, with muscles like an ox. People stepped aside for him.

"Put it there," said the cook, hardly looking up. "And don't drop it."

Bork didn't drop the keg. Nor did he resent the cook's expecting him to be clumsy. He had been told he was clumsy all his life, ever since it became plain at the age of three that he was going to be immense. Everyone knew that big people were clumsy. And it was true enough. Bork was so strong he kept doing things he never meant to do, accidentally. Like the time the swordmaster, admiring his strength, had invited him to learn to use the heavy battleswords. Bork hefted them easily, of course, though at the time he was only twelve and hadn't reached his full strength.

"Hit me," the swordmaster said.

"But the blade's sharp," Bork told him.

"Don't worry. You won't come near me." The swordmaster had taught a hundred knights to fight. None of them had come near him. And, in fact, when Bork swung the heavy sword the swordmaster had his shield up in plenty of time. He just hadn't counted on the terrible force of the blow. The shield was battered aside easily, and the blow threw the sword upward, so it cut off the swordmaster's left arm just below the shoulder, and only narrowly missed slicing deeply into his chest.

Clumsy, that was all Bork was. But it was the end of any hope of his becoming a knight. When the swordmaster finally recovered, he consigned Bork to the kitchen and the black-smith's shop, where they needed someone with enough strength to skewer a cow end to end and carry it to the fire; where it was convenient to have a man who, with a double-sized ax, could chop down a large tree in half an hour, cut it into logs, and carry a month's supply of firewood into the castle in an afternoon.

A page came into the kitchen. "There's a council, cook. The Count wants ale, and plenty of it."

The cook swore profusely and threw a carrot at the page. "Always changing the schedule! Always making me do extra work." As soon as the page had escaped, the cook turned on Bork. "All right, carry the ale out there, and be quick about it. Try not to drop it."

"I won't," Bork said.

"He won't," the cook muttered. "Clever as an ox, he is."

Bork manhandled the cask into the great hall. It was cold, though outside the sun was shining. Little light and little warmth reached the inside of the castle. And since it was spring, the huge logpile in the pit in the middle of the room lay cold and damp.

The knights were beginning to wander into the great hall and sit on the benches that lined the long, pock-marked slab of a table. They knew enough to carry their mugs—councils were always well-oiled with ale. Bork had spent years as a child watching the knights practice the arts of war, but the knights seemed more natural carrying their cups than holding their swords at the ready. They were more dedicated to their drinking than to war.

"Ho, Bork the Bully," one of the knights greeted him. Bork managed a half-smile. He had learned long since not to take offense.

"How's Sam the stableman?" asked another, tauntingly.

Bork blushed and turned away, heading for the door to the kitchen.

The knights were laughing at their cleverness. "Twice the body, half the brain," one of them said to the others. "Probably hung like a horse," another speculated, then quipped, "Which probably accounts for those mysterious deaths among the sheep this winter." A roar of laughter, and cups beating on the table. Bork stood in the kitchen, trembling. He could not escape the sound—the stones carried it echoing to him wherever he went.

The cook turned and looked at him. "Don't be angry, boy," he said. "It's all in fun."

Bork nodded and smiled at the cook. That's what it was. All in fun. And besides, Bork deserved it, he knew. It was only fair that he be treated cruelly. For he had earned the title Bork the Bully, hadn't he? When he was three, and already massive as a ram, his only friend, a beautiful young village boy named Winkle, had hit upon the idea of becoming a knight. Winkle had dressed himself in odds and ends of leather and tin, and made a makeshift lance from a hog prod.

"You're my destrier," Winkle cried as he mounted Bork and rode him for hours. Bork thought it was a fine thing to be a knight's horse. It became the height of his ambition, and he wondered how one got started in the trade. But one day Sam, the stableman's son, had taunted Winkle for his make-believe armor, and it had turned into a fist fight, and Sam had thoroughly bloodied Winkle's nose. Winkle screamed as if he were dying, and Bork sprang to his friend's defense, walloping Sam, who was three years older, along the side of his head.

Ever since then Sam spoke with a thickness in his voice, and often lost his balance; his jaw, broken in several places, never healed properly, and he had problems with his ear.

It horrified Bork to have caused so much pain, but Winkle assured him that Sam deserved it. "After all, Bork, he was twice my size, and he was picking on me. He's a bully. He had it coming."

For several years Winkle and Bork were the terror of the village. Winkle would constantly get into fights, and soon the village children learned not to resist him. If Winkle lost a fight, he would scream for Bork, and though Bork was never again so harsh as he was with Sam, his blows still hurt terribly. Winkle loved it. Then one day he tired of being a knight, dismissed his destrier, and became fast friends with the other children. It was only then that Bork began to hear himself called Bork the Bully; it was Winkle who convinced the other children that the only villain in the fighting had been Bork. "After all," Bork overheard Winkle say one day, "he's twice as strong as anyone else. Isn't fair for him to fight. It's a cowardly thing for him to do, and we mustn't have anything to do with him. Bullies must be punished."

Bork knew that Winkle was right, and ever after that he bore the burden of shame. He remembered the frightened looks in the other children's eyes when he approached them, the way they pleaded for mercy. But Winkle was always screaming and writhing in agony, and Bork always hit the child despite his terror, and for that bullying Bork was still paying. He paid in the ridicule he accepted from the knights; he paid in the solitude of all his days and nights; he paid by working as hard as he could, using his strength to serve instead of hurt.

But just because he knew he deserved the punishment did not mean he enjoyed it. There were tears in his eyes as he went about his work in the kitchen. He tried to hide them from the cook, but to no avail. "Oh, no, you're not going to cry, are you?" the cook asked. "You'll only make your nose run and then you'll get snot in the soup. Get out of the kitchen for a while!"

Which is why Bork was standing in the doorway of the great hall watching the council that would completely change his life.

* 　 * 　 *

"Well, where's the tribute money gone to?" demanded one of the knights. "The harvest was large enough last year!"

It was an ugly thing, to see the knights so angry. But the Count knew they had a right to be upset—it was they who would have to fight the Duke's men, and they had a right to know why.

"My friends," the Count said. "My friends, some things are more important than money. I invested the money in something more important than tribute, more important than peace, more important than long life. I invested the money in beauty. Not to create beauty, but to perfect it." The knights were listening now. For all their violent preoccupations, they all had a soft place in their hearts for true beauty. It was one of the requirements for knighthood. "I have been entrusted with a jewel, more perfect than any diamond. It was my duty to place that jewel in the best setting money could buy. I can't explain. I can only show you." He rang a small bell, and behind him one of the better-known secret doors in the castle opened, and a wizened old woman emerged. The Count whispered in her ear, and the woman scurried back into the secret passage.

"Who's she?" asked one of the knights.

"She is the woman who nursed my children after my wife died. My wife died in childbirth, you remember. But what you don't know is that the child lived. My two sons you know well. But I have a third child, my last child, whom you know not at all, and this one is not a son."

The Count was not surprised that several of the knights seemed to puzzle over this riddle. Too many jousts, too much practice in full armor in the heat of the afternoon.

"My child is a daughter."

"Ah," said the knights.

"At first I kept her hidden away because I could not bear to see her—after all, my most beloved wife had died in bearing her. But after a few years I overcame my grief, and went to see the child in the room where she was hidden, and lo! She was the most beautiful child I had ever seen. I named her Brunhilda, and from that moment on I loved her. I was the most devoted father you could imagine. But I did not let her leave the secret room. Why, you may ask?"

"Yes, why!" demanded several of the knights.

"Because she was so beautiful I was afraid she would be

stolen from me. I was terrified that I would lose her. Yet I saw her every day, and talked to her, and the older she got, the more beautiful she became, and for the last several years I could no longer bear to see her in her mother's cast-off clothing. Her beauty is such that only the finest cloths and gowns and jewels of Flanders, of Venice, of Florence would do for her. You'll see! The money was not ill-spent."

And the door opened again, and the old woman emerged, leading forth Brunhilda.

In the doorway, Bork gasped. But no one heard him, for all the knights gasped, too.

She was the most perfect woman in the world. Her hair was a dark red, flowing behind her like an auburn stream as she walked. Her face was white from being indoors all her life, and when she smiled it was like the sun breaking out on a stormy day. And none of the knights dared look at her body for very long, because the longer they looked the more they wanted to touch her, and the Count said, "I warn you. Any man who lays a hand on her will have to answer to me. She is a virgin, and when she marries she shall be a virgin, and a king will pay half his kingdom to have her, and still I'll feel cheated to have to give her up."

"Good evening, my lords," she said, smiling. Her voice was like the song of leaves dancing in the summer wind, and the knights fell to their knees before her.

None of them was more moved by her beauty than Bork, however. When she entered the room he forgot himself; there was no room in his mind for anything but the great beauty he had seen for the first time in his life. Bork knew nothing of courtesy. He only knew that, for the first time in his life, he had seen something so perfect that he could not rest until it was his. Not his to own, but his to be owned by. He longed to serve her in the most degrading ways he could think of, if only she would smile upon him; longed to die for her, if only the last moment of his life were filled with her voice saying, "You may love me."

If he had been a knight, he might have thought of a poetic way to say such things. But he was not a knight, and so his words came out of his heart before his mind could find a way to make them clever. He strode blindly from the kitchen door, his huge body casting a shadow in the torchlight that seemed to the knights like the shadow of death passing over them. They watched in uneasiness that soon turned to outrage as he came to the girl, reached out, and took her small white hands in his.

"I love you," Bork said to her, and tears came unbidden to his eyes. "Let me marry you."

At that moment several of the knights found their courage. They seized Bork roughly by the arms, meaning to pull him away and punish him for his effrontery. But Bork effortlessly tossed them away. They fell to the ground yards from him. He never saw them fall; his gaze never left the lady's face.

She looked wonderingly in his eyes. Not because she thought him attractive, because he was ugly and she knew it. Not because of the words he had said, because she had been taught that many men would say those words, and she was to pay no attention to them. What startled her, what amazed her, was the deep truth in Bork's face. That was something she had never seen, and though she did not recognize it for what it was, it fascinated her.

The Count was furious. Seeing the clumsy giant holding his daughter's small white hands in his was outrageous. He would not endure it. But the giant had such great strength that to tear him away would mean a full-scale battle, and in such a battle Brunhilda might be injured. No, the giant had to be handled delicately, for the moment.

"My dear fellow," said the Count, affecting a joviality he did not feel. "You've only just met."

Bork ignored him. "I will never let you come to harm," he said to the girl.

"What's his name?" the Count whispered to a knight. "I can't remember his name."

"Bork," the knight answered.

"My dear Bork," said the Count. "All due respect and everything, but my daughter has noble blood, and you're not even a knight."

"Then I'll become one," Bork said.

"It's not that easy, Bork, old fellow. You must do something exceptionally brave, and then I can knight you and we can talk about this other matter. But in the meantime, it isn't proper for you to be holding my daughter's hands. Why don't you go back to the kitchen like a good fellow?"

Bork gave no sign that he heard. He only continued looking into the lady's eyes. And finally it was she who was able to end the dilemma.

"Bork," she said, "I will count on you. But in the meantime, my father will be angry at you if you don't return to the kitchen."

Of course, Bork thought. Of course, she is truly concerned for me, doesn't want me to come to harm on her account. "For your sake," he said, the madness of love still on him. Then he turned and left the room.

The Count sat down, sighing audibly. "Should have got rid of him years ago. Gentle as a lamb, and then all of a sudden goes crazy. Get rid of him—somebody take care of that tonight, would you? Best to do it in his sleep. Don't want any casualties when we're likely to have a battle in the morning."

The reminder of the battle was enough to sober even those who were on their fifth mug of ale. The wizened old woman led Brunhilda away again. "But not to the secret room, now. To the chamber next to mine. And post a double guard outside her door, and keep the key yourself," said the Count.

When she was gone, the Count looked around at the knights. "The treasury has been emptied in a vain attempt to find clothing to do her justice. I had no other choice."

And there was not a knight who would say the money had been badly spent.

The Duke came late in the afternoon, and demanded the tribute, and the Count refused, of course. There was the usual challenge to come out of the castle and fight, but the Count, outnumbered ten to one, merely replied, rather saucily, that the Count should come in and get him. The messenger who delivered the sarcastic message came back with his tongue in a bag around his neck. The battle was thus begun grimly: and grimly it continued.

The guard watching on the south side of the castle was slacking. He paid for it. The Duke's archers managed to creep up to the huge oak tree and climb it without any alarm being given, and the first notice any of them had was when the guard fell from the battlements with an arrow in his throat.

The archers—there must have been a dozen of them—kept up a deadly rain of arrows. They wasted no shots. The squires dropped dead in alarming numbers until the Count gave orders for them to come inside. And when the human targets were all under cover, the archers set to work on the cattle and sheep milling about in their open pens. There was no way to protect the animals. By sunset, all of them were dead.

"Dammit," said the cook. "How can I cook all this before it spoils?"

"Find a way," said the Count. "That's our food supply. I refuse to let them starve us out."

So all night Bork worked, carrying the cattle and sheep inside, one by one. At first the villagers who had taken refuge in the castle tried to help him, but he could carry three animals inside the kitchen in the time it took them to drag one, and they soon gave it up.

The Count saw who was saving the meat. "Don't get rid of him tonight," he told his knights. "We'll punish him for his effrontery in the morning."

Bork only rested twice in the night, taking naps for an hour before the cook woke him again. And when dawn came, and the arrows began coming again, all the cattle were inside, and all but twenty sheep.

"That's all we can save," the cook told the Count.

"Save them all."

"But if Bork tries to go out there, he'll be killed!"

The Count looked the cook in the eyes. "Bring in the sheep or have him die trying."

The cook was not aware of the fact that Bork was under sentence of death. So he did his best to save Bork. A kettle lined with cloth and strapped onto the giant's head; a huge kettle lid for a shield. "It's the best we can do," the cook said.

"But I can't carry sheep if I'm holding a shield," Bork said.

"What can I do? The Count commanded it. It's worth your life to refuse."

Bork stood and thought for a few moments, trying to find a way out of his dilemma. He saw only one possibility. "If I can't stop them from hitting me, I'll have to stop them from shooting at all."

"How!" the cook demanded, and then followed Bork to the blacksmith's shop, where Bork found his huge ax leaning against the wall.

"Now's not the time to cut firewood," said the blacksmith.

"Yes it is," Bork answered.

Carrying the ax and holding the kettle lid between his body and the archers, Bork made his way across the courtyard. The arrows pinged harmlessly off the metal. Bork got to the drawbridge. "Open up!" he shouted, and the drawbridge fell away and dropped across the moat. Bork walked across, then made his way along the moat toward the oak tree.

In the distance the Duke, standing in front of his dazzling white tent with his emblem of yellow crosses on it, saw Bork emerge from the castle. "Is that a man or a bear?" he asked. No one was sure.

The archers shot at Bork steadily, but the closer he got to the tree the worse their angle of fire and the larger the shadow of safety the kettle lid cast over his body. Finally, holding the lid high over his head, Bork began hacking one-handed at the trunk. Chips of wood flew with each blow; with his right hand alone he could cut deeper and faster than a normal man with both hands free.

But he was concentrating on cutting wood, and his left arm grew tired holding his makeshift shield, and an archer was able to get off a shot that slipped past the shield and plunged into his left arm, in the thick muscle at the back.

He nearly dropped the shield. Instead, he had the presence of mind to let go of the ax and drop to his knees, quickly balancing the kettle lid between the tree trunk, his head, and the top of the ax handle. Gently he pulled at the arrow shaft. It would not come backward. So he broke the arrow and pushed the stub the rest of the way through his arm until it was out the other side. It was excruciatingly painful, but he knew he could not quit now. He took hold of the shield with his left arm again, and despite the pain held it high as he began to cut again, girdling the tree with a deep white gouge. The blood dripped steadily down his arm, but he ignored it, and soon enough the bleeding stopped and slowed.

On the castle battlements, the Count's men began to realize that there was a hope of Bork's succeeding. To protect him, they began to shoot their arrows into the tree. The archers were well-hidden, but the rain of arrows, however badly aimed, began to have its effect. A few of them dropped to the ground, where the castle archers could easily finish them off; the others were forced to concentrate on finding cover.

The tree trembled more and more with each blow, until finally Bork stepped back and the tree creaked and swayed. He had learned from his lumbering work in the forest how to make the tree fall where he wanted it; the oak fell parallel to the castle walls, so it neither bridged the moat nor let the Duke's archers scramble from the tree too far from the castle. So when the archers tried to flee to the safety of the Duke's lines, the castle bowmen were able to kill them all.

One of them, however, despaired of escape. Instead, though he already had an arrow in him, he drew a knife and charged at Bork, in a mad attempt to avenge his own death on the man who had caused it. Bork had no choice. He swung his ax through the air and discovered that men are nowhere near as sturdy as a tree.

In the distance, the Duke watched with horror as the giant cut a man in half with a single blow. "What have they got!" he said. "What is this monster?"

Covered with the blood that had spurted from the dying man, Bork walked back toward the drawbridge, which opened again as he approached. But he did not get to enter. Instead the Count and the fifty mounted knights came from the gate on horseback, their armor shining in the sunlight.

"I've decided to fight them in the open," the Count said. "And you, Bork, must fight with us. If you live through this, I'll make you a knight!"

Bork knelt. "Thank you, my Lord Count," he said.

The Count glanced around in embarrassment. "Well, then. Let's get to it. Charge!" he bellowed.

Bork did not realize that the knights were not even formed in a line yet. He simply followed the command and charged, alone, toward the Duke's lines. The Count watched him go, and smiled.

"My Lord Count," said the nearest knight. "Aren't we going to attack with him?"

"Let the Duke take care of him," the Count said.

"But he cut down the oak and saved the castle, my lord."

"Yes," said the Count. "An exceptionally brave act. Do you want him to try to claim my daughter's hand?"

"But my lord," said the knight, "if he fights beside us, we might have a chance of winning. But if he's gone, the Duke will destroy us."

"Some things," said the Count, with finality, "are more important than victory. Would you want to go on living in a world where perfection like Brunhilda's was possessed by such a man as that?"

The knights were silent, then, as they watched Bork approach the Duke's army, alone.

Bork did not realize he was alone until he stood a few feet away from the Duke's lines. He had felt a strange exhilaration as he walked across the fields, believing he was marching into battle with the knights he had long admired in their bright armor and deft instruments of war. Now the exhilaration was gone. Where were the others? Bork was afraid.

He could not understand why the Duke's men had not shot any arrows at him. Actually, it was a misunderstanding. If the Duke had known Bork was a commoner and not a knight at all, Bork would have had a hundred arrows bristling from his corpse. As it was, however, one of the Duke's men called out, "You, sir! Do you challenge us to single combat?"

Of course. That was it—the Count did not intend Bork to face an army, he intended him to face a single warrior. The whole outcome of the battle would depend on him alone! It was a tremendous honor, and Bork wondered if he could carry it off.

"Yes! Single combat!" he answered. "Your strongest, bravest man!"

"But you're a giant!" cried the Duke's man.

"But I'm wearing no armor." And to prove his sincerity, Bork took off his helmet, which was uncomfortable anyway, and stepped forward. The Duke's knights backed away, making an opening for him, with men in armor watching him pass from both sides. Bork walked steadily on, until he came to a cleared circle where he faced the Duke himself.

"Are you the champion?" asked Bork.

"I'm the Duke," he answered. "But I don't see any of my knights stepping forward to fight you."

"Do you refuse the challenge, then?" Bork asked, trying to sound as brave and scornful as he imagined a true knight would sound.

The Duke looked around at his men, who, if the armor had allowed, would have been shuffling uncomfortably in the morning sunlight. As it was, none of them looked at him.

"No," said the Duke. "I accept your challenge myself." The thought of fighting the giant terrified him. But he was a knight, and known to be a brave man; he had become Duke in the prime of his youth, and if he backed down before a giant now, his duchy would be taken from him in only a few years; his honor would be lost long before. So he drew his sword and advanced upon the giant.

Bork saw the determination in the Duke's eyes, and marveled at a man who would go himself into a most dangerous battle instead of sending his men. Briefly Bork wondered why the Count had not shown such courage; he determined at that moment that if he could help it the Duke would not

die. The blood of the archer was more than he had ever
wanted to shed. Nobility was in every movement of the Duke,
and Bork wondered at the ill chance that had made them
enemies.

The Duke lunged at Bork with his sword flashing. Bork hit
him with the flat of the ax, knocking him to the ground. The
Duke cried out in pain. His armor was dented deeply; there
had to be ribs broken under the dent.

"Why don't you surrender?" asked Bork.

"Kill me now!"

"If you surrender, I won't kill you at all."

The Duke was surprised. There was a murmur from his
men.

"I have your word?"

"Of course. I swear it."

It was too startling an idea.

"What do you plan to do, hold me for ransom?"

Bork thought about it. "I don't think so."

"Well, what then? Why not kill me and have done with it?"
The pain in his chest now dominated the Duke's voice, but he
did not spit blood, and so he began to feel some hope.

"All the Count wants you to do is go away and stop
collecting tribute. If you promise to do that, I'll promise that
not one of you will be harmed."

The Duke and his men considered this in silence. It was too
good to believe. So good it was almost dishonorable even to
consider it. Still—there was Bork, who had broken the Duke's
body with one blow, right through the armor. If he chose to
let them walk away from the battle, why argue?

"I give my word that I'll cease collecting tribute from the
Count, and my men and I will go away in peace."

"Well, then, that's good news," Bork said. "I've got to go
tell the Count." And Bork turned away and walked into the
fields, heading for where the Count's tiny army waited.

"I can't believe it," said the Duke. "A knight like that, and
he turns out to be generous. The Count could have his way
with the King, with a knight like that."

They stripped the armor off him, carefully, and began
wrapping his chest with bandages.

"If he were mine," the Duke said, "I'd use him to conquer
the whole land."

* * *

The Count watched, incredulous, as Bork crossed the field.

"He's still alive," he said, and he began to wonder what Bork would have to say about the fact that none of the knights had joined his gallant charge.

"My Lord Count!" cried Bork, when he was within range. He would have waved, but both his arms were exhausted now. "They surrender!"

"What?" the Count asked the knights near him. "Did he say they surrender?"

"Apparently," a knight answered. "Apparently he won."

"Damn!" cried the Count. "I won't have it!"

The knights were puzzled. "If anybody's going to defeat the Duke, *I* am! Not a damnable commoner! Not a giant with the brains of a cockroach! Charge!"

"What?" several of the knights asked.

"I said charge!" And the Count moved forward, his warhorse plodding carefully through the field, building up momentum.

Bork saw the knights start forward. He had watched enough mock battles to recognize a charge. He could only assume that the Count hadn't heard him. But the charge had to be stopped—he had given his word, hadn't he? So he planted himself in the path of the Count's horse.

"Out of the way, you damned fool!" cried the Count. But Bork stood his ground. The Count was determined not to be thwarted. He prepared to ride Bork down.

"You can't charge!" Bork yelled. "They surrendered!"

The Count gritted his teeth and urged the horse forward, his lance prepared to cast Bork out of the way.

A moment later the Count found himself in midair, hanging to the lance for his life. Bork held it over his head, and the knights laboriously halted their charge and wheeled to see what was going on with Bork and the Count.

"My Lord Count," Bork said respectfully. "I guess you didn't hear me. They surrendered. I promised them they could go in peace if they stopped collecting tribute."

From his precarious hold on the lance, fifteen feet off the ground, the Count said, "I didn't hear you."

"I didn't think so. But you *will* let them go, won't you?"

"Of course. Could you give a thought to letting me down, old boy?"

And so Bork let the Count down, and there was a peace treaty between the Duke and the Count, and the Duke's men rode away in peace, talking about the generosity of the giant knight.

"But he isn't a knight," said a servant to the Duke.

"What? Not a knight?"

"No. Just a villager. One of the peasants told me, when I was stealing his chickens."

"Not a knight," said the Duke, and for a moment his face began to turn the shade of red that made his knights want to ride a few feet further from him—they knew his rage too well already.

"We were tricked then," said a knight, trying to fend off his lord's anger by anticipating it.

The Duke said nothing for a moment. Then he smiled. "Well, if he's not a knight, he should be. He has the strength. He has the courtesy. Hasn't he?"

The knights agreed that he had.

"He's the moral equivalent of a knight," said the Duke. Pride assuaged, for the moment, he led his men back to his castle. Underneath, however, even deeper than the pain in his ribs, was the image of the Count perched on the end of a lance held high in the air by the giant, Bork, and he pondered what it might have meant, and what, more to the point, it might mean in the future.

Things were getting out of hand, the Count decided. First of all, the victory celebration had not been his idea, and yet here they were, riotously drunken in the great hall, and even villagers were making free with the ale, laughing and cheering among the knights. That was bad enough, but worse was the fact that the knights were making no pretense about it—the party was in honor of Bork.

The Count drummed his fingers on the table. No one paid any attention. They were too busy—Sir Alwishard trying to keep two village wenches occupied near the fire, Sir Silwiss pissing in the wine and laughing so loud that the Count could hardly hear Sir Braig and Sir Umlaut as they sang and danced along the table, kicking plates off with their toes in time with the music. It was the best party the Count had ever seen. And it wasn't for him, it was for that damnable giant who had made an ass of him in front of all his men and all the Duke's men and, worst of all, the Duke. He heard a strange growling sound, like a savage wolf getting ready to spring. In a lull in the bedlam he suddenly realized that the sound was coming from his own throat.

Get control of yourself, he thought. The real gains, the solid gains were not Bork's—they were mine. The Duke is gone, and instead of me paying him tribute from now on, he'll be paying me. Word would get around, too, that the Count had won a battle with the Duke. After all, that was the basis of power—who could beat whom in battle. A duke was just a man who could beat a count, a count someone who could beat a baron, a baron someone who could beat a knight.

But what was a person who could beat a duke?

"You should be king," said a tall, slender young man standing near the throne.

The Count looked at him, making a vague motion with his hidden hand. How had the boy read his thoughts?

"I'll pretend I didn't hear that."

"You heard it," said the young man.

"It's treason."

"Only if the king beats you in battle. If *you* win, it's treason *not* to say so."

The Count looked the boy over. Dark hair that looked a bit too carefully combed for a villager. A straight nose, a pleasant smile, a winning grace when he walked. But something about his eyes gave the lie to the smile. The boy was vicious somehow. The boy was dangerous.

"I like you," said the Count.

"I'm glad." He did not sound glad. He sounded bored.

"If I'm smart, I'll have you strangled immediately."

The boy only smiled more.

"Who are you?"

"My name is Winkle. And I'm Bork's best friend."

Bork. There he was again, that giant sticking his immense shadow into everything tonight. "Didn't know Bork the Bully had any friends."

"He has one. Me. Ask him."

"I wonder if a friend of Bork's is really a friend of mine," the Count said.

"I said I was his best friend. I didn't say I was a good friend." And Winkle smiled.

A thoroughgoing bastard, the Count decided, but he waved to Bork and beckoned for him to come. In a moment the giant knelt before the Count, who was irritated to discover that

when Bork knelt and the Count sat, Bork still looked down
on him.

"This man," said the Count, "claims to be your friend."

Bork looked up and recognized Winkle, who was beaming
down at him, his eyes filled with love, mostly. A hungry kind
of love, but Bork wasn't discriminating. He had the admira-
tion and grudging respect of the knights, but he hardly knew
them. This was his childhood friend, and at the thought that
Winkle claimed to be his friend Bork immediately forgave all
the past slights and smiled back. "Winkle," he said. "Of
course we're friends. He's my *best* friend."

The Count made the mistake of looking in Bork's eyes and
seeing the complete sincerity of his love for Winkle. It embar-
rassed him, for he knew Winkle too well already, from just
the moments of conversation they had had. Winkle was
nobody's friend. But Bork was obviously blind to that. For a
moment the Count almost pitied the giant, had a glimpse of
what his life must be like, if the predatory young villager was
his best friend.

"Your majesty," said Winkle.

"Don't call me that."

"I only anticipate what the world will know in a matter of
months."

Winkle sounded so confident, so sure of it. A chill went up
the Count's spine. He shook it off. "I won one battle, Winkle. I
still have a huge budget deficit and a pretty small army of
some fairly lousy knights."

"Think of your daughter, even if *you* aren't ambitious.
Despite her beauty she'll be lucky to marry a duke. But if she
were the daughter of a king, she could marry anyone in all
the world. And her own lovely self would be a dowry—no
prince would think to ask for more."

The Count thought of his daughter, the beautiful Brunhilda,
and smiled.

Bork also smiled, for he was also thinking the same thing.

"Your majesty," Winkle urged, "with Bork as your right-
hand man and me as your counselor, there's nothing to stop
you from being king within a year or two. Who would be
willing to stand against an army with the three of us marching at the head?"

"Why three?" asked the Count.

"You mean, why me. I thought you would already understand that—but then, that's what you need me for. You see,

your majesty, you're a good man, a godly man, a paragon of virtue. You would never think of seeking power and conniving against your enemies and spying and doing repulsive things to people you don't like. But kings *have* to do those things or they quickly cease to be kings."

Vaguely the Count remembered behaving in just that way many times, but Winkle's words were seductive—they *should* be true.

"Your majesty, where you are pure, I am polluted. Where you are fresh, I am rotten. I'd sell my mother into slavery if I had a mother and I'd cheat the devil at poker and win hell from him before he caught on. And I'd stab any of your enemies in the back if I got the chance."

"But what if my enemies aren't your enemies?" the Count asked.

"Your enemies are *always* my enemies. I'll be loyal to you through thick and thin."

"How can I trust you, if you're so rotten?"

"Because you're going to pay me a lot of money." Winkle bowed deeply.

"Done," said the Count.

"Excellent," said Winkle, and they shook hands. The Count noticed that Winkle's hands were smooth—he had neither the hard horny palms of a village workingman nor the slick calluses of a man trained to warfare.

"How have you made a living, up to now?" the Count asked.

"I steal," Winkle said, with a smile that said I'm joking and a glint in his eye that said I'm not.

"What about me?" asked Bork.

"Oh, you're in it, too," said Winkle. "You're the king's strong right arm."

"I've never met the king," said Bork.

"Yes you have," Winkle retorted. "That is the king."

"No he's not," said the giant. "He's only a count."

The words stabbed the Count deeply. *Only* a count. Well, that would end. "Today I'm only a count," he said patiently. "Who knows what tomorrow will bring? But Bork—I shall knight you. As a knight you must swear absolute loyalty to me and do whatever I say. Will you do that?"

"Of course I will," said Bork. "Thank you, my Lord Count." Bork arose and called to his new friends throughout the hall in a voice that could not be ignored. "My Lord Count has

decided I will be made a knight!" There were cheers and
applause and stamping of feet. "And the best thing is," Bork
said, "that now I can marry the Lady Brunhilda."

There was no applause. Just a murmur of alarm. Of course.
If he became a knight, he was eligible for Brunhilda's hand.
It was unthinkable—but the Count himself had said so.

The Count was having second thoughts, of course, but he
knew no way to back out of it, not without looking like a word
breaker. He made a false start at speaking, but couldn't
finish. Bork waited, expectantly. Clearly he believed the
Count would confirm what Bork had said.

It was Winkle, however, who took the situation in hand.
"Oh, Bork," he said sadly—but loudly, so that everyone could
hear. "Don't you understand? His majesty is making you a
knight out of gratitude. But unless you're a king or the son of
a king, you have to do something exceptionally brave to earn
Brunhilda's hand."

"But, wasn't I brave today?" Bork asked. After all, the
arrow wound in his arm still hurt, and only the ale kept him
from aching unmercifully all over from the exertion of the
night and the day just past.

"You were brave. But since you're twice the size and ten
times the strength of an ordinary man, it's hardly fair for you
to win Brunhilda's hand with ordinary bravery. No, Bork—
it's just the way things work. It's just the way things are
done. Before you're worthy of Brunhilda, you have to do
something ten times as brave as what you did today."

Bork could not think of something ten times as brave.
Hadn't he gone almost unprotected to chop down the oak
tree? Hadn't he attacked a whole army all by himself, and
won the surrender of the enemy? What could be ten times as
brave?

"Don't despair," the Count said. "Surely in all the battles
ahead of us there'll be *something* ten times as brave. And in
the meantime, you're a knight, my friend, a great knight,
and you shall dine at my table every night! And when we
march into battle, there you'll be, right beside me—"

"A few steps ahead," Winkle whispered discreetly.

"A few steps ahead of me, to defend the honor of my
county—"

"Don't be shy," whispered Winkle.

"No, not my county. My kingdom. For from today, you
men no longer serve a count! You serve a king!"

It was a shocking declaration, and might have caused sober reflection if there had been a sober man in the room. But through the haze of alcohol and torchlight and fatigue, the knights looked at the Count and he did indeed seem kingly. And they thought of the battles ahead and were not afraid, for they had won a glorious victory today and not one of them had shed a drop of blood. Except, of course, Bork. But in some corner of their collected opinions was a viewpoint they would not have admitted to holding, if anyone brought the subject out in the open. The opinion so well hidden from themselves and each other was simple: Bork is not like me. Bork is not one of us. Therefore, Bork is expendable.

The blood that still stained his sleeve was cheap. Plenty more where that came from.

And so they plied him with more ale until he fell asleep, snoring hugely on the table, forgetting that he had been cheated out of the woman he loved; it was easy to forget, for the moment, because he was a knight, and a hero, and at last he had friends.

It took two years for the Count to become King. He began close to home, with other counts, but soon progressed to the great dukes and earls of the kingdom. Wherever he went, the pattern was the same. The Count and his fifty knights would ride their horses, only lightly armored so they could travel with reasonable speed. Bork would walk, but his long legs easily kept up with the rest of them. They would arrive at their victim's castle, and three squires would hand Bork his new steel-headed ax. Bork, covered with impenetrable armor, would wade the moat, if there was one, or simply walk up to the gates, swing the ax, and begin chopping through the wood. When the gates collapsed, Bork would take a huge steel rod and use it as a crow, prying at the portcullis, bending the heavy iron like pretzels until there was a gap wide enough for a mounted knight to ride through.

Then he would go back to the Count and Winkle.

Throughout this operation, not a word would have been said; the only activity from the Count's other men would be enough archery that no one would be able to pour boiling oil or hot tar on Bork while he was working. It was a precaution, and nothing more—even if they set the oil on the fire the moment the Count's little army approached, it would scarcely be hot enough to make water steam by the time Bork was through.

"Do you surrender to his Majesty the King?" Winkle would cry.

And the defenders of the castle, their gate hopelessly breached and terrified of the giant who had so easily made a joke of their defenses, would usually surrender. Occasionally there was some token resistance—when that happened, at Winkle's insistence, the town was brutally sacked and the noble's family was held in prison until a huge ransom was paid.

At the end of two years, the Count and Bork and Winkle and their army marched on Winchester. The King—the real king—fled before them and took up his exile in Anjou, where it was warmer anyway. The Count had himself crowned king, accepted the fealty of every noble in the country, and introduced his daughter Brunhilda all around. Then, finding Winchester not to his liking, he returned to his castle and ruled from there. Suitors for his daughter's hand made a constant traffic on the roads leading into the country; would-be courtiers and nobles vying for positions filled the new hostelries that sprang up on the other side of the village. All left much poorer than they had arrived. And while much of that money found its way into the King's coffers, much more of it went to Winkle, who believed that skimming off the cream meant leaving at least a quarter of it for the King.

And now that the wars were done, Bork hung up his armor and went back to normal life. Not quite normal life, actually. He slept in a good room in the castle, better than most of the knights. Some of the knights had even come to enjoy his company, and sought him out for ale in the evenings or hunting in the daytime—Bork could always be counted on to carry home two deer himself, and was much more convenient than a packhorse. All in all, Bork was happier than he had ever thought he would be.

Which is how things were going when the dragon came and changed it all forever.

Winkle was in Brunhilda's room, a place he had learned many routes to get to, so that he went unobserved ever time. Brunhilda, after many gifts and more flattery, was on the verge of giving in to the handsome young adviser to the King when strange screams and cries began coming from the fields below. Brunhilda pulled away from Winkle's exploring hands and, clutching her half-open gown around her, rushed to the window to see what was the matter.

She looked down, to where the screams were coming from, and it wasn't until the dragon's shadow fell across her that she looked up. Winkle, waiting on the bed, only saw the claws reach in and, gently but firmly, take hold of Brunhilda and pull her from the room. Brunhilda fainted immediately, and by the time Winkle got to where he could see her, the dragon had backed away from the window and on great flapping wings was carrying her limp body off toward the north whence he came.

Winkle was horrified. It was so sudden, something he could not have foreseen or planned against. Yet still he cursed himself and bitterly realized that his plans might be ended forever. A dragon had taken Brunhilda who would be his means of legitimately becoming king; now the plot of seduction, marriage, and inheritance was ruined.

Ever practical, Winkle did not let himself lament for long. He dressed himself quickly and used a secret passage out of Brunhilda's room, only to reappear in the corridor outside it a moment later. "Brunhilda!" he cried, beating on the door. "Are you all right?"

The first of the knights reached him, and then the King, weeping and wailing and smashing anything that got in his way. Brunhilda's door was down in a moment, and the King ran to the window and cried out after his daughter, now a pinpoint speck in the sky many miles away. "Brunhilda! Brunhilda! Come back!" She did not come back. "Now," cried the King, as he turned back into the room and sank to the floor, his face twisted and wet with grief, "Now I have nothing, and all is in vain!"

My thoughts precisely, Winkle thought, but I'm not weeping about it. To hide his contempt he walked to the window and looked out. He saw, not the dragon, but Bork, emerging from the forest carrying two huge logs.

"Sir Bork," said Winkle.

The King heard a tone of decision in Winkle's voice. He had learned to listen to whatever Winkle said in that tone of voice. "What about him?"

"Sir Bork could defeat a dragon," Winkle said, "if any man could."

"That's true," the King said, gathering back some of the hope he had lost. "Of course, that's true."

"But will he?" asked Winkle.

"Of course he will. He loves Brunhilda, doesn't he?"

"He said he did. But Your Majesty, is he really loyal to you? After all, why wasn't he here when the dragon came? Why didn't he save Brunhilda in the first place?"

"He was cutting wood for the winter."

"Cutting wood? When Brunhilda's life was at stake?"

The King was outraged. The illogic of it escaped him—he was not in a logical mood. So he was furious when he met Bork at the gate of the castle.

"You've betrayed me!" the King cried.

"I have?" Bork was smitten with guilt. And he hadn't even meant to.

"You weren't here when we needed you. When *Brunhilda* needed you!"

"I'm sorry," Bork said.

"Sorry, sorry, sorry. A lot of good it does to say you're sorry. You swore to protect Brunhilda from any enemy, and when a really dangerous enemy comes along, how do you repay me for everything I've done for you? You hide out in the forest!"

"What enemy?"

"A dragon," said the King, "as if you didn't see it coming and run out into the woods."

"Cross my heart, Your Majesty, I didn't know there was a dragon coming." And then he made the connection in his mind. "The dragon—it took Brunhilda?"

"It took her. Took her half-naked from her bedroom when she leaped to the window to call to you for help."

Bork felt the weight of guilt, and it was a terrible burden. His face grew hard and angry, and he walked into the castle, his harsh footfalls setting the earth to trembling. "My armor!" he cried. "My sword!"

In minutes he was in the middle of the courtyard, holding out his arms as the heavy mail was draped over him and the breastplate and helmet were strapped and screwed in place. The sword was not enough—he also carried his huge ax and a shield so massive two ordinary men could have hidden behind it.

"Which way did he go?" Bork asked.

"North," the King answered.

"I'll bring back your daughter, Your Majesty, or die in the attempt."

"Damn well better. It's all your fault."

The words stung, but the sting only impelled Bork further. He took the huge sack of food the cook had prepared for him and fastened it to a belt, and without a backward glance strode from the castle and took the road north.

"I almost feel sorry for the dragon," said the King.

But Winkle wondered. He had seen how large the claws were as they grasped Brunhilda—she had been like a tiny doll in a large man's fingers. The claws were razor sharp. Even if she were still alive, could Bork really best the dragon? Bork the Bully, after all, had made his reputation picking on men smaller than he, as Winkle had ample reason to know. How would he do facing a dragon at least five times his size? Wouldn't he turn coward? Wouldn't he run as other men had run from *him?*

He might. But Sir Bork the Bully was Winkle's only hope of getting Brunhilda and the kingdom. If he could do anything to ensure that the giant at least *tried* to fight the dragon, he would do it. And so, taking only his rapier and a sack of food, Winkle left the castle by another way, and followed the giant along the road toward the north.

And then he had a terrible thought.

Fighting the dragon was surely ten times as brave as anything Bork had done before. If he won, wouldn't he have a claim on Brunhilda's hand himself?

It was not something Winkle wished to think about. Something would come to him, some way around the problem when the time came. Plenty of opportunity to plan something— *after* Bork wins and rescues her.

Bork had not rounded the second turn in the road when he came across the old woman, waiting by the side of the road. It was the same old woman who had cared for Brunhilda all those years that she was kept in a secret room in the castle. She looked wizened and weak, but there was a sharp look in her eyes that many had mistaken for great wisdom. It was not great wisdom. But she did know a few things about dragons.

"Going after the dragon, are you?" she asked in a squeaky voice. "Going to get Brunhilda back, are you?" She giggled darkly behind her hand.

"I am if anyone can," Bork said.

"Well, anyone can't," she answered.

"*I* can."

"Not a prayer, you big bag of wind!"

Bork ignored her and started to walk past.

"Wait!" she said, her voice harsh as a dull file taking rust from armor. "Which way will you go?"

"North," he said. "That's the way the dragon took her."

"A quarter of the world is north, Sir Bork the Bully, and a dragon is small compared to all the mountains of the earth. But I know a way you can find the dragon, if you're really a knight."

"What is it?" Bork asked. It would simplify everything if he had a sure way of finding where Brunhilda was being kept captive.

"Light a torch, man. Light a torch, and whenever you come to a fork in the way, the light of the torch will leap the way you ought to go. Wind or no wind, fire seeks fire, and there is a flame at the heart of every dragon."

"They *do* breathe fire, then?" he asked. He did not know how to fight fire.

"Fire is light, not wind, and so it doesn't come from the dragon's mouth or the dragon's nostrils. If he burns you, it won't be with his breath." The old woman cackled like a mad hen. "No one knows the truth about dragons anymore!"

"Except you."

"I'm an old wife," she said. "And I know. They don't eat human beings, either. They're strict vegetarians. But they kill. From time to time they kill."

"Why, if they aren't hungry for meat?"

"You'll see," she said. She started to walk away, back into the forest.

"Wait!" Bork called. "How far will the dragon be?"

"Not far," she said. "Not far, Sir Bork. He's waiting for you. He's waiting for you and all the fools who come to try to free the virgin." Then she melted away into the darkness.

Bork lit a torch and followed it all night, turning when the flame turned, unwilling to waste time in sleep when Brunhilda might be suffering unspeakable degradation at the monster's hands. And behind him, Winkle forced himself to stay awake, determined not to let Bork lose him in the darkness.

All night, and all day, and all night again Bork followed the light of the torch, through crooked paths long unused, until he came to the foot of a dry, tall hill, with rocks and crags along the top. He stopped, for here the flame leaped high, as if to say, "Upward from here." And in the silence he heard a sound that chilled him to the bone. It was Brunhilda, screaming as if she were being tortured in the cruelest imaginable way. And the screams were followed by a terrible roar. Bork cast aside the remnant of his food and made his way to the top of the hill. On the way he called out, to stop the dragon from whatever it was doing.

"Dragon! Are you there!"

The voice rumbled back to him with a power that made the dirt shift under Bork's feet. "Yes indeed."

"Do you have Brunhilda?"

"You mean the little virgin with the heart of an adder and the brain of a gnat?"

In the forest at the bottom of the hill, Winkle ground his teeth in fury, for despite his designs on the kingdom, he loved Brunhilda as much as he was capable of loving anyone.

"Dragon!" Bork bellowed at the top of his voice, "Dragon! Prepare to die!"

"Oh dear! Oh dear!" cried out the dragon. "Whatever shall I do!"

And then Bork reached the top of the hill, just as the sun topped the distant mountains and it became morning. In the light Bork immediately saw Brunhilda tied to a tree, her auburn hair glistening. All around her was the immense pile of gold that the dragon, according to custom, kept. And all around the gold was the dragon's tail.

Bork looked at the tail and followed it until finally he came to the dragon, who was leaning on a rock chewing on a tree trunk and smirking. The dragon's wings were clad with feathers, but the rest of him was covered with tough gray hide the color of weathered granite. His teeth, when he smiled, were ragged, long, and pointed. His claws were three feet long and sharp as a rapier from tip to base. But in spite of all this armament, the most dangerous thing about him was his eyes. They were large and soft and brown, with long lashes and gently arching brows. But at the center each eye held a sharp point of light, and when Bork looked at the eyes that light stabbed deep into him, seeing his heart and laughing at what it found there.

For a moment, looking at the dragon's eyes, Bork stood transfixed. Then the dragon reached over one wing toward

Brunhilda, and with a great growling noise he began to tickle her ear.

Brunhilda was unbearably ticklish, and she let off a blood-curdling scream.

"Touch her not!" Bork cried.

"Touch her what?" asked the dragon, with a chuckle. "I will not."

"Beast!" bellowed Bork. "I am Sir Bork the Big! I have never been defeated in battle! No man dares stand before me, and the beasts of the forest step aside when I pass!"

"You must be awfully clumsy," said the dragon.

Bork resolutely went on. He had seen the challenges and jousts—it was obligatory to recite and embellish your achievements in order to strike terror into the heart of the enemy. "I can cut down trees with one blow of my ax! I can cleave an ox from head to tail, I can skewer a running deer, I can break down walls of stone and doors of wood!"

"Why can't I ever get a handy servant like that?" murmured the dragon. "Ah well, you probably expect too large a salary."

The dragon's sardonic tone might have infuriated other knights; Bork was only confused, wondering if this matter was less serious than he had thought. "I've come to free Brunhilda, dragon. Will you give her up to me, or must I slay you?"

At that the dragon laughed long and loud. Then it cocked its head and looked at Bork. In that moment Bork knew that he had lost the battle. For deep in the dragon's eyes he saw the truth.

Bork saw himself knocking down gates and cutting down trees, but the deeds no longer looked heroic. Instead he realized that the knights who always rode behind him in these battles were laughing at him, that the King was a weak and vicious man, that Winkle's ambition was the only emotion he had room for; he saw that all of them were using him for their own ends, and cared nothing for him at all.

Bork saw himself asking for Brunhilda's hand in marriage, and he was ridiculous, an ugly, unkempt, and awkward giant in contrast to the slight and graceful girl. He saw that the King's hints of the possibility of their marriage were merely a trick, to blind him. More, he saw what no one else had been able to see—that Brunhilda loved Winkle, and Winkle wanted her.

And at last Bork saw himself as a warrior, and realized that in all the years of his great reputation and in all his many victories, he had fought only one man—an archer who ran at him with a knife. He had terrorized the weak and the small, but never until now had he faced a creature larger than himself. Bork looked in the dragon's eyes and saw his own death.

"Your eyes are deep," said Bork softly.

"Deep as a well, and you are drowning."

"Your sight is clear." Bork's palms were cold with sweat.

"Clear as ice, and you will freeze."

"Your eyes," Bork began. Then his mouth was suddenly so dry that he could barely speak. He swallowed. "Your eyes are filled with light."

"Bright and tiny as a star," the dragon whispered. "And see: your heart is afire."

Slowly the dragon stepped away from the rock, even as the tip of his tail reached behind Bork to push him into the dragon's waiting jaws. But Bork was not in so deep a trance that he could not see.

"I see that you mean to kill me," Bork said. "But you won't have me as easily as that." Bork whirled around to hack at the tip of the dragon's tail with his ax. But he was too large and slow, and the tail flicked away before the ax was fairly swung.

The battle lasted all day. Bork fought exhaustion as much as he fought the dragon, and it seemed the dragon only toyed with him. Bork would lurch toward the tail or a wing or the dragon's belly, but when his ax or sword fell where the dragon had been, it only sang in the air and touched nothing.

Finally Bork fell to his knees and wept. He wanted to go on with the fight, but his body could not do it. And the dragon looked as fresh as it had in the morning.

"What?" asked the dragon. "Finished already?"

Then Bork felt the tip of the dragon's tail touch his back, and the sharp points of the claws pressed gently on either side. He could not bear to look up at what he knew he would see. Yet neither could he bear to wait, not knowing when the blow would come. So he opened his eyes, and lifted his head, and saw.

The dragon's teeth were nearly touching him, poised to tear his head from his shoulders.

Bork screamed. And screamed again when the teeth touched

him, when they pushed into his armor, when the dragon lifted him with teeth and tail and talons until he was twenty feet above the ground. He screamed again when he looked into the dragon's eyes and saw, not hunger, not hatred, but merely amusement.

And then he found his silence again, and listened as the dragon spoke through clenched teeth, watching the tongue move massively in the mouth only inches from his head.

"Well, little man. Are you afraid?"

Bork tried to think of some heroic message of defiance to hurl at the dragon, some poetic words that might be remembered forever so that his death would be sung in a thousand songs. But Bork's mind was not quick at such things; he was not that accustomed to speech, and had no ear for gallantry. Instead he began to think it would be somehow cheap and silly to die with a lie on his lips.

"Dragon," Bork whispered, "I'm frightened."

To Bork's surprise, the teeth did not pierce him then. Instead, he felt himself being lowered to the ground, heard a grating sound as the teeth and claws let go of his armor. He raised his visor, and saw that the dragon was now lying on the ground, laughing, rolling back and forth, slapping its tail against the rocks, and clapping its claws together. "Oh, my dear tiny friend," said the dragon. "I thought the day would never dawn."

"What day?"

"Today," answered the dragon. It had stopped laughing, and it once again drew near to Bork and looked him in the eye. "I'm going to let you live."

"Thank you," Bork said, trying to be polite.

"Thank me? Oh no, my midget warrior. You won't thank me. Did you think my teeth were sharp? Not half so pointed as the barbs of your jealous, disappointed friends."

"I can go?"

"You can go, you can fly, you can dwell in your castle forever for all I care. Do you want to know why?"

"Yes."

"Because you were afraid. In all my life, I have only killed brave knights who knew no fear. You're the first, the very first, who was afraid in that final moment. Now go." And the dragon gave Bork a push and sent him down the hill.

Brunhilda, who had watched the whole battle in curious silence, now called after him. "Some kind of knight you are!

Coward! I hate you! Don't leave me!" The shouts went on until Bork was out of earshot.

Bork was ashamed.

Bork went down the hill and, as soon as he entered the cool of the forest, he lay down and fell asleep.

Hidden in the rocks, Winkle watched him go, watched as the dragon again began to tickle Brunhilda, whose gown was still open as it had been when she was taken by the dragon. Winkle could not stop thinking of how close he had come to having her. But now, if even Bork could not save her, her cause was hopeless, and Winkle immediately began planning other ways to profit from the situation.

All the plans depended on his reaching the castle before Bork. Since Winkle had dozed off and on during the day's battle, he was able to go farther—to a village, where he stole an ass and rode clumsily, half-asleep, all night and half the next day and reached the castle before Bork awoke.

The King raged. The King swore. The King vowed that Bork would die.

"But Your Majesty," said Winkle, "you can't forget that it is Bork who inspires fear in the hearts of your loyal subjects. You can't kill him—if he were dead, how long would you be king?"

That calmed the old man down. "Then I'll let him live. But he won't have place in this castle, that's certain. I won't have him around here, the coward. Afraid! Told the dragon he was afraid! Pathetic. The man has no gratitude." And the King stalked from the court.

When Bork got home, weary and sick at heart, he found the gate of the castle closed to him. There was no explanation—he needed none. He had failed the one time it mattered most. He was no longer worthy to be a knight.

And now it was as it had been before. Bork was ignored, despised, feared; he was completely alone. But still, when it was time for great strength, there he was, doing the work of ten men, and not thanked for it. Who would thank a man for doing what he must to earn his bread?

In the evenings he would sit in his hut, staring at the fire that pushed a column of smoke up through the hole in the roof. He remembered how it had been to have friends, but the memory was not happy, for it was always poisoned by the knowledge that the friendship did not outlast Bork's first

failure. Now the knights spat when they passed him on the
road or in the fields.

The flames did not let Bork blame his troubles on them,
however. The flames constantly reminded him of the dragon's eyes, and in their dance he saw himself, a buffoon who
dared to dream of loving a princess, who believed that he was
truly a knight. Not so, not so. I was never a knight, he
thought. I was never worthy. Only now am I receiving what I
deserve. And all his bitterness turned inward, and he hated
himself far more than any of the knights could hate him.

He had made the wrong choice. When the dragon chose to
let him go, he should have refused. He should have stayed
and fought to the death. He should have died.

Stories kept filtering into the village, stories of the many
heroic and famous knights who accepted the challenge of
freeing Brunhilda from the dragon. All of them went as
heroes. All of them died as heroes. Only Bork had returned
alive from the dragon, and with every knight who died Bork's
shame grew. Until he decided that he would go back. Better
to join the knights in death than to live his life staring into
the flames and seeing the visions of the dragon's eyes.

Next time, however, he would have to be better prepared.
So after the spring plowing and planting and lambing and
calving, where Bork's help was indispensable to the villagers, the giant went to the castle again. This time no one
barred his way, but he was wise enough to stay as much out
of sight as possible. He went to the one-armed swordmaster's
room. Bork hadn't seen him much since he accidentally cut
off his arm in sword practice years before.

"Come for the other arm, coward?" asked the swordmaster.

"I'm sorry," Bork said. "I was younger then."

"You weren't any smaller. Go away."

But Bork stayed, and begged the swordmaster to help him.
They worked out an arrangement. Bork would be the
swordmaster's personal servant all summer, and in exchange
the swordmaster would try to teach Bork how to fight.

They went out into the fields every day, and under the
swordmaster's watchful eye he practiced sword-fighting with
bushes, trees, rocks—anything but the swordmaster, who
refused to let Bork near him. Then they would return to the
swordmaster's rooms, and Bork would clean the floor and
sharpen swords and burnish shields and repair broken practice equipment. And always the swordmaster said, "Bork,

you're too stupid to do anything right!" Bork agreed. In a summer of practice, he never got any better, and at the end of the summer, when it was time for Bork to go out in the fields and help with the harvest and the preparations for winter, the swordmaster said, "It's hopeless, Bork. You're too slow. Even the bushes are more agile than you. Don't come back. I still hate you, you know."

"I know," Bork said, and he went out into the fields, where the peasants waited impatiently for the giant to come carry sheaves of grain to the wagons.

Another winter looking at the fire, and Bork began to realize that no matter how good he got with the sword, it would make no difference. The dragon was not to be defeated that way. If excellent swordplay could kill the dragon, the dragon would be dead by now—the finest knights in the kingdom had already died trying.

He had to find another way. And the snow was still heavy on the ground when he again entered the castle and climbed the long and narrow stairway to the tower room where the wizard lived.

"Go away," said the wizard, when Bork knocked at his door. "I'm busy."

"I'll wait," Bork answered.

"Suit yourself."

And Bork waited. It was late at night when the wizard finally opened the door. Bork had fallen asleep leaning on it—he nearly knocked the magician over when he fell inside.

"What the devil are you—you waited!"

"Yes," said Bork, rubbing his head where it had hit the stone floor.

"Well, I'll be back in a moment." The wizard made his way along a narrow ledge until he reached the place where the wall bulged and a hole opened onto the outside of the castle wall. In wartime, such holes were used to pour boiling oil on attackers. In peacetime, they were even more heavily used. "Go on inside and wait," the wizard said.

Bork looked around the room. It was spotlessly clean, the walls were lined with books, and here and there a fascinating artifact hinted at hidden knowledge and arcane powers—a sphere with the world on it, a skull, an abacus, beakers and tubes, a clay pot from which smoke rose, though there was no fire under it. Bork marveled until the wizard returned.

"Nice little place, isn't it?" the wizard asked. "You're Bork, the bully, aren't you?"

Bork nodded.

"What can I do for you?"

"I don't know," Bork asked. "I want to learn magic. I want to learn magic powerful enough that I can use it to fight the dragon."

The wizard coughed profusely.

"What's wrong?" Bork asked.

"It's the dust," the wizard said.

Bork looked around and saw no dust. But when he sniffed the air, it felt thick in his nose, and a tickling in his chest made him cough, too.

"Dust?" asked Bork. "Can I have a drink?"

"Drink," said the wizard. "Downstairs—"

"But there's a pail of water right here. It looks perfectly clean—"

"Please don't—"

But Bork put the dipper in the pail and drank. The water sloshed into his mouth, and he swallowed, but it felt dry going down, and his thirst was unslaked. "What's wrong with the water?" Bork asked.

The wizard sighed and sat down. "It's the problem with magic, Bork old boy. Why do you think the King doesn't call on me to help him in his wars? He knows it, and now you'll know it, and the whole world probably will know it by Thursday."

"You don't know any magic?"

"Don't be a fool! I know all the magic there is! I can conjure up monsters that would make your dragon look tame! I can snap my fingers and have a table set with food to make the cook die of envy. I can take an empty bucket and fill it with water, with wine, with gold—whatever you want. But try spending the gold, and they'll hunt you down and kill you. Try drinking the water and you'll die of thirst."

"It isn't real."

"All illusion. Handy, sometimes. But that's all. Can't create anything except in your head. That pail, for instance—" And the wizard snapped his fingers. Bork looked, and the pail was filled, not with water, but with dust and spider webs. That wasn't all. He looked around the room, and was startled to see that the bookshelves were gone, as were the other trappings of great wisdom. Just a few books on a table in a corner, some counters covered with dust and papers and half-decayed food, and the floor inches deep in garbage.

"The place is horrible," the wizard said. "I can't bear to look at it." He snapped his fingers, and the old illusion came back. "Much nicer, isn't it?"

"Yes."

"I have excellent taste, haven't I? Now, you wanted me to help you fight the dragon, didn't you? Well, I'm afraid it's out of the question. You see, my illusions only work on human beings, and occasionally on horses. A dragon wouldn't be fooled for a moment. You understand?"

Bork understood, and despaired. He returned to his hut and stared again at the flames. His resolution to return and fight the dragon again was undimmed. But now he knew that he would go as badly prepared as he had before, and his death and defeat would be certain. Well, he thought, better death than life as Bork the coward, Bork the bully who only has courage when he fights people smaller than himself.

The winter was unusually cold, and the snow was remarkably deep. The firewood ran out in February, and there was no sign of an easing in the weather.

The villagers went to the castle and asked for help, but the King was chilly himself, and the knights were all sleeping together in the great hall because there wasn't enough firewood for their barracks and the castle, too. "Can't help you," the King said.

So it was Bork who led the villagers—the ten strongest men, dressed as warmly as they could, yet still cold to the bone in the wind—and they followed in the path his body cut in the snow. With his huge ax he cut down tree after tree; the villagers set the wedges and Bork split the huge logs; the men carried what they could but it was Bork who made seven trips and carried most of the wood home. The village had enough to last until spring—more than enough, for, as Bork had expected, as soon as the stacks of firewood were deep in the village, the King's men came and took their tax of it.

And Bork, exhausted and frozen from the expedition, was carefully nursed back to health by the villagers. As he lay coughing and they feared he might die, it occurred to them how much they owed to the giant. Not just the firewood, but the hard labor in the farming work, and the fact that Bork had kept the armies far from their village, and they felt what no one in the castle had let himself feel for more than a few

moments—gratitude. And so it was that when he had mostly
recovered, Bork began to find gifts outside his door from time
to time. A rabbit, freshly killed and dressed; a few eggs; a
vast pair of hose that fit him very comfortably; a knife
specially made to fit his large grip and to ride with comfortable weight on his hip. The villagers did not converse with
him much. But then, they were not talkative people. The
gifts said it all.

Throughout the spring, as Bork helped in the plowing and
planting, with the villagers working alongside, he realized
that this was where he belonged—with the villagers, not with
the knights. They weren't rollicking good company, but there
was something about sharing a task that must be done that
made for stronger bonds between them than any of the rough
camaraderie of the castle. The loneliness was gone.

Yet when Bork returned home and stared into the flames
in the center of his hut, the call of the dragon's eyes became
even stronger, if that were possible. It was not loneliness that
drove him to seek death with the dragon. It was something
else, and Bork could not think what. Pride? He had none—he
accepted the verdict of the castle people that he was a coward.
The only guess he could make was that he loved Brunhilda
and felt a need to rescue her. The more he tried to convince
himself, however, the less he believed it.

He had to return to the dragon because, in his own mind,
he knew he should have died in the dragon's teeth, back
when he fought the dragon before. The common folk might
love him for what he did for them, but he hated himself for
what he was.

He was nearly ready to head back for the dragon's mountain when the army came.

"How many are there?" the King asked Winkle.

"I can't get my spies to agree," Winkle said. "But the lowest
estimate was two thousand men."

"And we have a hundred and fifty here in the castle. Well,
I'll have to call on my dukes and counts for support."

"You don't understand, Your Majesty. These *are* your dukes
and counts. This isn't an invasion. This is a rebellion."

The King paled. "How do they dare?"

"They dare because they heard a rumor, which at first they
didn't believe was true. A rumor that your giant knight had
quit, that he wasn't in your army anymore. And when they

found out for sure that the rumor was true, they came to cast you out and return the old King to his place."

"Treason!" the King shouted. "Is there no loyalty?"

"I'm loyal," Winkle said, though of course he had already made contact with the other side in case things didn't go well. "But it seems to me that your only hope is to prove the rumors wrong. Show them that Bork is still fighting for you."

"But he isn't. I threw him out two years ago. The coward was even rejected by the dragon."

"Then I suggest you find a way to get him back into the army. If you don't, I doubt you'll have much luck against that crowd out there. My spies tell me they're placing wagers about how many pieces you can be cut into before you die."

The King turned slowly and stared at Winkle, glared at him, gazed intently in his eyes. "Winkle, after all we've done to Bork over the years, persuading him to help us now is a despicable thing to do."

"True."

"And so it's your sort of work, Winkle. Not mine. You get him back in the army."

"I can't do it. He hates me worse than anyone, I'm sure. After all, I've betrayed him more often."

"You get him back in the army within the next six hours, Winkle, or I'll send pieces of you to each of the men in that traitorous group that you've made friends with in order to betray me."

Winkle managed not to look startled. But he was surprised. The King had somehow known about it. The King was not quite the fool he had seemed to be.

"I'm sending four knights with you to make sure you do it right."

"You misjudge me, Your Majesty," Winkle said.

"I hope so, Winkle. Persuade Bork for me, and you live to eat another breakfast."

The knights came, and Winkle walked with them to Bork's hut. They waited outside.

"Bork, old friend," Winkle said. Bork was sitting by the fire, staring in the flames. "Bork, you aren't the sort who holds grudges, are you?"

Bork spat into the flames.

"Can't say I blame you," Winkle said. "We've treated you ungratefully. We've been downright cruel. But you rather brought it on yourself, you know. It isn't *our* fault you turned coward in your fight with the dragon. Is it?"

Bork shook his head. "My fault, Winkle. But it isn't my fault the army has come, either. I've lost my battle. You lose yours."

"Bork, we've been friends since we were three—"

Bork looked up so suddenly, his face so sharp and lit with the glow of the fire, that Winkle could not go on.

"I've looked in the dragon's eyes," Bork said, "and I know who you are."

Winkle wondered if it was true, and was afraid. But he had courage of a kind, a selfish courage that allowed him to dare anything if he thought he would gain by it.

"Who I am? No one knows anything as it is, because as soon as it's known it changes. You looked in the dragon's eyes years ago, Bork. Today I am not who I was then. Today you are not who you were then. And today the King needs you."

"The King is a petty count who rode to greatness on my shoulders. He can rot in hell."

"The other knights need you, then. Do you want them to die?"

"I've fought enough battles for them. Let them fight their own."

And Winkle stood helplessly, wondering how he could possibly persuade this man, who would not be persuaded.

It was then that a village child came. The knights caught him lurking near Bork's hut; they roughly shoved him inside. "He might be a spy," a knight said.

For the first time since Winkle came, Bork laughed. "A spy? Don't you know your own village, here? Come to me, Laggy." And the boy came to him, and stood near him as if seeking protection from the giant. "Laggy's a friend of mine," Bork said. "Why did you come, Laggy?"

The boy wordlessly held out a fish. It wasn't large, but it was still wet from the river.

"Did you catch this?" Bork said.

The boy nodded.

"How many did you catch today?"

The boy pointed at the fish.

"Just the one? Oh, then I can't take this, if it's all you caught."

But as Bork handed the fish back, the boy retreated, refused to take it. He finally opened his mouth and spoke.

"For you," he said, and then he scurried out of the hut and into the bright morning sunlight.

And Winkle knew he had his way to get Bork into the battle.

"The villagers," Winkle said.

Bork looked at him quizzically.

And Winkle *almost* said, "If you don't join the army, we'll come out here and burn the village and kill all the children and sell the adults into slavery in Germany." But something stopped him; a memory, perhaps, of the fact that he was once a village child himself. No, not that. Winkle was honest enough with himself to know that what stopped him from making the threat was a mental picture of Sir Bork striding into battle, not in front of the King's army, but at the head of the rebels. A mental picture of Bork's ax biting deep into the gate of the castle, his huge crow prying the portcullis free. This was not the time to threaten Bork.

So Winkle took the other tack. "Bork, if they win this battle, which they surely will if you aren't with us, do you think they'll be kind to this village? They'll burn and rape and kill and capture these people for slaves. They hate us, and to them these villagers are part of us, part of their hatred. If you don't help us, you're killing them."

"I'll protect them," Bork said.

"No, my friend. No, if you don't fight with us, as a knight, they won't treat you chivalrously. They'll fill you full of arrows before you get within twenty feet of their lines. You fight with us, or you might as well not fight at all."

Winkle knew he had won. Bork thought for several minutes, but it was inevitable. He got up and returned to the castle, strapped on his old armor, took his huge ax and his shield, and kept his sword belted at his waist, and walked into the courtyard of the castle. The other knights cheered, and called out to him as if he were their dearest friend. But the words were hollow and they knew it, and when Bork didn't answer they soon fell silent.

The gate opened and Bork walked out, the knights on horseback behind him.

And in the rebel camp, they knew that the rumors were a lie—the giant still fought with the King, and they were doomed. Most of the men slipped away into the woods. But others, particularly the leaders who would die if they surrendered as surely as they would die if they fought, stayed.

Better to die valiantly than as a coward, they each thought, and so as Bork approached he still faced an army—only a few hundred men, but still an army.

They came out to meet Bork one by one, as the knights came to the dragon on his hill. And one by one, as they made their first cut or thrust, Bork's ax struck, and their heads flew from their bodies, or their chests were cloven nearly in half, or the ax reamed them end to end, and Bork was bright red with blood and a dozen men were dead and not one had touched him.

So they came by threes and fours, and fought like demons, but still Bork took them, and when even more than four tried to fight him at once they got in each other's way and he killed them more easily.

And at last those who still lived despaired. There was no honor in dying so pointlessly. And with fifty men dead, the battle ended, and the rebels laid down their arms in submission.

Then the King emerged from the castle and rode to the battleground, and paraded triumphantly in front of the defeated men.

"You are all sentenced to death at once," the King declared.

But suddenly he found himself pulled from his horse, and Bork's great hands held him. The King gasped at the smell of gore; Bork rubbed his bloody hands on the King's tunic, and took the King's face between his sticky palms.

"No one dies now. No one dies tomorrow. These men will all live, and you'll send them home to their lands, and you'll lower their tribute and let them dwell in peace forever."

The King imagined his own blood mingling with that which already covered Bork, and he nodded. Bork let him go. The King mounted his horse again, and spoke loudly, so all could hear. "I forgive you all. I pardon you all. You may return to your homes. I confirm you in your lands. And your tribute is cut in half from this day forward. Go in peace. If any man harms you, I'll have his life."

The rebels stood in silence.

Winkle shouted at them "Go! You heard the king! You're free! Go home!"

And they cheered, and long-lived-the-King, and then bellowed their praise to Bork.

But Bork, if he heard them, gave no sign. He stripped off his armor and let it lie in the field. He carried his great ax to the stream, and let the water run over the metal until it was clean. Then he lay in the stream himself, and the water carried off the last of the blood, and when he came out he was clean.

Then he walked away, to the north road, ignoring the calls of the King and his knights, ignoring everything except the dragon who waited for him on the mountain. For this was the last of the acts Bork would perform in his life for which he would feel shame. He would not kill again. He would only die, bravely, in the dragon's claws and teeth.

The old woman waited for him on the road.

"Off to kill the dragon, are you?" she asked in a voice that the years had tortured into gravel. "Didn't learn enough the first time?" She giggled behind her hand.

"Old woman, I learned everything before. Now I'm going to die."

"Why? So the fools in the castle will think better of you?"

Bork shook his head.

"The villagers already love you. For your deeds today, you'll already be a legend. If it isn't for love or fame, why are you going?"

Bork shrugged. "I don't know. I think he calls to me. I'm through with my life, and all I can see ahead of me are his eyes."

The old woman nodded. "Well, well, Bork. I think you're the first knight that the dragon won't be happy to see. We old wives know, Bork. Just tell him the truth, Bork."

"I've never known the truth to stop a sword," he said.

"But the dragon doesn't carry a sword."

"He might as well."

"No, Bork, no," she said, clucking impatiently. "You know better than that. Of all the dragon's weapons, which cut you the deepest?"

Bork tried to remember. The truth was, he realized, that the dragon had never cut him at all. Not with his teeth nor his claws. Only the armor had been pierced. Yet there had been a wound, a deep one that hadn't healed, and it had been cut in him, not by teeth or talons, but by the bright fires in the dragon's eyes.

"The truth," the old woman said. "Tell the dragon the truth. Tell him the truth, and you'll live!"

Bork shook his head. "I'm not going there to live," he said. He pushed past her, and walked on up the road.

But her words rang in his ears long after he stopped hearing her call after him. The truth, she had said. Well, then, why not? Let the dragon have the truth. Much good may it do him.

This time Bork was in no hurry. He slept every night, and paused to hunt for berries and fruit to eat in the woods. It was four days before he reached the dragon's hill, and he came in the morning, after a good night's sleep. He was afraid, of course; but still there was a pleasant feeling about the morning, a tingling of excitement about the meeting with the dragon. He felt the end coming near, and he relished it.

Nothing had changed. The dragon roared; Brunhilda screamed. And when he reached the top of the hill, he saw the dragon tickling her with his wing. He was not surprised to see that she hadn't changed at all—the two years had not aged her, and though her gown still was open and her breasts were open to the sun and the wind, she wasn't even freckled or tanned. It could have been yesterday that Bork fought with the dragon the first time. And Bork was smiling as he stepped into the flat space where the battle would take place.

Brunhilda saw him first. "Help me! You're the four hundred and thirtieth knight to try! Surely that's a lucky number!" Then she recognized him. "Oh, no. You again. Oh well, at least while he's fighting you I won't have to put up with his tickling."

Bork ignored her. He had come for the dragon, not for Brunhilda.

The dragon regarded him calmly. "You are disturbing my nap time."

"I'm glad," Bork said. "You've disturbed me, sleeping and waking, since I left you. Do you remember me?"

"Ah yes. You're the only knight who was ever afraid of me."

"Do you really believe that?" Bork asked.

"It hardly matters what I believe. Are you going to kill me today?"

"I don't think so," said Bork. "You're much stronger than I am, and I'm terrible at battle. I've never defeated anyone who was more than half my strength."

The lights in the dragon's eyes suddenly grew brighter, and the dragon squinted to look at Bork. "Is that so?" asked the dragon.

"And I'm not very clever. You'll be able to figure out my next move before I know what it is myself."

The dragon squinted more, and the eyes grew even brighter.

"Don't you want to rescue this beautiful woman?" the dragon asked.

"I don't much care," he said. "I loved her once. But I'm through with that. I came for you."

"You don't love her anymore?" asked the dragon.

Bork almost said, "Not a bit." But then he stopped. The truth, the old woman had said. And he looked into himself and saw that no matter how much he hated himself for it, the old feelings died hard. "I love her, dragon. But it doesn't do me any good. She doesn't love me. And so even though I desire her, I don't want her."

Brunhilda was a little miffed. "That's the stupidest thing I've ever heard," she said. But Bork was watching the dragon, whose eyes were dazzlingly bright. The monster was squinting so badly that Bork began to wonder if he could see at all.

"Are you having trouble with your eyes?" Bork asked.

"Do you think you ask the questions here? I ask the questions."

"Then ask."

"What in the world do I want to know from you?"

"I can't think of anything," Bork answered. "I know almost nothing. What little I do know, you taught me."

"Did I? What was it that you learned?"

"You taught me that I was not loved by those I thought had loved me. I learned from you that deep within my large body is a very small soul."

The dragon blinked, and its eyes seemed to dim a little.

"Ah," said the dragon.

"What do you mean, 'Ah'?" asked Bork.

"Just 'Ah,'" the dragon answered. "Does every ah have to mean something?"

Brunhilda sighed impatiently. "How long does this go on? Everybody else who comes up here is wonderful and brave. You just stand around talking about how miserable you are. Why don't you fight?"

"Like the others?" asked Bork.

"They're so brave," she said.

"They're all dead."

"Only a coward would think of that," she said scornfully.

"It hardly comes as a surprise to you," Bork said. "Everyone knows I'm a coward. Why do you think I came? I'm of no use to anyone, except as a machine to kill people at the command of a King I despise."

"That's my father you're talking about!"

"I'm nothing, and the world will be better without me in it."

"I can't say I disagree," Brunhilda said.

But Bork did not hear her, for he felt the touch of the dragon's tail on his back, and when he looked at the dragon's eyes they had stopped glowing so brightly. They were almost back to normal, in fact, and the dragon was beginning to reach out its claws.

So Bork swung his ax, and the dragon dodged, and the battle was on, just as before.

And just as before, at sundown Bork stood pinned between tail and claws and teeth.

"Are you afraid to die?" asked the dragon, as it had before.

Bork almost answered *yes* again, because that would keep him alive. But then he remembered that he had come in order to die, and as he looked in his heart he still realized that however much he might fear death, he feared life more.

"I came here to die," he said. "I still want to."

And the dragon's eyes leaped bright with light. Bork imagined that the pressure of the claws lessened.

"Well, then, Sir Bork, I can hardly do you such a favor as to kill you." And the dragon let him go.

That was when Bork became angry.

"You can't do this to me!" he shouted.

"Why not?" asked the dragon, who was now trying to ignore Bork and occupied itself by crushing boulders with its claws.

"Because I insist on my right to die at your hands."

"It's not a right, it's a privilege," said the dragon.

"If you don't kill me, then I'll kill you!"

The dragon sighed in boredom, but Bork would not be put off. He began swinging the ax, and the dragon dodged, and in the pink light of sunset the battle was on again. This time, though, the dragon only fell back and twisted and turned to avoid Bork's blows. It made no effort to attack. Finally Bork was too tired and frustrated to go on.

"Why don't you fight!" he shouted. Then he wheezed from the exhaustion of the chase.

The dragon was panting, too. "Come on now, little man, why don't you give it up and go home. I'll give you a signed certificate testifying that I asked you to go, so that no one thinks you're a coward. Just leave me alone."

The dragon began crushing rocks and dribbling them over its head. It lay down and began to bury itself in gravel.

"Dragon," said Bork, "a moment ago you had me in your teeth. You were about to kill me. The old woman told me that truth was my only defense. So I must have lied before, I must have said something false. What was it? Tell me!"

The dragon looked annoyed. "She had no business telling you that. It's privileged information."

"All I ever said to you was the truth."

"Was it?"

"Did I lie to you? Answer—yes or no!"

The dragon only looked away, its eyes still bright. It lay on its back and poured gravel over its belly.

"I did then. I lied. Just the kind of fool I am to tell the truth and still get caught in a lie."

Had the dragon's eyes dimmed? Was there a lie in what he had just said?

"Dragon," Bork insisted, "if you don't kill me or I don't kill you, then I might as well throw myself from the cliff. There's no meaning to my life, if I can't die at your hands!"

Yes, the dragon's eyes were dimming, and the dragon rolled over onto its belly, and began to gaze thoughtfully at Bork.

"Where is the lie in that?"

"Lie? Who said anything about a lie?" But the dragon's long tail was beginning to creep around so it could get behind Bork.

And then it occurred to Bork that the Dragon might not even know. That the dragon might be as much a prisoner of the fires of truth inside him as Bork was, and that the dragon wasn't deliberately toying with him at all. Didn't matter, of course. "Never mind what the lie is, then," Bork said. "Kill me now, and the world will be a better place!"

The dragon's eyes dimmed, and a claw made a pass at him, raking the air by his face.

It was maddening, to know there was a lie in what he was saying and not know what it was. "It's the perfect ending for my meaningless life," he said. "I'm so clumsy I even have to stumble into death."

He didn't understand why, but once again he stared into the dragon's mouth, and the claws pressed gently but sharply against his flesh.

The dragon asked the question of Bork for the third time. "Are you afraid, little man, to die?"

This was the moment, Bork knew. If he was to die, he had to lie to the dragon now, for if he told the truth the dragon would set him free again. But to lie, he had to know what the truth was, and now he didn't know at all. He tried to think of where he had gone astray from the truth, and could not. What had he said? It was true that he was clumsy; it was true that he was stumbling into death. What else then?

He had said his life was meaningless. Was that the lie? He had said his death would make the world a better place. Was that the lie?

And so he thought of what would happen when he died. What hole would his death make in the world? The only people who might miss him were the villagers. That was the meaning of his life, then—the villagers. So he lied.

"The villagers won't miss me if I die. They'll get along just fine without me."

But the dragon's eyes brightened, and the teeth withdrew, and Bork realized to his grief that his statement had been true after all. The villagers wouldn't miss him if he died. The thought of it broke his heart, the last betrayal in a long line of betrayals.

"Dragon, I can't outguess you! I don't know what's true and what isn't! All I learn from you is that everyone I thought loved me doesn't. Don't ask me questions! Just kill me and end my life. Every pleasure I've ever had turns to pain when you tell me the truth."

And now, when he had thought he was telling the truth, the claws broke his skin, and the teeth closed over his head, and he screamed. "Dragon! Don't let me die like this! What is the pleasure that your truth won't turn to pain? What do I have left?"

The dragon pulled away, and regarded him carefully. "I told you, little man, that I don't answer questions. I ask them."

"Why are you here?" Bork demanded. "This ground is littered with the bones of men who failed your tests. Why not mine? Why not mine? Why can't I die? Why did you keep sparing my life? I'm just a man, I'm just alive, I'm just trying to do the best I can in a miserable world and I'm sick of trying to figure out what's true and what isn't. End the game, dragon. My life has never been happy, and I want to die."

The dragon's eyes went black, and the jaws opened again, and the teeth approached, and Bork knew he had told his last lie, that this lie would be enough. But with the teeth inches from him Bork finally realized what the lie was, and the realization was enough to change his mind. "No," he said, and he reached out and seized the teeth, though they cut his fingers. "No," he said, and he wept. "I have been happy. I have." And, gripping the sharp teeth, the memories raced through his mind. The many nights of comradeship with the knights in the castle. The pleasures of weariness from working in the forest and the fields. The joy he felt when alone he won a victory from the Duke; the rush of warmth when the boy brought him the single fish he had caught; and the solitary pleasures, of waking and going to sleep, of walking and running, of feeling the wind on a hot day and standing near a fire in the deep of winter. They were all good, and they had all happened. What did it matter if later the knights despised him? What did it matter if the villagers' love was only a fleeting thing, to be forgotten after he died? The reality of the pain did not destroy the reality of the pleasure; grief did not obliterate joy. They each happened in their time, and because some of them were dark it did not mean that none of them was light.

"I have been happy," Bork said. "And if you let me live, I'll be happy again. That's what my life means, doesn't it? That's the truth, isn't it, dragon? My life matters because I'm alive, joy or pain, whatever comes, I'm alive and that's meaning enough. It's true, isn't it, dragon! I'm not here to fight you. I'm not here for you to kill me. I'm here to make myself alive!"

But the dragon did not answer. Bork was gently lowered to the ground. The dragon withdrew its talons and tail, pulled its head away, and curled up on the ground, covering its eyes with its claws.

"Dragon, did you hear me?"

The dragon said nothing.

"Dragon, look at me!"

The dragon sighed. "Man, I cannot look at you."

"Why not?"

"I am blind," the dragon answered. It pulled its claws away

from its eyes. Bork covered his face with his hands. The dragon's eyes were brighter than the sun.

"I feared you, Bork," the dragon whispered. "From the day you told me you were afraid, I feared you. I knew you would be back. And I knew this moment would come."

"What moment?" Bork asked.

"The moment of my death."

"Are you dying?"

"No," said the dragon. "Not yet. You must kill me."

As Bork looked at the dragon lying before him, he felt no desire for blood. "I don't want you to die."

"Don't you know that a dragon cannot live when it has met a truly honest man? It's the only way we ever die, and most dragons live forever."

But Bork refused to kill him.

The dragon cried out in anguish. "I am filled with all the truth that was discarded by men when they chose their lies and died for them. I am in constant pain, and now that I have met a man who does not add to my treasury of falsehood, you are the cruelest of them all."

And the dragon wept, and its eyes flashed and sparkled in every hot tear that fell, and finally Bork could not bear it. He took his ax and hacked off the dragon's head, and the light in its eyes went out. The eyes shriveled in their sockets until they turned into small, bright diamonds with a thousand facets each. Bork took the diamonds and put them in his pocket.

"You killed him," Brunhilda said wonderingly.

Bork did not answer. He just untied her, and looked away while she finally fastened her gown. Then he shouldered the dragon's head and carried it back to the castle, Brunhilda running to keep up with him. He only stopped to rest at night because she begged him to. And when she tried to thank him for freeing her, he only turned away and refused to hear. He had killed the dragon because it wanted to die. Not for Brunhilda. Never for her.

At the castle they were received with rejoicing, but Bork would not go in. He only laid the dragon's head beside the moat and went to his hut, fingering the diamonds in his pocket, holding them in front of him in the pitch blackness of his hut to see that they shone with their own light, and did not need the sun or any other fire but themselves.

The King and Winkle and Brunhilda and a dozen knights

came to Bork's hut. "I have come to thank you," the King said, his cheeks wet with tears of joy.

"You're welcome," Bork said. He said it as if to dismiss them.

"Bork," the King said. "Slaying the dragon was ten times as brave as the bravest thing any man has ever done. You can have my daughter's hand in marriage."

Bork looked up in surprise.

"I thought you never meant to keep your promise, Your Majesty."

The King looked down, then at Winkle, then back at Bork. "Occasionally," he said, "I keep my word. So here she is, and thank you."

But Bork only smiled, fingering the diamonds in his pocket. "It's enough that you offered, Your Majesty. I don't want her. Marry her to a man she loves."

The King was puzzled. Brunhilda's beauty had not waned in her years of captivity. She had the sort of beauty that started wars. "Don't you want *any* reward?" asked the King.

Bork thought for a moment. "Yes," he said. "I want to be given a plot of ground far away from here. I don't want there to be any count, or any duke, or any king over me. And any man or woman or child who comes to me will be free, and no one can pursue them. And I will never see you again, and you will never see me again."

"That's all you want?"

"That's all."

"Then you shall have it," the King said.

Bork lived all the rest of his life in his little plot of ground. People did come to him. Not many, but five or ten a year all his life, and a village grew up where no one came to take a king's tithe or a duke's fifth or a count's fourth. Children grew up who knew nothing of the art of war and never saw a knight or a battle or the terrible fear on the face of a man who knows his wounds are too deep to heal. It was everything Bork could have wanted, and he was happy all his years there.

Winkle, too, achieved everything he wanted. He married Brunhilda, and soon enough the King's sons had accidents and died, and the King died after dinner one night, and Winkle became King. He was at war all his life, and never went to sleep at night without fear of an assassin coming upon him in the darkness. He governed ruthlessly and thoroughly and was hated all his life; later generations, however, remembered him as a great King. But he was dead then, and didn't know it.

Later generations never heard of Bork.

He had only been out on his little plot of ground for a few months when the old wife came to him. "Your hut is much bigger than you need," she said. "Move over."

So Bork moved over, and she moved in.

She did not magically turn into a beautiful princess. She was foul-mouthed and nagged Bork unmercifully. But he was devoted to her, and when she died a few years later he realized that she had given him more happiness than pain, and he missed her. But the grief at her dying did not taint any of the joy of his memory of her; he just fingered the diamonds, and remembered that grief and joy were not weighed in the same scale, one making the other seem less substantial.

And at last he realized that Death was near; that Death was reaping him like wheat, eating him like bread. He imagined Death to be a dragon, devouring him bit by bit, and one night in a dream he asked Death, "Is my flavor sweet?"

Death, the old dragon, looked at him with bright and understanding eyes, and said, "Sweet and salt, bitter and rich. You sting and you soothe."

"Ah," Bork said, and was satisfied.

Death poised itself to take the last bite. "Thank you," it said.

"You're welcome," Bork answered, and he meant it.

L. FRANK BAUM

L. Frank Baum is known the world over as the creator of Dorothy from Kansas and the land of Oz, a series which began at the turn of the century as a vanity edition. (Publishers were convinced that *The Wonderful Wizard of Oz* would never sell.) But, in addition to these books, Baum also produced a number of other fantasies, including *The Master Key* and *The Surprising Adventures of the Magical Monarch of Mo*, from which the following charming adventure is taken.

THE KING'S HEAD
AND THE PURPLE DRAGON

by L. Frank Baum

A GOOD many years ago the Magical Monarch of Mo became annoyed by the Purple Dragon, which came down from the mountains and ate up a patch of his best chocolate caramels just as they were getting ripe.

So the King went out to the sword-tree and picked a long, sharp sword, and tied it to his belt and went away to the mountains to fight the Purple Dragon.

The people all applauded him, saying one to another:

"Our King is a good King. He will destroy this naughty Purple Dragon and we shall be able to eat the caramels ourselves."

But the Dragon was not alone naughty; it was big, and fierce, and strong, and did not want to be destroyed at all.

Therefore the King had a terrible fight with the Purple Dragon, and cut it with his sword in several places, so that the raspberry juice which ran in its veins squirted all over the ground.

It is always difficult to kill Dragons. They are by nature thick-skinned and tough, as doubtless every one has heard. Besides, you must not forget that this was a Purple Dragon, and all scientists who have studied deeply the character of Dragons say those of a purple color are the most disagreeable to fight with. So all the King's cutting and slashing had no other effect upon the monster than to make him angry. Forgetful of the respect due to a crowned King, the wicked Dragon presently opened wide its jaws and bit his Majesty's head clean off from his body. Then he swallowed it.

Of course the King realized it was useless to continue the fight after that, for he could not see where the Dragon was. So he turned and tried to find his way back to his people. But at every other step he would bump into a tree, which made

169

the naughty Dragon laugh at him. Furthermore, he could not
tell in which direction he was going, which is an unpleasant
feeling under any circumstances.

At last some of the people came to see if the King had
succeeded in destroying the Dragon, and found their monarch running around in a circle, bumping into trees and
rocks, but not getting a step nearer home. So they took his
hand and led him back to the palace, where every one was
filled with sorrow at the sad sight of the headless King.
Indeed, his devoted subjects, for the first time in their lives,
came as near to weeping as an inhabitant of the Valley of Mo
can.

"Never mind," said the King, cheerfully; "I can get along
very well without a head; and, as a matter of fact, the loss has
its advantages. I shall not be obliged to brush my hair, or
clean my teeth, or wash my ears. So do not grieve, I beg of
you, but be happy and joyful as you were before." Which
showed the King had a good heart; and, after all, a good heart
is better than a head, any day.

The people, hearing him speak out of the top of his neck
(for he had no mouth), immediately began to laugh, which in
a short time led to their being as happy as ever.

But the Queen was not contented.

"My love," she said to him, "I cannot kiss you any more,
and that will break my heart."

Thereupon the King sent word throughout the Valley that
any one who could procure for him a new head should wed
one of the princesses.

The princesses were all exceedingly pretty girls, and so it
was not long before one young man made a very nice head out
of candy and brought it to the King. It did not look exactly
like the old head, but the face was very sweet, nevertheless;
so the King put it on and the Queen kissed it at once with
much satisfaction.

The young man had put a pair of glass eyes in the head,
with which the King could see very well after he got used to
them.

According to the royal promise, the young man was now
called into the palace and asked to take his pick of the
princesses. They were all so sweet and ladylike that he had
some trouble in making a choice; but at last he took the
biggest, thinking that he would thus secure the greatest
reward, and they were married amid great rejoicing.

But, a few days afterward, the King was caught out in a rainstorm, and before he could get home his new head had melted in the great shower of lemonade that fell. Only the glass eyes were left, and these he put in his pocket and went sorrowfully to tell the Queen of his new misfortune.

Then another young man who wanted to marry a princess made the King a head out of dough, sticking in the glass eyes; and the King tried it on and found that it fitted very well. So the young man was given the next biggest princess.

But the following day the sun chanced to shine extremely hot, and when the King walked out it baked his dough head into bread, at which the monarch felt very light-headed. And when the birds saw the bread they flew down from the trees, perched upon the King's shoulder and quickly ate up his new head. All but the glass eyes.

Again the good King was forced to go home to the Queen without a head, and the lady firmly declared that this time her husband must have a head warranted to last at least as long as the honeymoon of the young man who made it; which was not at all unreasonable under the circumstances.

So a request was sent to all loyal subjects throughout the Valley asking them to find a head for their King that was neat and substantial.

In the meanwhile the King had a rather hard time of it. When he wished to go anyplace he was obliged to hold out in front of him, between his thumbs and fingers, the glass eyes, that they might guide his footsteps. This, as you may imagine, made his Majesty look rather undignified, and dignity is very precious to every royal personage.

At last a wood-chopper in the mountains made a head out of wood and sent it to the King. It was neatly carved, besides being solid and durable; moreover, it fitted the monarch's neck to a T. So the King rummaged in his pocket and found the glass eyes, and when these were put in the new head the King announced his satisfaction.

There was only one drawback—he couldn't smile, as the wooden face was too stiff; and it was funny to hear his Majesty laughing heartily while his face maintained a solemn expression. But the glass eyes twinkled merrily and every one knew that he was the same kind-hearted monarch of old, although he had become, of necessity, rather hard-headed.

Then the King sent word to the wood-chopper to come to

the palace and take his pick of the princesses, and preparations were at once begun for the wedding.

But the wood-chopper, on his way to the court, unfortunately passed by the dwelling of the Purple Dragon and stopped to speak to the monster.

Now it seems that when the Dragon had swallowed the King's head, the unusual meal made the beast ill. It was more accustomed to berries and caramels for dinner than to heads, and the sharp points of the King's crown (which was firmly fastened to the head) pricked the Dragon's stomach and made the creature miserable. After a few days of suffering the Dragon disgorged the head, and, not knowing what else to do with it, locked it up in a cupboard and put the key in its pocket.

When the Dragon met the wood-chopper and learned he had made a new head for the King, and as a reward was to wed one of the princesses, the monster became very angry. It resolved to do a wicked thing; which will not surprise you when you remember the beast's purple color.

"Step into my parlor and rest yourself," said the Dragon, politely. Wicked people are most polite when they mean mischief.

"Thank you, I'll stop for a few minutes," replied the wood-chopper; "but I cannot stay long, as I am expected at court."

When he had entered the parlor the Dragon suddenly opened its mouth and snapped off the poor wood-chopper's head. Being warned by experience, however, it did not swallow the head, but placed it in the cupboard. Then the Dragon took from a shelf the King's head and glued it on the wood-chopper's neck.

"Now," said the beast, with a cruel laugh, "you are the King! Go home and claim your wife and your kingdom."

The poor wood-chopper was much amazed; for at first he did not really know which he was, the King or the wood-chopper.

He looked in the mirror and, seeing the King, made a low bow. Then the King's head thought: "Who am I bowing to? There is no one greater than the King!" And so at once there began a conflict between the wood-chopper's heart and the King's head.

The Dragon was mightily pleased at the result of its wicked stratagem, and having pushed the bewildered wood-chopper out of the castle, immediately sent him on his way to the court.

When the poor man neared the town the people ran out and said: "Why, this is the King come back again. All hail, your Majesty!"

"All nonsense!" returned the wood-chopper. "I am only a poor man with the King's head on my shoulders. You can easily see it isn't mine, for it's crooked; the Dragon didn't glue it on straight."

"Where, then, is your own head?" they asked.

"Locked up in the Dragon's cupboard," replied the poor fellow, beginning to weep.

"Here," cried the King's head; "stop this. You mustn't cry out of my eyes! The King never weeps."

"I beg pardon, your Majesty," said the wood-chopper, meekly, "I'll not do it again."

"Well, see that you don't," returned the head more cheerfully.

The people were greatly amazed at this, and took the wood-chopper to the palace, where all was soon explained.

When the Queen saw the King's head she immediately kissed it; but the King rebuked her, saying she must kiss only him.

"But it is your head," said the poor Queen.

"Probably it is," replied the King; "but it is on another man. You must confine yourself to kissing my wooden head."

"I'm sorry," sighed the Queen, "for I like to kiss the real head best."

"And so you shall," said the King's head; "I don't approve your kissing that wooden head at all."

The poor lady looked from one to the other in perplexity. Finally a happy thought occurred to her.

"Why don't you trade heads?" she asked.

"Just the thing!" cried the King; and, the wood-chopper consenting, the exchange was made, and the Monarch of Mo found himself in possession of his own head again, whereat he was so greatly pleased that he laughed long and merrily.

The wood-chopper, however, did not even smile. He couldn't because of the wooden face. The head he had made for the King he now was compelled to wear himself.

"Bring hither the princesses," commanded the King. "This good man shall choose his bride at once, for he has restored to me my own head."

But when the princesses arrived and saw that the wood-chopper had a wooden head, they each and all refused to marry him, and begged so hard to escape that the King was in a quandary.

"I promised him one of my daughters," he argued, "and a King never breaks his word."

"But he hadn't a wooden head then," explained one of the girls.

The King realized the truth of this. Indeed, when he came to look carefully at the wooden head, he did not blame his daughers for not wishing to marry it. Should he force one of them to consent, it was not unlikely she would call her husband a blockhead—a term almost certain to cause trouble in any family.

After giving the matter deep thought, the King resolved to go to the Purple Dragon and oblige it to give up the wood-chopper's head.

So all the fighting men in the kingdom were got together, and, having picked ripe swords off the sword-trees, they marched in a great body to the Dragon's castle.

Now the Purple Dragon realized that if it attempted to fight all this army, it would perhaps be cut to pieces; so it retired within its castle and refused to come out.

The wood-chopper was a brave man.

"I'll go in and fight the Dragon alone," he said; and in he went. By this time the Dragon was both frightened and angry, and the moment it saw the man it rushed forward and made a snap at his head.

The wooden head came off at once, and the Dragon's long, sharp teeth got stuck in the wood and would not come out again; so the monster was unable to do anything but flop its tail and groan.

The wood-chopper now ran to the cupboard, took out his head and placed it upon his shoulders where it belonged. Then he proudly walked out of the castle and was greeted with loud shouts by the army, which carried him back in triumph to the King's palace.

And, now that he wore his own head again, one of the prettiest of the young princesses willingly agreed to marry him; so the wedding ceremony was performed amidst great rejoicing.

DEAN R. KOONTZ

In *How to Write Best Selling Fiction*, Dean R. Koontz discusses the advantages of shedding genre labels, as he now feels he has done. But later, as he offers suggestions about generating story titles, he confesses a fondness for the work reprinted here. And well he might, for although it was his first publication, it contains many of the elements, such as dark mood and experimental prose, which have contributed to his fame.

SOFT COME THE DRAGONS

By Dean R. Koontz

"AND WHAT will you do when the soft breezes come and the dragons drift in to spread death?"

Marshall wriggled in his seat, reached for another sugar packet to empty into his mug of coffee.

"I'll tell you what you'll do. You'll get up when the alarms sound and dress in your uniform and go down in the cellar complex like a red-eyed mole in flight from his own fear. You'll get up when the alarms sound and monitor everything as usual, hiding until the dragons float out and are gone."

"What am I supposed to do?" Marshall asked. "Maybe I should pet them and pour out milk?"

"You wouldn't pet, you'd club. The milk would have cyanide in it."

Marshall slammed his fist into the table. "You forget, Dante, that I am commander here and you are only third line officer."

Mario Alexander Dante snorted, picked up his folio, and walked out of the rec room. Mounting the twisting stairs, he climbed two floors, stepped out into a dark, narrow hallway, and ambled to the glass observation lounge that hung like a third story patio over the beach.

It was low tide. The sea stretched away across the horizon like poured glass, glittering like a queen's jewels or like a shattered church window. Only small waves lapped at the shore, depositing minute quantities of sand, etching out microscopic gullies in the orange beach as they dragged away a corresponding amount of other grains.

It seemed to Mare Dante that the ocean was the same on any world. It was the womb, the all-encompassing mother where men migrated at least once in their lives—like lemmings. He had walked to the edge of it on some nights, hoping to see a face. . . .

Just above the horizon floated the twin moons; their reflections stretched long across the ocean, cresting every wavelet with a tint of golden dew.

The trouble with Marshall, Dante reflected, was that he lacked imagination. He accepted everything at face value—tempered only by what his instruments told him. Being truthful with himself, he understood that he saw the old Mario Dante in the commander, and that this was why he disliked the man. The old Mario Dante, before the car crash that took Ellen and broke her body and tossed it into the ocean, before he lay in a hospital piecing together his shattered mind for seven months, the old Mario Dante had been lacking in sensitivity, in imagination. In unlocking his mental block so that he could accept the death of Ellen, the psychiatrist removed other things in passing, and opened a whole new portion of his mind.

But still, he disliked Marshall. And he was certain that the commander's Achilles heel would be struck by an arrow from the quiver of the dragons. The dragons that came daily with the tidal winds.

The dragons of emerald and vermilion and yellow and white of virgin bridal gown and devil black and jack-of-lantern orange.

The butterfly dragons that were twenty yards wide and seventy yards long—but weighed only two or three hundred pounds. The flimsy, gossamer dragons.

The dragons of beauty.

The dragons that killed with their eyes.

He sighed, turned from the windowside, and sat down in one of the black leather easy chairs, snapping on the small, high-intensity reading lamp in the arm. Lighting a cigarette, he looked over his newer poems.

The first three he tossed in the wastebasket without reviewing. The fourth he read, re-read, then read aloud for full effect.

> *"Discovery Upon Death"*
>
> *"dear mankind:*
> *am writing you from purgatory*
> *to say that i*

have made a discovery
that i wish you
would spread around up there.
god, now listen mankind,
god is a computer
and someone misprogrammed him . . ."

"Not bad," said a voice from the darkness. Abner stepped into the small circle of light around the chair. "But don't tell me the Pioneer Poet has doubts about life?"

"Please, the name is Mare."

Pioneer Poet. It was a name *Life* had coined when his first volume had been published and had won critical acclaim. He admitted it all seemed romantic: a space force surveyor drafted for three years, writing poetry on some alien world in some alien star system. But, Pioneer Poet?

"Heard about your fight with Marshall."

"It wasn't a fight."

"It was the way I heard it. What bothers you about him, Mare?"

"He doesn't understand things."

"Neither do any of us."

"Suffice it to say he might be a mirror in which I can see myself. And the reflection isn't a nice one."

They sat in silence a moment.

"You plan to sit up all night?" Abner asked.

"No, Pioneer Physician, I do not."

Abner grinned. "Dragon warnings should go up in six hours. You'll need your rest."

He folded his poems and rose, flicked off the light, and said: "Fine, but let us just look at the ocean a minute, huh?"

The snakes growing from her scalp hissed and bared fangs.

His hand burned with the dribbling of his own blood where their sharp teeth raked him.

Slowly, she turned, and the beauty was there in the face—and the horror was there.

In the eyes.

And his muscles, slowly but doubtlessly and without pause, began turning to granite.

"No!" he screamed. "I think I'm just beginning to see—"

His hair became individual strands of rock. Each cell of his face froze into eternity and became a part of something that could never die—that could only be eroded by wind and rain.

And finally his eyes, staring into hers, slipped into cataract, then to stone.

And he woke to the sound of screams in his ears.

Before opening his eyes, he could see her, pinned behind the wheel, mouth twisted in agony.

The flames licking at her face as he was tossed free, the tumbling, burning car, plunging over the cliff and away.

But when the waking dream was over, he still heard the screams. He fumbled for his bed light, and the flood of yellow fire made him squint. He looked at the clock. Five o'clock in the morning Translated Earth Time.

The dragon warning was in effect. They were not screams, but the wails of mechanical voices. "Beware and Run," they seemed to say.

Bewareandrun, bewareandrun, bewareandrun . . .

He had been sleeping in his duty suit, a uniform of shimmering purple synthe-fabric. The United Earth emblem graced his right arm: a dove sitting on a green globe. That was one symbol that always repulsed him. He pictured the dove loosening its bowels.

Stumbling across the room, he palmed open the door and stepped into the corridor, blinking away the remainders of sleep from his eyes.

Holden Twain was running down the hall, strapping his nylon belt around his waist. "I have some poetry for you to look at while we're in the shelter," he said breathlessly, coming to a halt at Dante's side.

Mario liked the kid. He was five years the poet's junior, but his innocence seemed to add to his immaturity—and charm. He had not met Hemingway's Discovery of Evil. He never understood "The Killers" when he read it. Dante made him plunge through it every few weeks, searching for that glint of understanding that would mean he saw it all.

"Fine," Mario said. "That'll help pass the hours in that dreadful hole."

They set out at a steady trot down the hall, past the large windows that peered out upon the alien landscape.

At the stairwell, Mario ushered the younger man down and waited at the head for the others from that corridor. He was captain of the block and was to be the last into the shelter from that particular accessway.

He glanced out of the nearest window. There was sure to be

wind. The spindly pine-palms were swaying erratically, some bent nearly to the snapping point in the gale. This was only the front of the tidal winds, he knew, and the soft breezes and the dragons would follow.

The dragons that looked so beautiful in pictures but which killed any man who looked directly into their eyes.

The dragons that seemed to live constantly in the air—without eating.

The dragons that killed with their eyes . . .

He had a vision of the first victims, their eyes crystallized, shrunken within the blackened sockets, the brain wilted within the skull. He shuddered.

Still, it did not seem right to hide when they came.

Though the specially designed lenses failed, though dozens of scientists died trying to prove that they wouldn't, that men's eyes could be protected from the deadly dragons, it did not seem right to hide.

Though gunnery officers could not shoot them down (because only a shot in the eye seemed to kill the beasts, and aiming at those misty, pupilless orbs was impossible), it did not seem right to squirrel away in the earth.

The last man in the corridor pounded down the stairs. Dante swung the door shut, sealed it, then flicked the shutters that would partially protect the windows.

The shelter was filled with men. The city's complement numbered sixty-eight. They were sixty-eight prepared to wait out another three hours of dragons and silence in the cellar.

Dante decided the entire affair got more ridiculous each time. It hardly seemed as if the planet were worth all the trouble. But then he knew it was. There were the Bakium deposits, and the planet itself was central to this galaxy. Someday, it would be built nearly as heavily as Earth. A grand population.

Certainly more than sixty-eight.

Sixty-seven.

"Sixty-seven!" The Secretary shrilled.

"Impossible!" Mashall shouted.

"Menchen. Menchen isn't here."

"Who has that corridor?"

"I, sir."

"Anamaxender. Why the hell didn't you notice he was missing?"

"Sorry, sir."

"You'll be damned sorry before this is over." Marshall turned to the other faces. "Who saw him last?"

"I believe just about everyone was asleep, commander," Dante said quietly. Marshall opened his mouth to speak, then thought better of it. He turned to Twain. "You know corridor F?"

"Yes, sir."

Every man was required to have a memorized floor plan of the installation buried deep in the emergency vaults of his mind. It was a ridiculous question.

"Go after Menchen. Go to his room and see if he needs help. At any cost, get him back here."

"But the dragons," someone said.

"They won't be out yet, and it will be another half hour before they gain access to the upper floors."

Twain was strapping on a radio set, fastening a blaster to his belt. He crossed to Dante and handed him a sheaf of eight papers. He smiled and was gone.

At the head of the stairs, there was a sucking of a door unsealing, then a second whine as it sealed again—behind Holden Twain.

Mare Dante had nothing to do. He could have sat and worried, but the commander had been right. Dragons would not break into the upper corridors for a while yet. Until things really started getting bad above, there was no reason to worry.

He sat down and opened the folded sheets of yellow papers.

> Hath a man not eyes?
> Can he feel not pain?
> Does the grass grow greener?
> Is God's blood rain?
>
> And so it goes,
> And so it is.
> Is there a soul?
> And if there is,
> Where is it?

M.A. Dante was jealous. *Jealousy?* When he translated that and deducted the source, he realized that Twain's poetry had taken a change for the better. It was no longer what

Dante called "tree and flower poetry." There was something of a philosophical note in those last three lines. At least, there was pessimism.

Pessimism, he strongly believed, was merely realism.

Suddenly, he was very worried about the boy—the man—upstairs.

He stood and approached Marshall. "Commander, I—"

Marshall turned, his eyes gleaming, immediately on the defensive. Between clenched teeth: "Dante. What is it now? Would you like to take over command of the operation? Would you like to—"

"Oh, shut up!" He turned up the volume on the receiver that would carry Twain's words back to them. "I am not an enemy of yours. I disagree with your methods and procedure. I do not lower myself to personal vendetta."

"Listen—"

The radio crackled, interrupting the building rage within Marshall. "Twain here. Menchen is in his room. Ill. I'm going to trundle him back."

"What about the dragons?" Marshall snapped into the mike.

"I can hear them bumping softly against the window shields, trying to get in. Like big moths. Creepy."

"None in the halls?"

"No. Starting back. Out."

The dragons that killed with their eyes. Beautiful dragons so the automatic cameras showed. But dragons that no man could look upon.

Somehow, men must be able to see, he thought. *The photos* —Dante's mind seemed dangling on the ravine of inspiration.

When Twain returned, he was quite relieved, forgot about Marshall, and lived the moments of good poetry the younger man had composed, commenting and discussing.

"Why do you write?"

Twain thought a moment. "To detail Truth."

"With a capital T?"

"Yes."

"There isn't such a thing. Don't interrupt. There is no such thing as Truth, no purity with a tag. It is a shade of gray somewhere between black and white. It is one thing to a slave, another to a monarch, and yet another to the monk who kneels alone in cloistered walls of towering granite, fingering beads. It is for no man to delineate, and for no man to criticize another's understanding of it. Truth, old son, is relative. And more than relative, it is nonexistent as a pure entity."

"But in the literature classes in college, they said we were to search for the truth. The textbooks on poetry say we should write to discover truth."

The sixty plus men muttered among themselves. Marshall followed his scopes, his dials, his unfailing measuring devices that justified the way of things to man.

"That's what they tell you, Mr. Twain. That is also what I will tell you. Write to delineate truth. Yet I warn you there is no such thing. Yet I tell you never to stop looking, never to forsake the search. Yet do I tell ye that ye shall never end the quest. Do you have guts enough to keep looking, Holden Twain?"

Twain looked at him, and silently without needing to explain, he walked off and sat in a corner, staring intently at the wall where it joined the ceiling.

The rest of the day he spent tramping in and out of Abner's clinic, checking on Menchen's progress.

The blue walls of the med room made him feel as if he were hanging, dangling precariously from the center of the sky. The thin silver instruments on the table, the stark functional furniture, the university degrees on the walls, the anatomical chart above the operating table as if the surgeon followed a paint-by-number method in removing an appendix—all seemed like flotsam and jetsam swirling around in the crystal sky, remnants of mankind's achievements hurled into the stratosphere after a violent swipe of a disgusted God's powerful hand.

"What does he have?"

Abner stared at the diagnostic machine's readings. "Could be a tumor."

"Could be?"

"Could be half a dozen other things. It's hidden in the maze of tissues in his bowels. Maybe I found it. Maybe not."

"What can you do?"

"Nothing."

"He'll die?"

"We don't have the most modern hospital devised by mankind at our disposal."

"I'm not blaming you, Abe."

"I am."

"He *will* die, then?"

"Yes. And because I don't understand. I don't understand."

At night, while Dante slept, Menchen died. But the poet didn't know. No one would know until the morning. And it would disturb no one's sleep. A thousand sparrows could fall at once . . .

A thousand sparrows, a million sparrows fell from the sky, between the snowflakes. They crashed silently into the pavement. They tangled in the telephone wires—looking like notes in a staff of copper, separated by pole-bars into economical musical measures. But there was no music.

After they fell, he stood, the collar of his coat turned up to ward off the cold, and looked at their bodies, broken and bleeding. And he did not understand.

Looking up into the gray sky from whence came the snow swirling like a thousand dandelion puffs blown on by children, he searched hopefully for the source of the coldness.

Far away, tires screeching . . .

Metal shredding . . .

Ghostly screams in the night, a woman in agony . . .

Perhaps, he thought, if I could look with a mirror, I could see and know. Perhaps, seeing everything backwards, the world makes sense. Maybe, if we change our perspective . . .

"Yes," said a voice.

He turned and looked at the snakes in her head, and he could not keep his eyes from dropping to hers. And slowly, forever and for always, he turned to stone, crying: "From another perspective you might be love and not hatred."

"Yes," she said, smiling.

Waking, sweating, he knew the answer. It was just crazy enough to work. But he could not say anything. Marshall would see his effort as an attempt to gain power. It would, of necessity, be a secret project.

He turned on the bed lamp, forced himself totally awake, and set to dismantling his dressing mirror.

He was the last down the stairway at the dragon warning:

"Did you hear?" Twain asked.

"Hear what?"

"Menchen died during the night."

"Now there might be your only truth. Death."

"What?"

"It is indisputable, inevitable, and impossible of misinterpretation."

He walked away from Twain and secreted himself in a corner, hoping to blend into oblivion. It was a corner near a stairwell. Roll was called, and all were found to be present. An hour into the warning, he rose, meandered through a clot of men to the edge of the stairs. Suddenly, like a tired apparition, he was gone.

At the head of the stairs, he unsealed the door, stepped into the corridor, closed the portal behind. Carefully, he removed the delicate, makeshift spectacles from his pocket. They were diamondlike, circus-prop spectacles of glittering looking glass and golden wire. They worked roughly like a periscope so that the wearer saw a mirror reflection of what was in front of him.

Sucking in his breath, he swung open the outside door and stepped onto the black soil.

The humming of giant wings sung above him.

Slowly, he turned his head to the skies.

The far-darting beams of the spirit, the un'loos'd dreams, he thought.

They were spirits and fairies above him. They were orange and magenta and coffee brown and crayon brown and pecan brown. They were white and chrome yellow and peach yellow and pear yellow.

They were thin, and in spots, through their silken wings, he glimpsed the sun. "Daedalus, your labyrinth was no more mystifying than a single wing of these creatures. And Icarus, turn from beside the sun, beauty is not up there. Look down and see."

They were dragons of the wind.

And with his lenses, their eyes did not burn him.

He walked forth, his mouth gaping. Other lines from Whiteman's "Passage to India" entered his mind.

I mark from on deck the strange landscape, the pure sky, the level sand in the distance . . .

Truly, there was something about the alien landscape that seemed fresh. In the sunlight filtered through gossamer wings, he seemed to see more detail. The strange way the chlorophyll was formed as a crystalline substance within the yellow-green leaves; the patterns in the sand that he had once considered only chance happenings. He looked around.

There were patterns to everything. The sky was delicately shaded in a soft-hued, artistic effect. There was a tasteful blending of all nature—something he had never seen before.

He could almost see the rays of sun like individual golden rivers, beaming into everything, showering back when reflected, soaking in and disappearing when refracted. The world was more real . . .

The gigantic dredging machines . . .

He saw the mining shafts and cranes, recognizing them as dredgers that sucked the scum of a planet, sent the base ores in gross tanker ships to run large, smoky factories on an overpopulated Earth where some lived in poverty and some in plenty. And they were no longer just mining tools . . .

I hear the echoes reverberate through the grandest scenery in the world . . .

From the air, vibrating the molecules of his body so that he heard with his eyes and ears and mouth and nose. So that he tasted the notes, the pitched wailings of melancholy and joy. So that joy was sweet and melancholy bittersweet. The dragons flocked above him and sang.

The music was soundless and all sound. It was the trumpets of the marching dead and the flutes of the living angels. They were strange songs.

Crossing the great desert, the alkaline plains, I behold the enchanting mirages of waters and meadows . . .

He stumbled over the sand, heedless of destination. Everything was new to him. A thousand times before had he looked at it. Never had he seen it.

The dragons sang of it, the why of it. The why.

Careening drunkenly to the mirages, he dipped his hands in cool water and there was no mirage. The meadows smelled fresh and grassy. They were real.

A spark within his mind was relighted; his search had ended.

Stumbling, laughing, seeing and hearing the gossamer butterfly-formed dragons, he reached the complex, went inside, and started for the shelter door.

They were all standing there looking when he came down the stairs. He threw the glasses at their feet and laughed loudly.

"He's insane," someone said.

"No!" Mare Dante shouted. "You're insane. All of you.

Crackier than a box of saltines. You hide while all of life waits for you out there with the Gods."

"The dragons?"

"The dragons, the Gods. I'm not sure yet."

"Someone grab him," Marshall shouted, working his way up front.

"And you," Mare said. "You are phony to the bottom of your being. You don't even want to be captain. You're afraid of the position. But you have to prove yourself; you're impotent—"

"Shut up!" Marshall screamed, his face white.

"Impotent because once when you were eight, your aunt—"

"Shut up!"

"I can't. It's in your eyes. God, can't the rest of you see it in his eyes?"

"How did you look at the dragons?" someone asked.

"Through a mirror."

"But other men had their eyes burned out."

"Because they could not face what they saw in the liquid eyes of the dragons. They were not killed by strange, burning rays. They simply folded and lost their souls. But it's beautiful. If you have always searched for it, you will find it in their eyes."

"What the hell are you talking about?" Abe asked.

"The dragons are not constituted of matter."

Abe stepped closer. "Talk sense, Mare. For God's sake, you'll be committed."

"When Menchen died, Abe, you told me you couldn't understand. You can understand if you will only let yourself. Your weight estimates on the dragons are incorrect. The dragons are weightless, for they are not formed of matter. The life forms on this planet are composed of what we call abstract ideas. The dragons are truth—Truth. Truth personified. Through them, you can understand *why*."

"He's insane."

"And there are other life forms here we haven't seen. The dragons were the only ones trying to contact us, to break down our shelter. There is an opposite life form living in the ground. We thought those desert holes were caves, but they are not. There are worms that burrow miles beneath us and fester. The worms are Hate. Hate personified."

Someone reached forward to grab him. He struggled and fell.

Miles below the sands, a long, caterpillar thing glowed momentarily and turned over.

The floor shook. Almost gleefully, the mob descended and covered Mario Dante until black swallowed and consumed him as he muttered lastly—"Ellen."

Upstairs, the pair of discarded spectacles clamped to his head, Holden Twain stepped forward into the outside world, a blaster on his hip, determined to seek out every cave, every wormhole. . . .

GORDON R. DICKSON

Perhaps most noted for his Dorsai series (*Soldier, Ask Not, Three to Dorsai*, etc.), Gordon R. Dickson has been producing well-crafted, entertaining fiction since the early 1950s. Much of his work concerns war, honor, and loyalty, but he is also capable of doing justice to a number of additional themes, as exemplified by such works as "Computers Don't Argue," "The Gift," and "The Mortal and the Monster." The following story marks the first reprinting of a charming parallel world quest which Dickson subsequently expanded into an award-winning novel.

ST. DRAGON AND THE GEORGE

by Gordon R. Dickson

I

A TRIFLE diffidently, Jim Eckert rapped with his claw on the blue-painted door.

Silence.

He knocked again. There was the sound of a hasty step inside the small, oddly peak-roofed house and the door was snatched open. A thin-faced old man with a tall pointed cap and a long, rather dingy-looking white beard peered out, irritably.

"Sorry, not my day for dragons!" he snapped. "Come back next Tuesday." He slammed the door.

It was too much. It was the final straw. Jim Eckert sat down on his haunches with a dazed thump. The little forest clearing with its impossible little pool tinkling away like Chinese glass wind chimes in the background, its well-kept greensward with the white gravel path leading to the door before him, and the riotous flower beds of asters, tulips, zinnias, roses and lilies-of-the-valley all equally impossibly in bloom at the same time about the white finger-post labeled S. CAROLINUS and pointing at the house—it all whirled about him. It was more than flesh and blood could bear. At any minute now he would go completely insane and imagine he was a peanut or a cocker spaniel. Grottwold Hanson had wrecked them all. Dr. Howells would have to get another teaching assistant for his English Department. Angie . . .

Angie!

Jim pounded on the door again. It was snatched open.

"Dragon!" cried S. Carolinus, furiously. "How would you like to be a beetle?"

"But I'm not a dragon," said Jim desperately.

The magician stared at him for a long minute, then threw up his beard with both hands in a gesture of despair, caught some of it in his teeth as it fell down and began to chew on it fiercely.

"Now where," he demanded, "did a dragon acquire the brains to develop the imagination to entertain the illusion that he is *not* a dragon? Answer me, O Ye Powers!"

"The information is psychically, though not physiologically correct," replied a deep brass voice out of thin air beside them and some five feet off the ground. Jim, who had taken the question to be rhetorical, started convulsively.

"Is that so?" S. Carolinus peered at Jim with new interest. "Hmm." He spat out a hair or two. "Come in, Anomaly—or whatever you call yourself."

Jim squeezed in through the door and found himself in a large single room. It was a clutter of mismatched furniture and odd bits of alchemical equipment.

"Hmm," said S. Carolinus, closing the door and walking once around Jim, thoughtfully. "If you aren't a dragon, what are you?"

"Well, my real name's Jim Eckert," said Jim. "But I seem to be in the body of a dragon named Gorbash."

"And this disturbs you. So you've come to me. How nice," said the magician, bitterly. He winced, massaged his stomach and closed his eyes. "Do you know anything that's good for a perpetual stomach-ache? Of course not. Go on."

"Well, I want to get back to my real body. And take Angie with me. She's my fiancée and I can send her back but I can't send myself back at the same time. You see, this Grottwold Hanson—well, maybe I better start from the beginning."

"Brilliant suggestion, Gorbash," said Carolinus. "Or whatever your name is," he added.

"Well," said Jim. Carolinus winced. Jim hurried on. "I teach at a place called Riveroak College in the United States— you've never heard of it—"

"Go on, go on," said Carolinus.

"That is, I'm a teaching assistant. Dr. Howells, who heads the English Department, promised me an instructorship over a year ago. But he's never come through with it; and Angie— Angie Gilman, my fiancée—"

"You mentioned her."

"Yes—well, we were having a little fight. That is, we were arguing about my going to ask Howells whether he was going

to give me the instructor's rating for next year or not. I didn't
think I should; and she didn't think we could get married—
well, anyway, in came Grottwold Hanson."

"In *where* came *who?*"

"Into the Campus Bar and Grille. We were having a drink
there. Hanson used to go with Angie. He's a graduate student
in psychology. A long, thin geek that's just as crazy as he
looks. He's always getting wound up in some new odd-ball
organization or other—"

"Dictionary!" interrupted Carolinus, suddenly. He opened
his eyes as an enormous volume appeared suddenly poised in
the air before him. He massaged his stomach. "Ouch," he
said. The pages of the volume began to flip rapidly back and
forth before his eyes. "Don't mind me," he said to Jim. "Go
on."

"—This time it was the Bridey Murphy craze. Hypnotism.
Well—"

"Not so fast," said Carolinus. *"Bridey Murphy . . . Hypnotism . . . yes . . ."*

"Oh, he talked about the ego wandering, planes of reality,
on and on like that. He offered to hypnotize one of us and
show us how it worked. Angie was mad at me, so she said yes.
I went off to the bar. I was mad. When I turned around, Angie
was gone. Disappeared."

"Vanished?" said Carolinus.

"Vanished. I blew my top at Hanson. She must have wandered, he said, not merely the ego, but all of her. Bring her
back, I said. I can't, he said. It seemed she wanted to go back
to the time of St. George and the Dragon. When men were
men and would speak up to their bosses about promotions.
Hanson'd have to send someone else back to rehypnotize her
and send her back home. Like an idiot I said I'd go. Ha! I
might've known he'd goof. He couldn't do anything right if he
was paid for it. I landed in the body of this dragon."

"And the maiden?"

"Oh, she landed here, too. Centuries off the mark. A place
where there actually were such things as dragons—fantastic."

"Why?" said Carolinus.

"Well, I mean—anyway," said Jim, hurriedly. "The point
is, they'd already got her—the dragons, I mean. A big brute
named Anark had found her wandering around and put her
in a cage. They were having a meeting in a cave about
deciding what to do with her. Anark wanted to stake her out

for a decoy, so they could capture a lot of the local people—only the dragons called people *georges*—"

"They're quite stupid, you know," said Carolinus, severely, looking up from the dictionary. "There's only room for one name in their head at a time. After the Saint made such an impression on them his name stuck."

"Anyway, they were all yelling at once. They've got tremendous voices."

"Yes, you have," said Carolinus, pointedly.

"Oh, sorry," said Jim. He lowered his voice. "I tried to argue that we ought to hold Angie for ransom—" He broke off suddenly. "Say," he said. "I never thought of that. Was I talking dragon, then? What am I talking now? Dragons don't talk English, do they?"

"Why not?" demanded Carolinus, grumpily. "If they're British dragons?"

"But I'm not a dragon—I mean—"

"But you *are* here!" snapped Carolinus. "You and this maiden of yours. Since all the rest of you was translated here, don't you suppose your ability to speak understandably was translated, too? Continue."

"There's not much more," said Jim, gloomily. "I was losing the argument and then this very big, old dragon spoke up on my side. Hold Angie for ransom, he said. And they listened to him. It seems he swings a lot of weight among them. He's a great-uncle of me—of this Gorbash who's body I'm in—and I'm his only surviving relative. They penned Angie up in a cave and he sent me off to the Tinkling Water here, to find you and have you open negotiations for ransom. Actually, on the side he told me to tell you to make the terms easy on the georges—I mean humans; he wants the dragons to work toward good relations with them. He's afraid the dragons are in danger of being wiped out. I had a chance to double back and talk to Angie alone. We thought you might be able to send us both back."

He stopped rather out of breath, and looked hopefully at Carolinus. The magician was chewing thoughtfully on his bread.

"Smrgol," he muttered. "Now there's an exception to the rule. Very bright for a dragon. Also experienced. Hmm."

"Can you help us?" demanded Jim. "Look, I can show you—"

Carolinus sighed, closed his eyes, winced and opened them again.

"Let me see if I've got it straight," he said. "You had a dispute with this maiden to whom you're betrothed. To spite you, she turned to this third-rate practitioner, who mistakenly exorcized her from the United States (whenever in the cosmos that is) to here, further compounding his error by sending you back in spirit only to inhabit the body of Gorbash. The maiden is in the hands of the dragons and you have been sent to me by your great-uncle Smrgol."

"That's sort of it," said Jim dubiously, "only—"

"You wouldn't," said Carolinus, "care to change your story to something simpler and more reasonable—like being a prince changed into a dragon by some wicked fairy stepmother? Oh, my poor stomach! No?" He sighed. "All right, that'll be five hundred pounds of gold, or five pounds of rubies, in advance."

"B-but—" Jim goggled at him. "But I don't have any gold—or rubies."

"What? What kind of a dragon are you?" cried Carolinus, glaring at him. "Where's your hoard?"

"I suppose this Gorbash has one," stammered Jim, unhappily. "But I don't know anything about it."

"Another charity patient!" muttered Carolinus, furiously. He shook his fist at empty space. "What's wrong with that auditing department? Well?"

"Sorry," said the invisible bass voice.

"That's the third in two weeks. See it doesn't happen again for another ten days." He turned to Jim. "No means of payment?"

"No. Wait—" said Jim. "This stomach-ache of yours. It might be an ulcer. Does it go away between meals?"

"As a matter of fact, it does. Ulcer?"

"High-strung people working under nervous tension get them back where I come from."

"People?" inquired Carolinus suspiciously. "Or dragons?"

"There aren't any dragons where I come from."

"All right, all right, I believe you," said Carolinus, testily. "You don't have to stretch the truth like that. How do you exorcise them?"

"Milk," said Jim. "A glass every hour for a month or two."

"Milk," said Carolinus. He held out his hand to the open air and received a small tankard of it. He drank it off, making a face. After a moment, the face relaxed into a smile.

"By the Powers!" he said. "By the Powers!" He turned to Jim, beaming. "Congratulations, Gorbash, I'm beginning to believe you about that college business after all. The bovine nature of the milk quite smothers the ulcer-demon. Consider me paid."

"Oh, fine. I'll go get Angie and you can hypnotize—"

"What?" cried Carolinus. "Teach your grandmother to suck eggs. Hypnotize! Ha! And what about the First Law of Magic, eh?"

"The what?" said Jim.

"The First Law—the First Law—didn't they teach you anything in that college? Forgotten it already, I see. Oh, this younger generation! The First Law: *for every use of the Art and Science, there is required a corresponding price.* Why do I live by my fees instead of by conjurations? Why does a magic potion have a bad taste? Why did this Hanson-amateur of yours get you all into so much trouble?"

"I don't know," said Jim. "Why?"

"No credit! No credit!" barked Carolinus, flinging his skinny arms wide. "Why, I wouldn't have tried what he did without ten years credit with the auditing department, and *I* am a Master of the Arts. As it was, he couldn't get anything more than your spirit back, after sending the maiden complete. And the fabric of Chance and History is all warped and ready to spring back and cause all kinds of trouble. We'll have to give a little, take a little—"

"GORBASH!" A loud thud outside competed with the dragon-bellow.

"And here we go," said Carolinus dourly. "It's already starting." He led the way outside. Sitting on the greensward just beyond the flower beds was an enormous old dragon Jim recognized as the great-uncle of the body he was in—Smrgol.

"Greetings, Mage!" boomed the old dragon, dropping his head to the ground in salute. "You may not remember me. Name's Smrgol—you remember the business about that ogre I fought at Gormely Keep? I see my grandnephew got to you all right."

"Ah, Smrgol—I remember," said Carolinus. "That was a good job you did."

"He had a habit of dropping his club head after a swing," said Smrgol. "I noticed it along about the fourth hour of

battle and the next time he tried it, went in over his guard.
Tore up the biceps of his right arm. Then—"

"I remember," Carolinus said. "So this is your nephew."

"Grandnephew," corrected Smrgol. "Little thick-headed and
all that," he added apologetically, "but my own flesh and
blood, you know."

"You may notice some slight improvement in him," said
Carolinus, dryly.

"I hope so," said Smrgol, brightening. "Any change, a
change for the better, you know. But I've bad news, Mage.
You know that inchworm of an Anark?"

"The one that found the maiden in the first place?"

"That's right. Well, he's stolen her again and run off."

"What?" cried Jim.

He had forgotten the capabilities of a dragon's voice.
Carolinus tottered, the flowers and grass lay flat, and even
Smrgol winced.

"My boy," said the old dragon reproachfully. "How many
times must I tell you not to shout. I said, Anark stole the
george."

"He means Angie!" cried Jim desperately to Carolinus.

"I know," said Carolinus, with his hands over his ears.

"You're sneezing again," said Smrgol, proudly. He turned
to Carolinus. "You wouldn't believe it. A dragon hasn't
sneezed in a hundred and ninety years. This boy did it the
first moment he set eyes on the george. The others couldn't
believe it. Sign of brains, I said. Busy brains make the nose
itch. Our side of the family—"

"Angie!"

"See there? All right now, boy, you've shown us you can do
it. Let's get down to business. How much to locate Anark and
the george, Mage?"

They dickered like rug-peddlers for several minutes, finally
settling on a price of four pounds of gold, one of silver, and a
flawed emerald. Carolinus got a small vial of water from the
Tinkling Spring and searched among the grass until he found
a small sandy open spot. He bent over it and the two dragons
sat down to watch.

"Quiet now," he warned. "I'm going to try a watch-beetle.
Don't alarm it."

Jim held his breath. Carolinus tilted the vial in his hand
and the crystal water fell in three drops—*Tink! Tink!* And
again—*Tink!* The sand darkened with the moisture and

began to work as if something was digging from below. A hole widened, black insect legs busily in action flickered, and an odd-looking beetle popped itself halfway out of the hole. Its forelimbs waved in the air and a little squeaky voice, like a cracked phonograph record repeating itself far away over a bad telephone connection, came to Jim's ears.

"Gone to the Loathly Tower! Gone to the Loathly Tower! Gone to the Loathly Tower!"

It popped back out of sight. Carolinus straightened up and Jim breathed again.

"The Loathly Tower!" said Smrgol. "Isn't that that ruined tower to the west, in the fens, Mage? Why, that's the place that loosed the blight on the mere-dragons five hundred years ago."

"It's a place of old magic," said Carolinus, grimly. "These places are like ancient sores on the land, scabbed over for a while but always breaking out with new evil when—the twisting of the Fabric by these two must have done it. The evilness there has drawn the evil in Anark to it—lesser to greater, according to the laws of nature. I'll meet you two there. Now, I must go set other forces in motion."

He began to twirl about. His speed increased rapidly until he was nothing but a blur. Then suddenly, he faded away like smoke; and was gone, leaving Jim staring at the spot where he had been.

A poke in the side brought Jim back to the ordinary world.

"Wake up, boy. Don't dally!" the voice of Smrgol bellowed in his ear. "We got flying to do. Come on!"

II

The old dragon's spirit was considerably younger than his body. It turned out to be a four-hour flight to the fens on the west seacoast. For the first hour or so Smrgol flew along energetically enough, meanwhile tracing out the genealogy of the mere-dragons and their relationship to himself and Gorbash; but gradually his steady flow of chatter dwindled and became intermittent. He tried to joke about his long-gone battle with the Ogre of Gormely Keep, but even this was too much and he fell silent with labored breath and straining wings. After a short but stubborn argument, Jim got him to admit that he would perhaps be better off taking a short breather and then coming on a little later. Smrgol let out a

deep gasping sigh and dropped away from Jim in weary
spirals. Jim saw him glide to an exhausted landing amongst
the purple gorse of the moors below and lie there, sprawled
out.

Jim continued on alone. A couple of hours later the moors
dropped down a long land-slope to the green country of the
fenland. Jim soared out over its spongy, grass-thick earth,
broken into causeways and islands by the blue water, which
in shallow bays and inlets was itself thick-choked with reeds
and tall marsh grass. Flocks of water fowl rose here and there
like eddying smoke from the glassy surface of one mere and
drifted over to settle on another a few hundred yards away.
Their cries came faintly to his dragon-sensitive ears and a
line of heavy clouds was piling up against the sunset in the
west.

He looked for some sign of the Loathly Tower, but the
fenland stretched away to a faint blue line that was probably
the sea, without showing sign of anything not built by
nature. Jim was beginning to wonder uneasily if he had not
gotten himself lost when his eye was suddenly caught by the
sight of a dragon-shape nosing at something on one of the
little islands amongst the meres.

Anark! he thought. And Angie!

He did not wait to see more. He nosed over and went into a
dive like a jet fighter, sights locked on Target Dragon.

It was a good move. Unfortunately Gorbash-Jim, having
about the weight and wingspread of a small flivver airplane,
made a comparable amount of noise when he was in a dive,
assuming the plane's motor to be shut off. Moreover, the
dragon on the ground had evidently had experience with the
meaning of such a sound; for, without even looking, he went
tumbling head over tail out of the way just as Jim slammed
into the spot where, a second before, he had been.

The other dragon rolled over onto his feet, sat up, took one
look at Jim, and began to wail.

"It's not fair! It's not fair!" he cried in a (for a dragon)
remarkably high-pitched voice. "Just because you're bigger
than I am. And I'm all horned up. It's the first good one I've
been able to kill in months and you don't need it, not at all.
You're big and fat and I'm so weak and thin and hungry—"

Jim blinked and stared. What he had thought to be Angie,
lying in the grass, now revealed itself to be an old and rather
stringy-looking cow, badly bitten up and with a broken neck.

"It's just my luck!" the other dragon was weeping. He was less than three-quarters Jim's size and so emaciated he appeared on the verge of collapse. "Every time I get something good, somebody takes it away. All I ever get to eat is fish—"

"Hold on," said Jim.

"Fish, fish, fish. Cold, nasty fi—"

"Hold on, I say! SHUT UP!" bellowed Jim, in Gorbash's best voice.

The other dragon stopped his wailing as suddenly as if his switch had been shut off.

"Yes, sir," he said, timidly.

"What's the matter? I'm not going to take this from you." The other dragon tittered uncertainly.

"I'm not," said Jim. "It's your cow. All yours."

"He-he-he!" said the other dragon. "You certainly are a card, your honor."

"Blast it, I'm serious!" cried Jim. "What's your name, anyway?"

"Oh, well—" the other squirmed. "Oh well, you know—"

"What's your name?"

"Secoh, your worship!" yelped the dragon, frightenedly. "Just Secoh. Nobody important. Just a little, unimportant mere-dragon, your highness, that's all I am. Really!"

"All right, Secoh, dig in. All I want is some directions."

"Well—if your worship really doesn't . . ." Secoh had been sidling forward in fawning fashion. "If you'll excuse my table manners sir. I'm just a mere-dragon—" and he tore into the meat before him in sudden, terrified, starving fashion.

Jim watched. Unexpectedly, his long tongue flickered out to lick his chops. His belly rumbled. He was astounded at himself. Raw meat? Off a dead animal—flesh, bones, hide and all? He took a firm grip on his appetites.

"Er, Secoh," he said. "I'm a stranger around these parts. I suppose you know the territory. . . . Say, how does that cow taste, anyway?"

"Oh, terrubble—mumpf—" replied Secoh, with his mouth full. "Stringy—old. Good enough for a mere-dragon like myself, but not—"

"Well, about these directions—"

"Yes, your highness?"

"I think . . . you know it's your cow . . ."

"That's what your honor said," replied Secoh, cautiously.

"But I just wonder . . . you know I've never tasted a cow like that."

Secoh muttered something despairingly under his breath.

"What?" said Jim.

"I said," said Secoh, resignedly, "wouldn't your worship like to taste it—"

"Not if you're going to cry about it," said Jim.

"I bit my tongue."

"Well, in that case . . ." Jim walked up and sank his teeth in the shoulder of the carcass. Rich juices trickled enticingly over his tongue. . . .

Some little time later he and Secoh sat back polishing bones with the rough uppers of their tongues which were as abrasive as steel files.

"Did you get enough to eat, Secoh?" asked Jim.

"More than enough, sir," replied the mere-dragon, staring at the white skeleton with a wild and famished eye. "Although, if your exaltedness doesn't mind, I've a weakness for marrow. . . ." He picked up a thighbone and began to crunch it like a stick of candy.

"Now," said Jim. "About this Loathly Tower. Where is it?"

"The wh-what?" stammered Secoh, dropping the thighbone.

"The Loathly Tower. It's in the fens. You know of it, don't you?"

"Oh, sir! Yes, sir. But you wouldn't want to go there, sir! Not that I'm presuming to give your lordship advice—" cried Secoh, in a suddenly high and terrified voice.

"No, no," soothed Jim. "What are you so upset about?"

"Well—of course I'm only a timid little mere-dragon. But it's a terrible place, the Loathly Tower, your worship, sir."

"How? Terrible?"

"Well—well, it just is." Secoh cast an unhappy look around him. "It's what spoiled all of us, you know, five hundred years ago. We used to be like other dragons—oh, not so big and handsome as you, sir. Then, after that, they say it was the Good got the upper hand and the Evil in the Tower was vanquished and the Tower itself ruined. But it didn't help us mere-dragons any, and I wouldn't go there if I was your worship, I really wouldn't."

"But what's so bad? What sort of thing is it?"

"Well, I wouldn't say there was any real *thing* there. Nothing your worship could put a claw on. It's just strange things go to it and strange things come out of it; and lately . . ."

"Lately what?"

"Nothing—nothing, really, your excellency!" cried Secoh. "Your illustriousness shouldn't catch a worthless little mere-dragon up like that. I only meant, lately the Tower's seemed more fearful than ever. That's all."

"Probably your imagination," said Jim, shortly. "Anyway, where is it?"

"You have to go north about five miles." While they had eaten and talked, the sunset had died. It was almost dark now; and Jim had to strain his eyes through the gloom to see the mere-dragon's foreclaw, pointing away across the mere. "To the Great Causeway. It's a wide lane of solid ground running east and west through the fens. You follow it west to the Tower. The Tower stands on a rock overlooking the sea-edge."

"Five miles . . ." said Jim. He considered the soft grass on which he lay. His armored body seemed undisturbed by the temperature, whatever it was. "I might as well get some sleep. See you in the morning, Secoh." He obeyed a sudden, birdlike instinct and tucked his ferocious head and long neck back under one wing.

"Whatever your excellency desires . . ." the mere-dragon's muffled voice came distantly to his ear. "Your excellency has only to call and I'll be immediately available. . . ."

The words faded out on Jim's ear, as he sank into sleep like a heavy stone into deep, dark waters.

When he opened his eyes, the sun was up. He sat up himself, yawned, and blinked.

Secoh was gone. So were the leftover bones.

"Blast!" said Jim. But the morning was too nice for annoyance. He smiled at his mental picture of Secoh carefully gathering the bones in fearful silence, and sneaking them away.

The smile did not last long. When he tried to take off in a northerly direction, as determined by reference to the rising sun, he found he had charley horses in both the huge wing-muscles that swelled out under the armor behind his shoulders. The result, of course, of yesterday's heavy exercise. Grumbling, he was forced to proceed on foot; and four hours later, very hot, muddy and wet, he pulled his weary body up onto the broad east-and-west-stretching strip of land which must, of necessity, be the Great Causeway. It ran straight as a Roman road through the meres, several feet higher than the rest of the fenland, and was solid enough to support good-sized trees. Jim collapsed in the shade of one with a heartfelt sigh.

He awoke to the sound of someone singing. He blinked and lifted his head. Whatever the earlier verses of the song had been, Jim had missed them; but the approaching baritone voice now caroled the words of the chorus merrily and clearly to his ear:

> "A right good sword, a constant mind,
> A trusty spear and true!
> The dragons of the mere shall find
> What Nevile-Smythe can do!"

The tune and words were vaguely familiar. Jim sat up for a better look and a knight in full armor rode into view on a large white horse through the trees. Then everything happened at once. The knight saw him, the visor of his armor came down with a clang, his long spear seemed to jump into his mailed hand and the horse under him leaped into a gallop, heading for Jim. Gorbash's reflexes took over. They hurled Jim straight up into the air, where his punished wing muscles cracked and faltered. He was just able to manage enough of a fluttering flop to throw himself into the upper branches of a small tree nearby.

The knight skidded his horse to a stop below and looked up through the spring-budded branches. He tilted his visor back to reveal a piercing pair of blue eyes, a rather hawklike nose and a jutting generous chin, all assembled into a clean-shaven young man's face. He looked eagerly up at Jim.

"Come down," he said.

"No thanks," said Jim, hanging firmly to the tree. There was a slight pause as they both digested the situation.

"Dashed caitiff mere-dragon!" said the night finally, with annoyance.

"I'm not a mere-dragon," said Jim.

"Oh, don't talk rot!" said the knight.

"I'm not," repeated Jim. He thought a minute. "I'll bet you can't guess who I really am."

The knight did not seem interested in guessing who Jim really was. He stood up in his stirrups and probed through the branches with his spear. The point did not quite reach Jim.

"Damn!" Disappointedly, he lowered the spear and became thoughtful. "I can climb the dashed tree," he muttered to himself. "But then what if he flies down and I have to fight him unhorsed, eh?"

"Look," called Jim, peering down—the knight looked up eagerly—"if you'll listen to what I've to say, first."

The knight considered.

"Fair enough," he said, finally. "No pleas for mercy, now!"

"No, no," said Jim.

"Because I shan't grant them, dammit! It's not in my vows. Widows and orphans and honorable enemies on the field of battle. But not dragons."

"No. I just want to convince you who I really am."

"I don't give a blasted farthing who you really are."

"You will," said Jim. "Because I'm not really a dragon at all. I've just been—uh—enchanted into a dragon."

The man on the ground looked skeptical.

"Really," said Jim, slipping a little in the tree. "You know S. Carolinus, the magician? I'm as human as you are."

"Heard of him," grunted the knight. "You'll say *he* put you under?"

"No, he's the one who's going to change me back—as soon as I can find the lady I'm—er—betrothed to. A real dragon ran off with her. I'm after him. Look at me. Do I look like one of these scrawny mere-dragons?"

"Hmm," said the knight. He rubbed his hooked nose thoughtfully.

"Carolinus found she's at the Loathly Tower. I'm on my way there."

The knight stared.

"The Loathly Tower?" he echoed.

"Exactly," said Jim, firmly. "And now you know, your honor as knight and gentleman demands you don't hamper my rescue efforts."

The knight continued to think it over for a long moment or two. He was evidently not the sort to be rushed into things.

"How do I know you're telling the truth?" he said at last.

"Hold your sword up. I'll swear on the cross of its hilt."

"But if you're a dragon, what's the good in that? Dragons don't have souls, dammit!"

"No," said Jim, "but a Christian gentleman has; and if I'm

a Christian gentleman, I wouldn't dare forswear myself like that, would I?"

The knight struggled visibly with this logic for several seconds. Finally, he gave up.

"Oh, well . . ." He held up his sword by the point and let Jim swear on it. Then he put the sword back in its sheath as Jim descended. "Well," he said, still a little doubtfully, "I suppose, under the circumstances, we ought to introduce ourselves. You know my arms?"

Jim looked at the shield which the other swung around for his inspection. It showed a wide X of silver—like a cross lying over sideways—on a red background and above some sort of black animal in profile which seemed to be lying down between the X's bottom legs.

"The gules, a saltire argent, of course," went on the knight, "are the Nevile of Raby arms. My father, as a cadet of the house, differenced with a hart lodged sable—you see it there at the bottom. Naturally, as his heir, I carry the family arms."

"Nevile-Smythe," said Jim, remembering the name from the song.

"Sir Reginald, knight bachelor. And you, sir?"

"Why, uh . . ." Jim clutched frantically at what he knew of heraldry. "I bear—in my proper body, that is—"

"Quite."

"A . . . gules, a typewriter argent, on a desk sable. Eckert, Sir James—uh—knight bachelor. Baron of—er—Riveroak."

Nevile-Smythe was knitting his brows.

"Typewriter . . ." he was muttering, "typewriter . . ."

"A local beast, rather like a griffin," said Jim, hastily. "We have a lot of them in Riveroak—that's in America, a land over the sea to the west. You may not have heard of it."

"Can't say that I have. Was it there you were enchanted into this dragon-shape?"

"Well, yes and no. I was transported to this land by magic as was the—uh—lady Angela. When I woke here I was bedragoned."

"Were you?" Sir Reginald's blue eyes bulged a little in amazement. "Angela—fair name, that! Like to meet her. Perhaps after we get this muddle cleared up, we might have a bit of a set-to on behalf of our respective ladies."

Jim gulped slightly.

"Oh, you've got one, too?"

"Absolutely. And she's tremendous. The Lady Elinor—" The knight turned about in his saddle and began to fumble about his equipment. Jim, on reaching the ground, had at once started out along the causeway in the direction of the Tower, so that the knight happened to be pacing alongside him on horseback when he suddenly went into these evolutions. It seemed to bother his charger not at all. "Got her favor here someplace—half a moment—"

"Why don't you just tell me what it's like?" said Jim, sympathetically.

"Oh, well," said Nevile-Smythe, giving up his search, "it's a kerchief, you know. Monogrammed. E. d'C. She's a deChauncy. It's rather too bad, though. I'd have liked to show it to you since we're going to the Loathly Tower together."

"We are?" said Jim, startled. "But—I mean, it's my job. I didn't think you'd want—"

"Lord, yes," said Nevile-Smythe, looking somewhat startled himself. "A gentleman of coat-armor like myself—and an outrage like this taking place locally. I'm no knight-errant, dash it, but I *do* have a decent sense of responsibility."

"I mean—I just meant—" stumbled Jim. "What if something happened to you? What would the Lady Elinor say?"

"Why, what could she say?" replied Nevile-Smythe in plain astonishment. "No one but an utter rotter dodges his plain duty. Besides, there may be a chance here for me to gain a little worship. Elinor's keen on that. She wants me to come home safe."

Jim blinked.

"I don't get it," he said.

"Beg pardon?"

Jim explained his confusion.

"Why, how do you people do things, overseas?" said Nevile-Smythe. "After we're married and I have lands of my own, I'll be expected to raise a company and march out at my lord's call. If I've no name as a knight, I'll be able to raise nothing but bumpkins and clodpoles who'll desert at the first sight of steel. On the other hand, if I've a name, I'll have good men coming to serve under my banner; because, you see, they know I'll take good care of them; and by the same token they'll take good care of me—I say, isn't it getting dark rather suddenly?"

Jim glanced at the sky. It was indeed—almost the dimness of twilight although it could, by rights, be no more than early afternoon yet. Glancing ahead up the Causeway, he became aware of a further phenomenon. A line seemed to be cutting across the trees and grass and even extending out over the waters of the meres on both sides. Moreover, it seemed to be moving toward them as if some heavy, invisible fluid was slowly flooding out over the low country of the fenland.

"Why—" he began. A voice wailed suddenly from his left to interrupt him.

"No! No! Turn back, your worship. Turn back! It's death in there!"

They turned their heads sharply. Secoh, the mere-dragon, sat perched on a half-drowned tussock about forty feet out in the mere.

"Come here, Secoh!" called Jim.

"No! No!" The invisible line was almost to the tussock. Secoh lifted heavily into the air and flapped off, crying. "Now it's loose! It's broken loose again. And we're all lost . . . lost . . . lost . . ."

His voice wailed away and was lost in the distance. Jim and Nevile-Smythe looked at each other.

"Now, that's one of our local dragons for you!" said the knight disgustedly. "How can a gentleman of coat armor gain honor by slaying a beast like that? The worst of it is when someone from the Midlands compliments you on being a dragon-slayer and you have to explain—"

At that moment either they both stepped over the line, or the line moved past them—Jim was never sure which; and they both stopped, as by one common, instinctive impulse. Looking at Sir Reginald, Jim could see under the visor how the knight's face had gone pale.

"In manus tuas Domine," said Nevile-Smythe, crossing himself.

About and around them, the serest gray of winter light lay on the fens. The waters of the meres lay thick and oily, still between the shores of dull green grass. A small, cold breeze wandered through the tops of the reeds and they rattled together with a dry and distant sound like old bones cast out into a forgotten courtyard for the wind to play with. The trees stood helpless and still, their new, small leaves now pinched and faded like children aged before their time while all about and over all the heaviness of dead hope and bleak despair lay on all living things.

"Sir James," said the knight, in an odd tone and accents

such as Jim had not heard him use before, "wot well that we
have this day set our hands to no small task. Wherefore I
pray thee that we should push forward, come what may, for
my heart faileth and I think me that it may well hap that I
return not, ne no man know mine end."

Having said this, he immediately reverted to his usual
cheerful self and swung down out of his saddle. "Clarivaux
won't go another inch, dash it!" he said. "I shall have to lead
him—by the bye, did you know that mere-dragon?"

Jim fell into step beside him and they went on again, but a
little more slowly, for everything seemed an extra effort
under this darkening sky.

"I talked to him yesterday," said Jim. "He's not a bad sort
of dragon."

"Oh, I've nothing against the beasts, myself. But one slays
them when one finds them, you know."

"An old dragon—in fact he's the granduncle of this body
I'm in," said Jim, "thinks that dragons and humans really
ought to get together. Be friends, you know."

"Extraordinary thought!" said Nevile-Smythe, staring at
Jim in astonishment.

"Well actually," said Jim, "why not?"

"Well, I don't know. It just seems like it wouldn't do."

"He says men and dragons might find common foes to fight
together."

"Oh, that's where he's wrong, though. You couldn't trust
dragons to stick by you in a bicker. And what if your enemy
had dragons of his own? They wouldn't fight each other. No.
No."

They fell silent. They had moved away from the grass onto
flat sandy soil. There was a sterile, flinty hardness to it. It
crunched under the hooves of Clarivaux, at once unyielding
and treacherous.

"Getting darker, isn't it?" said Jim, finally.

The light was, in fact, now down to a grayish twilight
through which it was impossible to see more than a dozen
feet. And it was dwindling as they watched. They had halted
and stood facing each other. The light fled steadily, and
faster. The dimness became blacker, and blacker—until finally
the last vestige of illumination was lost and blackness, total
and complete, overwhelmed them. Jim felt a gauntleted hand
touch one of his forelimbs.

"Let's hold together," said the voice of the knight. "Then

whatever comes upon us, must come upon us all at once."

"Right," said Jim. But the word sounded cold and dead in his throat.

They stood, in silence and in lightlessness, waiting for they did not know what. And the blankness about them pressed further in on them, now that it had isolated them, nibbling at the very edges of their minds. Out of the nothingness came nothing material, but from within them crept up one by one, like blind white slugs from some bottomless pit, all their inner doubts and fears and unknown weaknesses, all the things of which they had been ashamed and which they had tucked away to forget, all the maggots of their souls.

Jim found himself slowly, stealthily beginning to with-draw his forelimb from under the knight's touch. He no longer trusted Nevile-Smythe—for the evil that must be in the man because of the evil he knew to be in himself. He would move away . . . off into the darkness alone . . .

"Look!" Nevile-Smythe's voice cried suddenly to him, dis-tant and eerie, as if from someone already a long way off. "Look back the way we came."

Jim turned about. Far off in the darkness, there was a distant glimmer of light. It rolled toward them, growing as it came. They felt its power against the power of lightlessness that threatened to overwhelm them; and the horse Clarivaux stirred unseen beside them, stamped his hooves on the hard sand, and whinnied.

"This way!" called Jim.

"This way!" shouted Nevile-Smythe.

The light shot up suddenly in height. Like a great rod it advanced toward them and the darkness was rolling back, graying, disappearing. They heard a sound of feet close, and a sound of breathing, and then—

It was daylight again.

And S. Carolinus stood before them in tall hat and robes figured with strange images and signs. In his hand upright before him—as if it was blade and buckler, spear and armor all in one—he held a tall carven staff of wood.

"By the Powers!" he said. "I was in time. Look there!"

He lifted the staff and drove it point down into the soil. It went in and stood erect like some denuded tree. His long arm pointed past them and they turned around.

The darkness was gone. The fens lay revealed far and wide, stretching back a long way, and up ahead, meeting the thin dark line of the sea. The Causeway had risen until they now stood twenty feet above the mere-waters. Ahead to the west, the sky was ablaze with sunset. It lighted up all the fens and the end of the Causeway leading onto a long and bloody-looking hill, whereon—touched by that same dying light—there loomed above and over all, amongst great tumbled boulders, the ruined, dark and shattered shell of a Tower as black as jet.

III

"—why didn't you wake us earlier, then?" asked Jim.

It was the morning after. They had slept the night within the small circle of protection afforded by Carolinus' staff. They were sitting up now and rubbing their eyes in the light of a sun that had certainly been above the horizon a good two hours.

"Because," said Carolinus. He was sipping at some more milk and he stopped to make a face of distaste. "Because we had to wait for them to catch up with us."

"Who? Catch up?" asked Jim.

"If I knew *who*," snapped Carolinus, handing his empty milk tankard back to emptier air, "I would have said *who*. All I know is that the present pattern of Chance and History implies that two more will join our party. The same pattern implied the presence of this knight and—oh, so that's who they are."

Jim turned around to follow the magician's gaze. To his surprise, two dragon shapes were emerging from a clump of brush behind them.

"Secoh!" cried Jim. "And—Smrgol! Why—" His voice wavered and died. The old dragon, he suddenly noticed, was limping and one wing hung a little loosely, half drooping from its shoulder. Also, the eyelid on the same side as the loose wing and stiff leg was sagging more or less at half-mast. "Why, what happened?"

"Oh, a bit stiff from yesterday," huffed Smrgol, bluffly. "Probably pass off in a day or two."

"Stiff nothing!" said Jim, touched in spite of himself. "You've had a stroke."

"Stroke of bad luck, *I'd* say," replied Smrgol, cheerfully, trying to wink his bad eye and not succeeding very well. "No, boy, it's nothing. Look who I've brought along."

"I—I wasn't too keen on coming," said Secoh, shyly, to Jim. "But your granduncle can be pretty persuasive, your wo—you know."

"That's right!" boomed Smrgol. "Don't you go calling anybody your worship. Never heard of such stuff!" He turned to Jim. "And letting a george go in where he didn't dare go himself! Boy, I said to him, don't give me this *only a mere-dragon* and *just a mere-dragon*. Mere's got nothing to do with what kind of dragon you are. What kind of a world would it be if we were all like that?" Smrgol mimicked (as well as his dragon-basso would let him) someone talking in a high, simpering voice. "Oh, I'm just a plowland-and-pasture dragon—you'll have to excuse me I'm only a halfway-up-the-hill dragon—*Boy!*" bellowed Smrgol, "I said, you're a *dragon!* Remember that. And a dragon acts like a dragon or he doesn't act at all!"

"Hear! Hear!" said Nevile-Smythe, carried away by enthusiasm.

"Hear that, boy? Even the george here knows that. Don't believe I've met you, george," he added, turning to the knight.

"Nevile-Smythe, Sir Reginald. Knight bachelor."

"Smrgol. Dragon."

"Smrgol? You aren't the—but you couldn't be. Over a hundred years ago."

"The dragon who slew the Ogre of Gormely Keep? That's who I am, boy—george, I mean."

"By Jove! Always thought it was a legend, only."

"Legend? Not on your honor, george! I'm old—even for a dragon, but there was a time—well, well, we won't go into that. I've something more important to talk to you about. I've been doing a lot of thinking the last decade or so about us dragons and you georges getting together. Actually, we're really a lot alike—"

"If you don't mind, Smrgol," cut in Carolinus, snappishly, "we aren't out here to hold a parlement. It'll be noon in—when will it be noon, you?"

"Four hours, thirty-seven minutes, twelve seconds at the sound of the gong," replied the invisible bass voice. There was a momentary pause, and then a single mellow, chimed note. "Chime, I mean," the voice corrected itself.

"Oh, go back to bed!" cried Carolinus, furiously.

"I've been up for hours," protested the voice, indignantly. Carolinus ignored it, herding the party together and starting them off for the Tower. The knight fell in beside Smrgol.

"About this business of men and dragons getting together,"
said Nevile-Smythe. "Confess I wasn't much impressed until
I heard your name. D'you think it's possible?"

"Got to make a start sometime, george." Smrgol rumbled
on. Jim, who had moved up to the head of the column to walk
beside Carolinus, spoke to the magician.

"What lives in the Tower?"

Carolinus jerked his fierce old bearded face around to look
at him.

"What's *living* there?" he snapped. "I don't know. We'll find
out soon enough. What *is* there—neither alive nor dead, just
in existence at the spot—is the manifestation of pure evil."

"But how can we do anything against that?"

"We can't. We can only contain it. Just as you—if you're
essentially a good person—contain the potentialities for evil
in yourself, by killing its creatures, your evil impulses and
actions."

"Oh?" said Jim.

"Certainly. And since evil opposes good in like manner, its
creatures, the ones in the Tower, will try to destroy us."

Jim felt a cold lump in his throat. He swallowed.

"Destroy us?"

"Why no, they'll probably just invite us to tea—" The
sarcasm in the old magician's voice broke off suddenly with
the voice itself. They had just stepped through a low screen of
bushes and instinctively checked to a halt.

Lying on the ground before them was what once had been a
man in full armor. Jim heard the sucking intake of breath
from Nevile-Smythe behind him.

"A most foul death," said the knight softly, "most foul . . ."
He came forward and dropped clumsily to his armored knees,
joining his gauntleted hands in prayer. The dragons were
silent. Carolinus poked with his staff at a wide trail of slime
that led around and over the body and back toward the
Tower. It was the sort of trail a garden slug might have
left—if this particular garden slug had been two or more feet
wide where it touched the ground.

"A Worm," said Carolinus. "But Worms are mindless. No
Worm killed him in such cruel fashion." He lifted his head to
the old dragon.

"I didn't say it, Mage," rumbled Smrgol, uneasily.

"Best none of us say it until we know for certain. Come on."
Carolinus took up the lead and led them forward again.

They had come up off the Causeway onto the barren plain
that sloped up into a hill in which stood the Tower. They
could see the wide fens and the tide flats coming to meet
them in the arms of a small bay—and beyond that the sea,
stretching misty to the horizon.

The sky above was blue and clear. No breeze stirred; but,
as they looked at the Tower and the hill that held it, it
seemed that the azure above had taken on a metallic cast.
The air had a quivering unnaturalness like an atmosphere
dancing to heat waves, though the day was chill; and there
came on Jim's ears, from where he did not know, a high-
pitched dizzy singing like that which accompanies delirium,
or high fever.

The Tower itself was distorted by these things. So that
although to Jim it seemed only the ancient, ruined shell of a
building, yet, between one heartbeat and the next, it seemed
to change. Almost, but not quite, he caught glimpses of it
unbroken and alive and thronged about with fantastic, half-
seen figures. His heart beat stronger with the delusion; and
its beating shook the scene before him, all the hill and Tower,
going in and out of focus, in and out, *in* and *out* . . .

. . . And there was Angie, in the Tower's doorway, calling
him . . .

"*Stop!*" shouted Carolinus. His voice echoed like a clap of
thunder in Jim's ears; and Jim awoke to his senses, to find
himself straining against the barrier of Carolinus' staff, that
barred his way to the Tower like a rod of iron. "By the
Powers!" said the old magician, softly and fiercely. "Will you
fall into the first trap set for you?"

"Trap?" echoed Jim, bewilderedly. But he had no time to go
further, for at that moment there rose from among the giant
boulders at the Tower's base the heavy, wicked head of a
dragon as large as Smrgol.

The thunderous bellow of the old dragon beside Jim split
the unnatural air.

"*Anark!* Traitor—thief—inchworm! Come down here!"

Booming dragon-laughter rolled back an answer.

"Tell us about Gormely Keep, old bag of bones! Ancient
mudpuppy, fat lizard, scare us with words!"

Smrgol lurched forward; and again Carolinus' staff was
extended to bar the way.

"Patience," said the magician. But with one wrenching effort, the old dragon had himself under control. He turned, panting, to Carolinus.

"What's hidden, Mage?" he demanded.

"We'll see." Grimly, Carolinus brought his staff, endwise, three times down upon the earth. With each blow the whole hill seemed to shake and shudder.

Up among the rocks, one particularly large boulder tottered and rolled aside. Jim caught his breath and Secoh cried out, suddenly.

In the gap that the boulder revealed, a thick, sluglike head was lifting from the ground. It reared, yellow-brown in the sunlight, its two sets of horns searching and revealing a light external shell, a platelet with a merest hint of spire. It lowered its head and slowly, inexorably, began to flow downhill toward them, leaving its glistening trail behind it.

"Now—" said the knight. But Carolinus shook his head. He struck at the ground again.

"Come forth!" he cried, his thin, old voice piping on the quivering air. "By the Powers! Come forth!"

And then they saw it.

From behind the great barricade of boulders, slowly, there reared first a bald and glistening dome of hairless skin. Slowly this rose, revealing two perfectly round eyes below which they saw, as the whole came up, no proper nose, but two air-slits side by side as if the whole of the bare, enormous skull was covered with a simple sheet of thick skin. And rising still further, this unnatural head, as big around as a beach ball, showed itself to possess a wide and idiot-grinning mouth, entirely lipless and revealing two jagged, matching rows of yellow teeth.

Now, with a clumsy, studied motion, the whole creature rose to its feet and stood knee-deep in the boulders and towering above them. It was manlike in shape, but clearly nothing ever spawned by the human race. A good twelve feet high it stood, a rough patchwork kilt of untanned hides wrapped around its thick waist—but this was not the extent of its differences from the race of Man. It had, to begin with, no neck at all. That obscene beachball of a hairless, near-featureless head balanced like an apple on thick, square shoulders of gray, coarse-looking skin. Its torso was one straight trunk, from which its arms and legs sprouted with a disproportionate thickness and roundness, like sections of

pipe. Its knees were hidden by its kilt and its further legs by
the rocks; but the elbows of its oversize arms had unnatural
hinges to them, almost as if they had been doubled, and the
lower arms were almost as large as the upper and near-
wristless, while the hands themselves were awkward, thick-
fingered parodies of the human extremity, with only three
digits, of which one was a single, opposed thumb.

The right hand held a club, bound with rusty metal, that
surely not even such a monster should have been able to lift.
Yet one grotesque hand carried it lightly, as lightly as
Carolinus had carried his staff. The monster opened its
mouth.

"He!" it went. "He! He!"

The sound was fantastic. It was a bass titter, if such a thing
could be imagined. Though the tone of it was as low as the
lowest note of a good operatic basso, it clearly came from the
creature's upper throat and head. Nor was there any real
humor in it. It was an utterance with a nervous, habitual air
about it, like a man clearing his throat. Having sounded, it
fell silent, watching the advance of the great slug with its
round, light blue eyes.

Smrgol exhaled slowly.

"Yes," he rumbled, almost sadly, almost as if to himself.
"What I was afraid of. An ogre."

In the silence that followed, Nevile-Smythe got down from
his horse and began to tighten the girths of its saddle.

"So, so, Clarivaux," he crooned to the trembling horse. "So
ho, boy."

The rest of them were looking all at Carolinus. The magician leaned on his staff, seeming very old indeed, with the
deep lines carven in the ancient skin of his face. He had been
watching the ogre, but now he turned back to Jim and the
other two dragons.

"I had hoped all along," he said, "that it needn't come to
this. However," he crackled sourly, and waved his hand at
the approaching Worm, the silent Anark and the watching
ogre, "as you see . . . The world goes never the way we want
it by itself, but must be haltered and led." He winced,
produced his flask and cup, and took a drink of milk. Putting
the utensils back, he looked over at Nevile-Smythe, who was
now checking his weapons. "I'd suggest, Knight, that you
take the Worm. It's a poor chance, but your best. I know you'd

prefer that renegade dragon, but the Worm is the greater danger."

"Difficult to slay, I imagine?" queried the knight.

"Its vital organs are hidden deep inside it," said Carolinus, "and being mindless, it will fight on long after being mortally wounded. Cut off those eye-stalks and blind it first, if you can—"

"Wait!" cried Jim, suddenly. He had been listening bewilderedly. Now the word seemed to jump out of his mouth. "What're we going to do?"

"Do?" said Carolinus, looking at him. "Why, fight, of course."

"But," stammered Jim, "wouldn't it be better to go get some help? I mean—"

"Blast it, boy!" boomed Smrgol. "We can't wait for that! Who knows what'll happen if we take time for something like that? Hell's bell's, Gorbash, lad, you got to fight your foes when you meet them, not the next day, or the day after that."

"Quite right, Smrgol," said Carolinus, dryly. "Gorbash, you don't understand this situation. Every time you retreat from something like this, it gains and you lose. The next time the odds would be even worse against us."

They were all looking at him. Jim felt the impact of their curious glances. He did not know what to say. He wanted to tell them that he was not a fighter, that he did not know the first thing to do in this sort of battle, that it was none of his business anyway and that he would not be here at all, if it were not for Angie. He was, in fact, quite humanly scared, and floundered desperately for some sort of strength to lean on.

"What—what am I supposed to do?" he said.

"Why, fight the ogre, boy! Fight the ogre!" thundered Smrgol—and the inhuman giant up on the slope, hearing him, shifted his gaze suddenly from the Worm to fasten it on Jim. "And I'll take on that louse of an Anark. The george here'll chop up the Worm, the Mage'll hold back the bad influences—and there we are."

"Fight the ogre . . ." If Jim had still been possessed of his ordinary two legs, they would have buckled underneath him. Luckily his dragon-body knew no such weakness. He looked at the overwhelming bulk of his expected opponent, contrasted the ogre with himself, the armored, ox-heavy body of the Worm with Nevile-Smythe, the deep-chested oversize Anark with the crippled old dragon beside him—and a cry of protest rose from the very depths of his being. "But we can't win!"

He turned furiously on Carolinus, who, however, looked at him calmly. In desperation he turned back to the only normal human he could find in the group.

"Nevile-Smythe," he said. "You don't need to do this."

"Lord, yes," replied the knight, busy with his equipment. "Worms, ogres—one fights them when one runs into them, you know." He considered his spear and put it aside. "Believe I'll face it on foot," he murmured to himself.

"Smrgol!" said Jim. "Don't you see—can't you understand? Anark is a lot younger than you. And you're not well—"

"Er . . ." said Secoh, hesitantly.

"Speak up, boy!" rumbled Smrgol.

"Well," stammered Secoh, "it's just . . . what I mean is, I couldn't bring myself to fight that Worm or that ogre—I really couldn't. I just sort of go to pieces when I think of them getting close to me. But I *could*—well, fight another dragon. It wouldn't be quite so bad, if you know what I mean, if that dragon up there breaks my neck—" He broke down and stammered incoherently. "I know I sound awfully silly—"

"Nonsense! Good lad!" bellowed Smrgol. "Glad to have you. I—er—can't quite get into the air myself at the moment—still a bit stiff. But if you could fly over and work him down this way where I can get a grip on him, we'll stretch him out for the buzzards." And he dealt the mere-dragon a tremendous thwack with his tail by way of congratulation, almost knocking Secoh off his feet.

In desperation, Jim turned back to Carolinus.

"There is no retreat," said Carolinus, calmly, before Jim could speak. "This is a game of chess where if one piece withdraws, all fall. Hold back the creatures, and I will hold back the forces—for the creatures will finish me, if you go down, and the forces will finish you if they get me."

"Now, look here, Gorbash!" shouted Smrgol in Jim's ear. "That Worm's almost here. Let me tell you something about how to fight ogres, based on experience. You listening, boy?"

"Yes," said Jim, numbly.

"I know you've heard the other dragons calling me an old windbag when I wasn't around. But I *have* conquered an ogre—the only one in our race to do it in the last eight hundred years—and they haven't. So pay attention, if you want to win your own fight."

Jim gulped.

"All right," he said.

"Now, the first thing to know," boomed Smrgol, glancing at the Worm who was now less than fifty yards distant, "is about the bones in an ogre—"

"Never mind the details!" cried Jim. "Who do I do?"

"In a minute," said Smrgol. "Don't get excited, boy. Now, about the bones in an ogre. The thing to remember is that they're big—matter of fact in the arms and legs, they're mainly bone. So there's no use trying to bite clear through, if you get a chance. What you try to do is get at the muscle—that's tough enough as it is—and hamstring. That's point one." He paused to look severely at Jim.

"Now, point two," he continued, "also connected with bones. Notice the elbows on that ogre. They aren't like a george's elbows. They're what you might call double-jointed. I mean, they have two joints where a george has just the one. Why? Simply because with the big bones they got to have and the muscle on them, they'd never be able to bend an arm more than halfway up before the bottom part'd bump the top if they had a george-type joint. Now, the point of all this is that when it swings that club, it can only swing in one way with that elbow. That's up and down. If it wants to swing it side to side, it's got to use its shoulder. Consequently if you can catch it with its club down and to one side of the body, you got an advantage; because it takes two motions to get it back up and in line again—instead of one, like a george."

"Yes, yes," said Jim, impatiently, watching the advance of the Worm.

"Don't get impatient, boy. Keep cool. Keep cool. Now, the knees don't have that kind of joint, so if you can knock it off its feet you got a real advantage. But don't try that, unless you're sure you can do it; because once it gets you pinned, you're a goner. The way to fight it is in-and-out—fast. Wait for a swing, dive in, tear him, get back out again. Got it?"

"Got it," said Jim, numbly.

"Good. Whatever you do, don't let it get a grip on you. Don't pay attention to what's happening to the rest of us, no matter what you hear or see. It's every one for himself. Concentrate on your own foe; and *keep your head*. Don't let your dragon instinct to get in there and slug run away with you. That's why the georges have been winning against us as they have. Just remember you're faster than that ogre and your brains'll

win for you if you stay clear, keep your head and don't rush. I
tell you, boy—"

He was interrupted by a sudden cry of joy from Nevile-
Smythe, who had been rummaging around Clarivaux's saddle.

"I say!" shouted Nevile-Smythe, running up to them with
surprising lightness, considering his armor. "The most marvelous stroke of luck! Look what I found." He waved a wispy
stretch of cloth at them.

"What?" demanded Jim, his heart going up in one sudden
leap.

"Elinor's favor! And just in time, too. Be a good fellow, will
you," went on Nevile-Smythe, turning to Carolinus, "and tie
it about my vambrace here on the shield arm. Thank you,
Mage."

Carolinus, looking grim, tucked his staff into the crook of
his arm and quickly tied the kerchief around the armor of
Nevile-Smythe's lower left arm. As he tightened the final
knot and let his hands drop away, the knight caught up his
shield into position and drew his sword with his other hand.
The bright blade flashed like a sudden streak of lightning in
the sun, he leaned forward to throw the weight of his armor
before him, and with a shout of *"A Nevile-Smythe! Elinor!
Elinor!"* he ran forward up the slope toward the approaching
Worm.

Jim heard, but did not see, the clash of shell and steel that
was their coming together. For just then everything began to
happen at once. Up on the hill, Anark screamed suddenly in
fury and launched himself down the slope in the air, wings
spread like some great bomber gliding in for a crash landing.
Behind Jim, there was the frenzied flapping of leathery
wings as Secoh took to the air to meet him—but this was
drowned by a sudden short, deep-chested cry, like a wordless
shout; and, lifting his club, the ogre stirred and stepped clear
of the boulders, coming forward and straight down the hill
with huge, ground-covering strides.

"Good luck, boy," said Smrgol, in Jim's ear. "And, Gorbash—"
Something in the old dragon's voice made Jim turn his head
to look at Smrgol. The ferocious red mouth-pit and enormous
fangs were frighteningly open before him; but behind it Jim
read a strange affection and concern in the dark dragon-eyes.
"—remember," said the old dragon, almost softly, "that you
are a descendant of Ortosh and Agtval, and Gleingul who
slew the sea serpent on the tide-banks of the Gray Sands.

And be therefore valiant. But remember too, that you are my only living kin and the last of our line . . . and be careful."

Then Smrgol's head was jerked away, as he swung about to face the coming together of Secoh and Anark in mid-air and bellowed out his own challenge. While Jim, turning back toward the Tower, had only time to take to the air before the rush of the ogre was upon him.

He had lifted on his wings without thinking—evidently this was dragon instinct when attacked. He was aware of the ogre suddenly before him, checking now, with its enormous hairy feet digging deep into the ground. The rust-bound club flashed before Jim's eyes and he felt a heavy blow high on his chest that swept him backward through the air.

He flailed with his wings to regain balance. The oversize idiot face was grinning only a couple of yards off from him. The club swept up for another blow. Panicked, Jim scrambled aside, and saw the ogre sway forward a step. Again the club lashed out—*quick!*—how could something so big and clumsy-looking be so quick with its hands? Jim felt himself smashed down to earth and a sudden lance of bright pain shot through his right shoulder. For a second a gray, thick-skinned fore-arm loomed over him and his teeth met in it without thought.

He was shaken like a rat by a rat terrier and flung clear. His wings beat for the safety of altitude, and he found himself about twenty feet off the ground, staring down at the ogre, which grunted a wordless sound and shifted the club to strike upwards. Jim cupped air with his wings, to fling himself backward and avoid the blow. The club whistled through the unfeeling air; and, sweeping forward, Jim ripped at one great blocky shoulder and beat clear. The ogre spun to face him, still grinning. But now blood welled and trickled down where Jim's teeth had gripped and torn, high on the shoulder.

—And suddenly, Jim realized something:

He was no longer afraid. He hung in the air, just out of the ogre's reach, poised to take advantage of any opening; and a hot sense of excitement was coursing through him. He was discovering the truth about fights—and about most similar things—that it is only the beginning that is bad. Once the chips are down, several million years of instinct take over and there is no time for thought for anything but confronting the enemy. So it was with Jim—and then the ogre moved in on him again; and that was his last specific intellectual thought of the fight, for everything else was drowned in his overwhelming drive to avoid being killed and, if possible, to kill, himself. . . .

IV

It was a long, blurred time, about which later Jim had no clear memory. The sun marched up the long arc of the heavens and crossed the nooning point and headed down again. On the torn-up sandy soil of the plain he and the ogre turned and feinted, smashed and tore at each other. Sometimes he was in the air, sometimes on the ground. Once he had the ogre down on one knee, but could not press his advantage. At another time they had fought up the long slope of the hill almost to the Tower and the ogre had him pinned in the cleft between two huge boulders and had hefted its club back for the final blow that would smash Jim's skull. And then he had wriggled free between the monster's very legs and the battle was on again.

Now and then throughout the fight he would catch brief kaleidoscopic glimpses of the combats being waged about him; Nevile-Smythe now wrapped about by the blind body of the Worm, its eyestalks hacked away—and striving in silence to draw free his sword arm, which was pinned to his side by the Worm's encircling body. Or there would roll briefly into Jim's vision a tangled roaring tumble of flailing leathery wings and serpentine bodies that was Secoh, Anark and old Smrgol. Once or twice he had a momentary view of Carolinus, still standing erect, his staff upright in his hand, his long white beard flowing forward over his blue gown with the cabalistic golden signs upon it, like some old seer in the hour of Armageddon. Then the gross body of the ogre would blot out his vision and he would forget all but the enemy before him.

The day faded. A dank mist came rolling in from the sea and fled in little wisps and tatters across the plain of battle. Jim's body ached and slowed, and his wings felt leaden. But the ever-grinning face and sweeping club of the ogre seemed neither to weaken nor to tire. Jim drew back for a moment to catch his breath; and in that second, he heard a voice cry out.

"Time is short!" it cried, in cracked tones. "We are running out of time. The day is nearly gone!"

It was the voice of Carolinus. Jim had never heard him

raise it before with just such a desperate accent. And even as
Jim identified the voice, he realized that it came clearly to
his ears—and that for sometime now upon the battlefield,
except for the ogre and himself, there had been silence.

He shook his head to clear it and risked a quick glance
about him. He had been driven back almost to the neck of the
Causeway itself, where it entered onto the plain. To one side
of him, the snapped strands of Clarivaux's bridle dangled
limply where the terrified horse had broken loose from the
earth-thrust spear to which Nevile-Smythe had tethered it
before advancing against the Worm on foot. A little off from
it stood Carolinus, upheld now only by his staff, his old face
shrunken and almost mummified in appearance, as if the life
had been all but drained from it. There was nowhere else to
retreat to; and Jim was alone.

He turned back his gaze to see the ogre almost upon him.
The heavy club swung high, looking gray and enormous in
the mist. Jim felt in his limbs and wings a weakness that
would not let him dodge in time; and, with all his strength,
he gathered himself, and sprang instead, up under the monster's guard and inside the grasp of those cannon-thick arms.

The club glanced off Jim's spine. He felt the arms go
around him, the double triad of bone-thick fingers searching
for his neck. He was caught, but his rush had knocked the
ogre off his feet. Together they went over and rolled on the
sandy earth, the ogre gnawing with his jagged teeth at Jim's
chest and striving to break a spine or twist a neck, while
Jim's tail lashed futilely about.

They rolled against the spear and snapped it in half. The
ogre found its hold and Jim felt his neck begin to be slowly
twisted, as if it were a chicken's neck being wrung in slow
motion. A wild despair flooded through him. He had been
warned by Smrgol never to let the ogre get him pinned. He
had disregarded that advice and now he was lost, the battle
was lost. *Stay away,* Smrgol had warned, *use your brains . . .*

The hope of a wild chance sprang suddenly to life in him.
His head was twisted back over his shoulder. He could see
only the gray mist above him, but he stopped fighting the
ogre and groped about with both forelimbs. For a slow moment
of eternity, he felt nothing, and then something hard nudged
against his right foreclaw, a glint of bright metal flashِ d for
a second before his eyes. He changed his grip on what he

held, clamping down on it as firmly as his clumsy foreclaws
would allow—

—and with every ounce of strength that was left to him, he
drove the fore-part of the broken spear deep into the middle
of the ogre that sprawled above him.

The great body bucked and shuddered. A wild scream burst
from the idiot mouth alongside Jim's ear. The ogre let go,
staggered back and up, tottering to its feet, looming like the
Tower itself above him. Again, the ogre screamed, staggering
about like a drunken man, fumbling at the shaft of the spear
sticking from him.It jerked at the shaft, screamed again, and,
lowering its unnatural head, bit at the wood like a wounded
animal. The tough ash splintered between its teeth. It screamed
once more and fell to its knees. Then slowly, like a bad actor
in an old-fashioned movie, it went over on its side, and drew
up its legs like a man with the cramp. A final scream was
drowned in bubbling. Black blood trickled from its mouth
and it lay still.

Jim crawled slowly to his feet and looked about him.

The mists were drawing back from the plain and the first
thin light of late afternoon stretching long across the slope.
In its rusty illumination, Jim made out what was to be seen
there.

The Worm was dead, literally hacked in two. Nevile-Smythe,
in bloody, dinted armor, leaned wearily on a twisted sword not
more than a few feet off from Carolinus. A little farther off,
Secoh raised a torn neck and head above the intertwined,
locked-together bodies of Anark and Smrgol. He stared dazedly
at Jim. Jim moved slowly, painfully over to the mere-dragon.

Jim came up and looked down at the two big dragons.
Smrgol lay with his eyes closed and his jaws locked in
Anark's throat. The neck of the younger dragon had been
broken like the stem of a weed.

"Smrgol . . ." croaked Jim.

"No—" gasped Secoh. "No good. He's gone. . . . I led the
other one to him. He got his grip—and then he never let
go. . . ." The mere-dragon choked and lowered his head.

"He fought well," creaked a strange harsh voice which Jim
did not at first recognize. He turned and saw the Knight
standing at his shoulder. Nevile-Smythe's face was white as
sea-foam inside his helmet and the flesh of it seemed fallen in
to the bones, like an old man's. He swayed as he stood.

"We have won," said Carolinus, solemnly, coming up with

the aid of his staff. "Not again in our lifetimes will evil gather
enough strength in this spot to break out." He looked at Jim.
"And now," he said, "the balance of Chance and History
inclines in your favor. It's time to send you back."

"Back?" said Nevile-Smythe.

"Back to his own land, Knight," replied the magician.
"Fear not, the dragon left in this body of his will remember
all that happened and be your friend."

"Fear!" said Nevile-Smythe, somehow digging up a final
spark of energy to expend on hauteur. "I fear no dragon,
dammit. Besides, in respect to the old boy here"—he nodded
at the dead Smrgol—"I'm going to see what can be done about
this dragon-alliance business."

"He was great!" burst out Secoh, suddenly, almost with a
sob. "He—he made me strong again. Whatever he wanted, I'll
do it." And the mere-dragon bowed his head.

"You come along with me then, to vouch for the dragon end
of it," said Nevile-Smythe. "Well," he turned to Jim, "it's
goodby, I suppose, Sir James."

"I suppose so," said Jim. "Goodby to you, too. I—" Suddenly
he remembered.

"Angie!" he cried out, spinning around. "I've got to go get
Angie out of that Tower!"

Carolinus put his staff out to halt Jim.

"Wait," he said. "Listen. . . ."

"Listen?" echoed Jim. But just at that moment, he heard it,
a woman's voice calling, high and clear, from the mists that
still hid the Tower.

"Jim! Jim, where are you?"

A slight figure emerged from the mist, running down the
slope toward them.

"Here I am!" bellowed Jim. And for once he was glad of the
capabilities of his dragon-voice. "Here I am, Angie—"

—but Carolinus was chanting in a strange, singing voice,
words without meaning, but which seemed to shake the very
air about them. The mist swirled, the world rocked and
swung. Jim and Angie were caught up, were swirled about,
were spun away and away down an echoing corridor of
nothingness . . .

. . . and then they were back in the Grille, seated together
on one side of the table in the booth. Hanson, across from
them, was goggling like a bewildered accident victim.

"Where—where am I?" he stammered. His eyes suddenly

focused on them across the table and he gave a startled croak. "Help!" he cried, huddling away from them. "Humans!"

"What did you expect?" snapped Jim. "Dragons?"

"No!" shrieked Hanson. "Watch-beetles—like me!" And, turning about, he tried desperately to burrow his way through the wood seat of the booth to safety.

V

It was the next day after that Jim and Angie stood in the third floor corridor of Chumley Hall, outside the door leading to the office of the English Department.

"Well, are you going in or aren't you?" demanded Angie.

"In a second, in a second," said Jim, adjusting his tie with nervous fingers. "Just don't rush me."

"Do you suppose he's heard about Grottwold?" Angie asked.

"I doubt it," said Jim. "The Student Health Service says Hanson's already starting to come out of it—except that he'll probably always have a touch of amnesia about the whole afternoon. Angie!" said Jim, turning on her. "Do you suppose, all the time we were there, Hanson was actually being a watch-beetle underground?"

"I don't know, and it doesn't matter," interrupted Angie, firmly. "Honestly, Jim, now you've finally promised to get an answer out of Dr. Howells about a job, I'd think you'd want to get it over and done with, instead of hesitating like this. I just can't understand a man who can go about consorting with dragons and fighting ogres and then—"

"—still not want to put his boss on the spot for a yes-or-no answer," said Jim. "Hah! Let me tell you something." He waggled a finger in front of her nose. "Do you know what all this dragon-ogre business actually taught me? It wasn't not to be scared, either."

"All right," said Angie, with a sigh. "What was it then?"

"I'll tell you," said Jim. "What I found out . . ." He paused. "What I found out was not, not to be scared. It was that scared or not doesn't matter; because you just go ahead, anyway."

Angie blinked at him.

"And that," concluded Jim, "is why I agreed to have it out with Howells, after all. Now you know."

He yanked Angie to him, kissed her grimly upon her startled lips, and, letting go of her, turned about. Giving a final jerk to his tie, he turned the knob of the office door, opened it, and strode valiantly within.

THOMAS N. SCORTIA

Thomas N. Scortia is a former aerospace worker who began writing full-time in the early 1970s. Although much of his output is science fiction, his best-known work is a disaster novel (*The Glass Inferno*) which he co-authored with Frank M. Robinson and which formed much of the basis of the blockbuster film *The Towering Inferno*. Here, however, he is concerned with things on a quieter, smaller scale: childhood, dreams, and family relationships.

JOHN ROBERT AND THE DRAGON'S EGG

by Thomas N. Scortia

ON A warm sunny day in late June, John Robert walked through the dusty tobacco field of his Uncle Ben's farm toward the dirty white four-room farm house, carrying a dragon's egg wrapped in his faded blue denim shirt.

In all of his eight years he knew that nothing quite as wonderful had ever happened to him. Not even the time the merry-go-round truck had broken down in St. Basile in front of Beauchamp's General Store and the driver had let him peek at the enameled and gilded wooden horses through the heavy slats of their pine crates.

Not even the impossible joy of riding one of those great black and golden stallions could ever be quite as wonderful as this.

The first person John Robert saw, as he rounded the decaying double building that served as the chicken house and barn, was Grandpa Riley, sitting on the back porch, rocking and smoking his smelly black pipe.

"John Robert," the old man said, pulling his pipe from his mouth, "whut you doing 'thout your shirt on? You'll get your back blistered good and proper and then your Aunt Bess will really land on you."

"Ain't no fear o' that," John Robert said. "I'm good and brown already. See." He turned in a slow circle, exhibiting his back.

"Like plug tobacco," Grandpa agreed. "Whut you got in the shirt, John Robert?"

"It's a dragon's egg," John Robert said proudly.

"Do tell. Can't recollect ever seeing one o' them." The old man leaned forward in his rocker. "Unfold it and let's fetch a look," he demanded.

John Robert carefully folded back the layers of blue cloth.

The egg was about four inches long and looked very much like a large hen's egg except that its surface was wrinkled and glistened like wet leather.

"Huh, it's sort o' greenish," Grandpa Riley observed. "Where'd you get it?"

"Found it down in the swamp . . . on the bank in a sort o' mud nest."

"Better not tell your Aunt Bess. She tole you to stay away from that swamp. She'll whop you good."

"Don't tell Aunt Bess what?" Aunt Bess demanded as her thin form appeared at the sagging screen door and she stepped out, blinking into the sun.

"Now'll you catch it," Grandpa whispered.

"John Robert, whut you got in your nice clean shirt?" she demanded. John Robert saw her hands move to her hips in the familiar gesture of annoyance.

"Dragon's egg," he said in a small voice.

"Huh! More'n likely a dirty 'gator egg."

"It is not," he said. "They was tracks all around it. Big tracks with claws."

Aunt Bess frowned and Grandpa Riley started to move away.

"Dragon's tracks," John Robert added triumphantly.

" 'Gator tracks," Aunt Bess insisted. "Pa," she raised her voice, "you come back here and take this boy and make him get rid of that dirty egg."

"I was just gonna . . ."

"Never you mind. Get rid of that dirty egg." She opened the door and went into the kitchen, mumbling, "Where does that boy get such . . ."

"Pa," she called over her shoulder, "now mind." They heard her voice sink to an almost inaudible mutter of complaint.

"Well, John Robert," Grandpa Riley said. He shoved his pipe into his mouth so hard that John Robert heard it click against his store teeth.

"Do we have to?"

"Wouldn't dast keep it."

"I wanted to hatch it." John Robert bit his lip. "She don't need to know."

"Real dragon tracks, you say?" Grandpa Riley's voice sank to a whisper and the corners of his eyes crinkled.

"Uh, huh . . . With three toes and claws."

" 'Course, 'gator eggs is hard, not soft and wrinkly like

this'n." Grandpa paused in thought, then grabbed John Robert's arm and pulled him toward the deserted chicken house that leaned limply against the larger barn.

"Tell you what, John Robert," he said.

That evening at dinner John Robert sat silently opposite Grandpa Riley and slowly mashed the boiled potatoes into his plate with the worn fork and thought grand thoughts. Occasionally he would steal a secret look at Grandpa and think of the treasure wrapped carefully in layer on layer of flannel and hidden in a warm corner of the hen house.

Grandpa hadn't been sure if the egg needed warmth or whether it would hatch without extra heat as does a turtle's egg or an alligator's egg. However, since they had nothing to serve as an incubator, they had compromised on wrapping the egg in an old flannel nightshirt of Uncle Ben's and placing the bundle so that the sun would fall on the egg most of the day through one of the two windows in the hen house.

A kind of nervous excitement had seized John Robert and, though Aunt Bess complained tiredly at dinner to Uncle Ben, who had returned late from the cotton mill, John Robert scarcely heard her.

"Look at that boy," she fretted, "playing with his good food when prices is so high a body can barely make do." Uncle Ben gave a tired grunt and continued to eat. "He shore don't take after his ma and pa, God rest their souls, with him dreamin' and lazin' his time away. Why, would you believe it . . ."

And she was off on the incident of the dragon's egg. Grandpa Riley gave his daughter a pained look and attacked his food with new vigor.

Later, after the oil lamp had been lighted in the kitchen and they had washed and dried the dishes, John Robert sat on the porch, watching the glowing cinder of Grandpa Riley's pipe and listening to the creak of his rocker mingle with the shrill music of the crickets and the katydids. Uncle Ben sat inside at the kitchen table, reading his newspaper, while Aunt Bess, who never came out after dark because of the mosquitoes from the swamp, sat opposite him, sewing on the wedding ring quilt she was making. Occasionally, John Robert could hear her shrill voice raised in comment.

"Ain't Aunt Bess ever been happy?" John Robert asked.

"Well, I recollect she used to be different . . . maybe even a little like you, John Robert."

"Whut happened?"

Grandpa Riley sucked thoughtfully at his pipe.

"I guess she just grew up," he said.

They sat silently, savoring the heavy night air.

"Grandpa," John Robert asked at last, "where do dragons come from?"

"Oh, all places, John Robert."

"Where?"

"China, Japan, Araby, places you and me never even heard tell of. Maybe places nobody on this earth's heard tell of."

"Oh," John Robert was silent for a moment. Then he said, "Maybe he'll want to fly back there."

"Maybe . . . if he's the flyin' kind."

"Oh, he'll be the flyin' kind," John Robert insisted. "And maybe . . ."

"John Robert," Aunt Bess's voice pierced his words, "you get yourself in here and warsh them feet and get to bed."

John Robert spent the rest of the week in rising anticipation, stealing to the secret hiding place at every opportunity to observe the progress of the egg. It quickly became apparent that this was a very unusual egg indeed. For one thing the shell itself appeared to be elastic and, as the week progressed, the wrinkled surface filled out and the egg enlarged with surprising rapidity until it resembled a circus balloon, filled with water to the point of bursting. In addition, other, more startling changes became apparent.

"First time I ever seen an egg purple and gold," Grandpa Riley remarked with some excitement. The egg had indeed changed color from its original bilious green. By Friday the deepening shades of mottled purple and gold had assumed an iridescent sheen and the surface seemed to catch the light and throw it back into the eyes of the viewer in a rainbow shower of color.

"Like the wings of a butterfly," Grandpa observed. "Same color as a purple swallertail."

Aunt Bess noticed the increased tension and the furtive visits to the hen house. Since only the larger barn was still used and that only for storing a drum of kerosene for the household lamps, she demanded to know why John Robert and Grandpa Riley were "a-skulkin' around that place." For once Grandpa Riley managed to appear innocent under Aunt

Bess's sharp questioning and after a while she found something more immediate to occupy her thoughts.

The egg hatched on Sunday.

"Well," Grandpa admitted, "it sure ain't no 'gator."

"It ain't quite what I expected," John Robert said, holding the foot-long reptile in his lap and stroking it gently. The animal made a soft cooing sound every time his fingers brushed the soft fleshy ridge that ran from its forehead down its back to the tip of its tail. A tiny forked tongue darted out to brush John Robert's hand.

"Well, I told you he mightn't be the flyin' kind," Grandpa said.

"Maybe, these'll be wings." John Robert hopefully touched the filmy sac-like protrusions on each side of the fleshy ruff.

"Maybe," Grandpa admitted. "Whut'll we call him?"

"You 'member that book I used to have, the one with the green cover?"

Grandpa scratched his chin.

"You mean *The Laughing Dragon of Oz?*"

"That one. Let's call him Ozzie. You like that, Grandpa?"

"Uh, hm-m-m-m," Grandpa said thoughtfully. " 'Course, he'll have to grow some to fit that name."

Ozzie cooed indignantly.

"He'll get real big," John Robert said belligerently. "I know he will."

"Probably grow just like a weed, considerin' how fast the egg growed," Grandpa agreed. "Wonder what he eats?"

"People?" John Robert hazarded.

"Little small for that, don't you reckon? Anyway, don't know as how we could get any for him."

The problem of what to feed young Ozzie proved less difficult than they feared. John Robert tried him on carrots. Ozzie ate them, tops and all.

Grandpa tried potato peels. Ozzie munched them contentedly and then polished off the cardboard box in which Grandpa had smuggled them from the kitchen.

In rapid succession Ozzie demonstrated a taste for coffee grounds, buttons, hay, handkerchiefs, pipe tobacco and peanut butter and jelly sandwiches. He grew rapidly on this varied diet and by the end of the second week he was over three feet long from blunt nose to arrow-pointed tail.

The hen house was rapidly becoming too small to hold Ozzie, who, with increasing size, had become restless. John

Robert and Grandpa Riley discussed transferring him to the tool room in the rear half of the barn. This, of course, increased the hazard of Aunt Bess's stumbling onto their secret. The decision was finally forced upon them.

On Wednesday of the third week after the arrival of Ozzie, John Robert and Grandpa Riley sneaked into the hen house. Ozzie greeted them with a low bubbling moan. The cause of his anguish was easily discerned. He had devoured the lower six inches, nails and all, of three planks that made up one wall of the hen house.

"He sure has an appetite," John Robert observed. Ozzie rubbed his glistening back against John Robert's legs and groaned. He buried his muzzle in the boy's midsection and burped softly.

"Tarnation," Grandpa said, "ain't there nothing you won't eat?"

Ozzie eyed him reproachfully and his blunt head drooped.

"Tarnation," Grandpa Riley repeated, withdrawing his foot as Ozzie began to nibble on the leather of his left toe. From one scaly nostril dribbled the faintest wisp of gray smoke.

"That settles it," Grandpa said. "We'll have to use the tool shed and Bess be hanged if she finds out. Good thing the stone foundation comes up about four feet in back," he added, observing the smoke. "Wonder if he's going to start spurtin' fire?"

Ozzie was installed in his new home and, as his growth increased, John Robert and Grandpa Riley were increasingly thankful for the stone foundation of the barn. Ozzie, depending on his diet of the moment, would snort smoke and on occasion even small tongues of flame. With developing maturity, however, he showed no sign of the legendary fierceness of his kind. The growths on his back had enlarged to leathery sacs with the irregular appearance of wadded damp canvas. They did not share the shifting colors of his body, but remained a dirty gray. By the end of July they were as big as basketballs and growing daily. Ozzie was over fourteen feet long by then, a mottled golden, and increasingly difficult to contain in the tool room. It was inevitable that Aunt Bess should discover him.

It happened on the first Sunday of August, just a month before John Robert's scheduled return to school. Aunt Bess, still in her church dress and shoes, carried the old tin measuring cup with which she filled the oil lamps out to the barn

to get kerosene. John Robert and Grandpa Riley were standing warily on the porch, their fingers crossed, when they
heard a ragged scream which quickly choked into an inarticu-
late gurgle. Aunt Bess clawed her way through the double
doors of the barn. Her eyes were rolling wildly and she was
missing a shoe.

"It came through the wall," she wailed. "I was filling the
cup and it poked its head through the wall." She fell limply to
the porch as Uncle Ben thrust his head outside.

"What the Sam Hill's goin' on out here?" he demanded.

"There's a monster in the barn," Aunt Bess screamed. "It's
drinking my coal oil."

"Oh, my," said John Robert.

"Tarnation," said Grandpa and they ran for the barn.
Inside they found Ozzie, leaning against the drum of kerosene, his forked tongue darting out to pull in a growing
puddle under the open spigot. The fleshy ruff down his neck
was an inflamed brick red. He looked up as John Robert and
Grandpa Riley appeared and rumbled inquiringly.

"Get him outside before he burps," Grandpa yelled and
they circled to the rear of the dragon. John Robert nudged
him gently with his hands and then pushed harder. Ozzie
resisted feebly and then began to stumble for the open doors.

"Look," John Robert yelled, "he chewed his way right
through the wall."

"That ain't all," Grandpa said as Ozzie weaved into the
yard and Aunt Bess wailed another long sobbing wail. "The
critter's drank up every bit o' that coal oil."

They followed Ozzie into the open and quickly herded him
around the barn toward the open tobacco field. Just as the
dragon pushed through into the open field, he hiccoughed
wrackingly. Then he gave a monstrous burp. A six-foot jet of
smoky flame splashed down the furrows. Ozzie sank to the
rough ground and emitted a soft moan.

"Heh, heh," said Grandpa, "what a stomachache you're
gonna have."

"Stand back," Uncle Ben shouted, running around the
corner of the barn and flourishing a double-barreled shotgun
over his head. "Stand back whilst I blast the varmint."

"No," John Robert yelled.

"You'll do no such thing," Grandpa said, placing himself in
front of Uncle Ben's rush.

"Hic," Ozzie said and a thick oily cloud of smoke enveloped his head.

It was fully twenty minutes before John Robert and Grandpa Riley could persuade Uncle Ben that Ozzie was harmless. By that time the dragon had exhausted his charge of kerosene. Occasionally, he would give a low moan while a tendril of black smoke as from a dying fire would trickle from his nostrils.

"You mean that hellion's a pet?" Uncle Ben demanded.

"Yep," Grandpa said proudly. "John Robert and me hatched and raised him unbeknownst from an egg."

"He's real gentle. Honest," John Robert said. "Just kinda young."

"That critter young? Why, he'd make four horses."

"Just a pup, though," Grandpa insisted. "Only two months old."

"Whut you been feeding him? A cow a day?"

"Nope. Been on hay and grass for three weeks."

"Is it gone?" Aunt Bess asked, sticking her head around the barn.

She saw Ozzie and started to withdraw. Uncle Ben motioned her on.

"Come here, Bess," he commanded. "We got us an honest-to-bob dragon."

It rained that night for the first time in several weeks, a slow monotonous drizzle that collected in puddles in the backyard and turned the tobacco field behind the house into a soupy morass of yellow mud. John Robert and Grandpa Riley spent most of the evening after supper in the barn, ministering to Ozzie. The dragon was weak and shaken and his scales were a lusterless yellow. The enigmatic sacs on his back were pulsing feebly and they had become quite tender to the touch. At length Grandpa Riley was satisfied that they could do no more and they left Ozzie in a troubled sleep.

The next morning Uncle Ben announced that he was not going to work. Instead, he planned to be gone for several days on a trip to New Orleans to see a man whom he knew. Aunt Bess packed him a lunch in a shoe box and, after a whispered conversation in a corner of the kitchen with occasional glances in John Robert's and Grandpa's direction, she accompanied Uncle Ben to the door. Shortly thereafter, John Robert heard the coughing of Uncle Ben's aged pick-up truck recede into the distance.

At just a few minutes before ten, Grandpa Riley called John Robert to the barn.

"Real amazin'," he said as he ushered John Robert into the back. John Robert could scarcely believe his eyes. Ozzie was stretched out lazily on a mound of straw, basking in the sunlight that streamed through a window. The great sacs during the night had ruptured, releasing two membranous masses which, under the drying effect of the sun, were assuming form and rigidity.

"He is one of the flyin' kind," John Robert said ecstatically. "I told you so."

"Sure looks like it," Grandpa admitted.

After some conversation, they decided to brave Aunt Bess's displeasure and lead Ozzie into the yard to take better advantage of the sun.

The wings were large and rustled like wet leather when Ozzie moved. Under the open sun, they lost their early transparency and quickly became opaque, sharing the brilliancy of his scale coloration. By evening he was already making tentative flying motions and John Robert marveled at the great muscles that flexed in Ozzie's chest at each increasingly certain movement.

The evening meal was a silent one, full of tenseness and excitement. Aunt Bess sat silently opposite John Robert, her face strained and thoughtful.

"Bess, you're looking mighty nervous," Grandpa remarked.

"Well, who wouldn't with that thing out in the barn," she said, biting her lip.

"Now, Bess. Ozzie ain't no 'thing.' Just like a pet."

"Well, won't be no bother after this week," she said.

John Robert looked up from his plate in alarm.

"Whut's that supposed to mean?" Grandpa demanded.

"I ... well, you might as well know," Aunt Bess said slowly. "Ben says a dragon'd be worth a right smart to some folks. He's gone to see a circus man he knows. Figures we'll get enough maybe even to buy a new car."

John Robert jumped to his feet. "You can't do that," he protested. "Ozzie ain't yourn."

"Now, boy," Aunt Bess said nervously, "you got to look at it the practical way. Whut you want with a dragon anyway?"

"John Robert's right," Grandpa said. "Ozzie ain't yourn to sell."

"You keep still, Pa," Aunt Bess's voice became hard and firm. "Life's too hard for your and John Robert's fancy notions. Somebody's got to think of the bread and butter in this house. Besides, Ben's the head of the house. He pays the bills and I couldn't change his mind.

"Even if I wanted to," she added after a moment.

And she began to talk of the many fine things they would buy after they had sold Ozzie to the circus.

John Robert had little to say the rest of the evening. Several times he found Aunt Bess looking at him with the strangest expression on her face and he wondered what she must be thinking behind those silent eyes. He had never known her to be so silent and withdrawn. Her expression, he realized, seemed almost apologetic as though she were somehow a little sorry for what she was doing. But, if she felt any regret, he knew that this would not interfere with the harsh demands of her life that said Ozzie must be sold.

When bedtime finally arrived, he lay awake, tossing on his mattress on the kitchen floor. He could hear the creak of Grandpa's couch in the living room and he knew that the old man must be having as much difficulty as he in getting to sleep.

Finally he dozed, but he awoke again in the early morning before the dawn when the bright yellow light of the full moon fell through the kitchen window and on his lids. He lay, thinking of Ozzie in the barn and the sudden exciting freedom of his new wings. He saw him imprisoned in a circus cage, iron bars shutting him from the vastness of the upper air, and he felt sudden wetness on his lids.

A voice said, "Ps-s-t," and he sat up. Grandpa Riley was tiptoeing through the door, his shoes in his hands. He was fully dressed.

"Grandpa," John Robert demanded, "whut you doing up?"

"Not so loud," Grandpa shushed. "You know," he said in a low voice, "I been thinking."

"So have I," John Robert said. "About Ozzie. It ain't fair to him."

"John Robert," Grandpa said slowly, "there ain't really any place here for a young boy and an old man. Bess means well, but . . . Well, she don't see things the way you and me do."

"I know," John Robert said. "I like her and Uncle Ben, but she just don't seem to enjoy life any more."

"Maybe it's 'cause life's taken something out o' her," Grandpa said.

"You know," the old man said after a moment, "why don't you and me just take a little trip? They wouldn't miss us after a week or two."

John Robert jumped to his feet and began to pull on his clothes. They made their way silently through the moonlit yard to the barn. Ozzie awoke with a sleepy rumble and they led him outside.

"Think he can carry us both?" Grandpa asked.

" 'Course he can. Ozzie's the strongest dragon in creation."

They led him into the damp tobacco field.

"Needs a good long runway," Grandpa said. "Trifle muddy, though."

"Where'll we go?" John Robert laughed. "India? Araby?"

"Why, we'll go far away where no human's ever been before," Grandpa said. "He knows where."

They mounted, Grandpa in front, and held tightly to Ozzie's back. He sensed what was expected of him and eagerness poured into his body. The great muscles tensed, the clawed feet churned the muddy ground, found firm footing, and suddenly, with the smoothness of a skate slipping over ice, they soared up and up . . . over the tiny house and barn below, over the moon-flecked fields.

The wind whipped through John Robert's hair and he could barely breathe as he pressed himself forward against Grandpa Riley's thin frame.

"Egypt and Africa and Araby and all the faraway places where nobody but him and his kind know!" John Robert yelled into the wind. "What will Aunt Bess and Uncle Ben say?"

"They'll never tell anyone. Why, they won't ever guess the truth," Grandpa gasped, his voice whipping back into John Robert's ear.

"Oh, they will. They will. They'll know," John Robert shouted. "Look."

He pointed down below as they banked sharply and swooped back over the tiny house below. Even at their speed they could see clearly the line of heavy tracks that led into the moon-bright tobacco field, led into its very center and then mysteriously came to an end.

And they could even see the tiny human figure that stood by the house, her head turned upward, her eyes shaded by a bare arm.

"Goodbye!" Grandpa Riley yelled.

"Goodbye, goodbye, goodbye," John Robert called into the cold wind.

And below the small figure waved uncertainly—regretfully.

Then the field, the house, the dappled landscape of stippled fields and tiny buildings dissolved in a misty kaleidoscope of brilliant yellow as the great winged beast completed his turn and fled swiftly toward the already brightening east.

JANET FOX

Janet Fox is a graduate of the University of Kansas at Emporia who taught high school English for a number of years before deciding to try her hand at writing full-time. So far she had produced a novel and approximately a hundred stories, most of which are sword and sorcery or other types of fantasy. Her hobby is horseback riding, and that undoubtedly adds to the verisimilitude so strongly present in the following tale.

DEMON AND DEMOISELLE

by Janet Fox

ARCANA PULLED rein on a wooded mountainside and lifted her arm where the nervous falcon swayed heavily, clasping and unclasping his talons to steady his uncertain perch. His back and wing feathers were the sad color between blue and gray; his chest and legs were shadow-barred. She contemplated the vasty reach of sky for some moments and at last saw a pigeon flying. She hastily removed the black leather hood and the jesses and sent the falcon upward with an arm thrust and a cry. He climbed as if there were no such thing as gravity, and overtaking the pigeon in his speed, wheeled above it, windwalking. Just as he would have stooped to take the helpless bird in his talons, the falcon's body jerked, a few feathers drifting away on the wind. The great wings parachuted the fall, but to Arcana on the ground it took an inordinately long time for the body to fall to earth. She ran to where it lay among some trees and knelt beside the mound of rumpled feathers. Folly to think that one could be attached to a thing as stupid and rapacious as a bird of prey, but the beauty of its flight, the lofty power of it— The bird was transfixed by an arrow of ivory with peacock feathers on the end of the shaft; it looked like a decorative piece, not a weapon. She ran back into the open, to search for a bowman or fleeing horseman, but nothing moved on the mountainside. A dark wisp of hair by her ear moved, and she started, but decided that it was a gust of wind that had frightened her. Her huge black horse was pawing the earth, the feathers of his forelegs shaking like fine black fringe. "Sooo, Sable," she soothed him. "We're both spooked by nothing. Or we can hope it's nothing."

Sable's basin-sized hooves rattled the drawbridge and struck fire from the cobbles of the courtyard. She felt better when

245

the creaking machinery had lifted the bridge into a massive
wall behind her. She left the horse to the grooms and entered
the castle. She doubled herself as she entered, reflecting
darkly in the polished wood of the floor. Everything seemed
good, the blood-red hangings on the walls, the great hearth
blazing like Hell-Mouth, throwing off the chill of such a large
drafty room. Her Senechal Milston came in to personally
divest her of cloak and gauntlets.

"I watched you ride in just now as if someone pursued. And
where is your favorite, Windrider?"

Stony-visaged, Arcana dropped into a straightbacked chair
as large as a throne and every bit as uncomfortable. "He
was shot by—" her explanation halted while she rummaged
for mislaid reasons. "Some poacher hiding in the brush of the
mountainside," she finished lamely.

Milston said nothing, and drew his face into careful lines of
politeness, telling her that for all the world, he wouldn't pry.

"His wounds, Milston, of course it wasn't just any ordinary
poacher or huntsman. The arrow came from nowhere; I
misdoubt me it was shot from a bow at all. And it isn't just
that; a kind of dread haunts my bones like an ague. I must to
the tower."

The tower, in contrast to the chambers below, was a cold
and barren place. Spiders had left samples of their craft in
niches of the bare rock walls and rats' droppings collected in
the concave risers of the stone stairway. She produced a huge
iron key from inside her clothing, opened the massive lock
and let herself into the single round room where she practiced her craft. Yellowing scrolls and books with moldering,
flaking bindings were shelved along the walls. Bottles and
jars filled with questionable substances of every color and
texture filled the interstices between the books. On a rickety
wooden table an iron-bound book lay open to reveal slanting
lines of spidery black handwriting and a scrying glass half
filled with water. Alongside these was a toad, looking very
dry and petrified. Set in his back among the warty excrescences
of his skin was a red jewel, filled with fiery light. When she
moved the book the ancient toad hopped off silently, toadwise.

With a bit of charcoal she drew the pentagram on the
stones of the floor, recoloring a faded design that had often
been drawn there. Lighting five candles she placed them at
the corners of the pentagram and began the ritual, referring
now and again to the open book on the table. Sometime later

she dropped onto a wooden bench, pushing dark strands of hair off her damp forehead. Stolidly she rose to try again, because she had never failed at this before. Moments later the scrying glass and the book went flying off the table, one to splash and shatter on the stones, the other to fetch up against the wall, a broken black wing. "God's Little Body!" she swore. "Hrinegar, do you know aught of this?"

A small melancholic voice came from the floor and the aged toad hopped in its silkily silent progression, pausing at the sorceress' feet. "Mayhap your demon has been ensorceled by another mage."

"But that demon was the only one I could summon. It took years of study and experimentation to produce him. Without him, I can't even call myself sorceress. Who did it; do you know?"

"No, but if you hadn't acted in such haste, you may have scryed something on the matter."

"I'm too choleric to concentrate on that now."

"Then perhaps you don't care to know."

She gritted her teeth for a moment, then found another glass goblet and poured some water into it. Scrying consisted mainly of hours of staring and wasn't among Arcana's favorite activities, but she bent dutifully over the glass, and when she felt that her eyes were frozen in their sockets, an image began to form in the midst of clear water.

"I see," she said in a carefully controlled voice, so as to maintain her concentration.

"What do you see?" asked the toad peevishly (though everything he said sounded peevish).

"A face, old, more than old, seamed and eroded, hanks of greasy gray hair hanging about a bald pate, a nose long and drooping as an icicle, but his eyes—"

"Yes?"

"His eyes make it seem as if he is wearing a mask. They glow with the hot-bloodedness of youth, yet they also seem to be looking out of some other, unwholesome world." Her voice grew more excited. "In his hands he holds an ivory arrow. He's our man, but—who is he?"

"I should not tell you," said the toad in a voice more dismal (if that were possible) than heretofore.

"Why not? He has my demon and I want him back."

"That's why I dare not tell you, a neophyte, a beginner, a rank—"

"Of course you'll tell me, Hrinegar, old familiar." She stooped to grab him and he punished her toadfashion by wetting copiously.

She made a disgusted noise and dried her hands on the legs of her hunting costume. "But you *will* tell me." She grabbed him more carefully this time, and his skinny old legs thrashed comically.

"Ascarius, you fool, Ascarius. He has been an archimage longer than you have been a human, longer than I have been a toad, longer than the oak-giant in the forest has been a tree. He has read all the old books. He has written some of them before reading them. He commands seven demons!"

"Eight," she said, putting Hrinegar carefully onto the floor where he loped silently away, his stone spitting sparks. "That cony-catcher has preyed off his fellow mages for the last time. I'll to his keep and teach the old dodderer a lesson."

Arcana paused before the drawbridge, the massive head of the shire, Sable, poised above her shoulder as she pulled on her gauntlets. Though she had looked slim and feminine in the close-fitting hunting garb, with her long hair plaited, she now looked bulky in a leathern vest and thick broidered cloak, and beneath the flat cap her hair hung in bluntly cut tufts. Mil had suggested if she had to go, she go in the guise of a wandering scop. He had even found a battered old lute and hung it over her shoulder. He had done a good job disguising her, but still he hemmed and hawed and invented excuses to detain her.

"I'm pleased to know you fear for me," said Arcana, "but there's no need. Do you doubt my horsemanship?"

"Of course not, my Lady."

"Is it my skill with lance, with bow or dagger?"

"Oh no, my Lady."

"Then what is it?"

"Your cooking, my Lady. Take no offense, but I am afraid you may fall ill. Have you taken sufficient provisions?"

Arcana swung up and signaled the man on the parapet. "I'll worry about you, too," she said. "If the villagers below realize that I'm devoid of power, they'll arrange a torchlight procession and come up to tear apart my keep, stone by stone."

"We'll keep up appearances as long as possible. God speed."

"Fare thee well, Milston."

* * *

Many and many the miles Arcana rode in rain and sun.
And too diverse and blood-chilling were her adventures, up
hill and down dale, to tell the whole of them, but after her
travels had left her seasoned and wisened, she came to an inn
to pass the night.

As she prepared to enter she heard a terrible din. She
sidestepped a human projectile that careened out the door.
Waiting until the noise had subsided, she entered cautiously,
her hand on the hilt of her dagger. A ruffian was curled in a
corner in a posture too awkward for sleep. Another lay
beneath a table, his jerkin soaked with blood; luckily most of
it was streaming from his nose. She flattened herself against
the wall as a mace was slammed onto a heavy oaken table
with a rending crash. The man in armor dominated the room
like a monster of metal, but he clattered and clanged as he
swayed unsteadily.

A man hiding beneath a table waved her away. "He's taken
leave of his senses. Too much strong drink."

The man in armor began to growl deep in his throat as he
yanked at the mace, now inextricably one with the wood of
the table. "For the Holy Rood!" he bellowed. "Onward to the
grail."

Arcana began to move crabwise along the wall, but any
movement was a mistake. The night bore down on her like a
juggernaut. "Avaunt, pagan dog!"

The grid of a visor was thrust into her face, and a tang of
ale was wafted toward her. "Who be you, stranger?"

"Arcan, a scop, teller of thrilling tales of bold knights
and—" She thrust the lute between herself and him. His
metal glove plucked the strings with a discordant sound.

"By Saint Allidore, I'll hear some of your drivel, and it had
best be good."

Since in her travels she had neglected to learn to play the
instrument she banged the strings once or twice and began to
sing-song a tale that she devised on the spot. It was mostly
utter nonsense about a faithful knight and his lady who
sickened and died.

"Oh, my heart is broken. Oh my heart is sore. Verily,
verily, now I shall die," she finished, giving the lute a strum
for good measure. Having been caught up in her own creation,
she looked up to see how the crazed knight was taking it.

"Oh my heart is sore," echoed the knight. "That's the

saddest, most beautiful tale that ever I heard." He slumped onto a bench with a clang, his visored head resting in a pool of ale, his shoulders heaving.

"Thanks, stranger," said the hiding man, coming up to clap her on the shoulder.

"Verily," chimed in another who had been crouched by the hearth. "He'll be all right now. Simply boyish high spirits."

"Spirits of some type. Are any of you the innkeeper? I wish lodging for the night."

The knight lifted his head from the table and removed his helmet, displaying a pair of bleary blue eyes in a smiling red-bearded face. "You can share my room this night," he said, "for you cooled my madness with your song, and I fain would hear more of your tales."

"I must needs refuse this gentle offer."

What seemed a half ton of metal descended on her shoulders and she was dragged down an ill-smelling corridor and deposited half crushed in a dimly lit room.

The knight began noisily to remove his armor. "Help me, man, my squire is one who lies in the tavern bleeding."

Arcana unbuckled the greaves from his shins while he divested himself of the rest, tossing it into a dully gleaming pile on the floor.

"Make yourself comfortable, Sirrah. The bed's got plenty of room. I told the landlord if there're lice in it, I'll spit him like a capon."

"I'm comfortable as I am." Arcana lay back on the rustling straw mattress and watched as the night set up a tiny shrine and knelt before it.

A few moments later the bed creaked *in extremis* and the knight shouldered her aside. She was uncomfortable, but not too afraid, as he didn't seem the type to molest boys.

"A knight must never forget his spiritual duties. My name is Ethelred of Ironcastle, but they call me Quickspur."

"Well met," said Arcana.

"Where are you bound, balladeer?"

"Where the wind takes me."

"By Allidore's sainted relics, why not accompany me on my travels? You're a singer in search of songs, so why not celebrate me?"

"Why not indeed." Arcana felt laughter overcoming her. Would he spit her like a capon if he heard her laugh?

"There are sure to be adventures amany because my quest

takes me to the keep of a terrible magician, Ascarius. He holds captive the loveliest of maidens, Ermintrude, daughter of Lord Tabor. If I can rescue her, I shall receive her hand in marriage, though I know I am unworthy to touch the hem of her gown. A knight must adore his lady chastely, from afar."

Arcana had stopped shaking with laughter. "I'd be honored to accompany you, and to compose a saga at least of your victory over Ascarius." *And my own,* she added silently.

"Dragonslond," said Quickspur, gesturing toward a landscape of rocks and broken hills and stringy vegetation. The very trees were wind twisted and ugly as if the land itself were cursed. Arcana saw a goat-footed unicorn atop a shaft of stone, but when she tried to point it out, it was gone. They passed a massive circle of standing stones and had an argument over it, Quickspur asserting that it had been raised by giants in the youth of the world, Arcana theorizing that such heavy stones could only be magicked into place; she suggested the magic of sound.

"Maybe they were whistled into place," said Quickspur, laughing at her.

"Hsst, I hear something. It sounds like the clink of mail— perhaps we are pursued by robbers."

"If so, it'll be the last time they molest honest men."

"No, look!"

It continued its slow majestic progress across their field of vision, its taloned feet splaying under its great weight, the scales of its sides chinking and clinking as it walked, its pointed tail drawing a wide straight track behind it. The sunlight shivered off the scales, dark green, black, and bronze, here and there a glint of sapphire, a shimmer of ruby. Their horses began to dance and snort. The dragon turned his massive head in their direction, nictitating membranes flipping down over his lizard's eyes with chitinous click. A hiss issued from his maw and a dribble of smoke leaked out. A golden crest on head and shoulders began to rise.

"Let us flee," suggested Arcana. "Our horses are surely fleeter of foot than this weighty beast."

"Nonsense. Stand clear now."

"S'wounds, you're not going to—"

"Watch carefully, you'll want to chronicle this." Quickspur put spurs to his charger's sides and galloped toward the dragon, his lance at the ready. Arcana saw the dragon's corded belly flash icy-white as the thing reared up housetop high, towering over Quickspur and his tiny lance. Sparks began to shoot sideways from the jaws of the terrible worm, and as he huffed, a spurt of flame danced out, blasting the ground in front of Quickspur's horse's forefeet. The horse squalled and wheeled, Quickspur grabbing onto his neck. Somehow he managed to keep his seat and steer the crazed horse around to attack the dragon from the side, but his lance broke against the glittering scales, and the impact sent him flying to the ground, where he lay as helpless as an overturned lobster.

Arcana screamed and reined Sable forward. As Quickspur lay there kicking his feet, the dragon went after his horse. It moved lizard-swift for all its bulk and landed on the fleeing animal with splayed forefeet, bearing it to the ground. The great jaws closed on the horse's head, flames licking from its clamped jaws and a terrible smell of burnt flesh filling the air. Arcana reached Quickspur and tried to lever him up, but he was too heavy, and the dragon was returning at an impossibly rapid trot. "Stay down," she called and began to run, racing in a zig-zag pattern as she kept in mind the jetting flames. She was not quite quick enough, however, because a stream of fire spurted between her elbow and ribs, charring her vest and setting her sleeve on fire. But she had reached her goal, a sloping ridge of loose rock, larger boulders looming toward the top. She scrambled up it, ignoring the bruises to her ankles and shins. For a moment she crouched there in the sliding talus and beat out the flames on her clothing, while the monster bellowed and shot a stream of flame that crackled just out of reach. Then she began to climb again, almost too hastily, for she fell full length and began to slide down. With an effort that left her trembling with exhaustion, she found firm purchase for her feet and climbed to the top where boulders perched on layers of loose rock.

She put her shoulder behind one and pushed. She felt something break and prayed it was nothing of hers. She toppled herself backward as the whole hillside tore loose and fell to meet the dragon just as he was valiantly trying to climb the shaly slope. When she peered over the ridgetop the rock was bearing him down, and then with a muted roar, covered him completely, a dust-haze obscuring the scene.

For a moment she held her breath, thinking to see him digging out, but the largest stones must have done their

work. When she returned to Quickspur, she noticed that the
squire had taken to his heels. They were never to see him
again.

Arcana righted Quickspur as best she could so that he
could rise. He enfolded her in metallic embrace until she
cried out because of her burns. "For a singer of idle tales you
gave that dragon short shrift, but I didn't know if your plan
would work. If those rocks hadn't fallen—"

"I whistled them down."

Toward evening the wind came up blowing rain, so they
had to seek shelter in a cave. Arcana was afraid it might be a
dragon's den, but Quickspur insisted, so being too tired to
argue, she went inside. The entrance led through a narrow-
walled tunnel so dark she had to feel her way along damp
walls with her hands. In the darkness she suddenly felt
herself grabbed and held; a hand grabbed her jaw, twisted
her head around, then someone kissed her, full and forcefully
on the lips, a tongue warm and wet forcing itself between her
jaws. She was struggling when someone ran into her from
behind, and suddenly she was fighting nothing.

"What's wrong? Did you hear another dragon?" Quickspur's
voice matter-of-factly innocent.

Arcana stumbled forward. *Maybe he knows,* she thought, *or
maybe I was wrong. Maybe he likes boys.* But when they
reached a larger chamber of the cave, a dry and dragonfree
place, Quickspur lay chastely beside her.

"I have heard that Ermintrude is truly lovely—a goddess.
How dare that old lecher— My blood boils to think of it. I'll
carry her from the castle and be her humble slave forever. By
the bye, Arcan, if you compose a lay on our dragonslaying, I
hope you, uh, don't mention—"

"I'll sing of your triumph over the worm so that generations
will remember it," said Arcana, "but not now. I'm too sore,
and too tired."

"I'll recompense you for this, friend," said Quickspur, and
the arm about her shoulder was nothing but comradely.

Dragonslond dropped behind them, and they rode into a
greener, more wholesome country. They rode up to the door of
a country inn, looking like two scarecrows. The proprietor
ushered them inside where there was steaming food served
by red-cheeked peasant girls. "I knew I was missing some-

thing," said Quickspur, pinching a round bottom through voluminous homespun skirts. When Arcana gave him a scathing look he said confidingly, "There's something overdainty about you, lad. No offense, but it's time soneone helped you become more of a man."

"I'm as much man as I'll ever be, or need to be," said Arcana testily around a rare joint of meat that trickled bloody juices down her chin. "And what of your knightly vows of chivalry—chastity and reverence for womankind."

Quickspur looked wounded. "I have all proper reverence for ladies, beautiful ladies, high-born ladies, but these are tavern wenches. List while I give you a fatherly word on what to do with one of them."

Quickspur leaned over and whispered in her ear while she listened with narrowed eyes, a corner of her mouth turning up ever so slightly, as if she didn't know whether to laugh or to sneer.

"Oh, they might scream bloody murder, but it's the right thing to do. It's what they want after all." He began to work on his joint of meat, his eyes still on the serving girls.

Washed and wearing new clothes and lying back on a real bed, Arcana was feeling halfway human again and trying to plan a strategy that took into account Ascarius' power and Quickspur's impetuosity and her own cleverness, when the door began to vibrate as a booted foot was swung against it. "What can the dolt want now? If he wants to sleep in here I'll barricade the door. If he wants a song about his manly prowess with serving wenches I'll— Stop, you lout. You're splintering the door. Wait a moment and I'll open— Bodikins! No!"

Quickspur had knocked on the door with his foot because he had a serving girl under each arm. Arcana tried to slam the door but he was already striding inside. "This one's for you." He dropped half his burden on the bed, where she dissolved into giggles, hiding her red face with her hands.

"Remember the instructions I gave you, yearling. I'll have you strutting out of here like a gamecock."

"But I don't—"

"Someone must take you in hand, lad." He went out, closing the door securely. She heard the sound of a heavy piece of furniture being dragged against it.

The girl on the bed was now peeking coyly from between her fingers.

"This is going to be very difficult to explain," said Arcana, perching daintily on the edge of the bed. When she saw the flirting expression on the girl's face, she knew that explanation of any kind was impossible, so she untied the thongs of her vest and pulled up her jerkin.

Now that the stunned serving girl was open to explanations, Arcana told her everything and gave her a silver coin for the tale she was to relate to Quickspur on the morrow. "I don't suppose you play cards," said Arcana, producing a cunningly painted ivory deck from her waistband. "No? Well, I shall teach you—"

As they rode on their way the next day Arcana often found Quickspur looking at her surreptitiously. As they sat by their fire that night, he said, "That girl told me a story that curled my toes, but spill my spirit, if there's still not something girlified about you. The way the call of nature sends you skittering off behind rock or bush. Overnice, I call it. Mayhap—"

Arcana said no word in protest nor explanation; but rolled up in her cloak beside the pink coals of their fire. Wolves reminded them that the night was dark and this country lonely, but not even fear could stave off sleep.

She awoke from a dream in which someone was trying to ravish her. She had confused it somehow with the wolves' howls she had heard the evening before, and she fancied that sharp teeth had worried her neck and shoulders while blunt hands had touched and pawed at her breasts. She drew in her breath in a gasping half-scream and sat up. The thongs of her vest were untied, her jerkin rutched up as if her dream had come real. *No, I only struggled so in my dream to dislodge my clothing. Such a thing is nonsense* (or magic, insinuated a distant voice in her mind which she conveniently ignored). As she put her hand on her neck, she felt the stinging as of salt in a wound. When she looked at her hand there was a dull red smudge of blood on it. Beside where she slept in the moist earth was left, more a signature than a true spoor, one clear imprint of a wolf's paw. She erased it quickly with her hand.

Green land began to give way to black rock, scarps and canyons shelving ever upward, and at last they saw, bathed in a blue luminous haze that made it seem to float, Ascarius' keep set on a pinnacle of dull black rock. Sunlight drew streaks of light along its walls as if by some magic, the material had become vitrified. Only a narrow trail spiraled upward, easily defended, yet no defender appeared and they climbed with impunity, wind licking at their hair and the manes of the horses.

"Don't you have the feeling that the castle rises even as we climb toward it?" asked Quickspur.

"Yea, and looking down seems to confirm it. The ground is leagues away now. Perhaps we were rash—"

Hard fingers began to tickle her, and she struggled to be free of them and almost fell out of Sable's saddle and all that vast way to the ground. The same invisible hands kept her from falling and straightened her in the saddle. A moist whisper in her ear began to make obscene suggestions.

Another voice speaking from the air beside them interrupted. "Welcome to my domain. It has been most amusing, watching your futile struggles to arrive here, and there will be more festivities to come, I promise." Arcana saw light like blue needles surround Quickspur, his horse, shooting from Sable's bowed neck, from the fingers of her hands. And she could not move. Though her perceptions still seemed to work, she felt as if time had stopped for her, the wind frozen against her face. She knew that, if Ascarius chose, he could keep them thus for always, as the daystar dimmed to a pitted fire-coal, as the cliffs eroded, lost their diamond edges and collapsed into soft black earth. As she was possessed by this knowledge, she felt herself floating airy as a bubble (and as fragile). She didn't know about Quickspur, for her perceptions were fading as she floated upward, so lightly as if she would bump gently against the translucent blue porcelain of sky.

The floating sensation was gone, and she felt immensely heavy at first, but was immediately glad to have her senses, her mind and her body returned to her. She was sitting in a large chair, the arms of which were carved (or so she thought) in the likeness of serpents. As she watched, the coils twitched and writhed, twining about her arms. Ascarius was sitting in a companion chair (the arms static) opposite her, looking much as he had in the scrying glass, except immensely pleased with himself. His fingers fumbled in air for a moment as if seeking something lost in a pouch, and he retrieved a heavy golden goblet. "Drink this," he said, "a draught of reviving wine." When she looked down at her hands he made another gesture so rapidly his fingers seemed to blur and the serpents straightened into chair arms again. To gain time she sipped the wine slowly and tried to engage the sorcerer in conversation.

"Foolish, foolish. You should have realized when I pirated your demon that my magic is superior to yours. Oh we shall have some good games together, games of cat and mouse, of falcon and pigeon."

"I wish you'd call off your bedamned incubus. I can still feel him hovering around, breathing on me."

"Oh, he's taken quite an interest in his work. He finds you very exciting."

"All things considered, I can't say I'm flattered." She made a gesture as if to remove something repellent, something clinging.

"We mustn't spoil his diversion."

"At least you could release Quickspur. He won't afford you any amusement."

"On the contrary. I'm sure he will be vastly entertaining on the field of combat." He waved his hand and an armored knight strode into the room, his joints creaking maddeningly. But there was something wrong about the sound, the way he moved. Suddenly the visor flipped up with a clang, opening upon empty air. "I ween he will find this a true test of his knighthood. Unfortunately, the end of the tourney is in no doubt; he'll find no vulnerable spot in this perfect knight." The suit stalked out, inhabited by nothing more than an implacable sense of purpose.

"What of Ermintrude? She's done nothing to cause harm."

"Oh no, nothing to cause harm. Oh no." A wild look came into the magician's eyes. "She's securely behind walls and will stay so. I will admit I blundered in bringing her here, but how was I to know? Oh she's quite safe, quite safe. And now, I give you the freedom of my castle. Unfortunately, it's not untenanted, in fact, it's crowded, with my demons." He made himself disappear, from the feet up, in a leisurely way that made Arcana fume with jealousy. Some day she might have learned to do that, if she hadn't gone out willy-nilly, like a certain hotheaded knight.

No sooner was Ascarius gone than she felt a body pressing against her own, lips set delicately, lingeringly, against her throat and clever fingers working at the fastenings of her clothing. The hands were clinging and pervasive; she felt a

far-off languor stealing toward her. When she closed her
eyes, the body felt solid enough. Eyes squeezed shut, she
kicked. And was rewarded by a solid connection with flesh
and bone and a muffled grunt of pain. He had been too
involved in his games to dematerialize. Still in darkness, she
located the clinging, stroking hands, caught them by solid
wrists, and tore them from her, pushing herself away in a
stumbling run. Once into the corridor she ran to more purpose, hearing hollow footsteps pursuing.

Along the passageway there was a narrow, doorless opening; she almost missed it in her flight. Wheeling around she
fled into it and almost found herself falling upward against a
flight of naked stone steps that led steeply and crookedly
upward.

"If there's a donjon above, that may be where he's imprisoned Ermintrude." She climbed. This seemed to be an odd
time to be thinking of rescuing someone else, but her head
buzzed and sputtered and she found it hard to think logically.
There had been a note of ... something ... in Ascarius'
voice when he spoke of the Demoiselle, and he had said she
was "safely" imprisoned. She fetched up against a great
wooden door banded in metal. A tiny slot at eye level allowed
her to peer inside. She saw a girl of pale, ethereal beauty,
tight golden ringlets standing around her head in a filmy
halo, her dress of yellow silk drooping petal-like around her
as she sat, chin on fist, beside a barred window. One heavy
wooden bar held the door, and Arcana tried to force it
upward. At last she worked it free, worrying that her strength
appeared to be waning and wondering why she should feel so
drained and listless.

As she entered the cell, Ermintrude looked up out of
immense glassy blue eyes. "Who are you, Good Sir?"

"I've come to release you."

"Oh bless you." Her eyes shimmered, magnified by tears. "I
don't know why Ascarius was so mean to lock me up here in
this cold metal place when he knows I'm too weak and
helpless to do him any harm. I was as nice to him as I knew
how to be, both to him and to that nice friend of his that
nobody can see; well, this is how he treats me."

Arcana looked around and saw that indeed the prison was
sheathed in plates of lead. She couldn't imagine why, but it
was getting harder for her to link one thought with another.

"I thank you prettily, Good Young Sir. Though I had

waited and hoped that a gallant knight—no matter." She
made a little curtsey.

"There is a knight below," said Arcana, "who came to
rescue you."

"How *exciting!*" She put her hands together in front of her
face.

"Come, we'll search for him together." Arcana ran her
hand across her eyes, for she had gone through a mesh of
cobwebs and her vision was burning and blurring. Odd, but
there were no strands of cobweb there. "Drugged wine!" she
shouted aloud. "For sooth, I am a very babe in Ascarius'
sight." Ermintrude was descending the staircase, a dollop of
sunlight, growing larger, growing smaller. Arcana teetered
at the top of the stairs and would have gone toppling over
except that someone caught her and swung her up, one arm
under her shoulders, one under her knees. Surefootedly he
descended the stairs. "Safe," she thought and her eyes opened.
No one carried her; she floated on empty air like a conjurer's
trick. She could see no face but that didn't stop her from
tearing it with her nails. There was a stifled yelp, and with a
jolt, she found herself sitting on the floor. She scrambled to
her feet and began to run, but it was in the way one runs in
dreams, drenched in fear-sweat over something, one knows
not what, that always pursues, and feet sliding through leaden
sliminess, trying one's best to run, but going nowhere.

She found herself running more freely and shouted in
exhilaration. The walls of the passage narrowed and burned
with a velvet violet light. She burst through into noonday,
feeling light as air and unencumbered, floating upward, but
why—? She stopped, looking backward (and downward) in
her flight. She became confused to see her heavy earthen
body, lying in a crumpled posture, the mouth slackly open,
the eyes closed. But why such a clumsy body of dull earth-
bound hues when she saw herself milky pale and filled with
coruscating light of rainbow color? She was so light she could
bound above the trees. She looked more closely as she passed
over their branching tops, but they were not tree-like at all,
but had a cauliflower texture and were dusted with a glistening greenish powder that gave them a fungoid appearance.

Below, something invisible was lifting the body and bearing it away. She would have thought she had died except that
the mouth and hands moved in drunken protest. And she
could feel herself (when she concentrated on it) being carried.

So she was not dead, only separated. And she remembered being in this state once before while experimenting with a potion she had read of in a scroll half-eaten by worms. Ascarius had played the fool this time, for she was in demonland and free of her clinging earth-shape, but not totally free, for she could feel herself being lowered to the softness of a bed.

She seemed to need no direction in this land where fungoid trees rose in minutes, collapsing as rapidly, falling in upon themselves with a gust of shining green powder, beneath an immense red sun that stood always at noon, casting down a shadowless light. She met a shape like a wavering pillar of smoke. "Arcana, I never thought to see you again."

"Ungratefulness, I call it," she said, hovering over him, an opalescent light now and again sending out a streamer of anger.

The smokewisp shrugged, though without shoulders it was hard to recognize the gesture. "How could I help it? His magic overshadows yours. Even out of the body when you meet him mind to mind, he will surely defeat you."

In this shadowless land a dim coolness slid over them and looking above Arcana saw a great black cloud gathering, lightning playing along its flanks.

In the real world her clothes were being removed garment by garment, invisible hands gloating over the bare flesh. She felt herself struggle weakly, held in the jesses of the drug, then she shrugged it off her consciousness as a horse twitches away a fly.

Ascarius was speaking from the cloud, "I did not know you could go out of the body with such facility. I meant only to allow my demon a little pleasure. I would have watched with interest. But perhaps this is better—mind against mind, demon against demons." The innards of the cloud swirled as if it were birthing a tornado. "Who? How? Don't look at me so out of those cow eyes. Stop making them go so blank, and for the gods' sakes suck in that pouting rosy little lip."

"It's the thing," said the Demon.

"Thing?" said Arcana with a dawning awareness.

"I don't know what it is, really, a geas, perhaps. It is a terrible blank chaos that works to suck up Ascarius' power like a sponge."

"Come now, Child, I'm not really an 'old meanie.' Let me return you to your tower room. Don't dart about so!"

Arcana shot upward into the center of the thundercloud. Mind clashed against mind, and she felt an alien chill, tasting the length of his life, the *otherness* of it. Fear flashed and anger rumbled, and Arcana felt his wrath strike her like acid rain, burning, pitting, scarring, so that she knew after this battle she would be irrevocably changed.

The demon's lips made snail tracks across her breasts, his hands ran like fiery silk along her thighs. Chemically cocooned in anger and pleasure, she could only move as in a bad dream.

Her mind felt Ascarius' death grip weaken, and she reaffirmed her own more solidly. "Truce!" he called then. "You yellow-headed witch, I am destroyed!"

Arcana did not dare trust him in a truce, not when his power so overtowered her own. Her teeth were on his windpipe and she could not let go.

"Treachery!" he said in the thinnest of wind sounds, for he was dispersing, boiling, disappearing, and the red sun was burning through his grimy tatters.

Arcana's Demon backed away from the scarlet helix that had been coiling around and through him, and watched it, too, disappear. She and the Demon did a floating, bounding dance of joy. Then she remembered herself: "The incubus!"

"We can dispel him now," suggested the Demon.

"We can't leave me in a state like that," said Arcana. "No, we'll have to let him finish, and—"

Like a shapeless bird she dived downward, through enclosing gloom, through the violet fires, entering with a wrenching click in time to experience the penultimate madness, the violent release, the floating warmth.

Awakening later, all in one piece, she watched light and shadow moving on the ceiling. She was alone, the incubus dispersed. She began to collect things that were scattered, her cast-aside clothing littering the floor. She collected Ermintrude, who was still asking what had happened to the eccentric old granther with the fetching eyes. Unfortunately, or fortunately (who ever knew?), Ermintrude's wits were permanently fled to the four winds and could never be gathered. They went out into the courtyard, fearful that Quickspur's limbs would be what must needs be gathered next. He lay on the cobbles, as one dead, his armor sorely dented, but upon surveying the scene, Arcana saw lying here and there the component parts of Ascarius' perfect knight. Quickspur sat up suddenly, pushing up his visor. "He wasn't human, but I kept bashing away at him till one part fell off and then another. He was a hell of a fightingman, I thought, till I found out there wasn't anyone in there at all, just a suit of armor that walked like a man."

At that point he saw Ermintrude, her small hands clasped in adoration and the most appalling blankness in her blank blue eyes. "My lady," he intoned, rising only to kneel at her feet. He gingerly picked up the hem of her skirt and pressed it to his lips. "I know I am all unworthy to touch a hair on your lovely head or to beg a smile from your pearl-like teeth, but if you'll allow it, I'll return you to your father, defending you to the death, if need be."

Arcana sat in a dank chamber of the catacombs where Ascarius practiced his sorcery. She banged the lute and chanted in a nasal voice. "Oh my heart is laden. Oh my heart is full of—"

"Oh my ears are broken," echoed a still small voice above the faded pentagram that Ascarius had chalked on the floor. "Fair Demoiselle, is your heart fully broken?"

She felt for it, as to check if it were still pumping. "I think not. But to think that Quickspur—that lout will depart not even knowing that I am a woman and that I lay next to him all those nights we searched so long. If I told him now it would naught but scare him out of his iron pants. Besides, he has eyes for her only."

"Her eyes are mirrors in which he sees himself as he wishes to be seen. Have you any sorceries as strong as that?"

She twanged the lute at him, snapping a string that curled up in a discordant sound. "That incubus—he couldn't have been you by any chance?"

Muted retching sounds.

"I was wondering, but— Good, we shall pack up all Ascarius' books, gredients and magicks. I will learn all that he knew, and then—"

"You will attempt to rule the world," said the Demon approvingly. "To control the ocean tides and the four winds."

"I was thinking more of summoning the incubus."

The Demon reeled out pale tentacles of angry smoke as she dived behind a workbench, her sardonic laughter hanging demonlike in empty air.

ANNE MCCAFFREY

Anne McCaffrey is an American who has lived for several years in Ireland. She has written a wide variety of fantasy and science fiction, but her most popular works are a series of science fantasy stories about the remnants of an earth colony who have formed a symbiotic relationship with Pern's indigenous population of dragonlike creatures in order to battle a common enemy. These adventures include *Dragonflight*, *Dragonquest*, *Dragonsong*, *Dragonsinger*, and *The White Dragon*.

WEYR SEARCH

by Anne McCaffrey

WHEN IS a legend legend? Why is a myth a myth? How old and disused must a fact be for it to be relegated to the category: Fairy tale? And why do certain facts remain incontrovertible, while others lose their validity to assume a shabby, unstable character?

Rukbat, in the Sagittarian sector, was a golden G-type star. It had five planets, plus one stray it had attracted and held in recent millennia. Its third planet was enveloped by air man could breathe, boasted water he could drink, and possessed a gravity which permitted man to walk confidently erect. Men discovered it, and promptly colonized it, as they did every habitable planet they came to and then—whether callously or through collapse of empire, the colonists never discovered, and eventually forgot to ask—left the colonies to fend for themselves.

When men first settled on Rukbat's third world, and named it Pern, they had taken little notice of the stranger-planet, swinging around its primary in a wildly erratic elliptical orbit. Within a few generations they had forgotten its existence. The desperate path the wanderer pursued brought it close to its stepsister every two hundred [Terran] years at perihelion.

When the aspects were harmonious and the conjunction with its sister-planet close enough, as it often was, the indigenous life of the wanderer sought to bridge the space gap to the more temperate and hospitable planet.

It was during the frantic struggle to combat this menace dropping through Pern's skies like silver threads that Pern's contact with the mother-planet weakened and broke. Recollections of Earth receded further from Pernese history with each successive generation until memory of their origins degenerated past legend or myth, into oblivion.

*To forestall the incursions of the dreaded Threads, the
Pernese, with the ingenuity of their forgotten Yankee forebears
and between first onslaught and return, developed a highly
specialized variety of a life form indigenous to their adopted
planet—the winged, tailed, and fire-breathing dragons, named
for the Earth legend they resembled. Such humans as had a
high empathy rating and some innate telepathic ability were
trained to make use of and preserve this unusual animal
whose ability to teleport was of immense value in the fierce
struggle to keep Pern bare of Threads.*

*The dragons and their dragonmen, a breed apart, and the
shortly renewed menace they battled, created a whole new
group of legends and myths.*

*As the menace was conquered the populace in the Holds of
Pern settled into a more comfortable way of life. Most of the
dragon Weyrs eventually were abandoned, and the descen-
dants of heroes fell into disfavor, as the legends fell into
disrepute.*

*This, then, is a tale of legends disbelieved and their restora-
tion. Yet—how goes a legend? When is myth?*

> Drummer, beat, and piper, blow,
> Harper, strike, and soldier, go.
> Free the flame and sear the grasses
> Till the dawning Red Star passes.

Lessa woke, cold. Cold with more than the chill of the
everlastingly clammy stone walls. Cold with the prescience
of a danger greater than when, ten full Turns ago, she had
run, whimpering, to hide in the watch-wher's odorous lair.

Rigid with concentration, Lessa lay in the straw of the
redolent cheese room, sleeping quarters shared with the
other kitchen drudges. There was an urgency in the ominous
portent unlike any other forewarning. She touched the awareness of the watch-wher, slithering on its rounds in the courtyard. It circled at the choke-limit of its chain. It was restless,
but oblivious to anything unusual in the predawn darkness.

The danger was definitely not within the walls of Hold
Ruath. Nor approaching the paved perimeter without the
Hold where relentless grass had forced new growth through
the ancient mortar, green witness to the deterioration of the
once stone-clean Hold. The danger was not advancing up the
now little used causeway from the valley, nor lurking in the

craftsmen's stony holdings at the foot of the Hold's cliff. It did not scent the wind that blew from Tillek's cold shores. But still it twanged sharply through her senses, vibrating every nerve in Lessa's slender frame. Fully roused, she sought to identify it before the prescient mood dissolved. She cast outward, towards the Pass, farther than she had ever pressed. Whatever threatened was not in Ruatha . . . yet. Nor did it have a familiar flavor. It was not, then, Fax.

Lessa had been cautiously pleased that Fax had not shown himself at Hold Ruath in three full Turns. The apathy of the craftsmen, the decaying farmholds, even the green-etched stones of the Hold infuriated Fax, self-styled Lord of the High Reaches, to the point where he preferred to forget the reason why he had subjugated the once proud and profitable Hold.

Lessa picked her way among the sleeping drudges, huddled together for warmth, and glided up the worn steps to the kitchen-proper. She slipped across the cavernous kitchen to the stableyard door. The cobbles of the yard were icy through the thin soles of her sandals and she shivered as the predawn air penetrated her patched garment.

The watch-wher slithered across the yard to greet her, pleading, as it always did, for release. Glancing fondly down at the awesome head, she promised it a good rub presently. It crouched, groaning, at the end of its chain as she continued to the grooved steps that led to the rampart over the Hold's massive gate. Atop the tower, Lessa stared towards the east where the stony breasts of the Pass rose in black relief against the gathering day.

Indecisively she swung to her left, for the sense of danger issued from that direction as well. She glanced upward, her eyes drawn to the red star which had recently begun to dominate the dawn sky. As she stared, the star radiated a final ruby pulsation before its magnificence was lost in the brightness of Pern's rising sun.

For the first time in many Turns, Lessa gave thought to matters beyond Pern, beyond her dedication to vengeance on the murderer Fax for the annihilation of her family. Let him but come within Ruath Hold now and he would never leave.

But the brilliant ruby sparkle of the Red Star recalled the Disaster Ballads—grim narratives of the heroism of the dragonriders as they braved the dangers of *between* to breathe fiery death on the silver Threads that dropped through Pern's skies. Not one Thread must fall to the rich soil, to burrow deep and multiply, leaching the earth of minerals and fertility. Straining her eyes as if vision would bridge the gap between periol and person, she stared intently eastward. The watch-wher's thin, whistled question reached her just as the prescience waned.

Dawnlight illumined the tumbled landscape, the unplowed fields in the valley below. Dawnlight fell on twisted orchards, where the sparse herds of milchbeasts hunted stray blades of spring grass. Grass in Ruatha grew where it should not, died where it should flourish. An odd brooding smile curved Lessa's lips. Fax realized no profit from his conquest of Ruatha . . . nor would he, while she, Lessa, lived. And he had not the slightest suspicion of the source of this undoing.

Or had he? Lessa wondered, her mind still reverberating from the savage prescience of danger. East lay Fax's ancestral and only legitimate Hold. Northeast lay little but bare and stony mountains and Benden, the remaining Weyr, which protected Pern.

Lessa stretched, arching her back, inhaling the sweet, untainted wind of morning.

A cock crowed in the stableyard. Lessa whirled, her face alert, eyes darting around the outer Hold lest she be observed in such an uncharacteristic pose. She unbound her hair, letting it fall about her face concealingly. Her body drooped into the sloppy posture she affected. Quickly she thudded down the stairs, crossing to the watch-wher. It lurred piteously, its great eyes blinking against the growing daylight. Oblivious to the stench of its rank breath, she hugged the scaly head to her, scratching its ears and eye ridges. The watch-wher was ecstatic with pleasure, its long body trembling, its clipped wings rustling. It alone knew who she was or cared. And it was the only creature in all Pern she trusted since the day she had blindly sought refuge in its dark stinking lair to escape Fax's thirsty swords that had drunk so deeply of Ruathan blood.

Slowly she rose, cautioning it to remember to be as vicious to her as to all should anyone be near. It promised to obey her, swaying back and forth to emphasize its reluctance.

The first rays of the sun glanced over the Hold's outer wall. Crying out, the watch-wher darted into its dark nest. Lessa crept back to the kitchen and into the cheese room.

*   *   *

From the Weyr and from the Bowl
Bronze and brown and blue and green
Rise the dragonmen of Pern,
Aloft, on wing, seen, then unseen.

F"lar on bronze Mnementh's great neck appeared first in
the skies above the chief Hold of Fax, so-called Lord of the
High Reaches. Behind him, in proper wedge formation, the
wingmen came into sight. F"lar checked the formation automatically; as precise as at the moment of entry to *between*.

As Mnementh curved in an arc that would bring them to
the perimeter of the Hold, consonant with the friendly nature
of this visitation, F"lar surveyed with mounting aversion the
disrepair of the ridge defenses. The firestone pits were empty
and the rock-cut gutters radiating from the pits were green-
tinged with a mossy growth.

Was there even one lord in Pern who maintained his Hold
rocky in observance of the ancient Laws? F"lar's lips tightened to a thinner line. When this Search was over and the
Impression made, there would have to be a solemn, punitive
Council held at the Weyr. And by the golden shell of the
queen, he, F"lar, meant to be its moderator. He would replace
lethargy with industry. He would scour the green and dangerous scum from the heights of Pern, the grass blades from
its stoneworks. No verdant skirt would be condoned in any
farmhold. And the tithings which had been so miserly, so
grudgingly presented would, under pain of firestoning, flow
with decent generosity into the dragon Weyr.

Mnementh rumbled approvingly as he vaned his pinions to
land lightly on the grass-etched flagstones of Fax's Hold. The
bronze dragon furled his great wings, and F"lar heard the
warning claxon in the Hold's Great Tower. Mnementh dropped
to his knees as F"lar indicated he wished to dismount. The
bronze rider stood by Mnementh's huge wedge-shaped head,
politely awaiting the arrival of the Hold lord. F"lar idly gazed
down the valley, hazy with warm spring sunlight. He ignored
the furtive heads that peered at the dragonman from the
parapet slits and the cliff windows.

F"lar did not turn as a rush of air announced the arrival of
the rest of the wing. He knew, however, when F"nor, the
brown rider, his half-brother, took the customary position on
his left, a dragon-length to the rear. F"lar caught a glimpse of

F'nor's boot-heel twisting to death the grass crowding up between the stones.

An order, muffled to an intense whisper, issued from within the great court, beyond the open gates. Almost immediately a group of men marched into sight, led by a heavy-set man of medium height.

Mnementh arched his neck, angling his head so that his chin rested on the ground. Mnementh's many-faceted eyes, on a level with F'lar's head, fastened with disconcerting interest on the approaching party. The dragons could never understand why they generated such abject fear in common folk. At only one point in his life span would a dragon attack a human and that could be excused on the grounds of simple ignorance. F'lar could not explain to the dragon the politics behind the necessity of inspiring awe in the holders, lord and craftsman alike. He could only observe that the fear and apprehension showing in the faces of the advancing squad which troubled Mnementh was oddly pleasing to him, F'lar.

"Welcome, Bronze Rider, to the Hold of Fax, Lord of the High Reaches. He is at your service," and the man made an adequately respectful salute.

The use of the third person pronoun could be construed, by the meticulous, to be a veiled insult. This fit in with the information F'lar had on Fax; so he ignored it. His information was also correct in describing Fax as a greedy man. It showed in the restless eyes which flicked at every detail of F'lar's clothing, at the slight frown when the intricately etched sword-hilt was noticed.

F'lar noticed, in his own turn, the several rich rings which flashed on Fax's left hand. The overlord's right hand remained slightly cocked after the habit of the professional swordsman. His tunic, of rich fabric, was stained and none too fresh. The man's feet, in heavy wher-hide boots, were solidly planted, weight balanced forward on his toes. A man to be treated cautiously, F'lar decided, as one should the conqueror of five neighboring Holds. Such greedy audacity was in itself a revelation. Fax had married into a sixth . . . and had legally inherited, however unusual the circumstances, the seventh. He was a lecherous man by reputation.

Within these seven Holds, F'lar anticipated a profitable Search. Let R'gul go southerly to pursue Search among the indolent, if lovely, women there. The Weyr needed a strong

woman this time; Jora had been worse than useless with
Nemorth. Adversity, uncertainty: those were the conditions
that bred the qualities F'lar wanted in a weyrwoman.

"We ride in Search," F'lar drawled softly, "and request the
hospitality of your Hold, Lord Fax."

Fax's eyes widened imperceptibly at mention of Search.

"I had heard Jora was dead," Fax replied, dropping the
third person abruptly as if F'lar had passed some sort of test
by ignoring it. "So Nemorth has a new queen, hm-m-m?" he
continued, his eyes darting across the rank of the ring, noting
the disciplined stance of the riders, the healthy color of the
dragons.

F'lar did not dignify the obvious with an answer.

"And, my Lord—?" Fax hesitated, expectantly inclining his
head slightly towards the dragonman.

For a pulse beat, F'lar wondered if the man were deliberately provoking him with such subtle insults. The name of
bronze riders should be as well known throughout Pern as
the name of the Dragonqueen and her Weyrwoman. F'lar
kept his face composed, his eyes on Fax's.

Leisurely, with the proper touch of arrogance, F'nor stepped
forward, stopping slightly behind Mnementh's head, one
hand negligently touching the jaw hinge of the huge beast.

"The Bronze Rider of Mnementh, Lord F'lar, will require
quarters for himself. I, F'nor, brown rider, prefer to be lodged
with the wingmen. We are, in number, twelve."

F'lar liked that touch of F'nor's, totting up the wing strength,
as if Fax were incapable of counting. F'nor had phrased it so
adroitly as to make it impossible for Fax to protest the insult.

"Lord F'lar," Fax said through teeth fixed in a smile, "the
High Reaches are honored with your Search."

"It will be to the credit of the High Reaches," F'lar replied
smoothly, "if one of its own supplies the Weyr."

"To our everlasting credit," Fax replied as suavely. "In the
old days, many notable weyrwomen came from my Holds."

"Your Holds?" asked F'lar, politely smiling as he empha-
sized the plural. "Ah, yes, you are now overlord of Ruatha,
are you not? There have been many from that Hold."

A strange tense look crossed Fax's face. "Nothing good
comes from Ruath Hold." Then he stepped aside, gesturing
F'lar to enter the Hold.

*   *   *

Fax's troop leader barked a hasty order and the men formed two lines, their metal-edged boots flicking sparks from the stones.

At unspoken orders, all the dragons rose with a great churning of air and dust. F'lar strode nonchalantly past the welcoming files. The men were rolling their eyes in alarm as the beasts glided above to the inner courts. Someone on the higher tower uttered a frightened yelp as Mnementh took his position on that vantage point. His great wings drove phosphoric-scented air across the inner court as he maneuvered his great frame onto the inadequate landing space.

Outwardly oblivious to the consternation, fear and awe the dragons inspired, F'lar was secretly amused and rather pleased by the effect. Lords of the Holds needed this reminder that they must deal with dragons, not just with riders, who were men, mortal and murderable. The ancient respect for dragonmen as well as dragonkind must be reinstilled in modern breasts.

"The Hold has just risen from table, Lord F'lar, if . . ." Fax suggested. His voice trailed off at F'lar's smiling refusal.

"Convey my duty to your lady, Lord Fax," F'lar rejoined, noticing with inward satisfaction the tightening of Fax's jaw muscles at the ceremonial request.

"You would prefer to see your quarters first?" Fax countered.

F'lar flicked an imaginary speck from his soft wher-hide sleeve and shook his head. Was the man buying time to sequester his ladies as the old-time lords had?

"Duty first," he said with a rueful shrug.

"Of course," Fax all but snapped and strode smartly ahead, his heels pounding out the anger he could not express otherwise. F'lar decided he had guessed correctly.

F'lar and F'nor followed at a slower pace through the double-doored entry with its massive metal panels, into the great hall, carved into the cliffside.

"They eat not badly," F'nor remarked casually to F'lar, appraising the remnants still on the table.

"Better than the Weyr, it would seem," F'lar replied dryly.

"Young roasts and tender," F'nor said in a bitter undertone, "while the stringy, barren beasts are delivered up to us."

"The change is overdue," F'lar murmured, then raised his voice to conversational level. "A well-favored hall," he was saying amiably as they reached Fax. Their reluctant host stood in the portal to the inner Hold, which, like all such

Holds, burrowed deep into stone, traditional refuge of all in time of peril.

Deliberately, F'lar turned back to the banner-hung Hall. "Tell me, Lord Fax, do you adhere to the old practices and mount a dawn guard?"

Fax frowned, trying to grasp F'lar's meaning.

"There is always a guard at the Tower."

"An easterly guard?"

Fax's eyes jerked towards F'lar, then to F'nor.

"There are always guards," he answered sharply, "on all the approaches."

"Oh, just the approaches," and F'lar nodded wisely to F'nor.

"Where else?" demanded Fax, concerned, glancing from one dragonman to the other.

"I must ask that of your harper. You do keep a trained harper in your Hold?"

"Of course. I have several trained harpers," and Fax jerked his shoulders straighter.

F'lar affected not to understand.

"Lord Fax is the overlord of six other Holds," F'nor reminded his wingleader.

"Of course," F'lar assented, with exactly the same inflection Fax had used a moment before.

The mimicry did not go unnoticed by Fax but as he was unable to construe deliberate insult out of an innocent affirmative, he stalked into the glow-lit corridors. The dragonmen followed.

The women's quarters in Fax's Hold had been moved from the traditional innermost corridors to those at cliff-face. Sunlight poured down from three double-shuttered, deep-casement windows in the outside wall. F'lar noted that the bronze hinges were well oiled, and the sills regulation spear-length. Fax had not, at least, diminished the protective wall.

The chamber was richly hung with appropriately gentle scenes of women occupied in all manner of feminine tasks. Doors gave off the main chamber on both sides into smaller sleeping alcoves and from these, at Fax's bidding, his women hesitantly emerged. Fax sternly gestured to a blue-gowned woman, her hair white-streaked, her face lined with disappointments and bitterness, her body swollen with pregnancy. She advanced awkwardly, stopping several feet from her

lord. From her attitude, F'lar deduced that she came no closer
to Fax than was absolutely necessary.

"The Lady of Crom, mother of my heirs," Fax said without
pride or cordiality.

"My Lady—" F'lar hesitated, waiting for her name to be
supplied.

She glanced warily at her lord.

"Gemma," Fax snapped curtly.

F'lar bowed deeply. "My Lady Gemma, the Weyr is on
Search and requests the Hold's hospitality."

"My Lord F'lar," the Lady Gemma replied in a low voice,
"you are most welcome."

F'lar did not miss the slight slur on the adverb nor the fact
that Gemma had no trouble naming him. His smile was
warmer than courtesy demanded, warm with gratitude and
sympathy. Looking at the number of women in these quarters, F'lar thought there might be one or two Lady Gemma
could bid farewell without regret.

Fax preferred his women plump and small. There wasn't a
saucy one in the lot. If there once had been, the spirit had
been beaten out of her. Fax, no doubt, was stud, not lover.
Some of the covey had not all winter long made much use of
water, judging by the amount of sweet oil gone rancid in their
hair. Of them all, if these were all, the Lady Gemma was the
only willful one; and she, too old.

The amenities over, Fax ushered his unwelcome guests
outside, and led the way to the quarters he had assigned the
bronze rider.

"A pleasant room," F'lar acknowledged, stripping off gloves
and wher-hide tunic, throwing them carelessly to the table.
"I shall see to my men and the beasts. They have been fed
recently," he commented, pointing up Fax's omission in inquiring. "I request liberty to wander through the crafthold."

Fax sourly granted what was a dragonman's traditional
privilege.

"I shall not further disrupt your routine, Lord Fax, for you
must have many demands on you, with seven Holds to super-
vise." F'lar inclined his body slightly to the overlord, turning
away as a gesture of dismissal. He could imagine the infuriated expression on Fax's face from the stamping retreat.

F'nor and the men had settled themselves in a hastily
vacated barrackroom. The dragons were perched comfortably

on the rocky ridges above the Hold. Each rider kept his
dragon in light, but alert, charge. There were to be no
incidents on a Search.

As a group, the dragonmen rose at F'lar's entrance.

"No tricks, no troubles, but look around closely," he said
laconically. "Return by sundown with the names of any
likely prospects." He caught F'nor's grin, remembering how
Fax had slurred over some names. "Descriptions are in order
and craft affiliation."

The men nodded, their eyes glinting with understanding.
They were flatteringly confident of a successful Search even
as F'lar's doubts grew now that he had seen Fax's women. By
all logic, the pick of the High Reaches should be in Fax's chief
Hold—but they were not. Still, there were many large
craftholds not to mention the six other High Holds to visit.
All the same . . .

In unspoken accord F'lar and F'nor left the barracks. The
men would follow, unobtrusively, in pairs or singly, to recon-
noiter the crafthold and the nearer farmholds. The men were
as overtly eager to be abroad as F'lar was privately. There
had been a time when dragonmen were frequent and favored
guests in all the great Holds throughout Pern, from southern
Fort to high north Igen. This pleasant custom, too, had died
along with other observances, evidence of the low regard in
which the Weyr was presently held. F'lar vowed to correct
this.

He forced himself to trace in memory the insidious changes.
The Records, which each Weyrwoman kept, were proof of
the gradual, but perceptible, decline, traceable through the
past two hundred full Turns. Knowing the facts did not
alleviate the condition. And F'lar was of that scant handful
in the Weyr itself who did credit Records and Ballad alike.
The situation might shortly reverse itself radically if the old
tales were to be believed.

There was a reason, an explanation, a purpose, F'lar felt,
for every one of the Weyr laws from First Impression to the
Firestone: from the grass-free heights to ridge-running gutters. For elements as minor as controlling the appetite of a
dragon to limiting the inhabitants of the Weyr. Although
why the other five Weyrs had been abandoned, F'lar did not
know. Idly he wondered if there were records, dusty and
crumbling, lodged in the disused Weyrs. He must contrive to

check when next his wings flew patrol. Certainly there was
no explanation in Benden Weyr.

"There is industry but no enthusiasm," F'nor was saying,
drawing F'lar's attention back to their tour of the crafthold.

They had descended the guttered ramp from the Hold into
the crafthold proper, the broad roadway lined with cottages
up to the imposing stone crafthalls. Silently F'lar noted
moss-clogged gutters on the roofs, the vines clasping the
walls. It was painful for one of his calling to witness the
flagrant disregard of simple safety precautions. Growing
things were forbidden near the habitations of mankind.

"News travels fast," F'nor chuckled, nodding at a hurrying
craftsman, in the smock of a baker, who gave them a mum-
bled good day. "Not a female in sight."

His observation was accurate. Women should be abroad at
this hour, bringing in supplies from the storehouses, washing
in the river on such a bright warm day, or going out to the
farmholds to help with planting. Not a gowned figure in
sight.

"We used to be preferred mates," F'nor remarked caustically.

"We'll visit the Clothmen's Hall first. If my memory serves
me right . . ."

"As it always does . . ." F'nor interjected wryly. He took no
advantage of their blood relationship but he was more at ease
with the bronze rider than most of the dragonmen, the other
bronze riders included. F'lar was reserved in a close-knit
society of easy equality. He flew a tightly disciplined wing
but men maneuvered to serve under him. His wing always
excelled in the Games. None ever floundered in *between* to
disappear forever and no beast in his wing sickened, leaving
a man in dragonless exile from the Weyr, a part of him numb
forever.

"L'tol came this way and settled in one of the High Reaches,"
F'lar continued.

"L'tol?"

"Yes, a green rider from S'lel's wing. You remember."

An ill-timed swerve during the Spring Games had brought
L'tol and his beast into the full blast of a phosphene emission
from S'lel's bronze Tuenth. L'tol had been thrown from his
beast's neck as the dragon tried to evade the blast. Another
wingmate had swooped to catch the rider but the green
dragon, his left wing crisped, his body scorched, had died of
shock and phosphene poisoning.

"L'tol would aid our Search," F'nor agreed as the two dragonmen walked up to the bronze doors of the Clothmen's Hall. They paused on the threshold, adjusting their eyes to the dimmer light within. Glows punctuated the wall recesses and hung in clusters above the larger looms where the finer tapestries and fabrics were woven by master craftsmen. The pervading mood was one of quiet, purposeful industry.

Before their eyes had adapted, however, a figure glided to them, with a polite, if curt, request for them to follow him.

They were led to the right of the entrance, to a small office, curtained from the main hall. Their guide turned to them, his face visible in the wallglows. There was that air about him that marked him indefinably as a dragonman. But his face was lined deeply, one side seamed with old burn-marks. His eyes, sick with a hungry yearning, dominated his face. He blinked constantly.

"I am now Lytol," he said in a harsh voice.

F'lar nodded acknowledgment.

"You would be F'lar," Lytol said, "and you, F'nor. You've both the look of your sire."

F'lar nodded again.

Lytol swallowed convulsively, the muscles in his face twitching as the presence of dragonmen revived his awareness of exile. He essayed a smile.

"Dragons in the sky! The news spread faster than Threads."

"Nemorth has a new queen."

"Jora dead?" Lytol asked concernedly, his face cleared of its nervous movement for a second.

F'lar nodded.

Lytol grimaced bitterly. "R'gul again, huh." He stared off in the middle distance, his eyelids quiet but the muscles along his jaw took up the constant movement. "You've the High Reaches? All of them?" Lytol asked, turning back to the dragonman, a slight emphasis on "all."

F'lar gave an affirmative nod again.

"You've seen the women." Lytol's disgust showed through the words. It was a statement, not a question, for he hurried on. "Well, there are no better in all the High Reaches," and his tone expressed utmost disdain.

"Fax likes his women comfortably fleshed and docile," Lytol rattled on. "Even the Lady Gemma has learned. It'd be different if he didn't need her family's support. Ah, it would be different indeed. So he keeps her pregnant, hoping to kill her in childbed one day. And he will. He will."

Lytol drew himself up, squaring his shoulders, turning full to the two dragonmen. His expression was vindictive, his voice low and tense.

"Kill that tyrant, for the sake and safety of Pern. Of the Weyr. Of the queen. He only bides his time. He spreads discontent among the other lords. He"—Lytol's laughter had an hysterical edge to it now—"he fancies himself as good as dragonmen."

"There are no candidates then in this Hold?" F'lar said, his voice sharp enough to cut through the man's preoccupation with his curious theory.

Lytol stared at the bronze rider. "Did I not say it?"

"What of Ruath Hold?"

Lytol stopped shaking his head and looked sharply at F'lar, his lips curling in a cunning smile. He laughed mirthlessly.

"You think to find a Torene, or a Moreta, hidden at Ruath Hold in these times? Well, all of that Blood are dead. Fax's blade was thirsty that day. He knew the truth of those harpers' tales, that Ruathan lords gave full measure of hospitality to dragonmen and the Ruathan were a breed apart. There were, you know," Lytol's voice dropped to a confiding whisper, "exiled Weyrmen like myself in that Line."

F'lar nodded gravely, unable to contradict the man's pitiful attempt at self-esteem.

"No," and Lytol chuckled softly. "Fax gets nothing from that Hold but trouble. And the women Fax used to take . . ." his laugh turned nasty in tone. "It is rumored he was impotent for months afterwards."

"Any families in the holdings with Weyr blood?"

Lytol frowned, glanced surprised at F'lar. He rubbed the scarred side of his face thoughtfully.

"There were," he admitted slowly. "There were. But I doubt if any live on." He thought a moment longer, then shook his head emphatically.

F'lar shrugged.

"I wish I had better news for you," Lytol murmured.

"No matter," F'lar reassured him, one hand poised to part the hanging in the doorway.

Lytol came up to him swiftly, his voice urgent.

"Heed what I say, Fax is ambitious. Force R'gul, or whoever is Weyrleader next, to keep watch on the High Reaches."

Lytol jabbed a finger in the direction of the Hold. "He scoffs openly at tales of the Threads. He taunts the harpers for the stupid nonsense of the old ballads and has banned from their repertoire all dragonlore. The new generation will grow up totally ignorant of duty, tradition and precaution."

F'lar was surprised to hear that on top of Lytol's other disclosures. Yet the Red Star pulsed in the sky and the time was drawing near when they would hysterically reavow the old allegiances in fear for their very lives.

"Have you been abroad in the early morning of late?" asked F'nor, grinning maliciously.

"I have," Lytol breathed out in a hushed, choked whisper. "I have . . ." A groan was wrenched from his guts and he whirled away from the dragonmen, his head bowed between hunched shoulders. "Go," he said, gritting his teeth. And, as they hesitated, he pleaded, *"Go!"*

F'lar walked quickly from the room, followed by F'nor. The bronze rider crossed the quiet dim Hall with long strides and exploded into the startling sunlight. His momentum took him into the center of the square. There he stopped so abruptly that F'nor, hard on his heels, nearly collided with him.

"We will spend exactly the same time within the other Halls," he announced in a tight voice, his face averted from F'nor's eyes. F'lar's throat was constricted. It was difficult, suddenly, for him to speak. He swallowed hard, several times.

"To be dragonless . . ." murmured F'nor, pityingly. The encounter with Lytol had roiled his depths in a mournful way to which he was unaccustomed. That F'lar appeared equally shaken went far to dispel F'nor's private opinion that his half-brother was incapable of emotion.

"There is no other way once First Impression has been made. You know that," F'lar roused himself to say curtly. He strode off to the Hall bearing the Leathermen's device.

> The Hold is barred
> The Hall is bare.
> And men vanish.
> The soil is barren,
> The rock is bald.
> All hope banish.

*   *   *

Lessa was shoveling ashes from the hearth when the agitated messenger staggered into the Great Hall. She made herself as inconspicuous as possible so the Warder would not dismiss her. She had contrived to be sent to the Great Hall that morning, knowing that the Warder intended to brutalize the Head Clothman for the shoddy quality of the goods readied for shipment to Fax.

"Fax is coming! With dragonmen!" the man gasped out as he plunged into the dim Great Hall.

The Warder, who had been about to lash the Head Clothman, turned, stunned, from his victim. The courier, a farmholder from the edge of Ruatha, stumbled up to the Warder, so excited with his message that he grabbed the Warder's arm.

"How dare you leave your Hold?" and the Warder aimed his lash at the astonished holder. The force of the first blow knocked the man from his feet. Yelping, he scrambled out of reach of a second lashing. "Dragonmen indeed! Fax? Ha! He shuns Ruatha. There!" The Warder punctuated each denial with another blow, kicking the helpless wretch for good measure, before he turned breathless to glare at the clothman and the two underwarders. "How did he get in here with such a threadbare lie?" The Warder stalked to the great door. It was flung open just as he reached out for the iron handle. The ashen-faced guard officer rushed in, nearly toppling the Warder.

"Dragonmen! Dragons! All over Ruatha!" the man gibbered, arms flailing wildly. He, too, pulled at the Warder's arm, dragging the stupefied official towards the outer courtyard, to bear out the truth of his statement.

Lessa scooped up the last pile of ashes. Picking up her equipment, she slipped out of the Great Hall. There was a very pleased smile on her face under the screen of matted hair.

A dragonman at Ruatha! She must somehow contrive to get Fax so humiliated, or so infuriated, that he would renounce his claim to the Hold, in the presence of a dragonman. Then she could claim her birthright.

But she would have to be extraordinarily wary. Dragonriders were men apart. Anger did not cloud their intelligence. Greed did not sully their judgment. Fear did not dull their reactions. Let the dense-witted believe human sacrifice, unnatural lusts, insane revel. She was not so gullible. And those stories went against her grain. Dragonmen were still human and there was Weyr blood in *her* veins. It was the same color as that of anyone else; enough of hers had been spilled to prove that.

She halted for a moment, catching a sudden shallow breath. Was this the danger she had sensed four days ago at dawn? The final encounter in her struggle to regain the Hold? No—there had been more to that portent than revenge.

The ash bucket banged against her chins as she shuffled down the low-ceilinged corridor to the stable door. Fax would find a cold welcome. She had laid no new fire on the hearth. Her laugh echoed back unpleasantly from the damp walls. She rested her bucket and propped her broom and shovel as she wrestled with the heavy bronze door that gave into the new stables.

They had been built outside the cliff of Ruatha by Fax's first Warder, a subtler man than all eight of his successors. He had achieved more than all others and Lessa had honestly regretted the necessity of his death. But he would have made her revenge impossible. He would have caught her out before she had learned how to camouflage herself and her little interferences. What had his name been? She could not recall. Well, she regretted his death.

The second man had been properly greedy and it had been easy to set up a pattern of misunderstanding between Warder and craftsmen. That one had been determined to squeeze all profit from Ruathan goods so that some of it would drop into his pocket before Fax suspected a shortage. The craftsmen who had begun to accept the skillful diplomacy of the first Warder bitterly resented the second's grasping, high-handed ways. They resented the passing of the Old Line and, even more so, the way of its passing. They were unforgiving of insult to Ruatha; its now secondary position in the High Reaches; and they resented the individual indignities that holders, craftsmen and farmers alike, suffered under the second Warder. It took little manipulation to arrange for matters at Ruatha to go from bad to worse.

The second was replaced and his successor fared no better. He was caught diverting goods, the best of the goods at that. Fax had had him executed. His bony head still hung in the main firepit above the great Tower.

The present incumbent had not been able to maintain the Hold in even the sorry condition in which he had assumed its management. Seemingly simple matters developed rapidly

into disasters. Like the production of cloth . . . contrary to
his boasts to Fax, the quality had not improved, and the
quantity had fallen off.

Now Fax was here. And with dragonmen! Why dragonmen?
The import of the question froze Lessa, and the heavy door
closing behind her barked her heels painfully. Dragonmen
used to be frequent visitors at Ruatha, that she knew, and even
vaguely remembered. Those memories were like a harper's
tale, told of someone else, not something within her own
experience. She had limited her fierce attention to Ruatha
only. She could not even recall the name of Queen or
Weyrwoman from the instructions of her childhood, nor could
she recall hearing mention of any Queen or Weyrwoman by
anyone in the Hold these past ten Turns.

Perhaps the dragonmen were finally going to call the lords
of the Holds to task for the disgraceful show of greenery
about the Holds. Well, Lessa was to blame for much of that in
Ruatha but she defied even a dragonman to confront her with
her guilt. Did all Ruatha fall to the Threads it would be
better than remaining dependent to Fax! The heresy shocked
Lessa even as she thought it.

Wishing she could as easily unburden her conscience of
such blasphemy, she ditched the ashes on the stable midden.
There was a sudden change in air pressure around her. Then
a fleeting shadow caused her to glance up.

From behind the cliff above glided a dragon, its enormous
wings spread to their fullest as he caught the morning
updraft. Turning effortlessly, he descended. A second, a
third, a full wing of dragons followed in soundless flight and
patterned descent, graceful and awesome. The claxon rang
belatedly from the Tower and from within the kitchens there
issued the screams and shrieks of the terrified drudges.

Lessa took cover. She ducked into the kitchen where she
was instantly seized by the assistant cook and thrust with a
buffet and a kick towards the sinks. There she was put to
scrubbing grease-encrusted serving bowls with cleansing sand.

The yelping canines were already lashed to the spitrun,
turning a scrawny herdbeast that had been set to roast. The
cook was ladling seasonings on the carcass, swearing at
having to offer so poor a meal to so many guests, and some of
them high-rank. Winter-dried fruits from the last scanty
harvest had been set to soak and two of the oldest drudges
were scraping roots.

An apprentice cook was kneading bread; another, carefully spicing a sauce. Looking fixedly at him, she diverted his hand from one spice box to a less appropriate one as he gave a final shake to the concoction. She added too much wood to the wall oven, insuring ruin for the breads. She controlled the canines deftly, slowing one and speeding the other so that the meat would be underdone on one side, burned on the other. That the feast should be a fast, the food presented found inedible, was her whole intention.

Above in the Hold, she had no doubt that certain other measures, undertaken at different times for this exact contingency, were being discovered.

Her fingers bloodied from a beating, one of the Warder's women came shrieking into the kitchen, hopeful of refuge there.

"Insects have eaten the best blankets to shreds! And a canine who had littered on the best linens snarled at me as she gave suck! And the rushes are noxious, the best chambers full of debris driven in by the winter wind. Somebody left the shutters ajar. Just a tiny bit, but it was enough . . ." the woman wailed, clutching her hand to her breast and rocking back and forth.

Lessa bent with great industry to shine the plates.

> Watch-wher, watch-wher,
> In your lair,
> Watch well, watch-wher!
> Who goes there?

"The watch-wher is hiding something," F'lar told F'nor as they consulted in the hastily cleaned Great Hall. The room delighted to hold the wintry chill although a generous fire now burned on the hearth.

"It was but gibbering when Canth spoke to it," F'nor remarked. He was leaning against the mantel, turning slightly from side to side to gather some warmth. He watched his wingleader's impatient pacing.

"Mnementh is calming it down," F'lar replied. "He may be able to sort out the nightmare. The creature may be more senile than aware, but . . ."

"I doubt it," F'nor concurred helpfully. He glanced with apprehension up at the web-hung ceiling. He was certain he'd found most of the crawlers, but he didn't fancy their sting.

Not on top of the discomforts already experienced in this forsaken Hold. If the night stayed mild, he intended curling up with Canth on the heights. "That would be more reasonable than anything Fax or his Warder have suggested."

"Hm-m-m," F'lar muttered, frowning at the brown rider.

"Well, it's unbelievable that Ruatha could have fallen to such disrepair in ten short Turns. Every dragon caught the feeling of power and it's obvious the watch-wher had been tampered with. That takes a good deal of control."

"From someone of the Blood," F'lar reminded him.

F'nor shot his wingleader a quick look, wondering if he could possibly be serious in the light of all information to the contrary.

"I grant you there is power here, F'lar," F'nor conceded. "It could easily be a hidden male of the old Blood. But we need a female. And Fax made it plain, in his inimitable fashion, that he left none of the old Blood alive in the Hold the day he took it. No, no." The brown rider shook his head, as if he could dispel the lack of faith in his wingleader's curious insistence that the Search would end in Ruath with Ruathan blood.

"That watch-wher is hiding something and only someone of the Blood of its Hold can arrange that," F'lar said emphatically. He gestured around the Hall and towards the walls, bare of hangings. "Ruatha has been overcome. But she resists . . . subtly. I say it points to the old Blood, *and* power. Not power alone."

The obstinate expression in F'lar's eyes, the set of his jaw, suggested that F'nor seek another topic.

"The pattern was well-flown today," F'nor suggested tentatively. "Does a dragonman good to ride a flaming beast. Does the beast good, too. Keeps the digestive process in order."

F'lar nodded sober agreement. "Let R'gul temporize as he chooses. It is fitting and proper to ride a firespouting beast and these holders need to be reminded of Weyr power."

"Right now, anything would help our prestige," F'nor commented sourly. "What had Fax to say when he hailed you in the Pass?" F'nor knew his question was almost impertinent but if it were, F'lar would ignore it.

F'lar's slight smile was unpleasant and there was an ominous glint in his amber eyes.

"We talked of rule and resistance."

"Did he not also draw on you?" F'nor asked.

F'lar's smile deepened. "Until he remembered I was dragon-mounted."

"He's considered a vicious fighter," F'nor said.

"I am at some disadvantage?" F'lar asked, turning sharply on his brown rider, his face too controlled.

"To my knowledge, no," F'nor reassured his leader quickly. F'lar had tumbled every man in the Weyr, efficiently and easily. "But Fax kills often and without cause."

"And because we dragonmen do not seek blood, we are not to be feared as fighters?" snapped F'lar. "Are you ashamed of your heritage?"

"I? No!" F'nor sucked in his breath. "Nor any of our wing!" he added proudly. "But there is that in the attitude of the men in this progression of Fax's that . . . that makes me wish some excuse to fight."

"As you observed today, Fax seeks some excuse. And," F'lar added thoughtfully, "there is something here in Ruatha that unnerves our noble overlord."

He caught sight of Lady Tela, whom Fax had so courteously assigned him for comfort during the progression, waving to him from the inner Hold portal.

"A case in point. Fax's Lady Tela is some three months gone."

F'nor frowned at the insult to his leader.

"She giggles incessantly and appears so addlepated that one cannot decide whether she babbles out of ignorance or at Fax's suggestion. As she has apparently not bathed all winter, and is not, in any case, my ideal, I have"—F'lar grinned maliciously—"deprived myself of her kind offices."

F'nor hastily cleared his throat and his expression as Lady Tela approached them. He caught the unappealing odor from the scarf or handkerchief she waved constantly. Dragonmen endured a great deal for the Weyr. He moved away, with apparent courtesy, to join the rest of the dragonmen entering the Hall.

F'lar turned with equal courtesy to Lady Tela as she jabbered away about the terrible condition of the rooms which Lady Gemma and the other ladies had been assigned.

"The shutters, both sets, were ajar all winter long and you should have seen the trash on the floors. We finally got two of the drudges to sweep it all into the fireplace. And then that smoked something fearful till a man was sent up." Lady Tela

giggled. "He found the access blocked by a chimney stone
fallen aslant. The rest of the chimney, for a wonder, was in
good repair."

She waved her handkerchief. F'lar held his breath as the
gesture wafted an unappealing odor in his direction.

He glanced up the Hall towards the inner Hold door and
saw Lady Gemma descending, her steps slow and awkward.
Some subtle difference about her gait attracted him and he
stared at her, trying to identify it.

"Oh, yes, poor Lady Gemma," Lady Tela babbled, sighing
deeply. "We are so concerned. Why Lord Fax insisted on her
coming, I do not know. She is not near her time and yet . . ."
The lighthead's concern sounded sincere.

F'lar's incipient hatred for Fax and his brutality matured
abruptly. He left his partner chattering to thin air and
courteously extended his arm to Lady Gemma to support her
down the steps and to the table. Only the brief tightening of
her fingers on his forearm betrayed her gratitude. Her face
was very white and drawn, the lines deeply etched around
mouth and eyes, showing the effort she was expending.

"Some attempt has been made, I see, to restore order to the
Hall," she remarked in a conversational tone.

"Some," F'lar admitted dryly, glancing around the grandly
proportioned Hall, its rafters festooned with the webs of
many Turns. The inhabitants of those gossamer nests dropped
from time to time, with ripe splats, to the floor, onto the table
and into the serving platters. Nothing replaced the old ban-
ners of the Ruathan Blood, which had been removed from the
stark brown stone walls. Fresh rushes did obscure the greasy
flagstones. The trestle tables appeared recently sanded and
scraped, and the platters gleamed dully in the refreshed
glows. Unfortunately, the brighter light was a mistake for it
was much too unflattering.

"This was such a graceful Hall," Lady Gemma murmured
for F'lar's ears alone.

"You were a friend?" he asked, politely.

"Yes, in my youth." Her voice dropped expressively on the
last word, evoking for F'lar a happier girlhood. "It was a
noble line!"

"Think you *one* might have escaped the sword?"

Lady Gemma flashed him a startled look, then quickly
composed her features, lest the exchange be noted. She gave
a barely perceptible shake of her head and then shifted her

awkward weight to take her place at the table. Graciously
she inclined her head towards F'lar, both dismissing and
thanking him.

F'lar returned to his own partner and placed her at the
table on his left. As the only person of rank who would dine
that night at Ruath Hold, Lady Gemma was seated on his
right; Fax would be beyond her. The dragonmen and Fax's
upper soldiery would sit at the lower tables. No guildmen had
been invited to Ruatha. Fax arrived just then with his
current lady and two underleaders, the Warder bowing them
effusively into the Hall. The man, F'lar noticed, kept a good
distance from his overlord—as well as a Warder might whose
responsibility was in this sorry condition. F'lar flicked a
crawler away. Out of the corner of his eye, he saw Lady
Gemma wince and shudder.

Fax stamped up to the raised table, his face black with
suppressed rage. He pulled back his chair roughly, slamming
it into Lady Gemma's before he seated himself. He pulled the
chair to the table with a force that threatened to rock the
none too stable trestle-top from its supporting legs. Scowling,
he inspected his goblet and plate, fingering the surface, ready
to throw them aside if they displeased him.

"A toast and fresh bread, Lord Fax, and such fruits and
roots as are left. Had I but known of your arrival, I could
have sent to Crom for . . ."

"Sent to Crom?" roared Fax, slamming the plate he was
inspecting into the table so forcefully the rim bent under his
hands. The Warder winced again as if he himself had been
maimed.

"The day one of my Holds cannot support itself *or* the visit
of its rightful overlord, I shall renounce it."

Lady Gemma gasped. Simultaneously the dragons roared.
F'lar felt the unmistakable surge of power. His eyes instinctively sought F'nor at the lower table. The brown rider—all
the dragonmen—had experienced that inexplicable shaft of
exultation.

"What's wrong, Dragonman?" snapped Fax.

F'lar, affecting unconcern, stretched his legs under the
table and assumed an indolent posture in the heavy chair.

"Wrong?"

"The dragons!"

"Oh, nothing. They often roar . . . at the sunset, at a flock of passing wherries, at mealtimes," and F'lar smiled amiably at the Lord of the High Reaches. Beside him his tablemate gave a squeak.

"Mealtimes? Have they not been fed?"

"Oh, yes. Five days ago."

"Oh. Five . . . days ago? And are they hungry . . . now?" Her voice trailed into a whisper of fear, her eyes grew round.

"In a few days," F'lar assured her. Under cover of his detached amusement, F'lar scanned the Hall. That surge had come from nearby. Either in the Hall or just outside. It must have been from within. It came so soon upon Fax's speech that his words must have triggered it. And the power had had an indefinably feminine touch to it.

One of Fax's women? F'lar found that hard to credit. Mnementh had been close to all of them and none had shown a vestige of power. Much less, with the exception of Lady Gemma, any intelligence.

One of the Hall women? So far he had seen only the sorry drudges and the aging females the Warder had as house-keepers. The Warder's personal woman? He must discover if that man had one. One of the Hold guards' women? F'lar suppressed an intense desire to rise and search.

"You mount a guard?" he asked Fax casually.

"Double at Ruath Hold!" he was told in a tight, hard voice, ground out from somewhere deep in Fax's chest.

"Here?" F'lar all but laughed out loud, gesturing around the sadly appointed chamber.

"Here! Food!" Fax changed the subject with a roar.

Five drudges, two of them women in brown-gray rags such that F'lar hoped they had had nothing to do with the preparation of the meal, staggered in under the emplattered herdbeast. No one with so much as a trace of power would sink to such depths, unless . . .

The aroma that reached him as the platter was placed on the serving table distracted him. It reeked of singed bone and charred meat. The Warder frantically sharpened his tools as if a keen edge could somehow slice acceptable portions from this unlikely carcass.

Lady Gemma caught her breath again and F'lar saw her hands curl tightly around the armrests. He saw the convulsive movement of her throat as she swallowed. He, too, did not look forward to this repast.

The drudges reappeared with wooden trays of bread. Burnt crusts had been scraped and cut, in some places, from the loaves before serving. As other trays were borne in, F'lar tried to catch sight of the faces of the servitors. Matted hair obscured the face of the one who presented a dish of legumes swimming in greasy liquid. Revolted, F'lar poked through the legumes to find properly cooked portions to offer Lady Gemma. She waved them aside, her face ill-concealing her discomfort.

As F'lar was about to turn and serve Lady Tela, he saw Lady Gemma's hand clutch convulsively at the chair arms. He realized that she was not merely nauseated by the unappetizing food. She was seized with labor contractions.

F'lar glanced in Fax's direction. The overlord was scowling blackly at the attempts of the Warder to find edible portions of meat to serve.

F'lar touched Lady Gemma's arm with light fingers. She turned just enough to look at F'lar from the corner of her eye. She managed a socially correct half-smile.

"I dare not leave just now, Lord F'lar. He is always dangerous at Ruatha. And it may only be false pangs."

F'lar was dubious as he saw another shudder pass through her frame. The woman would have been a fine Weyrwoman, he thought ruefully, were she but younger.

The Warder, his hands shaking, presented Fax the sliced meats. There were slivers of overdone flesh and portions of almost edible meats, but not much of either.

One furious wave of Fax's broad fist and the Warder had the plate, meats and juice, square in the face. Despite himself, F'lar sighed, for those undoubtedly constituted the only edible portions of the entire beast.

"You call this food? *You call this food?*" Fax bellowed. His voice boomed back from the bare vault of the ceiling, shaking crawlers from their webs as the sound shattered the fragile strands. "Slop! *Slop!*"

F'lar rapidly brushed crawlers from Lady Gemma, who was helpless in the throes of a very strong contraction.

"It's all we had on such short notice," the Warder squealed, juices streaking down his cheeks. Fax threw the goblet at him and the wine went streaming down the man's chest. The steaming dish of roots followed and the man yelped as the hot liquid splashed over him.

"My lord, my lord, had I but known!"

"Obviously, Ruatha *cannot* support the visit of its Lord. You must renounce it," F'lar heard himself saying.

His shock at such words issuing from his mouth was as great as that of everyone else in the Hall. Silence fell, broken by the splat of falling crawlers and the drip of root liquid from the Warder's shoulders to the rushes. The grating of Fax's bootheel was clearly audible as he swung slowly around to face the bronze rider.

As F'lar conquered his own amazement and rapidly tried to predict what to do next to mend matters, he saw F'nor rise slowly to his feet, hand on dagger hilt.

"I did not hear you correctly?" Fax asked, his face blank of all expression, his eyes snapping.

Unable to comprehend how he could have uttered such an arrant challenge, F'lar managed to assume a languid pose.

"You did mention," he drawled, "that if any of your Holds could not support itself and the visit of its rightful overlord, you would renounce it."

Fax stared back at F'lar, his face a study of swiftly suppressed emotions, the glint of triumph dominant. F'lar, his face stiff with the forced expression of indifference, was casting swiftly about in his mind. In the name of the Egg, had he lo t all sense of discretion?

Pretending utter unconcern, he stabbed some vegetables onto his knife and began to munch on them. As he did so, he noticed F'nor glancing slowly around the Hall, scrutinizing everyone. Abruptly F'lar realized what had happened. Somehow, in making that statement, he, a dragonman, had responded to a covert use of the power. F'lar, the bronze rider, was being put into a position where he would *have* to fight Fax. Why? For what end? To get Fax to renounce the Hold? Incredible! But, there could be only one possible reason for such a turn of events. An exultation as sharp as pain swelled within F'lar. It was all he could do to maintain his pose of bored indifference, all he could do to turn his attention to thwarting Fax, should he press for a duel. A duel would serve no purpose. He, F'lar, had no time to waste on it.

A groan escaped Lady Gemma and broke the eye-locked stance of the two antagonists. Irritated, Fax looked down at her, fist clenched and half-raised to strike her for her temerity in interrupting her lord and master. The contraction that contorted the swollen belly was as obvious as the woman's pain. F'lar dared not look towards her but he wondered if she had deliberately groaned aloud to break the tension.

Incredibly, Fax began to laugh. He threw back his head, showing big, stained teeth, and roared.

"Aye, renounce it, in favor of her issue, if it is male . . . and lives!" he crowed, laughing raucously.

"Heard and witnessed!" F'lar snapped, jumping to his feet and pointing to his riders. They were on their feet in the instant. "Heard and witnessed!" they averred in the traditional manner.

With that movement, everyone began to babble at once in nervous relief. The other women, each reacting in her way to the imminence of birth, called orders to the servants and advice to each other. They converged towards Lady Gemma, hovering undecidedly out of Fax's range, like silly wherries disturbed from their roosts. It was obvious they were torn between their fear of the lord and their desire to reach the laboring woman.

He gathered their intentions as well as their reluctance and, still stridently laughing, knocked back his chair. He stepped over it, strode down to the meatstand and stood hacking off pieces with his knife, stuffing them, juice dripping, into his mouth without ceasing his guffawing.

As F'lar bent towards Lady Gemma to assist her out of her chair, she grabbed his arm urgently. Their eyes met, hers clouded with pain. She pulled him closer.

"He means to kill you, Bronze Rider. He loves to kill," she whispered.

"Dragonmen are not easily killed, but I am grateful to you."

"I do not want you killed," she said, softly, biting at her lip. "We have so few bronze riders."

F'lar stared at her, startled. Did she, Fax's lady, actually believe in the Old Laws?

F'lar beckoned to two of the Warder's men to carry her up into the Hold. He caught Lady Tela by the arm as she fluttered past him.

"What do you need?"

"Oh, oh," she exclaimed, her face twisted with panic; she was distractedly wringing her hands. "Water, hot. Clean cloths. And a birthing-woman. Oh, yes, we must have a birthing-woman."

F'lar looked about for one of the Hold women, his glance

sliding over the first disreputable figure who had started to
mop up the spilled food. He signaled instead for the Warder
and peremptorily ordered him to send for the woman. The
Warder kicked at the drudge on the floor.

"You . . . you! Whatever your name is, go get her from the
crafthold. You must know who she is."

The drudge evaded the parting kick the Warder aimed in
her direction with a nimbleness at odds with her appearance
of extreme age and decrepitude. She scurried across the Hall
and out the kitchen door.

Fax sliced and speared meat, occasionally bursting out with
a louder bark of laughter as his inner thoughts amused him.
F'lar sauntered down to the carcass and, without waiting for
invitation from his host, began to carve neat slices also,
beckoning his men over. Fax's soldiers, however, waited until
their lord had eaten his fill.

> Lord of the Hold, your charge is sure
> In thick walls, metal doors and no verdure.

Lessa sped from the Hall to summon the birthing-woman,
seething with frustration. So close! So close! How could she
come so close and yet fail? Fax should have challenged the
dragonman. And the dragonman was strong and young, his
face that of a fighter, stern and controlled. He should not
have temporized. Was all honor dead in Pern, smothered by
green grass?

And why, oh why, had Lady Gemma chosen that precious
moment to go into labor? If her groan hadn't distracted Fax,
the fight would have begun and not even Fax, for all his
vaunted prowess as a vicious fighter, would have prevailed
against a dragonman who had her—Lessa's—support! The
Hold must be secured to its rightful Blood again. Fax must
not leave Ruatha, alive, again!

Above her, on the High Tower, the great bronze dragon
gave forth a weird croon, his many-faceted eyes sparkling in
the gathering darkness.

Unconsciously she silenced him as she would have done the
watch-wher. Ah, that watch-wher. He had not come out of his
den at her passing. She knew the dragons had been at him.
She could hear him gibbering in panic.

The slant of the road towards the crafthold lent impetus to
her flying feet and she had to brace herself to a sliding stop at

the birthing-woman's stone threshold. She banged on the closed door and heard the frightened exclamation within.

"A birth. A birth at the Hold," Lessa cried.

"A birth?" came the muffled cry and the latches were thrown up on the door. "At the Hold?"

"Fax's lady and, as you love life, hurry! For if it is male, it will be Ruatha's own lord."

That ought to fetch her, thought Lessa, and in that instant, the door was flung open by the man of the house. Lessa could see the birthing-woman gathering up her things in haste, piling them into her shawl. Lessa hurried the woman out, up the steep road to the Hold, under the Tower gate, grabbing the woman as she tried to run at the sight of a dragon peering down at her. Lessa drew her into the Court and pushed her, resisting, into the Hall.

The woman clutched at the inner door, balking at the sight of the gathering there. Lord Fax, his feet up on the trestle table, was paring his fingernails with his knife blade, still chuckling. The dragonmen in their wher-hide tunics were eating quietly at one table while the soldiers were having their turn at the meat.

The bronze rider noticed their entrance and pointed urgently towards the Inner Hold. The birthing-woman seemed frozen to the spot. Lessa tugged futilely at her arm, urging her to cross the Hall. To her surprise, the bronze rider strode to them.

"Go quickly, woman, Lady Gemma is before her time," he said, frowning with concern, gesturing imperatively towards the Hold entrance. He caught her by the shoulder and led her, all unwilling, Lessa tugging away at her other arm.

When they reached the stairs, he relinquished his grip, nodding to Lessa to escort her the rest of the way. Just as they reached the massive inner door, Lessa noticed how sharply the dragonman was looking at them—at her hand, on the birthing-woman's arm. Warily, she glanced at her hand and saw it, as if it belonged to a stranger: the long fingers, shapely despite dirt and broken nails; her small hand, delicately boned, gracefully placed despite the urgency of the grip. She blurred it and hurried on.

> Honor those the dragons heed,
> In thought and favor, word and deed.
> Worlds are lost or worlds are saved
> By those dangers dragonbraved.

> Dragonman, avoid excess;
> Greed will bring the Weyr distress;
> To the ancient Laws adhere,
> Prospers thus the Dragon weyr.

An unintelligible ululation raised the waiting men to their
feet, startled from private meditations and diversion of
Bonethrows. Only Fax remained unmoved at the alarm, save
that the slight sneer, which had settled on his face hours
past, deepened to smug satisfaction.

"Dead-ed-ed," the tidings reverberated down the rocky
corridors of the Hold. The weeping lady seemed to erupt out
of the passage from the Inner Hold, flying down the steps to
sink into an hysterical heap at Fax's feet. "She's dead. Lady
Gemma is dead. There was too much blood. It was too soon.
She was too old to bear more children."

F'lar couldn't decide whether the woman was apologizing
for, or exulting in, the woman's death. She certainly couldn't
be criticizing her Lord for placing Lady Gemma in such peril.
F'lar, however, was sincerely sorry at Gemma's passing. She
had been a brave, fine woman.

And now, what would be Fax's next move? F'lar caught
F'nor's identically quizzical glance and shrugged expressively.

"The child lives!" a curiously distorted voice announced,
penetrating the rising noise in the Great Hall. The words
electrified the atmosphere. Every head slewed round sharply
towards the portal to the Inner Hold where the drudge, a
totally unexpected messenger, stood poised on the top step.

"It is male!" This announcement rang triumphantly in the
still Hall.

Fax jerked himself to his feet, kicking aside the wailer at
his feet, scowling ominously at the drudge. "What did you
say, woman?"

"The child lives. It is male," the creature repeated, descending the stairs.

Incredulity and rage suffused Fax's face. His body seemed
to coil up.

"Ruatha has a new lord!" Staring intently at the overlord,
she advanced, her mien purposeful, almost menacing.

The tentative cheers of the Warder's men were drowned by
the roaring of the dragons.

Fax erupted into action. He leaped across the intervening
space, bellowing. Before Lessa could dodge, his fist crashed

down across her face. She fell heavily to the stone floor, where she lay motionless, a bundle of dirty rags.

"Hold, Fax!" F'lar's voice broke the silence as the Lord of the High Reaches flexed his leg to kick her.

Fax whirled, his hand automatically closing on his knife hilt.

"It was heard and witnessed, Fax," F'lar cautioned him, one hand outstretched in warning, "by dragonmen. Stand by your sworn and witnessed oath!"

"Witnessed? By dragonmen?" cried Fax with a derisive laugh. "Dragonwomen, you mean," he sneered, his eyes blazing with contempt, as he made one sweeping gesture of scorn.

He was momentarily taken aback by the speed with which the bronze rider's knife appeared in his hand.

"Dragonwomen?" F'lar queried, his lips curled back over his teeth, his voice dangerously soft. Glowlight flickered off his circling knife as he advanced on Fax.

"Women! Parasites on Pern. The Weyr power is over. Over!" Fax roared, leaping forward to land in a combat crouch.

The two antagonists were dimly aware of the scurry behind them, of tables pulled roughly aside to give the duelists space. F'lar could spare no glance at the crumpled form of the drudge. Yet he was sure, through and beyond instinct sure, that she was the source of power. He had felt it as she entered the room. The dragons' roaring confirmed it. If that fall had killed her . . . He advanced on Fax, leaping high to avoid the slashing blade as Fax unwound from the crouch with a powerful lunge.

F'lar evaded the attack easily, noticing his opponent's reach, deciding he had a slight advantage there. But not much. Fax had had much more actual hand-to-hand killing experience than had he, whose duels had always ended at first blood on the practice floor. F'lar made due note to avoid closing with the burly lord. The man was heavy-chested, dangerous from sheer mass. F'lar must use agility as his weapon, not brute strength.

Fax feinted, testing F'lar for weakness, or indiscretion. The two crouched, facing each other across six feet of space, knife hands weaving, their free hands, spread-fingered, ready to grab.

Again Fax pressed the attack. F'lar allowed him to close,

just near enough to dodge away with a backhanded swipe. Fabric ripped under the tip of his knife. He heard Fax snarl. The overlord was faster on his feet than his bulk suggested and F'lar had to dodge a second time, feeling Fax's knife score his wher-hide jerkin.

Grimly the two circled, each looking for an opening in the other's defense. Fax plowed in, trying to corner the lighter, faster man between raised platform and wall.

F'lar countered, ducking low under Fax's flailing arm, slashing obliquely across Fax's side. The overlord caught at him, yanking savagely, and F'lar was trapped against the other man's side, straining desperately with his left hand to keep the knife arm up. F'lar brought up his knee, and ducked away as Fax gasped and buckled from the pain in his groin, but Fax struck in passing. Sudden fire laced F'lar's left shoulder.

Fax's face was red with anger and he wheezed from pain and shock. But the infuriated lord straightened up and charged. F'lar was forced to sidestep quickly before Fax could close with him. F'lar put the meat table between them, circling warily, flexing his shoulder to assess the extent of the knife's slash. It was painful, but the arm could be used.

Suddenly Fax scooped up some fatty scraps from the meat tray and hurled them at F'lar. The dragonman ducked and Fax came around the table with a rush. F'lar leaped sideways. Fax's flashing blade came within inches of his abdomen, as his own knife sliced down the outside of Fax's arm. Instantly the two pivoted to face each other again, but Fax's left arm hung limply at his side.

F'lar darted in, pressing his luck as the Lord of the High Reaches staggered. But F'lar misjudged the man's condition and suffered a terrific kick in the side as he tried to dodge under the feinting knife. Doubled with pain, F'lar rolled frantically away from his charging adversary. Fax was lurching forward, trying to fall on him, to pin the lighter dragonman down for a final thrust. Somehow F'lar got to his feet, attempting to straighten to meet Fax's stumbling charge. His very position saved him. Fax overreached his mark and staggered off balance. F'lar brought his right hand over with as much strength as he could muster and his blade plunged through Fax's unprotected back until he felt the point stick in the chest plate.

The defeated lord fell flat to the flagstones. The force of his

descent dislodged the dagger from his chestbone and an inch
of bloody blade reemerged.

F'lar stared down at the dead man. There was no pleasure
in killing, he realized, only relief that he himself was still
alive. He wiped his forehead on his sleeve and forced himself
erect, his side throbbing with the pain of that last kick and
his left shoulder burning. He half-stumbled to the drudge, still
sprawled where she had fallen.

He gently turned her over, noting the terrible bruise spreading across her cheek under the dirty skin. He heard F'nor
take command of the tumult in the Hall.

The dragonman laid a hand, trembling in spite of an effort
to control himself, on the woman's breast to feel for a heartbeat. . . . It was there, slow but strong.

A deep sigh escaped him, for either blow or fall could have
proved fatal. Fatal, perhaps, for Pern as well.

Relief was colored with disgust. There was no telling under
the filth how old this creature might be. He raised her in his
arms, her light body no burden even to his battle-weary
strength. Knowing F'nor would handle any trouble efficiently, F'lar carried the drudge to his own chamber.

Putting the body on the high bed, he stirred up the fire and
added more glows to the bedside bracket. His gorge rose at
the thought of touching the filthy mat of hair but nonetheless
and gently, he pushed it back from the face, turning the head
this way and that. The features were small, regular. One
arm, clear of rags, was reasonably clean above the elbow but
marred by bruises and old scars. The skin was firm and
unwrinkled. The hands, when he took them in his, were
filthy but well-shaped and delicately boned.

F'lar began to smile. Yes, she had blurred that hand so
skillfully that he had actually doubted what he had first
seen. And yes, beneath grime and grease, she was young.
Young enough for the Weyr. And no born drab. There was no
taint of common blood here. It was pure, no matter whose the
line, and he rather thought she was indeed Ruathan. One
who had by some unknown agency escaped the massacre ten
Turns ago and bided her time for revenge. Why else force Fax
to renounce the Hold?

Delighted and fascinated by this unexpected luck, F'lar
reached out to tear the dress from the unconscious body and
found himself constrained not to. The girl had roused. Her

great, hungry eyes fastened on his, not fearful or expectant; wary.

A subtle change occurred in her face. F'lar watched, his smile deepening, as she shifted her regular features into an illusion of disagreeable ugliness and great age.

"Trying to confuse a dragonman, girl?" he chuckled. He made no further move to touch her but settled against the great carved post of the bed. He crossed his arms sternly on his chest, thought better of it immediately, and eased his sore arm. "Your name, girl, and rank, too."

She drew herself upright slowly against the headboard, her features no longer blurred. They faced each other across the high bed.

"Fax?"

"Dead. Your name!"

A look of exulting triumph flooded her face. She slipped from the bed, standing unexpectedly tall. "Then I reclaim my own. I am of the Ruathan Blood. I claim Ruath," she announced in a ringing voice.

F'lar stared at her a moment, delighted with her proud bearing. Then he threw back his head and laughed.

"This? This crumbling heap?" He could not help but mock the disparity between her manner and her dress. "Oh, no. Besides, Lady, we dragonmen heard and witnessed Fax's oath renouncing the Hold in favor of his heir. Shall I challenge the babe, too, for you? And choke him with his swaddling cloth?"

Her eyes flashed, her lips parted in a terrible smile.

"There is no heir. Gemma died, the babe unborn. I lied."

"Lied?" F'lar demanded, angry.

"Yes," she taunted him with a toss of her chin. "I lied. There was no babe born. I merely wanted to be sure you challenged Fax."

He grabbed her wrist, stung that he had twice fallen to her prodding.

"You provoked a dragonman to fight? To kill? *When he is on Search?*"

"Search? Why should I care about a Search? I've Ruatha as my Hold again. For ten Turns, I have worked and waited, schemed and suffered for that. What could your Search mean to me?"

F'lar wanted to strike that look of haughty contempt from her face. He twisted her arm savagely, bringing her to her feet before he released his grip. She laughed at him, and scuttled to one side. She was on her feet and out the door before he could give chase.

Swearing to himself, he raced down the rocky corridors, knowing she would have to make for the Hall to get out of the Hold. However, when he reached the Hall, there was no sign of her fleeing figure among those still loitering.

"Has that creature come this way?" he called to F'nor, who was, by chance, standing by the door to the Court.

"No. Is she the source of power after all?"

"Yes, she is," F'lar answered, galled all the more. "And Ruathan Blood at that!"

"Oh ho! Does she depose the babe, then?" F'nor asked, gesturing towards the birthing-woman who occupied a seat close to the now blazing hearth.

F'lar paused, about to return to search the Hold's myriad passages. He stared, momentarily confused, at this brown rider.

"Babe? What babe?"

"The male child Lady Gemma bore," F'nor replied, surprised by F'lar's uncomprehending look.

"It lives?"

"Yes. A strong babe, the woman says, for all that he was premature and taken forcibly from his dead dame's belly."

F'lar threw back his head with a shout of laughter. For all her scheming, she had been outdone by truth.

At that moment, he heard Mnementh roar in unmistakable elation and the curious warble of other dragons.

"Mnementh has caught her," F'lar cried, grinning with jubilation. He strode down the steps, past the body of the former Lord of the High Reaches and out into the main court.

He saw that the bronze dragon was gone from his Tower perch and called him. An agitation drew his eyes upward. He saw Mnementh spiraling down into the Court, his front paws clasping something. Mnementh informed F'lar that he had seen her climbing from one of the high windows and had simply plucked her from the ledge, knowing the dragonman sought her. The bronze dragon settled awkwardly onto his hind legs, his wings working to keep him balanced. Carefully he set the girl on her feet and formed a precise cage around her with his huge talons. She stood motionless within that circle, her face towards the wedge-shaped head that swayed above her.

The watch-wher, shrieking terror, anger and hatred, was lunging violently to the end of its chain, trying to come to Lessa's aid. It grabbed at F'lar as he strode to the two.

"You've courage enough, girl," he admitted, resting one hand casually on Mnementh's upper claw. Mnementh was enormously pleased with himself and swiveled his head down for his eye ridges to be scratched.

"You did not lie, you know," F'lar said, unable to resist taunting the girl.

Slowly she turned towards him, her face impassive. She was not afraid of dragons, F'lar realized with approval.

"The babe lives. And it is male."

She could not control her dismay and her shoulders sagged briefly before she pulled herself erect.

"Ruatha is mine," she insisted in a tense low voice.

"Aye, and it would have been, had you approached me directly when the wing arrived here."

Her eyes widened. "What do you mean?"

"A dragonman may champion anyone whose grievance is just. By the time we reached Ruath Hold, I was quite ready to challenge Fax given any reasonable cause, despite the Search." This was not the whole truth but F'lar must teach this girl the folly of trying to control dragonmen. "Had you paid any attention to your harper's songs, you'd know your rights. And," F'lar's voice held a vindictive edge that surprised him, "Lady Gemma might not now lie dead. She suffered far more at that tyrant's hand than you."

Something in her manner told him that she regretted Lady Gemma's death, that it had affected her deeply.

"What good is Ruatha to you now?" he demanded, a broad sweep of his arm taking in the ruined courtyard and the Hold, the entire unproductive valley of Ruatha. "You have indeed accomplished your ends; a profitless conquest and its conqueror's death." F'lar snorted: "All seven Holds will revert to their legitimate Blood, and time they did. One Hold, one lord. Of course, you might have to fight others, infected with Fax's greed. Could you hold Ruatha against attack . . . now . . . in her decline?"

"Ruatha is mine!"

"Ruatha?" F'lar's laugh was derisive. "When you could be Weyrwoman?"

"Weyrwoman?" she breathed, staring at him.

"Yes, little fool. I said I rode in Search . . . it's about time you attended to more than Ruatha. And the object of my Search is . . . you!"

She stared at the finger he pointed at her as if it were dangerous.

"By the first Egg, girl, you've power in you to spare when you can turn a dragonman, all unwitting, to do your bidding. Ah, but never again, for now I am on guard against you."

Mnementh crooned approvingly, the sound a soft rumble in his throat. He arched his neck so that one eye was turned directly on the girl, gleaming in the darkness of the court.

F'lar noticed with detached pride that she neither flinched nor blanched at the proximity of an eye greater than her own head.

"He likes to have his eye ridges scratched," F'lar remarked in a friendly tone, changing tactics.

"I know," she said softly and reached out a hand to do that service.

"Nemorth's queen," F'lar continued, "is close to death. This time we must have a strong Weyrwoman."

"This time—the Red Star?" the girl gasped, turning frightened eyes to F'lar.

"You understand what it means?"

"There is danger . . ." she began in a bare whisper, glancing apprehensively eastward.

F'lar did not question by what miracle she appreciated the imminence of danger. He had every intention of taking her to the Weyr by sheer force if necessary. But something within him wanted very much for her to accept the challenge voluntarily. A rebellious Weyrwoman would be even more dangerous than a stupid one. This girl had too much power and was too used to guile and strategy. It would be a calamity to antagonize her with injudicious handling.

"There is danger for all Pern. Not just Ruatha," he said, allowing a note of entreaty to creep into his voice. "And *you* are needed. Not by Ruatha," a wave of his hand dismissed that consideration as a negligible one compared to the total picture. "We are doomed without a strong Weyrwoman. Without you."

"Gemma kept saying *all* the bronze riders were needed," she murmured in a dazed whisper.

What did she mean by that statement? F'lar frowned. Had she heard a word he had said? He pressed his argument, certain only that he had already struck one responsive chord.

"You've won here. Let the babe," he saw her startled rejection of that idea and ruthlessly qualified it, ". . . Gemma's babe . . . be reared at Ruatha. You have command of all the Holds as Weyrwoman, not ruined Ruatha alone. You've accomplished Fax's death. Leave off vengeance."

She stared at F'lar with wonder, absorbing his words.

"I never thought beyond Fax's death," she admitted slowly. "I never thought what should happen then."

Her confusion was almost childlike and struck F'lar forcibly. He had no time, or desire, to consider her prodigious accomplishment. Now he realized some measure of her indomitable character. She could not have been much over ten Turns of age herself when Fax had murdered her family. Yet somehow, so young, she had set herself a goal and managed to survive both brutality and detection long enough to secure the usurper's death. What a Weyrwoman she would be! In the tradition of those of Ruathan blood. The light of the paler moon made her look young and vulnerable and almost pretty.

"You can be Weyrwoman," he insisted gently.

"Weyrwoman," she breathed, incredulous, and gazed round the inner court bathed in soft moonlight. He thought she wavered.

"Or perhaps you enjoy rags?" he said, making his voice harsh, mocking. "And matted hair, dirty feet and cracked hands? Sleeping in straw, eating rinds? You are young . . . that is, I assume you are young," and his voice was frankly skeptical. She glared at him, her lips firmly pressed together. "Is this the be-all and end-all of your ambition? What are you that this little corner of the great world is *all* you want?" He paused and with utter contempt added, "The blood of Ruatha has thinned, I see. You're afraid!"

"I am Lessa, daughter of the Lord of Ruath," she countered, stung. She drew herself erect. Her eyes flashed. "I am afraid of nothing!"

F'lar contented himself with a slight smile.

Mnementh, however, threw up his head, and stretched out his sinuous neck to its whole length. His full-throated peal rang out down the valley. The bronze dragon communicated his awareness to F'lar that Lessa had accepted the challenge. The other dragons answered back, their warbles shriller than Mnementh's bellow. The watch-wher which had cowered at the end of its chain lifted its voice in a thin, unnerving screech until the Hold emptied of its startled occupants.

"F'nor," the bronze rider called, waving his wingleader to him. "Leave half the flight to guard the Hold. Some nearby lord might think to emulate Fax's example. Send one rider to the High Reaches with the glad news. You go directly to the Cloth Hall and speak to L'tol . . . Lytol." F'lar grinned. "I think he would make an exemplary Warder and Lord Surrogate for this Hold in the name of the Weyr and the babe."

The brown rider's face expressed enthusiasm for his mission as he began to comprehend his leader's intentions. With Fax dead and Ruatha under the protection of dragonmen, particularly that same one who had dispatched Fax, the Hold would have wise management.

"She caused Ruatha's deterioration?" he asked.

"And nearly ours with her machinations," F'lar replied, but having found the admirable object of his Search, he could now be magnanimous. "Suppress your exultation, brother," he advised quickly as he took note of F'nor's expression. "The new queen must also be Impressed."

"I'll settle arrangements here. Lytol is an excellent choice," F'nor said.

"Who is this Lytol?" demanded Lessa pointedly. She had twisted the mass of filthy hair back from her face. In the moonlight the dirt was less noticeable. F'lar caught F'nor looking at her with an all too easily read expression. He signaled F'nor, with a peremptory gesture, to carry out his orders without delay.

"Lytol is a dragonless man," F'lar told the girl, "no friend to Fax. He will ward the Hold well and it will prosper." He added persuasively with a quelling stare full on her, "Won't it?"

She regarded him somberly, without answering, until he chuckled softly at her discomfiture.

"We'll return to the Weyr," he announced, proffering a hand to guide her to Mnementh's side.

The bronze one had extended his head toward the watchwher, who now lay panting on the ground, its chain limp in the dust.

"Oh," Lessa sighed, and dropped beside the grotesque beast. It raised its head slowly, lurring piteously.

"Mnementh says it is very old and soon will sleep itself to death."

Lessa cradled the bestial head in her arms, scratching it behind the ears.

"Come, Lessa of Pern," F'lar said, impatient to be up and away.

She rose slowly but obediently. "It saved me. It knew me."

"It knows it did well," F'lar assured her, brusquely, wondering at such an uncharacteristic show of sentiment in her.

He took her hand again, to help her to her feet and lead her back to Mnementh. As they turned, he glimpsed the watchwher, launching itself at a dead run after Lessa. The chain, however, held fast. The beast's neck broke, with a sickeningly audible snap.

Lessa was on her knees in an instant, cradling the repulsive head in her arms.

"Why, you foolish thing, why?" she asked in a stunned whisper as the light in the beast's green-gold eyes dimmed and died out.

Mnementh informed F'lar that the creature had lived this long only to preserve the Ruathan line. At Lessa's imminent departure, it had welcomed death.

A convulsive shudder went through Lessa's slim body. F'lar watched as she undid the heavy buckle that fastened the metal collar about the watch-wher's neck. She threw the tether away with a violent motion. Tenderly she laid the watchwher on the cobbles. With one last caress to the clipped wings, she rose in a fluid movement and walked resolutely to Mnementh without a single backward glance. She stepped calmly to the dragon's raised leg and seated herself, as F'lar directed, on the great neck.

F'lar glanced around the courtyard at the remainder of his wing which had reformed there. The Hold folk had retreated back into the safety of the Great Hall. When his wingmen were all astride, he vaulted to Mnementh's neck, behind the girl.

"Hold tightly to my arms," he ordered her as he took hold of the smallest neck ridge and gave the command to fly.

Her fingers closed spasmodically around his forearm as the great bronze dragon took off, the enormous wings working to achieve height from the vertical takeoff. Mnementh preferred to fall into flight from a cliff or tower. Like all dragons, he tended to indolence. F'lar glanced behind him, saw the other dragonmen form the flight line, spread out to cover those still on guard at Ruatha Hold.

When they had reached a sufficient altitude, he told Mnementh to transfer, going *between* to the Weyr.

Only a gasp indicated the girl's astonishment as they hung *between*. Accustomed as he was to the sting of the profound cold, to the awesome utter lack of light and sound, F'lar still found the sensations unnerving. Yet the uncommon transfer spanned no more time than it took to cough thrice.

Mnementh rumbled approval of this candidate's calm reaction as they flicked out of the eerie *between*.

And then they were above the Weyr, Mnementh setting his wings to glide in the bright daylight, half a world away from night-time Ruatha.

As they circled above the great stony trough of the Weyr, F'lar peered at Lessa's face, pleased with the delight mirrored there; she showed no trace of fear as they hung a thousand lengths above the high Benden mountain range. Then, as the seven dragons roared their incoming cry, an incredulous smile lit her face.

The other wingmen dropped into a wide spiral, down, down while Mnementh elected to descend in lazy circles. The dragonmen peeled off smartly and dropped, each to his own tier in the caves of the Weyr. Mnementh finally completed his leisurely approach to their quarters, whistling shrilly to himself as he braked his forward speed with a twist of his wings, dropping lightly at last to the ledge. He crouched as F'lar swung the girl to the rough rock, scored from thousands of clawed landings.

"This leads only to our quarters," he told her as they entered the corridor, vaulted and wide for the easy passage of great bronze dragons.

As they reached the huge natural cavern that had been his since Mnementh achieved maturity, F'lar looked about him with eyes fresh from his first prolonged absence from the Weyr. The huge chamber was unquestionably big, certainly larger than most of the halls he had visited in Fax's procession. Those halls were intended as gathering places for men, not the habitations of dragons. But suddenly he saw his own quarters were nearly as shabby as all Ruatha. Benden was, of a certainty, one of the oldest dragon weyrs, as Ruatha was one of the oldest Holds, but that excused nothing. How many dragons had bedded in that hollow to make solid rock conform to dragon proportions! How many feet had worn the

path past the dragon's weyr into the sleeping chamber, to the
bathing room beyond where the natural warm spring provided ever-fresh water! But the wall hangings were faded
and unraveling and there were grease stains on lintel and
floor that should be sanded away.

He noticed the wary expression on Lessa's face as he
paused in the sleeping room.

"I must feed Mnementh immediately. So you may bathe
first," he said, rummaging in a chest and finding clean
clothes for her, discards of other previous occupants of his
quarters, but far more presentable than her present covering.
He carefully laid back in the chest the white wool robe that
was traditional Impression garb. She would wear that later.
He tossed several garments at her feet and a bag of sweetsand,
gesturing to the hanging that obscured the way to the bath.

He left her, then, the clothes in a heap at her feet, for she
made no effort to catch anything.

Mnementh informed him that F'nor was feeding Canth and
that he, Mnementh, was hungry, too. *She* didn't trust F'lar
but she wasn't afraid of himself.

"Why should she be afraid of you?" F'lar asked. "You're
cousin to the watch-wher who was her only friend."

Mnementh informed F'lar that he, a fully matured bronze
dragon, was no relation to any scrawny, crawling, chained,
and wing-clipped watch-wher.

F'lar, pleased at having been able to tease the bronze one,
chuckled to himself. With great dignity, Mnementh curved
down to the feeding ground.

> By the Golden Egg of Faranth
> By the Weyrwoman, wise and true,
> Breed a flight of bronze and brown wings,
> Breed a flight of green and blue.
> Breed riders, strong and daring,
> Dragon-loving, born as hatched,
> Flight of hundreds soaring skyward,
> Man and dragon fully matched.

Lessa waited until the sound of the dragonman's footsteps
proved he had really gone away. She rushed quickly through
the big cavern, heard the scrape of claw and the *whoosh* of
the mighty wings. She raced down the short passageway,
right to the edge of the yawning entrance. There was the

bronze dragon circling down to the wider end of the mile-long barren oval that was Benden Weyr. She had heard of the Weyrs, as any Pernese had, but to be in one was quite a different matter.

She peered up, around, down that sheer rock face. There was no way off but by dragon wing. The nearest cave mouths were an unhandy distance above her, to one side, below her on the other. She was neatly secluded here.

Weyrwoman, he had told her. His woman? In his weyr? Was that what he had meant? No, that was not the impression she got from the dragon. It occurred to her, suddenly, that it was odd she had understood the dragon. Were common folk able to? Or was it the dragonman blood in her line? At all events, Mnementh had implied something greater, some special rank. She remembered vaguely that, when dragonmen went on Search, they looked for certain women. Ah, certain women. She was one, then, of several contenders. Yet the bronze rider had offered her the position as if she and she, alone, qualified. He had his own generous portion of conceit, that one, Lessa decided. Arrogant he was, though not a bully like Fax.

She could see the bronze dragon swoop down to the running herdbeasts, saw the strike, saw the dragon wheel up to settle on a far ledge to feed. Instinctively she drew back from the opening, back into the dark and relative safety of the corridor.

The feeding dragon evoked scores of horrid tales. Tales at which she had scoffed but now . . . Was it true, then, that dragons did eat human flesh? Did . . . Lessa halted that trend of thought. Dragonkind was no less cruel than mankind. The dragon, at least, acted from bestial need rather than bestial greed.

Assured that the dragonman would be occupied awhile, she crossed the larger cave into the sleeping room. She scooped up the clothing and the bag of cleansing sand and proceeded to the bathing room.

To be clean! To be completely clean and to be able to stay that way. With distaste, she stripped off the remains of the rags, kicking them to one side. She made a soft mud with the sweetsand and scrubbed her entire body until she drew blood from various half-healed cuts. Then she jumped into the pool, gasping as the warm water made the sweetsand foam in the lacerations.

It was a ritual cleansing of more than surface soil. The luxury of cleanliness was ecstasy.

Finally satisfied she was as clean as one long soaking could make her, she left the pool, reluctantly. Wringing out her hair she tucked it up on her head as she dried herself. She shook out the clothing and held one garment against her experimentally. The fabric, a soft green, felt smooth under her water-shrunken fingers, although the nap caught on her roughened hands. She pulled it over her head. It was loose but the darker-green over-tunic had a sash which she pulled in tight at the waist. The unusual sensation of softness against her bare skin made her wriggle with voluptuous pleasure. The skirt, no longer a ragged hem of tatters, swirled heavily around her ankles. She smiled. She took up a fresh drying cloth and began to work on her hair.

A muted sound came to her ears and she stopped, hands poised, head bent to one side. Straining, she listened. Yes, there were sounds without. The dragonman and his beast must have returned. She grimaced to herself with annoyance at this untimely interruption and rubbed harder at her hair. She ran fingers through the half-dry tangles, the motions arrested as she encountered snarls. Vexed, she rummaged on the shelves until she found, as she had hoped to, a coarse-toothed metal comb.

Dry, her hair had a life of its own suddenly, crackling about her hands and clinging to face and comb and dress. It was difficult to get the silky stuff under control. And her hair was longer than she had thought, for, clean and unmatted, it fell to her waist—when it did not cling to her hands.

She paused, listening, and heard no sound at all. Apprehensively, she stepped to the curtain and glanced warily into the sleeping room. It was empty. She listened and caught the perceptible thoughts of the sleepy dragon. Well, she would rather meet the man in the presence of a sleepy dragon than in a sleeping room. She started across the floor and, out of the corner of her eye, caught sight of a strange woman as she passed a polished piece of metal hanging on the wall.

Amazed, she stopped short, staring, incredulous, at the face the metal reflected. Only when she put her hands to her prominent cheekbones in a gesture of involuntary surprise and the reflection imitated the gesture, did she realize she looked at herself.

Why, that girl in the reflector was prettier than Lady Tela,

than the clothman's daughter! But so thin. Her hands of their
own volition dropped to her neck, to the protruding collar-
bones, to her breasts which did not entirely accord with the
gauntness of the rest of her. The dress was too large for her
frame, she noted with an unexpected emergence of conceit
born in that instant of delighted appraisal. And her hair . . .
it stood out around her head like an aureole. It wouldn't lie
contained. She smoothed it down with impatient fingers,
automatically bringing locks forward to hang around her
face. As she irritably pushed them back, dismissing a need
for disguise, the hair drifted up again.

A slight sound, the scrape of a boot against stone, caught
her back from her bemusement. She waited, momentarily
expecting him to appear. She was suddenly timid. With her
face bare to the world, her hair behind her ears, her body
outlined by a clinging fabric, she was stripped of her accustomed anonymity and was, therefore, in her estimation,
vulnerable.

She controlled the desire to run away—the irrational fear.
Observing herself in the looking metal, she drew her shoulders back, tilted her head high, chin up; the movement
caused her hair to crackle and cling and shift about her head.
She was Lessa of Ruatha, of a fine old Blood. She no longer
needed artifice to preserve herself; she must stand proudly
bare-faced before the world . . . and that dragonman.

Resolutely she crossed the room, pushing aside the hanging on the doorway to the great cavern.

He was there, beside the head of the dragon, scratching its
eye ridges, a curiously tender expression on his face. The
tableau was at variance with all she had heard of dragonmen.

She had, of course, heard of the strange affinity between
rider and dragon but this was the first time she realized that
love was part of that bond. Or that this reserved, cold man
was capable of such deep emotion.

He turned slowly, as if loath to leave the bronze beast. He
caught sight of her and pivoted completely round, his eyes
intense as he took note of her altered appearance. With
quick, light steps, he closed the distance between them and
ushered her back into the sleeping room, one strong hand
holding her by the elbow.

"Mnementh has fed lightly and will need quiet to rest," he

said in a low voice. He pulled the heavy hanging into place across the opening.

Then he held her away from him, turning her this way and that, scrutinizing her closely, curious and slightly surprised.

"You wash up ... pretty, yes, almost pretty," he said, amused condescension in his voice. She pulled roughly away from him, piqued. His low laugh mocked her. "After all, how could one guess what was under the grime of ... ten full Turns?"

At length he said, "No matter. We must eat and I shall require your services." At her startled exclamation, he turned, grinning maliciously now as his movement revealed the caked blood on his left sleeve. "The least you can do is bathe wounds honorably received fighting your battle."

He pushed aside a portion of the drape that curtained the inner wall. "Food for two!" he roared down a black gap in the sheer stone.

She heard a subterranean echo far below as his voice resounded down what must be a long shaft.

"Nemorth is nearly rigid," he was saying as he took supplies from another drape-hidden shelf, "and the Hatching will soon begin anyhow."

A coldness settled in Lessa's stomach at the mention of a Hatching. The mildest tales she had heard about that part of dragonlore were chilling, the worst dismayingly macabre. She took the things he handed her numbly.

"What? Frightened?" the dragonman taunted, pausing as he stripped off his torn and bloodied shirt.

With a shake of her head, Lessa turned her attention to the wide-shouldered, well-muscled back he presented her, the paler skin of his body decorated with random bloody streaks. Fresh blood welled from the point of his shoulder, for the removal of his shirt had broken the tender scabs.

"I will need water," she said and saw she had a flat pan among the items he had given her. She went swiftly to the pool for water, wondering how she had come to agree to venture so far from Ruatha. Ruined though it was, it had been hers and was familiar to her from Tower to deep cellar. At the moment the idea had been proposed and insidiously prosecuted by the dragonman, she had felt capable of anything, having achieved, at last, Fax's death. Now, it was all she could do to keep the water from slopping out of the pan that shook unaccountably in her hands.

She forced herself to deal only with the wound. It was a nasty gash, deep where the point had entered and torn downward in a gradually shallower slice. His skin felt smooth under her fingers as she cleansed the wound. In spite of herself, she noticed the masculine odor of him, compounded not unpleasantly of sweat, leather, and an unusual muskiness which must be from close association with dragons.

She stood back when she had finished her ministration. He flexed his arm experimentally in the constricting bandage and the motion set the muscles rippling along side and back.

When he faced her, his eyes were dark and thoughtful.

"Gently done. My thanks." His smile was ironic.

She backed away as he rose but he only went to the chest to take out a clean, white shirt.

A muted rumble sounded, growing quickly louder.

Dragons roaring? Lessa wondered, trying to conquer the ridiculous fear that rose within her. Had the Hatching started? There was no watch-wher's lair to secrete herself in, here.

As if he understood her confusion, the dragonman laughed good-humoredly and, his eyes on hers, drew aside the wall covering just as some noisy mechanism inside the shaft propelled a tray of food into sight.

Ashamed of her unbased fright and furious that he had witnessed it, Lessa sat rebelliously down on the fur-covered wall seat, heartily wishing him a variety of serious and painful injuries which she could dress with inconsiderate hands. She would not waste future opportunities.

He placed the tray on the low table in front of her, throwing down a heap of furs for his own seat. There was meat, bread, a tempting yellow cheese and even a few pieces of winter fruit. He made no move to eat nor did she, though the thought of a piece of fruit that was ripe, instead of rotten, set her mouth to watering. He glanced up at her, and frowned.

"Even in the Weyr, the lady breaks bread first," he said, and inclined his head politely to her.

Lessa flushed, unused to any courtesy and certainly unused to being first to eat. She broke off a chunk of bread. It was nothing she remembered having tasted before. For one thing, it was fresh-baked. The flour had been finely sifted, without trace of sand or hull. She took the slice of cheese he proffered her and it, too, had an uncommonly delicious sharpness.

Made bold by this indication of her changed status, Lessa reached for the plumpest piece of fruit.

"Now," the dragonman began, his hand touching hers to get her attention.

Guiltily she dropped the fruit, thinking she had erred. She stared at him, wondering at her fault. He retrieved the fruit and placed it back in her hand as he continued to speak. Wide-eyed, disarmed, she nibbled, and gave him her full attention.

"Listen to me. You must not show a moment's fear, whatever happens on the Hatching Ground. And you must not let her overeat." A wry expression crossed his face. "One of our main functions is to keep a dragon from excessive eating."

Lessa lost interest in the taste of the fruit. She placed it carefully back in the bowl and tried to sort out not what he had said, but what his tone of voice implied. She looked at the dragonman's face, seeing him as a person, not a symbol, for the first time.

There was a blackness about him that was not malevolent; it was a brooding sort of patience. Heavy black hair, heavy black brows; his eyes, a brown light enough to seem golden, were all too expressive of cynical emotions, or cold hauteur. His lips were thin but well-shaped and in respose almost gentle. Why must he always pull his mouth to one side in disapproval or in one of those sardonic smiles? At this moment, he was completely unaffected.

He meant what he was saying. He did not want her to be afraid. There was no reason for her, Lessa, *to* fear.

He very much wanted her to succeed. In keeping whom from overeating what? Herd animals? A newly hatched dragon certainly wasn't capable of eating a full beast. That seemed a simple enough task to Lessa. . . . Main function? *Our* main function?

The dragonman was looking at her expectantly.

"Our main function?" she repeated, an unspoken request for more information inherent in her inflection.

"More of that later. First things first," he said, impatiently waving off her other questions.

"But what happens?" she insisted.

"As I was told so I tell you. No more, no less. Remember these two points. No fear, and no overeating."

"But . . ."

"You, however, need to eat. Here." He speared a piece of

meat on his knife and thrust it at her, frowning until she managed to choke it down. He was about to force more on her but she grabbed up her half-eaten fruit and bit down into the firm sweet sphere instead. She had already eaten more at this one meal than she was accustomed to having all day at the Hold.

"We shall soon eat better at the Weyr," he remarked, regarding the tray with a jaundiced eye.

Lessa was surprised. This was a feast, in her opinion.

"More than you're used to? Yes, I forgot you left Ruatha with bare bones indeed."

She stiffened.

"You did well at Ruatha. I mean no criticism," he added, smiling at her reaction. "But look at you," and he gestured at her body, that curious expression crossing his face, half-amused, half-contemplative. "I should not have guessed you'd clean up pretty," he remarked. "Nor with such hair." This time his expression was frankly admiring.

Involuntarily she put one hand to her head, the hair crackling over her fingers. But what reply she might have made him, indignant as she was, died aborning. An unearthly keening filled the chamber.

The sounds set up a vibration that ran down the bones behind her ear to her spine. She clapped both hands to her ears. The noise rang through her skull despite her defending hands. As abruptly as it started, it ceased.

Before she knew what he was about, the dragonman had grabbed her by the wrist and pulled her over to the chest.

"Take those off," he ordered, indicating dress and tunic. While she stared at him stupidly, he held up a loose white robe, sleeveless and beltless, a matter of two lengths of fine cloth fastened at shoulder and side seams. "Take it off, or do I assist you?" he asked, with no patience at all.

The wild sound was repeated and its unnerving tone made her fingers fly faster. She had no sooner loosened the garments she wore, letting them slide to her feet, than he had thrown the other over her head. She managed to get her arms in the proper places before he grabbed her wrist again and was speeding with her out of the room, her hair whipping out behind her, alive with static.

As they reached the outer chamber, the bronze dragon was standing in the center of the cavern, his head turned to watch the sleeping room door. He seemed impatient to Lessa; his great eyes, which fascinated her so, sparkled iridescently. His manner breathed an inner excitement of great proportions and from his throat a high-pitched croon issued, several octaves below the unnerving cry that had roused them all.

With a yank that rocked her head on her neck, the dragonman pulled her along the passage. The dragon padded beside them at such speed that Lessa fully expected they would all catapult off the ledge. Somehow, at the crucial stride, she was a-perch the bronze neck, the dragonman holding her firmly about the waist. In the same fluid movement, they were gliding across the great bowl of the Weyr to the higher wall opposite. The air was full of wings and dragon tails, rent with a chorus of sounds, echoing and re-echoing across the stony valley.

Mnementh set what Lessa was certain would be a collision course with other dragons, straight for a huge round blackness in the cliff-face, high up. Magically, the beasts filed in, the greater wingspread of Mnementh just clearing the sides of the entrance.

The passageway reverberated with the thunder of wings. The air compressed around her thickly. Then they broke out into a gigantic cavern.

Why, the entire mountain must be hollow, thought Lessa, incredulous. Around the enormous cavern, dragons perched in serried ranks, blues, greens, browns and only two great bronze beasts like Mnementh, on ledges meant to accommodate hundreds. Lessa gripped the bronze neck scales before her, instinctively aware of the imminence of a great event.

Mnementh wheeled downward, disregarding the ledge of the bronze ones. Then all Lessa could see was what lay on the sandy floor of the great cavern; dragon eggs. A clutch of ten monstrous, mottled eggs, their shells moving spasmodically as the fledglings within tapped their way out. To one side, on a raised portion of the floor, was a golden egg, larger by half again the size of the mottled ones. Just beyond the golden egg lay the motionless ocher hulk of the old queen.

Just as she realized Mnementh was hovering over the floor in the vicinity of that egg, Lessa felt the dragonman's hands on her, lifting her from Mnementh's neck.

Apprehensively, she grabbed at him. His hands tightened and inexorably swung her down. His eyes, fierce and gray, locked with hers.

"Remember, Lessa!"

Mnementh added an encouragement, one great compound eye turned on her. Then he rose from the floor. Lessa half-raised one hand in entreaty, bereft of all support, even that of the sure inner compulsion which had sustained her in her struggle for revenge on Fax. She saw the bronze dragon settle on the first ledge, at some distance from the other two bronze beasts. The dragonman dismounted and Mnementh curved his sinuous neck until his head was beside his rider. The man reached up absently, it seemed to Lessa, and caressed his mount.

Loud screams and wailings diverted Lessa and she saw more dragons descend to hover just above the cavern floor, each rider depositing a young woman until there were twelve girls, including Lessa. She remained a little apart from them as they clung to each other. She regarded them curiously. The girls were not injured in any way she could see, so why such weeping? She took a deep breath against the coldness within her. Let *them* be afraid. She was Lessa of Ruatha and did not need to be afraid.

Just then, the golden egg moved convulsively. Gasping as one, the girls edged away from it, back against the rocky wall. One, a lovely blonde, her heavy plait of golden hair swinging just above the ground, started to step off the raised floor and stopped, shrieking, backing fearfully towards the scant comfort of her peers.

Lessa wheeled to see what cause there might be for the look of horror on the girl's face. She stepped back involuntarily herself.

In the main section of the sandy arena, several of the handful of eggs had already cracked wide open. The fledglings, crowing weakly, were moving towards . . . and Lessa gulped . . . the young boys standing stolidly in a semicircle. Some of them were no older than she had been when Fax's army had swooped down on Ruath Hold.

The shrieking of the women subsided to muffled gasps. A fledgling reached out with claw and beak to grab a boy.

Lessa forced herself to watch as the young dragon mauled the youth, throwing him roughly aside as if unsatisfied in some way. The boy did not move and Lessa could see blood seeping onto the sand from dragon-inflicted wounds.

A second fledgling lurched against another boy and halted,

flapping its damp wings impotently, raising its scrawny neck
and croaking a parody of the encouraging croon Mnementh
often gave. The boy uncertainly lifted a hand and began to
scratch the eye ridge. Incredulous, Lessa watched as the
fledgling, its crooning increasingly more mellow, ducked its
head, pushing at the boy. The child's face broke into an
unbelieving smile of elation.

Tearing her eyes from this astounding sight, Lessa saw
that another fledgling was beginning the same performance
with another boy. Two more dragons had emerged in the
interim. One had knocked a boy down and was walking over
him, oblivious to the fact that its claws were raking great
gashes. The fledgling who followed its hatch-mate stopped by
the wounded child, ducking its head to the boy's face, crooning anxiously. As Lessa watched, the boy managed to struggle to his feet, tears of pain streaming down his cheeks. She
could hear him pleading with the dragon not to worry, that
he was only scratched a little.

It was over very soon. The young dragons paired off with
boys. Green riders dropped down to carry off the unaccept-
able. Blue riders settled to the floor with their beasts and led
the couples out of the cavern, the young dragons squealing,
crooning, flapping wet wings as they staggered off, encour-
aged by their newly acquired Weyrmates.

Lessa turned resolutely back to the rocking golden egg,
knowing what to expect and trying to divine what the successful boys had, or had not, done that caused the baby
dragons to single them out.

A crack appeared in the golden shell and was greeted by
the terrified screams of the girls. Some had fallen into little
heaps of white fabric, others embraced tightly in their mutual
fear. The crack widened and the wedge-head broke through,
followed quickly by the neck, gleaming gold. Lessa wondered
with unexpected detachment how long it would take the beast
to mature, considering its by no means small size at birth.
For the head was larger than that of the male dragons and
they had been large enough to overwhelm sturdy boys of ten
full Turns.

Lessa was aware of a loud hum within the Hall. Glancing
up at the audience, she realized it emanated from the watching bronze dragons, for this was the birth of their mate, their
queen. The hum increased in volume as the shell shattered

into fragments and the golden, glistening body of the new
female emerged. It staggered out, dipping its sharp beak into
the soft sand, momentarily trapped. Flapping its wet wings,
it righted itself, ludicrous in its weak awkwardness. With
sudden and unexpected swiftness, it dashed towards the
terror-stricken girls.

Before Lessa could blink, it shook the first girl with such
violence her head snapped audibly and she fell limply to the
sand. Disregarding her, the dragon leaped towards the second girl but misjudged the distance and fell, grabbing out
with one claw for support and raking the girl's body from
shoulder to thigh. The screaming of the mortally injured girl
distracted the dragon and released the others from their
horrified trance. They scattered in panicky confusion, racing,
running, tripping, stumbling, falling across the sand towards
the exit the boys had used.

As the golden beast, crying piteously, lurched down from
the raised arena towards the scattered women, Lessa moved.
Why hadn't that silly clunk-headed girl stepped aside, Lessa
thought, grabbing for the wedge-head, at birth not much
larger than her own torso. The dragon's so clumsy and weak
she's her own worst enemy.

Lessa swung the head round so that the many-faceted eyes
were forced to look at her . . . and found herself lost in that
rainbow regard.

A feeling of joy suffused Lessa, a feeling of warmth, ten-
derness, unalloyed affection and instant respect and admira-
tion flooded mind and heart and soul. Never again would
Lessa lack an advocate, a defender, an intimate, aware
instantly of the temper of her mind and heart, of her desires.
How wonderful was Lessa, the thought intruded into Lessa's
reflections, how pretty, how kind, how thoughtful, how brave
and clever!

Mechanically, Lessa reached out to scratch the exact spot
on the soft eye ridge.

The dragon blinked at her wistfully, extremely sad that she
had distressed Lessa. Lessa reassuringly patted the slightly
damp, soft neck that curved trustingly towards her. The
dragon reeled to one side and one wing fouled on the hind
claw. It hurt. Carefully, Lessa lifted the erring foot, freed the
wing, folding it back across the dorsal ridge with a pat.

The dragon began to croon in her throat, her eyes following

Lessa's every move. She nudged at Lessa and Lessa obediently attended the other eye ridge.

The dragon let it be known she was hungry.

"We'll get you something to eat directly," Lessa assured her briskly and blinked back at the dragon in amazement. How could she be so callous? It was a fact that this little menace had just now seriously injured, if not killed, two women.

She wouldn't have believed her sympathies could swing so alarmingly towards the beast. Yet it was the most natural thing in the world for her to wish to protect this fledgling.

The dragon arched her neck to look Lessa squarely in the eyes. Ramoth repeated wistfully how exceedingly hungry she was, confined so long in that shell without nourishment.

Lessa wondered how she knew the golden dragon's name and Ramoth replied: Why shouldn't she know her own name since it was hers and no one else's? And then Lessa was lost again in the wonder of those expressive eyes.

Oblivious to the descending bronze dragons, uncaring of the presence of their riders, Lessa stood caressing the head of the most wonderful creature on all Pern, fully prescient of troubles and glories, but most immediately aware that Lessa of Pern was Weyrwoman to Ramoth the Golden, for now and forever.